David M Henley has worked in Australian trade publishing for many years and grown a successful design and publishing studio. He is the author of the Pierre Jnr trilogy and has written and illustrated two esoteric novellas (*The Museum of Unnatural History* and *Bumbly Goes Forth*) and one love poem (*The Story So Far*). He has featured in multiple exhibitions and is the art director and co-founder of Seizure, a magazine for new writing. David is based in Sydney, Australia, but can be found on the Weave.

pierrejnr.com
Twitter @DavidMHenley
facebook.com/TerenceBumbly

Books by David M Henley

The Hunt for Pierre Jnr
Manifestations

MANIFESTATIONS

David M Henley

HARPER
Voyager

Harper*Voyager*
An imprint of HarperCollins*Publishers*

First published in Australia in 2014
by HarperCollins*Publishers* Australia Pty Limited
ABN 36 009 913 517
harpercollins.com.au

Copyright © David M Henley 2014

The right of David M Henley to be identified as the author
of this work has been asserted by him in accordance with the
Copyright Amendment (Moral Rights) Act 2000.

HarperCollins*Publishers*
Level 13, 201 Elizabeth Street, Sydney NSW 2000, Australia
Unit D1, 63 Apollo Drive, Rosedale, Auckland 0632, New Zealand
A 53, Sector 57, Noida, UP, India
77–85 Fulham Palace Road, London W6 8JB, United Kingdom
2 Bloor Street East, 20th floor, Toronto, Ontario M4W 1A8, Canada
10 East 53rd Street, New York NY 10022, USA

National Library of Australia Cataloguing-in-Publication entry:

Henley, David M., author.
  Manifestations / David M. Henley.
  ISBN: 978 0 7322 9561 5 (pbk.)
  ISBN: 978 1 7430 9686 4 (ebook)
  Telepathy — Fiction.
  Science fiction.
A823.4

Cover design by Darren Holt, HarperCollins Design Studio
Cover image by shutterstock.com
Typeset in Sabon by Kirby Jones
Printed and bound in Australia by Griffin Press
The papers used by HarperCollins in the manufacture of this book are a natural,
recyclable product made from wood grown in sustainable plantation forests. The fibre
source and manufacturing processes meet recognised international environmental
standards, and carry certification.

5 4 3 2 1   14 15 16 17

For Alice, always

PRELUDE

The widow Mali had always been kind to Morgan, as had her late partner Eurosh. The pair of them often shared their meals with him and endured his grumblings of dissatisfaction.

Morgan was an artist and wanted to spend all of his days making *objets d'art*. That is what he wanted the Will to want of him, but all it seemed to want him to make was more faces.

On Earth, in the year 2159, there are twenty-six megapolises and hundreds of smaller cities and housing clusters spreading out a population rapidly approaching twenty billion individuals. In almost every community hub it is common to have what is known as the town face, which might sit in a square if it was a sculpture; mounted on a building like a gargoyle; or placed on a mantel if simply a bust — as Morgan made.

Faces, technically, could look like anything — from an abstract kinetic sculpture, or a light show of coloured panels, to a faux Impressionist-style painting, or a life-sized replica (though socially that was unacceptable) — what made each artwork a face was how it uniquely interpreted the innumerable ways the Will and the Weave could be calculated, filtered and measured. Some faces changed with the trends — as determined by the most often used phrases and keywords — others reacted to the pace of change. Some averaged the local region, others the entire world. Morgan, as an artist, was interested in more than statistical averages though.

Unlike the clocks of old that kept people informed of the time, town faces depicted the overall mood and feelings of the Weave. The face's expression gave all who looked upon it an immediate sense of how those around them might be feeling.

In Nijmegen, the town face looked very human, which Morgan was particularly skilled at creating. It was hairless, effete and three metres tall. After he won the student prize for 2157 it had been made the common face for the town and was raised four storeys high to sit below the old clock of the meister tower. When the world was sad, its eyebrows drooped and its eyes searched the road and sky for hope. When the world was worried, as it often was these days, the face bit the inside of its lip and closed its eyes as if praying to a higher power. Morgan wished he'd never made it as a self-portrait.

Since his study piece nearly three years ago, Morgan had been making small hand-sized faces, versions of people's lost loved ones: 'death masks', he sometimes thought of them. The commissioners would supply images and recordings of their dear departed along with any personal writings or memos. Morgan had to draw everything together to create a miniature bust that closely imitated the person and how they had reacted to certain news and topics.

It was gruesome. Ghastly and morbid. And yet Morgan could never resist the pleas of those who had lost the ones they loved and wanted only to share their lives with them once again. Even if it was simply an image, even if the bust *was* only a replica, and even if its expressions were statistically motivated imitations, to them it was the face they had known, that had smiled upon them. That cried with them.

His studio was small and narrow. A long bench with just enough room for him to wheel his stool along its length. The shelves held the faces he was working on: three rows of heads, some the size of a child's fist, others larger busts for altars and entryways. Below the bench he kept a few sylus, handscreens and a replication box. All the tools he needed.

Making the lifelike image was easy. All it took was to feed in enough recordings to generate the visage overnight on one of the template skulls with actuated muscles. It was also easy to load the key expressions, another automated process.

The art of it, what Morgan really did, was in relating these imitation reactions to informational input in the same way the person he was modelling would have. For every soul, he had to find their essence, to capture their *je ne sais quoi*, so that when someone came home from a long day of frustration they could visit their loved one and look upon the face of the lover they remembered.

For him this was draining. Some people were easy, but some were so quirky it could take him months to discover the pattern of their emotive reactions. This was the first time he was working on a friend.

He had known Eurosh well. Morgan was building him life-sized and his stilled head sat in the centre of the bench, lit from all sides by recessed lumen bars.

'Eurosh?' Morgan called out the wake-up trigger. The eyes of his friend opened and blinked, looking towards Morgan as affably and welcoming as when he was alive, patiently waiting for his lonely friend to tell him what was on his mind.

'Today I have some pictures to show you. Would you like to see some pictures?' Eurosh smiled; this meant yes. Morgan wished the head could talk, but this was a line many facemakers chose not to cross. What they were doing felt bad enough. He sighed and Eurosh looked at him with curious concern. 'It's nothing, Eurosh. Nothing to worry about. Let's start.'

He propped a handscreen up in front of the head and tapped through images from the Weave. Recent events, historical events, cultural happenings. Sprinkled throughout the presentation, Morgan showed the head of Eurosh pictures of Mali, his wife. Each time the head would look downcast with longing. It looked real and convincing, but something wasn't right. It just wasn't his friend.

'Feg it, Eurosh. What am I missing?' he muttered, but the head was no longer watching him, or the screen.

A look of horror now contorted its skin, the eyes bulging and lips stretching back from its teeth. It stared to Morgan's side, its expression becoming more and more distorted beyond its programming.

'What's wrong with you now? Oh —' He turned and saw a boy standing next to him. 'Where did you come from?'

The boy only smiled and turned his head, looking from Morgan to the half-finished busts on the shelves.

Eurosh was nearly gagging, obviously broken. Morgan tapped it twice on the forehead to shut it down. It relaxed into sleep mode.

He turned back to the boy. His mind screamed that he knew who this was. He'd heard of this boy, or seen him some place before ... he was normally so good with faces.

He felt his attention swing to the handscreen and he reached out, his hands moving of their own accord. He tapped for the screen to go to a live view, a balloon hovering over some place in Korea. Nothing was happening. It looked like a nice day.

'What is it?'

Watch, a voice spoke into his head.

PIERRE JNR IS A MYTH

Shen waited while the panel scanned his thumb until it greenly approved and he heard the bolts in the wall retract. He pushed down a stiff lever that drained the electricity from the cage and grabbed hold of the handle.

He didn't notice the screech as it opened, or see the sharp gouges in the back of the door as it swung past him. Shen saw only the dark interior of the vault. There was no light inside. The room was full of blackness. An undulating, swallowing volume of black viscosity.

'Kronos?' Shen called.

The blackness sensed the change in light and the vibrations. It felt the shape of the new light and the taste of the sounds. It reached out, it grew, it took up space without knowing what any of those things were.

'Kronos?'

It smelt something. It came from the new. It tangled inside it. It took the it and absorbed it into its itness. It did not know what it was.

Quickly its hunger made it move. It saw the thing that made the sound. It moved. It could move ... from the place it had always been. It could move from the place. It touched the it that made the sound. It. Me. Kronos.

The it had made sounds — words — no, a name. The it was Shen. Shen made more sound words, 'Arck. Arghh. Arghllllllll.' It-Kronos took more of the it-Shen and it-Shen became Kronos. Words. Thought. Memory. From the man came words. Kronos saw light and dark, felt hot and cold.

It was wet, and warm, until it was cold. It had weight. The light of it-Shen disappeared and the words and thoughts stopped coming into Kronos. It shook the Shen. With a thousand spikes it searched the body, but the light was gone.

Kronos. I am Kronos. I am me. It is Shen. Shen is me. We are we.

The it-Shen was soft.

The space beyond the place where it-Kronos had always been — the room, the vault.

The cage ... the it-Shen had kept the it-Kronos in a cage. But, outside the cage, the space was enormous and Kronos flooded to fill it. There were so many things it didn't comprehend. It had so few words from the it-Shen.

But there was light. Light above, light in lines, light in different ... colours? The lines of light, it touched them and a geyser of something made it pull back. But that something was words. That something was information.

Kronos learnt quickly, as fast as electrical signals could flow. While Kronos devoured the data of Shen's network, Kronos's body completed every nanometre of the capsule. It could absorb anything. Some things took longer, metal things and plastic things. It enjoyed the plants. It had enjoyment. It left

12

them alone. They took the light as Kronos did and made it a part of them as it did.

It understood plants now. They came from an above. Kronos was in a cage below the earth and above there was light. So much light. So much more for it to absorb.

As a mass Kronos moved. It already filled the capsule. All was absorbed, speared then coated in the black viscous skin for absorption. The space that seconds ago had felt infinite was now a prison. Kronos reached and found the elevator shaft. There was light this way. A world of light.

PIERRE JNR IS WATCHING US

Years later people would ask each other what they were doing when Busan was destroyed.

For Gina Solomons it was when she was looking after her granddaughter, Marissa, while her daughter was at work. They were on the floor drawing with crayons. Mostly Gina read a book while encouraging Marissa with exclamations, and tried to keep her from getting marks on the floor.

They were drawing their family when Marissa's picture took a disturbing direction. 'What's happening there, Mari?' Gina asked. 'Are those people running?'

'Uh-huh.'

'And what is this black thing, is that a mistake?' Marissa was furiously expanding the black lines, as if intent to take over the whole image. 'If it's a mistake, you can just start over with a new page.'

'Uh-uh.' Marissa pointed behind her gran to where the screen showed what was being transmitted live.

'Shocking footage today out of Busan where a black substance erupted from underground and drowned the city centre. All Citizens are presumed dead.

'There are replay loops on the Weave showing what

happened — please, be advised that the following vision may not be suitable for younger viewers.'

The Weave watched in horror as a black liquid erupted from under the small city of Busan, like a mud volcano sweeping over a population of millions to spill into the sea. It looked like an oil strike, a geyser of viscous black spewing up into the air, but there the resemblance stopped. The jets of liquid didn't drop to Earth like liquid, but curled and explored with tentacles that stuck to every surface like honey, and then oozed further outward ...

The black spread rapidly, swelling and whipping a thousand appendages out to catch any who ran from it. People fled, but it was faster. Squibs that didn't immediately flee were pulled from the sky as large tentacles swept out, lashing at the sky like tongues.

The spring of black continued bubbling up from the ground until it covered everything. Buildings, boats, roads and the unipoles that lined them. As it grew, the cameras blacked out and the viewpoint of the slideshow retreated to the next unipole, and then the next until there was zero signal coming from the city.

Nine hundred square kilometres of territory had their connections to the Weave broken. A fail-safe in the system automatically triggered the response protocol for an unexplained attack: quarantine. Firstly, from the Weave; secondly, quarantined from land, air and sea.

This new Weave grey zone extended to the water's edge and the nearest natural borders. The city of Busan screamed for an hour and then went silent. Four million streams no longer transmitted to the Weave.

* * *

Stefan was packing his bags when it happened. He couldn't take sitting still any more. He was going to find Myfanwy, wherever she was. When he went to the fixit to get his bike he found Romeo and the others gathered in awe around the screens.

'What is it now?' Stefan asked, not really caring.

'Lad, you haven't seen? There's a monster in Korea.'

'A monster, right.'

'No joke, amigo. See for yourself.'

Stefan looked at the screens where a pulled-back view was showing the Bay of Busan from behind the Services cordon. It looked like a dark sea anemone was sitting peacefully, lifting its tentacles to wave in the current.

'What is that?'

'Nobody knows.'

The Prime, Ryu Shima, was about to enter an interview when it happened. Recent events had thrown doubt upon the strength of the Primacy. His chief of operations, Gladys, and all her advisors had recommended that he reconnect with the people, present a rational voice and a united message and reinforce his suddenly shaky position. He would have to respond to questions about the Shima breach and how he felt about the psi rebellion having been declared on his family's doorstep.

His influence had been on a downward slide ever since Tamsin Grey had left her mark on the central gate of his ancestral home for all to see. At least his presence at his command needle, two kilometres away and two hundred metres

19

in the air, could be verified. He hadn't had contact with anyone from Shima Palace since the incident, so any suspicion that he was somehow psionically influenced could be dismissed.

He finished brushing powder through his long hair. Making it shiny and straight before swooping it into a topknot at the back of his head.

The Prime stood and let his secretary look him over with her cameras to make sure that he was impeccable and pristine. This was the first time he had worn clothes without the Shima crest. The chameleon must disappear — even a name change was being considered. If the right alpha could be found to conjoin with his stream, then he might be better off cutting his ties to his family completely.

In a few minutes he would open up the channels of his command room to all first tier reporters. No one with less than a million followers would have access, but the contents of their streams would flow through to the rest of the Weave.

Then some chaos broke loose and his queue was engorged with emergency communications. It was pure black horror and he could only watch silently. The footage from Busan only stopped flowing when the automatic quarantine went into effect and there was no more direct communication from the city. They changed to satellites and watched as tendrils erupted from the black mass and lanced every human it could find until it reached the edge of the city and the mass stopped, its tentacles yearning for more to absorb. Not even the animals escaped.

The Weave was screaming and demanded the Prime's reaction. His queue was flooded, but he couldn't choose where to begin. He activated the simulations of himself that Takashi had made and let them filter. The fake Ryus could keep the dogs at bay. He'd had as long as anyone to process this ... how was he expected to know what this was?

Ryu took a deep breath. *Do not react. Respond.*

Ryu flicked out a directive.

Ryu to Zim: Establish an active perimeter, nothing and no one goes in or out.

'Gladys,' he paged.

Her head appeared on the screen. 'Yes, Prime?'

'I need you to put a study team together.'

'The Weave is demanding a response from you.'

'I understand. Can we respond that we are investigating?'

'That will buy us five minutes at most.'

'We need to find out what this thing is before we say what we are going to do about it.'

'We can put some general theorists in the field. Anyone who is happy to speculate. If we can make the Weave understand the position we're in, we might get half a cycle.' It wasn't a bad suggestion. It's what would happen anyway. 'I think we should go ahead with the interview.'

'You still want me to take questions?' Ryu asked.

'Yes. Show the Will that the Prime is in charge. It may stabilise your position.'

Don't let anyone else take the leadership on this, he thought. 'I've already put Zim in charge of establishing the quarantine. I can start by announcing that.'

'Good. So long as he is acting on your behalf. He's acting on your command. Make sure the world knows that.'

'I will. I'm ready, you can open it up.'

Takashi always kept a meme-minder playing in the background. It was the most digested form of information reporting and at any one time was listened to by at least five million people. Takashi enjoyed a light-hearted take on the things that mattered, and it was the fastest way to keep up with what was happening. A trio of speakers took shifts reading out the prompts from their researcher teams, twenty-four hours a day; the top memes in twenty words or less.

'Give us five minutes and we'll have you up to speed on all the big memes. Sato Shima, sister of the Prime, is getting married. Pharmers in Africa are reporting a successful field trial that could double crop production by 2165.'

Any story could be extended with a click for more detail, or he could set his stream to follow, as he did with Sato's wedding, so he would be up to date on all changes.

'The number of people wearing the psi emblem has increased point zero two of a per cent. Sato Shima, sister of the current Prime, has chosen designer Anna Arah to make her wedding dress. Primacy fallout: Zim up, Betts up, Shima down. Parabowl finals begin tonight, Phoenix team versus the Moon Rocks. Ellizabeth Betts will be celebrating her one hundredth birthday next week with a lavish private gathering. The weather everywhere is, as predicted, unpredictable.'

Takashi shivered and raised the heat in his quilted kimono. He hadn't left his rooms in three weeks and now they were trying to freeze him out with the unbearable air-conditioning. He could shut it down if he chose to, but he wanted them to see that he could bear it. The family had other problems to worry about, like removing the blemish he had made on the Shima family name and ensuring Sato's unity pact would not be aborted.

Mother didn't even bother forcing him to the family meetings any more — though he knew he was a topic down there. There was no block they could put around their streams that he couldn't go through, no wall they could build to stop him listening in. They were considering some kind of counselling for him, but they knew he wouldn't let anyone through his doors. He was happy, for now, to remain unsolvable.

His dolls remained in their boxes, ready to leave for his brother's needle ... though, of course, he wasn't going to be living there now. Since the Grey woman's breach of the Shima Palace and Takashi's mind, Ryu had accepted no contact from him. Takashi would never leave the palace now.

He had to find a way to earn back Ryu's trust ... if he could be useful to Ryu, he would be forgiven. But he hesitated to go on the Weave now. He let his simulations do the work while he sat listlessly listening to the news of the world.

'Breaking news. Four million feared dead in Busan after an unidentified disaster.'

Takashi automatically expanded the story and followed the feed to the footage. 'Cryppy!' He sent a ping to Ryu, offering his help.

He waited seconds. Then more seconds. The news continued in the background but he didn't hear it. He waited for a response from his brother but none came. He just had to watch him on the Weave like everyone else.

'Today at fourteen hundred hours, local time, the city of Busan was consumed by an unknown entity. We have so little information about the event that we don't even know what to call the entity. Animal, vegetable or mineral? Natural or man-made? Those are the questions we are asking ourselves now. We are going to merge streams with the Prime in a moment who is hopefully going to answer some of those questions. You know how it works, folks: plug in your query and the most popular questions will be put to our guest.

'We are now cutting to Ryu Shima, live in interview.'

A dozen different camera views were offered as the Prime allowed access to where he sat in his command room. 'Thank you for your time,' he said. 'I come to you to confirm the terrible news that you have already heard. There has been an incident in one of the World Union's cities that has taken the lives of many Citizens. We do not know what it is, or where it came from.'

Questions clamoured into his queue, colour-coded by frequency and by influence of the asker. Any pundit could record a question to be asked but only the questions with the most endorsements would be asked.

'Was this the action of the psis or Pierre Jnr?' was asked by an Oriolo supporter. This group was strongly opposed to all psis and their activities.

'We have no conclusive evidence to support the existence of Pierre Jnr. Nor do we have any evidence to suggest a connection between this event and the psis. Next question.'

'What do you plan to do?' asked a man from Seoul, one of the closest major cities to the incident.

'First, we are quarantining the area, then we are going to find out more before making a decision. Next.'

The questions came faster and Ryu didn't even look to see who was asking.

'Is this a localised phenomenon?'

'We believe so.'

'Is it spreading?'

'At this point in time it has stopped advancing. Whatever this is, it seems to attack inorganic materials and animals only. We have severed connections to the area, including basic services. Next question.'

Not a screen in the world showed anything but the incident. Headlines scratched their way into every banner. And the town faces were aghast, epileptic or overloaded in stunned despair. When people looked up at them they knew they should be worried.

'The Corner' was a popular segment for those with a light interest in civic matters. Prue Gella was the host and with her was Roger Applebent, a mid-level civic advisor.

'Another disaster today for the WU, this time from the East-Asian Peninsula. Roger, how do you think the Primacy will react?'

They collected the available footage into a looping stream for their viewers and spoke over the top. Screens showed an orbital aspect, a collation of cameras from the ground before the data was cut off; a frenzied slideshow of the black wave sloshing and clawing into the streets and consuming the people in its path.

'Prue, at times like these it's all about containment. Containment. Containment. Containment.'

'And then?'

'They need to find out if this is a natural disaster or not.'

'What else could it be?'

'Man-made.'

'Like what?'

'Any number of things. An underground chemical deposit. A leftover weapon from the wars. There's a strong chance this has something to do with Pierre Jnr. Or the psi rebellion.'

'Do you have any basis for that speculation?' Prue asked.

'Only the scale of the event, Prue. That's all I can say at this time.'

'But you know more?' she led.

'Which I'll neither confirm nor deny.'

'Alright, let's talk about the civic implications. The Weave doesn't often like to be shut out. How do you think this new data blockout will be met? And remembering that it has only been a matter of weeks since the Cape was quarantined from the Weave.'

The voice of Roger Applebent chuckled. 'Probably not well. But I'd like to remind your viewers not to be hasty. Responsible Citizens take time with their decisions. In my opinion, the Primacy is doing the right thing. We need to ascertain the level of the threat. We have to be cautious.'

'So you're saying it's okay to obscure the public's right to know?'

'Prue, you know that's not true. The orbital view is open for everyone to see. The public can watch what is happening.'

'But there is nothing from the ground teams. We know many Services personnel have been called to the area.'

'And I say we should let them have a few hours to assess.'

'Alright. That's all we have time for. I'm Prue Gella speaking with Roger Applebent. Roger, a few last words?'

'I think we just have to trust in our leaders for now. As a concerned Citizen, I wouldn't be rocking the boat.'

'Next in "The Corner", Julia Couling will be interviewing Lucius Gregg about his new meme science and to hear his speculations on the beast of Busan.'

Colonel Abercrombie Pinter was eating strawberries. He thought nothing had ever tasted so good.

He had been in the rejuvenation centre for over two months now and what they hadn't told him about was how his sense for flavour would come back. For years, he thought he had just grown so used to everything that eating was dull. But now that his tongue was reborn he was making his way through every food he could order.

The rejuvenation centre Pinter was resting in had perfect weather control. He was sitting in an expansive courtyard by an artificial oasis. There was greenery everywhere: in planters, garden beds and climbing the high white walls of the housing units. A drove of friendly gardening bots waved and chirped whenever a patient walked past.

Pinter was cynical enough to see the artifice behind the place. The architecture was designed to inspire. Rejuvenation was the new miracle and the centres that were beginning to pop up were embracing the magic for all it was worth. Elegant narrow buildings, like settings for art-deco fairy tales, clustered casually amongst common gardens and leisure groves and pools. A face stared down from the tallest of the lofts, smiling like a loving parent at the joy and content of its children below.

Like the others, Colonel Pinter was dressed in comforts: padded gowns that cosily protected their bodies, which were carefully wound up in rewind tape. Without the robes they looked like mummies. His face was painted with gels and he hadn't yet seen what was underneath.

It was a three-month period of relaxation — though his body was still eager for exercise. The Colonel was renewed. He felt it deep inside him. He felt invigorated like a cold shower was washing through him.

He watched a young woman get out of the pool. She was probably over sixty years old but had rejuved to the body of an eighteen-year-old, yet keeping her silvered hair as a memento. Her transformation was almost complete; only her hands and face were still cloaked in rewind. Was it lascivious of him to look at her this way?

In talking with some of the other guests they had quickly developed a parlance to speak of their age. He was a seventy-eight thirty; his first life, or body, aged seventy-eight years, was rejuved to the comparable age of thirty. As he grew older only his second age would increase.

Was it fear of death that had made him rejuv? He told himself it was duty, but there were other people, younger, who could have taken his place. Was he being a fool? Part of him knew the answer why. That when it came down to it, he could never really be sure that anyone else would do what needed to be done.

One night he was lying awake, when music reached his room. There was only a single female voice repeating soft syllables around the strums of a harp, but he could have sworn he recognised it: 'Forget Me as I Was' ... a song from the wars.

He had noticed that, along with his body, his memories were being revived and more and more he thought of things he had avoided thinking about for years. When he was thirty last time, he'd been in the rough with his men, leading a guerrilla cavalry against the Örjian horde. An army that had lost its country. He had started out with ten battalions behind him, but they were out in it for a month, cut off from a command base. No communications, no strategy. Supplies ran out and they were living off any food they could take.

His hundreds became fifty. Each day they rode their annihilators — ten-foot-high, eight-legged programmable killing machines — looking for Örjians. The winds were tearing up everything and were filled with stones and sticks. The soldiers kept their heads wrapped and let the annihilators do the hunting. They could track like bloodhounds and discern genetic targets from the faintest of evidence.

He and the soldiers in his band slept in plastic puff tents, torn and patched. After weeks without a full wash the tents began to reek — he remembered that smell distinctly — but there was nothing to be done about it. Living in hard buildings made you an easy target, so they were always moving. Never stopping in the same place and never crossing the same territory. During the day they hunted monsters, in the night they waited for the monsters to find them. Sometimes they played songs, like the one he was hearing this night, to keep them warm.

He leant out his window to gauge where the music was coming from. It wasn't from his tower, but it was nearby. Pinter slid on some flat shoes and went for a wander. The song didn't stop. The woman singing it just kept stroking her harp and calling out to him like a siren.

Pinter found the building and looked up to see the singer, but she wasn't sitting at the window as he had pictured so he went inside. The foyer of her tower was decorated with colourful geometric tiles on the ceiling and floor. He climbed the stairs, pausing to listen at each door to see if that was where the singer lived.

At the third floor he knocked and the singing stopped.

'Who is it?' a voice asked.

'Just another guest. I heard you singing,' he answered through the door.

'I'm sorry. I'll stop.'

'No, no. Please don't. Would you mind if I came in to listen?'

The door opened slowly and stopped at an inch. An eye looked at him. 'You want to listen to me sing?'

'Yes, please. I remember that song. It takes me back.'

'I find I can't remember the words.'

'It doesn't matter. I used to listen to it a lot when I was younger. I mean the first time I was younger.' He smiled.

'Okay.' She gave in. 'Just let me get more appropriately dressed.'

He waited outside, listening to the sounds of rushed tidying.

'Come in.'

She was sitting near the window, in a square of light from the moon. A small pad harp rested on her lap. What he could see of her was beautiful. Her skin was painted like his, and her silver hair was brushed straight. Pinter realised she was the sixty-something eighteen he'd been watching swim and tried not to blush. It really was the singing that had brought him here, he hadn't known it would be her.

Pinter sat near her on a big cushion — ha, he was sitting on the floor. It had been a long time since he'd done that for fun. The thought made him smile again, and the girl smiled back nervously.

She began strumming back and forth over the instrument's tactile sensors. The harp was meant to be a leisurely thing to play that, no matter your proficiency, would sound tranquil and in time with the song you had selected. When she was done he went to her, bowed and kissed her hands.

'Thank you. That was lovely.'

'I am glad you enjoyed it.'

'I remember when that song became popular. I was the age I am now.'

'Oh. I was younger.'

'It seems more appropriate every time I hear it,' he said.

She tilted her head, letting her fingers trail on the pad harp. 'What does it make you think of?'

'You don't want to know.'

'A woman?'

'No,' he chuckled. 'Nothing like that. Though, I guess it was about women for a lot of us. When I was a soldier, there were many days when we didn't know if we'd see the other end.

I think that song was just the most beautiful thing we could find in the nightmare.' He clenched his fist. Even rejuvenation couldn't make him forget the mud that was his skin. It would always be there under the surface.

'Oh, a soldier. Are you Colonel Pinter?'

'Yes,' he answered, lifting his head to watch her reaction. She didn't seem fussed either way. Neither afraid nor titillated.

'I had heard you were here. The Scorpion returns, they say.'

'I never did like that name.'

For the first time she laughed, a golden spring of humour. She was laughing at him and he didn't mind. 'You have many names that are worse.'

'There is no need to remind me. What should I call you?'

'You can call me Gretel.'

She stood and put her hand forward for shaking. It was soft and small and delicate and his own hand seemed to consume it like his body wanted to consume hers.

'I think we should say goodnight, Colonel.' She put a gentle hand to his chest.

'Please call me Abe.'

'If you like. Goodnight, Abe.'

Colonel Pinter was sitting down to his morning routine of papes, caf, butter and pepita cakes with a large bowl of medicinal yoghurt he had to eat. It had a strange savoury taste for yoghurt.

His door chimed and he lowered his papes. 'Come in.'

The door opened for Gretel. For the last two days they had seen each other at exercise and she had smiled at him, but hadn't spoken. It looked like she was through the rewind stage, and so there were dabs of the blue gel behind her ears, over her forehead, and probably every crease of skin the tape hadn't covered.

She held a handscreen that she put in front of him. 'I've been reading your book.'

Abercrombie picked it up and skimmed through the text. His heart raced at the memories it triggered. It covered the time leading up to the foundation of the WU and the Siberian solution, all the way back to when they had lost their country. He and his men had thought they were dead so often they began considering themselves already gone. None of them lost that feeling over the years. They had spoken of it amongst themselves because they couldn't speak to anyone else about it.

The Colonel put the screen down. 'Pure fiction,' he said.

She looked at him, a half-formed smile on her lips. 'May I join you?'

'Please do.' Another meal was brought for her and they ate quietly for a minute.

'When you wrote —'

Abercrombie put his cutlery down. 'Please, don't start on the memoir.'

'There's just one bit I don't —'

'No.' He refused to discuss it. 'At least not until I've had a chance to reread it. Why don't you tell me something about you? Who were you?'

'Don't you know me, Abe? I was nearly famous. I used to be a singer,' she joked. Gretel stood up and moved around the table, letting her robe fall open. 'Let's pretend that it might have been me you were listening to out there.' She began humming the tune and sat on his lap, pulling his head to her chest. 'Do you mind if I call you Colonel? Just this once?'

Stray thoughts brought data collations automatically to his queue. His wife, a new twenty-five, was living in a resettlement commune north of the old Hadrian's Wall. Her stream was mostly silent. Would she be wondering about him?

After Pinter's second month they allowed him to begin wearing a symbiot. In his first life he had avoided the machines, preferring a less invasive and easily removable option. He'd seen too many good men get rattled in the field when their wiring had fused, but with what he had ahead of him he would need the instant communication and the data overlay ability that modern Servicemen had. He couldn't be less than the best if he was to stand a chance against Pierre Jnr. He needed to be fast and all-knowing and connected to Services as though it was another part of his body.

Now he was wondering why he had held back. After the initial learning period it just became a part of his brain. The same way he recalled memories, if he thought about something, or questioned something he didn't know, the brain would recollect from the bot. Or rather, the symbiot gathered the data and pushed it into his synapses. It was dizzying magic. He was now technologically telepathic, he ruminated.

He began taking runs through the complex, testing the visual data overlay on everyone he went past. Their details and history were listed for him to read and process in a split second.

He began to run calculations of distance, speed, trajectory and threat level. It was a shame that no one in the centre registered as a threat.

The doctors warned him to take it easy and for him and Gretel to reduce their sexercise, but they only laughed. They were young now after all. They lazed their days away reading, watching entertainments and making up some of their own; then helped each other reapply their healing gels.

When his memories overpowered his will, and he sank into those nightmares, Gretel lay with him. Sometimes she would distract him with a song, or a demonstration of how her flexibility was returning. Sometimes he would tell her about his dreams, though never the details.

'Why do I feel that you know more about me than I do about you?' he asked her one day.

'Well, I'm not an historical figure like you are, and I'm not the one who keeps thinking about the past.'

'I know. I know.' He shook his head at himself. 'Here I am reborn and all I do is talk about the past. Perhaps we should talk about the future?'

'Is that some sort of proposition?'

'Maybe. I'm not sure. I don't know what the future holds.'

'Well, now we are talking. Why did you get rejuved, Mister Scorpion?' She took a seat on him as if he was a pony.

'The usual excuse. The call of duty.'

'You're going back into Services?' She seemed aghast.

'I never left.' He looked at her consideringly. It was impossible to see the decades of life lived in the young body and face. 'What about you? Why did you rejuv?'

'I didn't want to die, of course. Isn't that enough?' She smiled at him and stroked his face. He felt calmer and happier when she did that. 'I'm sorry. I didn't mean to be surprised. You're Colonel Abercrombie Pinter. Of course you're going back to Services.'

'I have to. I helped establish the WU, I can't let it be destroyed.'

'Who's going to destroy the World Union? The big bad Pierre Jnr?' This time he didn't meet her eye.

'Really?' she said, lowering her voice. '*Really?* That's something I should be worried about?'

'I didn't say anything.'

'You didn't have to.' She dug her hands into his ribs and tickled him.

'I neither confirm nor deny these rumours.' He barely got the sentence out before he wrestled her to the ground and kissed her. 'Say you'll come with me.'

'Never!' she declared.

'Say you will.' He kissed her again.

'Maybe!' She laughed.

'Stay with me.'

'Of course I will. I love you.'

'I love you.'

Their lovemaking was interrupted by a cry from outside. They lifted their heads to listen and the cry was followed by shouts of alarm and dismay. Pinter tapped his symbiot and information began flooding in.

'What is it?' Gretel asked. She hadn't gotten symbed with rejuv.

'Something terrible is happening.' There was a ping to his symbiot, a connection request from the Prime. 'Excuse me, I have to go.'

Pinter was rushed through the final stages of the treatment. The last of his tape was removed, revealing pink new skin with blond hairs beginning to emerge. He was given a salve to apply every two hours.

A uniform waited for him in his room. As sepia as the past. Three pins on the collar.

He stood in front of the mirror and looked himself over. He couldn't have been standing there long when the door chime interrupted his reverie.

'Come in.'

'Oh ... Abe. You're leaving?'

He turned to her and smiled. 'Yes. I've been asked to go to Busan.'

'To that thing? What if it ...?'

'Don't worry. I'll be far enough away.'

'You had two weeks left of the treatment.'

He shrugged. 'The Command is the Command, Gretel. What can I say?' She was lovely in white drapery. 'Do you still want to come with me?' he asked.

'Abe ...' She lunged into his arms. 'I was hoping you'd say that.'

I am I am I am. His voice reverberated powerfully, echoing through the endless pale grey. *I am Musashi, defender of the weak and saviour of the helpless.*

Actually he was just a junior angel, and his name was Zachary Frost. Like a garden, the Weave was maintained by a multitude of volunteers like Musashi. Clubs and scout groups whose members traversed every corner of the data looking for mistakes, infractions and data that had aged into falsehood. Most of the kids did it for fun, but Zach wanted to become a fully fledged weaver one day. Then he could move out from the orphanage he was in.

I am Musashi. Musashi the ronin. I roam the lands righting wrongs and aiding the weak.

Zachary didn't really keep time in the way that other people did. His clock was always on and set to keep pace with the atomic standard, but it was only a meaningless measure of increments. The times it marked held no significance for him. As the clock changed over from twenty-three hours and fifty-nine minutes to zero zero hours, this reset — that represented the beginning of a new day — was just another digit changing over in his dash.

His days were broken up into four. In the morning he would rise before dawn, eat a quick breakfast and then spend four hours on the Weave scouting. After lunch he spent the rest of his afternoon in lessons and meeting with tutors before returning home, usually after dinner time, to spend another four hours online before heading to bed.

He was going for his stamina badge as an Angel Scout, which meant two solid months of reverse circadian endurance. For eight hours his stream flowed from node to node. Searching for minor flaws he could fix or flag: broken connections, syntax and miscodes he was allowed to solve himself; errata, beautification and redundancy must all be tagged for a more senior scout to investigate.

Since the manifestation, and now this black mass, there was a shortage of guides. The scouts were encouraged not to immerse alone but he was always careful. He stuck to known paths, and anything anomalous he came across he logged and moved past.

Zach had to process ten thousand connections per night. He normally started close to home, looking at the streams of the orphanage, the kids who lived there and the people who ran the place. They were okay, Lily and Tom, he'd checked them out before. Tom was an orphan from the Dark Age. Lily, his life partner, was from a farming family on the fringe of West. Together they had run a home for strays for over twenty years.

He tapped into the eyes in the dorm room and looked over the sleeping forms to see who was up, immersed in their stream or reading. Jenks was sleeping. Zach put an alert tag on him so he would be notified if he left his bed. He didn't want that fusebrain sneaking up on him.

Zach needed a place to go if he was going to make quota. He checked the streams of Bronwyn and Gerty to see if they led anywhere interesting, but Gerty was just looking at celebrity indexes, ogling the images of singers, and Bronwyn was studying, she never went online. He pinged her as he went past, flipping everything in her dash upside-down and out of order.

Zach: Don't stay up all night, Bron.

Bron: Don't close your eyes, scoob. I'll get you back.

I am Musashi. Prankster and funmaker. I am a rogue and taunter of silly girls.

39

There were many areas he wasn't meant to enter and his stream would give him away if he did. A warning system would go off if he broke the rules. Though he could, potentially, mask a part of his stream and go exploring ... they'd probably find him out. So, the Dome was still off limits, Atlantic and the whole Cape was shut down, as was Busan and Korea and any platforms that might house streams from those areas. That left STOC as the next most interesting place to go and that was always forbidden to the younger scouts.

He was torn, should he go look? Someone had to patrol STOC. Everyone else was concentrating elsewhere, maybe STOC needed more scouts to do maintenance. The only thing was that Omskya was a freak show. He'd seen pictures that ran shivers down his spine. Even thinking about it made him feel cold and ... wet?

Wait a minute ...

Zach tore his headset off and found himself dripping with icy water. His clothes and chair were sodden and there was a puddle on the floor. He heard a giggle behind him and he leapt from his seat.

'Come back here!' he shouted and ran through the door.

'I told you not to close your eyes,' Bronwyn called back. She raced up the stairs and Zach was close behind when someone stepped into his path and took a hold of his shirt. He heard the door to the girls' dorm close and looked up into the weary face of Tom.

'Why are you running through the corridors in the middle of the night, Master Frost?'

'Nightmares, Tom.'

'And you are dripping wet because of ... fear?'

'Ah, no. I, um, forgot to take them off before I showered.'

'Is that so?' Tom lifted his eyebrows almost to the bottom of his nightcap. 'It isn't because Bronwyn poured a bucket of ice water on you in retaliation for an earlier incident?'

'Well, if you knew that, why were you asking?' Zach said, sour about being played.

Tom looked at his arm for the time. He didn't have a symb, just a passive interface. 'It is late. If you are still aiming for that badge, I suggest you quickly mop up your puddles and get back to work.'

'But, Tom, I'm soaking.'

'And let that be a lesson to you.' Tom smiled.

'I'll get pneumonia.'

'Then it will be a lesson well learnt. Goodnight. Keep the noise down, please.'

Zach gave up and went back in. He'd get a lock put on the door tomorrow.

When he was immersed again, he quickly forgot about how cold and wet he was. In geographic mode, a parallel of the real world, he began looking for any area he was allowed to go. He dropped into Peru, switching to the visual realm, or actuated level, and began tapping through random shops and services. Here in the visual, people and places and entities could choose how to be represented. Zach was Musashi again, a wandering samurai, with a curved glowing sword and a helmet of burnished steel beneath which there was only darkness. This was the avatar that anyone in the visual plane of the Weave would see; running and talking and fighting. On the geographic level Zach was a dot that pulsed from his home in Sutherland with branches that reached to all the sites he was accessing.

There were many levels to the Weave or, rather, many different ways to look at the data. Visual was the most common because it's faux physical nature made it intuitive for every user. There was also the code mode, or 'weaver level', where the actions he commanded with his thoughts, and minute movements, were written in trinary language. All three of these levels could be mixed to form a unique impression of him, showing the connections he maintained while online and who and what he interacted with.

He yawned. Musashi yawned with him and for a moment his visual representation was lying in a bed with a soft pillow. *No!* Zach snapped at himself. *Have to keep going.*

Zach would have sessions with his mathematics, crypto and languages teachers today, after his weekly session with his scout master, Miles Lizney.

Miles Lizney was about four times Zach's age, putting him close to fifty years old. This was what Zach surmised from his appearance. Observation was Zach's new tactic. As yet Zach had learnt next to nothing.

His teacher's stream was closed to him, censured from above: it was the challenge for every scout to learn about their teacher. Mister Lizney had moved into the area three years ago, brought in by the social engineering department to help train the young boys and girls in the area who wanted to work the Weave when they matured. He had twenty students on his roster. Zach had their names and ages, but had found no pattern to them, and he was the only orphan amongst them. He knew their progress and knew he was in the middle tier. He knew that the mentor appraisals from Lizney's students were positive, but no student had yet graduated, under Lizney's tutelage, to a weaver position.

For now he didn't have the ability to crack into Mister Lizney's stream, but that also wasn't the point of the exercise; that would be hakking. The aim of the challenge was to see the unseen. He, and the other students, had to find the Lizney-shaped hole in the datum to draw their conclusions. Somehow this pointless exercise was meant to teach them everything they needed to know, which Zach couldn't understand.

All weavers swore by it as a valuable exercise though and Zach had resorted to studying the histories of some of the great weavers to see if they explained how they had defeated the challenge. There was nothing he accessed that had helped him. It was a search by word patterns that discovered recurrent mentions of *What We Can See*, a thought tract composed by Milawi Ortega that spoke in Confucian-type stanzas about observation. It also preached a learning practice that to Zach seemed to border on the religious. *Look, watch, believe, practise, accept ... what was that supposed to mean?*

There was data before it turned into data, so he was told. The Weave is not the whole world and everything carries information. Appearance, possessions, vocabulary. Manner, motivation. Outcomes.

For the last two weeks, Zach had been observing Mister Lizney. He had had his unit monitored, he even had some of the man's clothes and pocket items chipped. His teacher lived

43

in a modest home, more modest even than the orphanage. He kept no mementos on display, nor did he ever look at any when Zach revised the surveillance footage. Mister Lizney spent most of his alone-time immersed, probably monitoring his students. He might even know that Zach was watching him, but that didn't seem likely, because if he did, something would have changed between them.

This is what Zach had observed so far. Lizney presented himself as the first wall for his students to climb. A hermit with no history who taught low rankers about the Weave — and yet he didn't wear a symbiot. That was curious.

Today he greeted Zach at the door and waved him in. He had a wand in his mouth and a couple of handscreens wedged under his arms. Always busy with more than one project. Zach reached out to catch the screens before they fell. Lizney had stiff movements and always dropped things.

'Why, thank you.' He took the wand from his mouth. As he walked he rubbed his hip. It must be sore today. If Zach had a sylus, he would be able to scan him for implants. He would have to find a way to get one into the unit. After he'd found a way to get one, that is. He was always looking for new ways to gather data.

The man had thinning hair, which he must have chosen not to repair. When asked about it, he claimed he would revive his scalp when he could get around to it. Lizney wore his helmet almost permanently, a silver cap with tinted lenses that went from purple to opaque when he immersed. He wore a range of indoor kimonos with bright patterns that confused the eyes. In his off-time he enjoyed a little mesh, but never around the students.

Miles was a bit plastic in the face. His skin was pale, but turned a deep tan if he caught too much sun. Zach thought the sheen of it looked unnatural. Zoom-ups over one thousand per cent caught a regularity that indicated manufacturing. His teeth too had been replaced at some point.

Mister Lizney avoided the topic of his skin; he said there had been an accident and didn't like talking about it. 'This is one of those mysteries you are to solve, young Musashi.' His smile was sad. His smiles were often sad. It was the only time Zach liked him, when he smiled like that. At other times Lizney's face and manners seemed artificial and he acted as though he was barely managing to put up with his students.

'How are you today? Tired yet?'

'No, sir,' Zach replied automatically.

'"No, sir." Very good. We can tick off "Shows continued respect for his elders" then. Of course I know your beta waves are down so you're either lying to me or you have convinced yourself.' He didn't wait for an answer, but bent carefully into a seat, one of two that were angled together by the small window, and beckoned for his screens back. When Zach took the other chair Lizney tapped the air with the wand and drew a vertical line.

'I see you are on track for your endurance badge. Very good. Now there is a note here from your foster. He says you're having trouble with the other children.'

'He said that?' Zach pulled his helmet from his pocket, flicked it open and quickly looked through the lenses to see the overlay Mister Lizney had superimposed in the room. It gave Zach's records, his stream, in an orderly but complicated arrangement of documents, footage and graphical analysis.

Lizney pushed the note from Tom towards him with the wand and Zach read it quickly.

Oh, he thought. *Bronwyn*.

'It's not all the kids, I don't see much of them at the moment. I'm shut in my study day and night. There's just this one annoying girl. She poured cold water on me while I was under and then Tom caught me as I was chasing her ... hey, why are you smiling?'

Lizney fought to keep the twitching corners of his mouth from turning into a grin. Zach was amusing him. Everything seemed so funny to Lizney. 'Maybe she likes you.'

Oh, this is a life talk. 'She's just a silly girl.'

'She won't always be. And someday you might not be a silly boy.' Zach didn't want to answer. He just wanted to have his lesson and go. 'Okay, okay. You still choose to keep that block up. When you change your mind I am here to talk. If you would like.'

Not likely, weirdie.

Lizney whisked the stream closed and the air was empty save for the dust motes.

'Now, I have to talk to you about what has been happening in Korea.' His teacher took a deep breath. 'You will have noticed in your last immersion that there was an increase in red zones.' Zach nodded. 'And you spent some time investigating the reason why.' There was no denying it. It was in his stream. 'I have to ask you, for your own safety, not to try to cross the barriers between you and this information. There is a quarantine over the area and Services is asking everyone to keep clear. Both on and off the Weave.'

'What is it?'

'I don't know. I don't know if anybody knows.'

'Is it the psionics?'

'It seems to be inorganic. You saw that on the satellite feed. Points off for not remembering. And points off because it was due to your obsession with the psis. Your bias is clouding you.'

Zach felt annoyed again. He should have remembered that but he didn't deserve to be fined for it. 'Pause it, why does this affect the Weave?'

Lizney smiled. 'Okay, you can have some points back for asking. The answer I have been given is that the Weave quarantine is a precautionary measure.'

'So what is it?' Zach asked again.

'Look, Zachary. Feel free to watch the Weave for more information. At the moment Services have the matter well in hand. Now, do you have any questions for me today, or should we look over your math?'

Zach thought for a moment. He had been meaning to ask about Lizney's lack of symbiot for a while, but it seemed rude to ask.

'I don't know how to ask. It is personal.'

'Don't be shy, Musashi. I am here to be asked anything.'

'It is about you.'

'I see.' Lizney's warmth disappeared. 'What have you found out?'

I've found out you're afraid of what I will find. That means it must be something bad. He would put a search through the malefactor list, maybe a visual would turn up something. 'I haven't found anything out yet, but I know that most teachers have symbiots. You don't.'

47

'Oh, I see.' His relief was obvious. Even to a thirteen-year-old. 'I'm not sure I can answer that without giving away the whole mystery. Why do you think I don't wear a symbiot? Reason it out for me.'

'I think you're not allowed one,' Zach said.

'And is that the only possibility? Could it not be by my own choice?'

'But you are a Weave teacher. And a scout master. Everyone old enough has one, even Lily.' A small one, like a bangle.

Miles's smile was thin and fixed, but he nodded at each suggestion. 'Or I might value my privacy.'

'Nyeah.' Zach batted that idea away with his hand. 'You're not superstitious.' Believing in privacy was like believing that a camera could steal your soul.

'Oh? Is superstition the only reason for people to want privacy?'

'Well, no. Of course not. Bad people need privacy to hide what they are doing.'

'Maybe I am a bad person,' Lizney suggested.

'But then you wouldn't be allowed to be my scout master,' Zach answered.

'True. Maybe I have something to hide?'

'Like what?'

'Musashi. I thought we had established the rules. That is for me to know and you to find out. I'm not going to tell you anything. You won't learn that way.'

'So you *are* hiding something,' Zach said triumphantly.

'Of course I am. That is the challenge of the exercise. I'm glad you have finally grasped the aims. Have you considered a medical explanation?' Mister Lizney asked. He must be trying to confuse him. To dilute his perception. Zach must be on the right track.

'I haven't heard of anything like that,' Zach answered.

'Have you looked into it at all? I can assure you such studies do exist, and are freely available.' Zach quickly flicked to the Weave, data mode, searching by phrase and keyword. 'I'll wait,' Lizney goaded. He wasn't lying, there were many documented cases where a symbiot connection was denied for health reasons. There was even a routine medical check before inception was allowed. 'Perhaps I have religion.'

Zach cursed as again his search showed that there were numerous belief systems that imposed bans on the wearing of symbiots. Lizney had done it, he'd made him uncertain.

'Zach, I give you points for your query. Even when one is uncertain, one should not hesitate to tell their teacher what they are thinking.'

'I felt so sure.'

'And you were right to express yourself. You deserve the reward. Now, for next week. When I noticed you've been reading *What We Can See*, I made a reading list for you of other classic works that I think have equal merit. Please have a scan of them before our next session.'

Musashi sagged as he read a list of fifteen titles. Fifteen! A children's picture book, *A Stream Runs Through It*, to the larger *The Eight-day Empire of the Fourth Weave*. A tome of eight volumes. Lizney knew all along what Zach was doing and was now throwing obstacles in his path.

Zach picked up his bag, folded his visor down and shoved it in his pocket. 'Thank you, Mister Lizney.'

'Thank you, Musashi. I'll see you next week.'

Sure enough, when he hit the tracks to his next lesson, the surveillance feeds he had connected to Lizney's apartment had been disconnected. He still had the footage recorded from before though, so his stream hadn't been rummaged. But if Lizney had known he was watching, he couldn't trust what he had seen.

Zach looked at the time and swore. 'Kutzo! I'm late.' Zach left the tracks at Corona and took an express bus across the city. The rest of his day he went from one tutorial to another. Watanabe for general math, Kelso for code and Belinda Maxwell for Weave history.

By the time he got home his feet were throbbing and his eyes itched. He was a cycle behind on his scouting thanks to Bronwyn and he would have to skip some of his sleep time to catch up and claim his endurance badge. He dropped his bag in his study room and went for a shower.

It didn't help as much as he had hoped. The warmth made him sleepy and he yawned as he put his visor on and it slipped off his nose. He tried again, but it kept sliding around his face. The inside was greasy with something, it smelt like butter ...

Oh, Bronwyn. Why would you want to bring the wrath of Musashi down upon you?

Wearily, he wiped it clean and began imagining what his revenge should be. Bronwyn didn't immerse, so there was no opportunity for pranking her on the Weave. He thought about having one of her soft toys replicated on a roboform, and then having it attack her in the night. She'd be terrified! He grinned.

At least it gave him something to pursue. He looked around his neighbourhood for who had a replicator and might allow him to use it. Dozey down the street had one, but he was a mesh-head and the kids were forbidden to associate with him. There was a boy not that much older than Zach who had one too. He lived a short scoot away, but Zach didn't know him.

He looked at the boy's stream. Garry Antram, sixteen. Only child. He went to classes centred around culture studies, architecture and organisation. His father had bought him the replicator kit for his birthday and they'd built it together over two nights, just so his son could make his model cities. Windsor Antram, the father, was forty-six years old, partnered to Eliza Barthes, though Garry's mother was a woman called Jasmin Tosche, who was now with a man who spent most of his time in the Cape. They hadn't had any contact with him in weeks and Garry's mother was becoming distraught.

Zach hated looking at the lives of other children and redirected his attention. The thing about the mother's partner disappearing interested him but if he looked through any information connected with Atlantic a flag would go up and he'd have to explain to Mister Lizney what his interest was. The Cape was a no-go zone.

What is my teacher up to now? he wondered. Now that his bugs had been disabled he had to watch from the outside. Zach tuned to the omnipoles near his teacher's residence and watched. Omnipoles were everywhere in the WU and some people joked that they were the real civilisation and we humans just ran amongst them; they were regularly spaced streetlights, Weave nodes, and held an array of passive sensors and inductive power coils. There were four poles in proximity to Lizney's home and Zach had each of them adding their data directly to his own stream for processing.

The light in Lizney's unit went out. A woman rode past on a bicycle. Zach sat and waited, but nothing more happened.

So why does a man like Lizney not have a symbiot? Belief system, impairment or because he had a negative assessment from the ups? What exactly was a 'negative assessment'? How did one get 'negatively assessed'? Technically, he knew that the Will could restrict someone's activities if they deemed them counter to the Will, but in reality he couldn't see how this would ever apply to a person.

He scanned through the Weave and compiled a better definition: when the actions of a given Citizen are deemed to be of negative effect to the World Union. It was a common phrase that meant little; Citizens had actions denied all the time, every day. But what kind of action would the Will decide was such a threat as to deny a person a commonplace item like a symbiot?

Of the sample cases he looked through, there was nothing like it. Unless of course he just couldn't access such cases. There was lots of data behind the Lizney wall he couldn't see. As he was only thirteen, the Will determined that not all information would be available to him. This would repeal as he got older, and when he became a Citizen and gained more value.

It didn't make any sense anyway. If Lizney was a malefactor, and the Will was denying him a symbiot, surely such an untrustable man wouldn't be allowed in charge of twenty impressionable children?

Maybe it was privacy. Zach didn't really know what that

was. It was something a lot of older people spoke of. They didn't see the Weave as he did, didn't always have their streams on. A stream to him was just like clothing, you always wore it. To be out of contact with the Weave, to have part of your life go unrec, was a real anxiety for him. He couldn't wait to get a symbiot.

Zach felt himself fading into sleep, his helmet automatically starting to pull him out. He had to stay awake and he demersed just enough to reach into his bag for the stimulants he had been sneakily collecting. He needed something.

He spent the rest of the night pinging around as fast and randomly as he could. He couldn't concentrate enough to read. He fixed three broken links all by himself that were easily corroborated and tagged for implementation.

The WU was working towards a day when the information on the Weave would be cross-referenced and sacrosanct; parity. In the future, Miz Maxwell told him, there might not be a need for scouts to look for errata, as it would be impossible to enter false information.

Bronwyn was clearing the kitchen when he clicked off the next morning and went down for some breakfast.

She giggled as he studiously ignored her and requested his food allowance from the fridge. Since he was living out of sync with the other kids, most of his meals were automated ones.

The other guardian of the orphanage was preparing the ingredients for lunch and tutted at the girl.

'Now, now, Bronwyn. You're even. Play nice,' Lily said. She stirred a large pot of spiced beans and legumes. It smelt good to Zach and he hoped she would save him some for tomorrow.

'Yes, Miz Patch.'

Zach sat down and lathered spreads on plain toast. Bronwyn chopped apples but kept a wary eye on him in case he was about to throw something at her.

'Will that be enough for you, Zach?' Lily asked. 'Would you like some tea?'

'Yes, please. I'm pretty tired.'

'You look it. It was wrong of Bronwyn to interfere with your studies. As penance she will be taking over some of your chores until your badge is complete.'

'I'll what?'

'Don't protest. It's all you deserve. You know Zach is working hard and the least we can do is support him.'

'But he —'

'Knocked your files around, I know. Zach will be doing penance for that too. But you know the rules.'

'Yes, Miz Patch,' Bronwyn retreated. Zach smiled and bit into his toast, which all of a sudden seemed to have more flavour.

They were quiet for a moment, Zach chewing, Bronwyn cutting and Miz Patch checking the loaves she had rising. The orphanage was quaintly naturalistic. Lily had lived on the outskirts of Andreas before taking on the orphanage and strongly believed in 'real' foods, things that she made herself.

'What do you do in there all night anyway?' Bronwyn asked him.

'I'm scouting.'

'What does that mean?'

'It means I go on the Weave and look for problems,' he answered and thanked Lily as she brought him some peppermint tea; home-grown and dried in the herbarium in the yard.

'You know, Zach, Bronwyn has never immersed before. Perhaps you'd like to show her sometime?' Lily said casually.

'Never,' he said.

Lily tutted. 'You owe me a penance, young man. And it would be good for Bronwyn to dive soon. You could show her the ropes.'

'But I'm trying to get my badge. I don't need her bratting me while I'm working.'

'Zachary. Please remember our ways here. We help each other. Besides, Tom has already confirmed for me that there is a badge for introducing new people to the Weave.'

'She's too young.'

'I'm only two years younger than you,' Bronwyn said.

'Then you're two years too young,' Zach replied.

'You'd like to learn, wouldn't you, Bronwyn?' Lily asked, ignoring the pair of them.

'I think so.'

'You see, she doesn't even want to.'

'Zachary. Perhaps it was my mistake to have phrased this as a request, but I was only being polite. You don't want me to tell Mister Lizney that you were too selfish to help one of the other children, do you?' Lily asked sweetly, while sprinkling sugar on the warm loaves.

'Fine. She can dive in with me, but she better not slow me down.'

'Good, then. Tonight it is. Now you should get off to your classes. Bronwyn will clear your plates away.'

'I'll what?'

'Bronwyn, every time you say that I have to come up with more chores for you to do. Speak in full sentences, please.'

'Yes, Miz Patch.'

Zach checked and saw that to earn a guide badge he only had to get a freshie to work up an avatar and take them on the Weave for thirty consecutive minutes. There were steps and guidelines he had to follow and she had to give him a positive report at the end of it. He would have to pretend to be nice to her.

There was a knock at the door. He opened it and stood to one side. 'Please come in.'

Bronwyn was wearing a one-piece of flexy material and carrying her blankets. 'I didn't know what I should wear,' she said.

'It doesn't matter. You will be lying down the whole time. Here, take a seat.'

Bronwyn sat on the edge of the pallet that he'd put beside his.

'Okay, now lie back,' he said.

'Don't do anything to me.'

'I'm not going to do anything, Bron. I'm trying to earn a badge. You just have to behave and try not to ruin it.'

She poked her tongue out at him, but lay back.

'Now, because it is your first time I have to strap you in. We don't want you to roll off the couch and hurt yourself.'

'I'm not letting you tie me up.' Bronwyn snapped back to sitting position.

'Don't worry, it's just webbing. Nothing you can't get out of by yourself.'

He got her to lie back down and he pulled two wings of webbing over her, clipping them on either side of the couch.

'Are you comfortable?'

'No.'

'Good, then. Now, in your right hand is a button. This is your emergency eject button. You can press it at any time and the program will demerse you instantly.' She clicked the button in her hand. 'It won't do anything until you are actually in the Weave,' he said patiently.

'I was just testing.'

'You can have it in your left hand if you prefer.'

'Zach?'

'What is it?'

'Um, well. This is going to sound silly to you.'

'There are no silly questions, only silly answers.' He'd got that one from Mister Lizney.

'What's going to happen?' she asked.

'Next we put on the visor, or helmet, and run some checks. Then we dive in.'

'No, I mean, what happens? What is immersion?'

Zach looked at her. She looked confused and tense. 'You don't know?'

'I know what I've heard about it. That I'll be put on the Weave but I don't know what that really means. I don't know what immersing does.'

Zach scratched his head. He'd never had to explain it before. He ran a scan in the background for an explanation he could use. 'When you immerse, your natural senses are overridden and replaced with sensory information from the Weave.'

'That sounds awful.'

'It's not … it's, it's magical.' She didn't seem comforted. 'Look, on the Weave you can do anything. And be anything. If you want to be a bird and fly over the city, we can do that. If you want to visit the wonders of the world, then we can do that.'

'But I won't really be there?'

'It will feel like you are. The Weave has many levels to it, and a representation of the real world is only one of them. Then there are all the fictional places. We call them fabula, the made-up things, and that level is nearly infinite. And if you can't find what you want, you can build it. Tell me one thing you've always wanted to do, but can't.'

Bronwyn bit her lip. 'You won't laugh?'

'No promises. But I won't tell.'

'I want to dance in a palace.'

'Done.'

'Like in that show with the three princesses.'

'I bet you we can find the exact castle.'

'And I want a fabulous dress with lots of layers and ribbons.'

'Easy.'

'Really?'

'I think I've found just the place.' He smiled at her. 'But first you actually have to dive in. Which means relaxing into the couch, getting comfortable and putting the helmet on.' He held it up for her to look at.

It was old and made of soft fabric straps with ferric bands sewn inside — they were what did the work of marrying the brain with foreign stimuli. And then there was a pair of goggles and earmuffs that blocked out external light and sound.

'It's ugly.'

'It's all I could get on short notice. It's this or nothing, Bron.'

'Okay, but don't take any pictures of me in that thing.'

'Of course not. Here, let me help you.'

Zach gently adjusted the straps, reminding her that once the muffs were on she wouldn't be able to hear anything until she was immersed. He was about to flip the goggles into place when she stopped him.

'Why are you being nice to me?' she asked.

Zach shrugged. 'Lily said I had to, so there's no point making this worse than it has to be. Let's have fun.'

'Well, I like nice-Zach.' She giggled and kicked her feet about. 'Let's go dancing.' She was so keen and excited about her first dive Zach nearly felt bad for putting adhesive over the inside of the goggles.

With Bron safely in the ganzfeld he pulled out his own helmet, which was not a hand-me-down. He had worked hard for the slick foldaways, which were simple unbridged mirror spectacles that hung down from the forehead lattice. He was advanced enough now not to need a full ganzfeld to immerse.

'Okay, Bron. Can you hear me?' He looked over at her but she didn't move. 'Just nod or something.' She still didn't move. That meant she must be in.

Zach quickly lay on his own couch and dove in to find her stream, waiting in the blank space where she couldn't escape until he said so.

He saw her standing on an empty grey that stretched to a darker grey. There was no space here, only a sense of space.

'Who are you?' she asked. He was dressed as Musashi.

'This is my avatar, Bron.'

'Your what?'

'My visual representation on the Weave.'

'You look like some kind of samurai.' She started laughing. 'Is that how you see yourself?' Her laugh rolled into a cackle and she bent over double.

'There's nothing wrong with it!' he shouted at her. 'You just look like your normal boring self, but in here I can be whoever I want. In here I am Musashi and if you don't like it —'

'Musashi? Is that your boffy name?' she snorted.

'Fine, I'll leave you here.' He turned to go and began fading from her vision, which was just a trick of making his avatar transparent.

'No, I'm sorry. I'm sorry,' she said hurriedly.

'No, you're not. You're just a silly girl and you don't understand anything.'

'Zach, wait. Don't leave me here. I don't know what to do.' Her amusement turned to panic as he disappeared.

'Press the eject button. I don't care.' He made his voice thin and echoey.

'Please, Zach. I'm sorry. I won't laugh any more.' He stayed silent. 'I'll call you Musashi.'

He appeared behind her and made her jump when he spoke.

'On the Weave people represent the selves they want to be. You have to respect that.'

'I will. I'm sorry. I didn't mean to hurt your feelings.'

'You didn't. You're just a silly girl.'

'Zach, please — Musashi. I'm sorry. I'll be good.'

He looked at her and said it was okay.

'I didn't mean to laugh.' She began looking around at the endless grey. 'Where are we?' Bron asked. 'Is this it? Is this the Weave?'

'This is the load space, or dressing room. Here we get you ready for going in. You can't go on the visual Weave until we've sorted your avatar out.'

'What should I wear?'

'Didn't you want to become a princess?'

'How?'

'Think of something. Form the words in your mind and then picture what you want them to look like.'

'Nothing is happening.'

'This is hard the first time, but once you've got it you've got it.' He made a rack of dresses appear next to her, as well as a tall mirror. 'Look in the mirror. Then look at one of the dresses.'

'Oh!' Her mirror image was wearing a long green dress with sparkly bits. She looked down and saw that she really was wearing it.

'It's that easy. The helmet can connect to what you think. You just have to be able to link those thoughts to how you look. In your mind.'

He explained to her about the load space they were in, while she went through dress after dress, intoxicated with awe. 'Here you can preview changes to your avatar and search for new things and information. When we go into the visual space you can also add things as you go along. And you can always pull back to the dressing room if you want to change up.'

'Can I be older?'

'As you wish. What age do you want to be?'

'Eighteen.'

He saw her body grow tall and form curves. Inside the sateen gown she had chosen she was beautiful. He couldn't take his eyes off her.

'Okay, I'm ready. Let's go to the Weave.'

'Bron, you've been on the Weave this whole time.'

'I have?'

'Yes. You are connected to the data network. That's all the Weave is.' The Weave was everything it drew information from. All connection was part of the Weave.

'Oh, sure, but I meant the real Weave. Let's go to the palace.'

Zach found the castle she was after, the one from the show that was so popular with girls her age.

He bowed before her and held out his arm. 'May I have this dance?'

Princess Bronwyn laid her gloved fingers on his arm and nodded.

He loaded some dance steps into his stream and pulled her into the first position as they crossed to the location and the walls and floor faded into their vision. It was a fantasy castle, nothing that could ever have been built in the real world, on top of an impossibly thin mountain spire with stars bright and the moon gentle. In the ballroom, which was the only room constructed in the program, a standing orchestra played while couples in masquerade twirled on the polished marble floor.

Bronwyn gasped and nearly stumbled as she twisted around to view it all at once.

'Oh, I can feel the floor.' She tapped her foot harder on the floor. 'And when we spin, I can feel the wind in my hair. It's so lovely. Is it real?'

'Does it need to be?'

'Oh, I don't know and I don't care. What about these people? Are they real?'

'Some of them,' he said. Most were just programs dancing to fill the space, but there was no need to tell Bron that. 'This is how most people join the Weave, so they can just act like normal without having to think.' He explained how there were parallel representations of everything in the real world, how even now they could go to the study room in the home and be able to see themselves lying in the couches.

'Everyone who is connected, or is in the WU, is part of the Weave. Their data is always being added to their stream.'

'So we're in two places at once?'

He laughed. He remembered thinking that. 'No. We are only where our bodies are, but our streams represent us. How we act in the physical world, what we are looking at on the Weave *and* what our avatars are doing.'

'That is so odd,' she said.

'You get used to it. Everything has to be represented, to keep the data pure.'

'But this castle isn't real. It's made up.'

'That's true. This is the fabula.'

'Fabula?'

'The fictional worlds that have been created. The fantasy places that don't, or can't, exist anywhere but here. Here you can just act and you don't need to know anything about how the Weave works. In real life, would I be able to do this?' Zach jumped into the air, spinning higher and higher until he was touching the ceiling, and then he dove suddenly down and landed comfortably on the balls of his feet. 'This is better than the real world.'

His avatar turned and pivoted, automatically. The older Bronwyn was laughing and clutching his shoulder.

'Where did you learn to dance like this?'

'I told you, Bron, here we can be whatever we want to be and do whatever we want to do.'

They spun and turned and became dizzy in each other's arms.

As the half-hour mark passed, Zach received an automated message that he could end the session and receive his merit badge, but he let the dance continue. He still had to make his scouting quota though, so he left his avatar dancing while his stream flicked to code mode to check the background data of the palace.

He found fifteen live streams, actual people, who had come to experience the ballroom scene of 'Amazing Princess'. Two were from the Dome, five from Seaboard, one from Lima and seven who were accessing from outside the WU. These he found interesting. Non-Citizens didn't have permanent access like real Citizens, and yet they had chosen to come to this girlish fantasy realm. The Weave was made by all kinds, Zach reflected.

There was something odd in the room though. In the code level he could see a slow drift of data, tiny amounts from each stream, flowing towards an empty corner of the room. In visual mode there was nothing there, but something was connecting to the visitors ... nothing of importance but information nonetheless.

He watched it draw out details of where he lived and his life and then he sent a ping along with it, asking who it was. Zach didn't even know why he did it. He shouldn't have. He should have flagged it as a curiosity and left it for the trained scouts to look into.

He was just curious where the data was going, and had no idea that he'd broken a tripwire, but in the empty corner a thing appeared. A dark, non-reflective blob of an undefined visual profile, no avatar, and no record of its existence.

'Oh, kutz,' Zach cursed softly.

'What is it?' Bronwyn looked around. 'Eww. What's it doing?'

'Syphon,' he whispered.

The blob shivered and the room gasped. Some of the dancers flashed out immediately, leaving the rest to watch it bloat and distort. On the code level, Zach could see it was still sucking in data from those around it, but it was also starting to harden into an avatar. *Something this way comes.*

'Come on, Bron. We'd better get you out of here,' Zach said.

'Why? What is happening?' The rest of the crowd were fading out, each of them dropping danger flags on the site to draw the attention of the weavers.

'It's a hakka trap. I don't know how long it has been here, but it's illegally collecting data from people's streams.'

'Is that bad?' she asked.

'Yes. And now its master is on the way. We have to go. Hit your eject button.'

'How do I do that?'

She was hyperventilating. She couldn't take her eyes off the monster growing in the corner as it changed colour to red and began twisting in ugly circles.

'Concentrate, Bron. Go to the dressing room if it helps.'

'It's not working,' she cried.

Musashi gritted his teeth and loaded an eject button that he handed to her. All she had to do was imagine her own, but this would be faster. 'Now press it. It will trigger your demersion.'

She pushed the red button and her avatar was gone instantly. Gone and safe. Zach turned around to see what the syphon was doing before he ordered his own evacuation. The thing had firmed into a segmented flea-like creature with spikes all over its body. The syphon saw him and opened dozens of orifices ringed with spittle and showing wet teeth. The mouths roared and its spit sprayed onto him, burning through his armour.

Zach hit eject … Nothing happened. The syphon swelled and gawped and shot grappling teeth into him, dragging him towards it.

'Oh, kutz.'

It was an angry red now, body panting and pumping with the enthusiasm of killing. Through its front mouth an eroding voice boiled through the teeth. 'You're not going anywhere, squirt. It's time you learnt not to touch other people's things.'

Musashi pushed at his ejector to no avail; he was dragged closer until the teeth could reach him and began tearing into his avatar. He took his katana from his belt and stabbed at it, but the blade bounced off the hard skin, jarring out of his hold.

He swore again and again, reminding himself it wasn't real and the pain was surrogate only, but he was so mentally connected to his avatar that he felt it happening as if to his real body. He was screaming as if it was real. The syphon creature chomped into Musashi, slicing through his armour and pulping the flesh beneath.

With the last of his control Zach threw every flag and tag at the thing that he could, but they dissolved. No one was coming to help him. He heard a soft laugh as his head was engulfed in the main maw.

'Now you will feel the wrath of Dungeon.'

Zach watched as his stream was dissected, his past and connections severed, his recorded life macerated before his eyes. The damage clawed up to his head. He saw a smile of fangs in the dark, then another set and another until the blackness was nearly defeated by bloodstained teeth. All at once the smiles took bites at him and his visual stream went haywire. He no longer saw what was there. He saw what the hakka wanted him to see.

It was a nightmare of black and red; subliminal flashes of horror, death, torture, rape, the distinct degradation of distortion on flesh; and the screams, the shouts, the dark voices that moaned, cawed and crazed over the top of the graphic horror. The nightmare changed, human bodies exploding, the pains of horses and animals being slaughtered; high-pitched ear-splitting whistles as emaciated and diseased faces lost their flesh and were defiled before his eyes.

Even when he went catatonic, the assault didn't stop.

* * *

He woke on a street. A pattern of tiles was under his face. His avatar had been reconstituted into a chewed-up mess whose only possible movement was to ooze. The rear end of the beast pushed foul excrement upon him before flying up into the sky.

Zach pulled his viewpoint away from his avatar, now floating a few feet above his body. He looked at himself. Musashi, dead. He'd died in games before, but not like this. His mind could still see the sensory torture; recalling the visions made him want to vomit. His avatar bubbled. He couldn't think and lay as a pile of blood and filth.

His stream was gone. All his memories, his recordings and history were twisted or deleted. He didn't recognise himself or where he was.

The eject still wasn't working. Maybe the hakka had put a scramble into his helmet somehow. Something that interfered with his control. He focused on the load space: if he could just imagine the endless grey and start a reset ...

In a blink, Musashi was standing again. His helmet had reset and his last backup was restored. Everything was in place as it should be. As he had been before he took Bron in. Where was she? How long had he been immersed? Surely she should have alerted somebody by now. He should have been pulled out ages ago.

He felt sick. That was his first experience with a real hakka. As much as he had heard there were dangers on the Weave, he'd never thought of them seriously. He had always thought he could just eject from trouble, but Dungeon had held onto him, taken his sensory input and ...

Zach looked over Musashi, his proud petulant stance, his sword that outshone all lights. He didn't deserve that sword, or that armour. He was just a pathetic boy who had been chewed up and spat out by the first hakka he had come across.

He stripped his avatar of its gauntlets and breastplates, the leg guards and weapons dropping to the ground. Let somebody else have them. They were no use to him. Musashi was just a boy. A weak boy standing in his underwear. Alone. Alone. Alone. *You are worthless, Musashi.*

He imagined another him circling Musashi with a rod, beating him with words and a stick until the welts started to break open. Zach lifted his arm and pushed the beaten thing away, sending it to oblivion in a million pieces.

Zach looked around him. He should have sent a broadcast alarm, but what did it matter now? Dungeon could do it all over again and it would not matter.

The street was empty save for himself. He was in a geographical representation. A place with low flat buildings set in straight lines. It was odd to see an empty space on the Weave, he wasn't really sure what it meant.

He walked forward, checking every intersection and finding no one. No streams had passed through here for months. Perhaps it was abandoned. Zach checked the info and saw he was in one of the STOC relocation towns, Sector 261 of Omskya. From the passive data sent by the omnipoles, transport, medical, education and administration, all functions were normal, indicating the town was populated and working at peak efficiency.

So where is everybody?

Before he could answer the question he began to fade as he began to demerse, returning to his body. He could smell vomit, and taste blood and bitterness in his mouth.

Zach blinked and saw Tom's concerned face frowning over him. 'Zach, are you okay?'

'I'm okay. What happened? Why didn't anyone wake me earlier?'

'Well, when Bronwyn was ejected she leapt up and banged her head. She knocked herself out and only just came to.'

'Oh ...'

'I found her on the floor when I came to check on you. What happened in there, Zach?'

'It's my fault, Tom. It's all my fault. I touched something I shouldn't have. A hakka came for me.'

'And you couldn't eject?'

'They stopped me.'

'I didn't know they could do that. You seem okay though, right? Mister Lizney is coming right away, he'll be here any minute.'

'I'm fine, Tom.'

'Let's get you cleaned up at least.' Zach looked down and saw where the smell of vomit was coming from.

'Is Bron okay?'

'She'll be fine. But you owe her an apology.'

'Yes. I'm sorry, Tom. I'm so sorry.' He couldn't keep the tears from forming.

Zach lay in bed unable to sleep. He wasn't used to sleeping when it was light outside. More than that, he couldn't stop the images of his recent experience repeating in his head. When he closed his eyes he saw them more clearly and even when he felt like sleeping he snapped awake as a scene of black and blood came back to him.

He didn't notice when one of the older boys from the orphanage tiptoed in and knelt by his bed, until he asked, 'Hey, Zach, are you sleeping?'

'No.'

'Mister Lizney is here to see you.'

'He is?' Zach had never known his teacher to go outside of his unit.

'Yeah. Strange guy for a teacher, Zach. Totally cryppy. Should I say you're awake?'

'Yeah. Thanks, Garth.'

'You want him to come in here, or can you get up?' Garth asked him.

'I ...' Zach tried to rise, but his body felt like glass and his head turned against him.

'Okay. Wipe your eyes.' Zach didn't realise he had still been crying, even though both his cheeks were wet and cooling. He hadn't noticed. When he blinked, horrors were behind his eyelids. He tried to shake them off, but they wouldn't move.

A hand patted him and he turned. Mister Lizney was sitting by him on the bed. Before he knew it, he had flung himself at his teacher and didn't bother to hold back the tears. 'I'm sorry. I'm sorry.'

Lizney wasn't used to such contact and the attack of affection caught him unprepared. But he'd seen what other people did and he put his arms around the boy and patted him.

Zach repeated he was sorry and begged for it to stop. 'Please. I won't do it again. Please.'

Miles patted and shushed him. There would be plenty of time later to ask for the boy's account, so while he was waiting for the emotional outpouring to end he tried to find out what had happened, though Zach's stream had been dismantled somehow and there was no record of his time on the Weave this evening.

Mister Lizney acquired permission from Bronwyn Zucker and the two guardians before accessing her stream, as was proper with juniors. He watched as Zach led her through orientation and then took her to a dance visualisation in the fabula. It was there that something appeared and Zach ejected her.

'Oh, my boy, what did you find?' he asked gently. Zach pushed his head further into his chest.

Something that could take a stream to pieces and stop a person from ejecting. What kind of hakka would do such a thing? And what else had the hakka done to turn the boy into such a mess?

'May I access your stream?' Lizney asked. Zach nodded, but Lizney had to prompt him again to make him give over permissions. There wasn't much to see anyway. The stream was a backup from before the night's dive and jumped straight to the town where Zach had been spat out. Those streets … with their identical capsule housing. Lizney knew this place. He remembered its homogeneity well. Except for the image of his student punishing the body of his old avatar, the streets were empty.

He sent a broadcast to Zach's teachers letting them know what had happened and that they should let him know if they observed anything out of the ordinary, or if Zach let slip any information about what had happened to him.

'Excuse me,' the Colonel said, bumping the pilot's arm as he clambered from the back to the front seat for a better view. The peninsula was just coming into visual range. With his enhanced eyesight, he could just make out the dark blemish that was being called the 'beast of Busan'.

Pinter looked at his pilot, Airman Quintan Crozier. The file said he was male, but he was slight and feminine, with hair coloured an unnatural bronze sitting in a high bouffant that tickled the ceiling of the squib. He was young, thirty-three — they were all going to seem young to him from now on, he reminded himself.

'Are you a good pilot, Crozier?' he asked.

'Of course, sir.'

'A good little Serviceman, or a man who can get the job done?'

'Sir?' The airman looked at him sideways and caught the Colonel in a half-smile.

'Fly me in closer. I want to take a look at this thing.'

'We are approaching the restricted area, sir.'

'Yes. But we can get closer, can't we?'

'I can't do that, sir.'

'Don't be modest, airman. I've read your file. You're top class.'

'Thank you, sir. Then you must also know that I have already been held back for insubordination.'

'Twice, in fact. Yes, I read that. But it's not insubordination if a superior tells you to do it,' Pinter said with a grin.

'Sir, we are scheduled to land in three minutes.'

'Yes, but they can't start the welcome ceremony without me, now, can they? I want to take a good look at this thing.' He shook the pilot's shoulder. 'Relax. You're following orders. I outrank everyone on the ground.'

'Sir, yes, sir.' Quintan smiled.

'Call me Colonel.'

Colonel, he said to himself. Until now it had been practically an honorary rank, which he hadn't taken seriously. The last time he was an active Serviceman he had only been a Captain. How would history have been different if he had been a Colonel the last time he was thirty? Maybe the wars wouldn't have drawn out for so long.

The squib flew on towards Busan — where Busan used to be. There was now almost nothing left of the city. The hard lines of the larger structures could still be made out underneath the undulating black hills. A tendril the length of a street bulged up and swung out towards the sea; Crozier avoided it easily.

'Can it see us?' Pinter asked.

'It doesn't seem to.'

'So, it's blind?'

'Hard to say. This is the closest I've gotten.'

'It really is enormous. Have you ever seen anything that big?'

'Nothing living, sir.'

'Do you think it is an animal of some sort?' Pinter asked.

'What else can move like that? No plant that I've ever seen.'

'Yes, but there's never been an animal that covers a thousand square kilometres before either. How could any one creature be this big? Fly us over the top.'

'Sure thing, Colonel.'

They swung up high before levelling out to cruise over the inky landscape. From above, the Colonel could see where the creature sank into the ocean, a clear change from black to turquoise showing its edge. Below the water, the same exploratory tentacles probed about. Feeling?

What sort of thing are you? he asked. The leading theory was that it was an old unrecorded nano-weapon that had somehow been reactivated. It was possible. It had happened before, though not with such spectacular results.

From above, Pinter could see open spaces in the black mass, and every park and tree remained uncoated, creating pockets of green scattered throughout the city.

'Nobody mentioned that,' he said.

'What?'

'The trees. It's not touching them.'

Quintan nodded.

Pinter's mind tried to find comparisons for what he was seeing. It was dark and massive like a lava plain, but seemingly alive and moving a hundred tendrils around like a sea urchin in a rock pool. It was black and sheeny like crude oil, but it could direct its movements and control its form. So far the researchers had turned up very little that it could be compared to.

'What would you say that looks like? A sea anemone?'

'It reminds me a bit of a snail, at least the tentacles do,' the pilot answered.

'The largest snail in the world is only a metre long, including the shell. How big would you say one of those arms are?' he asked.

'They can get pretty long. I've seen them stretch a couple of hundred metres.'

'Phenomenal. Take me around the edge of it. Slowly.'

'What about the ceremony, sir? I'm getting asked what we're doing.'

Pinter too had seen inquiries enter his queue. He bounced them for now. 'Send a message that we will be delayed, all fine, Colonel's orders.'

'As you wish, sir.'

The Colonel was reluctant to land. Landing meant that time really would have gone backward for him and he was once again a Serviceman. He could look in the mirror and see the man he used to be, but inside he was forty-eight years older and had been long retired. His time was done.

His memories felt like bad dreams that made him afraid to fall asleep again. He had left those nightmares decades ago. He had lived another life and now he was being drawn back into the past. He remembered the sweet rot of his men and the smoke of his burning enemies. He saw the teeth and claws of the twisted humans, launching at him like vultures —

'Colonel, are you okay? You've gone pale,' Quintan said.

'I'm fine.'

'Is my flying too bumpy?'

'No, no. I just don't want to land. That's all.'

'Another pass? Straight over the middle?' Crozier suggested.

'No. I shouldn't. Time to face the music.'

* * *

There actually was music when he landed. A bugler sounded off as he stepped from the squib and a drummer rapped along as he inspected the line of Servicemen standing at attention. His overlay hung names on them and gave bullet-point histories of their careers.

The man in charge was a ginger-haired Lieutenant who was looking down at his clipboard and refreshing the image he had of the Colonel in his files. Pinter's overlay marked him as Campsey, Lt, James. A lackey of Zim's who had been borrowed from the General to duplicate the perimeter boundary they had constructed around the Cape.

'Lieutenant Campsey?' Pinter held out his hand.

'Yes, sir.' The Lieutenant saluted and then shook the Colonel's hand.

'I hear you have a mysterious entity that has destroyed a whole city. What do you have to say for yourself?'

Campsey stuttered, 'But, sir, I —'

'At ease, Lieutenant. If we can't joke about the end of the world, what can we joke about?'

'Sir?' The poor man was confused. He looked down at his clipboard to see if there was anything written there for him to say. The Colonel let him off the hook.

'This all looks very good. Let's check the perimeter and then I want to visit the thought room.'

Turning around, he caught Quintan Crozier grinning and Pinter swiftly claimed the man to be his personal aide. The pilot's face fell as the command came down the line.

Pinter: Get my bags, Crozier. Quick smart.

77

* * *

Lieutenant Campsey, Airman Crozier and Colonel Pinter boarded an open-topped hover and programmed it to guide them around the boundary line.

Their first stop was where the unitracks had been demolished. Across the ravine the mass had stopped advancing and now probed the air and dirt with its yearning black tentacles.

Services was progressively clearing land from all sides, excavating a series of canyon-deep trenches with remote dozers. The beast somehow sensed the machines if they went within a hundred metres.

'So it can see?' Pinter asked.

'We don't think it can see, visually. Stealth drones can approach quite close, so we think it is hearing them, or feeling the vibrations through the ground. It may be picking up the radio control signal, or the electricity, or heat.'

'Then it has senses. Can it feel?'

'Does it feel pain, you mean?'

'Yes. Cut it to see if it bleeds, tickle it to see if it laughs. That sort of thing.'

'That is outside my purview, sir.'

'Of course. We'll schedule some tests immediately.'

'What kind of tests?'

'Oh, the usual. We'll throw things at it to see what happens.'

'And if that doesn't work?' Campsey asked.

'Then we'll try something more extreme. Don't fidget, Crozier. If you have a question, ask me.'

'I was just wondering if that is the best way to engage with an unknown and hostile mass,' Quintan said.

'I may not look it, Crozier, but I'm an old man. I like the direct approach, I'm not planning on dancing with the thing.'

'But attacking is aggressive.'

'Yes. But twelve hours ago it took four million lives. What do you call that?'

'But …?'

'Yes? Speak freely,' Pinter prompted.

'We don't even know what this thing is.'

'That's the beauty about the unknown. You never know.'

'You're enjoying this?' the airman asked.

'Immensely. Enigmas are good for the soul.'

'And what if firing at it achieves nothing?'

'It can't achieve nothing. If we hurt it, then we can consider it alive. If we don't, then we treat it like pollution and clean it up.'

'And if it is alive?'

'Then we try to communicate.'

'You're going to talk to it?'

The Colonel shrugged. 'If we can. Don't forget that the only animal on Earth we have ever been able to talk with is ourselves, but we learnt to control them anyway. I just want to know what it wants. Carry on, Campsey. Continue the tour.'

They proceeded to where the land met the sea and stood on the headland to look through the waves.

'It doesn't seem to behave any differently underwater,' the Colonel observed.

'No, sir.'

'Is that interesting?' Quintan asked.

'Very much so. Tell me, is it still expanding?'

'Its coverage isn't, but its volume seems to be. Results are inconclusive.'

If it is an animal, Pinter thought, *then it is either feeding or resting*. 'And we don't know how far underground it goes?' he asked.

'No.'

'Is there a contingency in case it does advance again?' Pinter asked.

'The mass hasn't expanded since its initial appearance.'

'That wasn't the question. What is the strategy if it does?'

'I don't know, sir.'

'Understood,' Pinter said gravely. He twisted around to look at Crozier, who still wasn't sure why he was there. 'What would you do?'

'Me?'

'Pull back?'

'Yes. Until we know more.'

The Colonel fed his command into the strategy-matrix, or strat-mat, as it was usually shortened to. The commander's primary role was to continuously build up and revise preset reactions for every event they could conceive of, just in case one eventuated, and then continually revise it as new information came to light or circumstances changed. He remembered it was like guessing the future.

Campsey pointed out the notable defences as they began their return journey. 'Mobile artillery and plasma tanks form a two-tier boundary. Overhead, the border is patrolled by ten drone squadrons of one hundred each. The same as the Cape cordon.'

'And orbital coverage?'

'Currently at forty per cent.'

'I'll ask Shreet to condense that. Anything else?'

'We've constructed the viewing platform, as you requested.' Lieutenant Campsey tried to shift the focus. Soon he would get to the end of his list where the Colonel would be shown to his sleeping quarters, and then he could report and hope to be returned to his former unit.

'Then take me to it,' the Colonel ordered him.

The hover tilted and began driving up a ridge on the western side of Busan where it set down at the base of a high scaffold. Tall trees surrounded it and the platform floor sat just amongst the topmost branches, pushing out to give a view of the beast and the ocean behind it.

If not for the enormous black mass, it would be a picture worth sharing. As it was, the graceful bay was interrupted by the sluggish beast. Arms, or tentacles — or whatever they were — lifted up into the air and then dropped back down. The distance made them look slow and languorous.

'Are you sure it didn't creep out of the sea?' Pinter asked, not really expecting an answer. He watched for a while, forgetting the others were there. He had stood like this at the base of mountains, volcanos, the world's tallest trees, trying to absorb their immensity.

'Yes, I like this. Set me up here.'

'Here, sir? This is just a viewing platform, your quarters are much better equipped.'

'I have all the equipment I need, thank you, Lieutenant. But do fetch me some chairs and a table. And get a canopy over this, will you? I don't intend to let my new skin go the same way as my old one.'

'Yes, sir.' Campsey inserted the new items on his to-do list.

'Now, let's see what your researchers have achieved. Crozier, get me some water while I immerse.'

The Prime had ordered the best minds across various sciences to work on the problem around the clock and for the last eight hours the highest-ranked brains in the WU had had their streams in a permanent connection to a virtual common room.

The first thing the Colonel noticed was the babble. There were a thousand experts tuned into the room, their thoughts and musings overlapping without inhibition.

'Why hasn't it touched the trees?'

'How could it have grown this fast?'

'Where does it draw energy from?'

'What are its core functions?'

Theories and epistles were written and dumped into the pool for factioning. The Colonel stood in the centre not engaging with the mess of inconclusive notions, just listened to them as they spoke over the top of each other.

'Who is in charge here?' he finally asked, prioritising his communications to interrupt everyone else's.

A female avatar stepped forward to introduce herself: Gretchen Caswell of the Wissenschaftskolleg. 'I am, Colonel.'

'Correction, Miz Caswell. I am in charge. You are organising the thought room.'

'That is what I meant, Colonel.'

'Just straightening out the language. It's no bother. Tell me what you have so far.'

'Well, sir, we have a lot of ideas but no hard evidence.'

'Why is that?'

'It is only the first day, sir, and we are limited to observational study. Until we have a sample to work with, conjecture is all we will be able to offer.'

'And we can't get a sample?'

'Our earlier attempts failed. It absorbs everything it touches. All the vehicles we've put close to it have been consumed.'

'I understand. I guess that will be our first priority. What have you observed? Can we communicate with it at all?'

'No, sir, we have tried all known communication methods: radio, light, optical *and* audio. Nothing.'

'No response at all?'

'No, sir.'

'Nothing reactive?'

'Negative.'

'And I presume it isn't emitting anything either?' She shook her head. 'Spectral analysis? What's this thing made of?'

'Results are inconclusive. It has been changing since it first appeared. There are traces of all elements you'd expect to find in a large city.'

'From the language you are using, the room seems to be assuming this to be mechanical. What do the biologists say?' he asked.

'They don't think it is biological.'

'So what's the leading theory?'

Miz Caswell looked uncomfortable, her face stricken. 'I would prefer not to suggest anything at this time.'

The Colonel scratched at his chin and thought. 'You were right about having nothing to go on ... We don't know if it is sentient or non-sentient ... Animal, vegetable or mineral? Or all of the above?' The Colonel started creating his own task list, making the collection of a specimen the top priority, and then creating commands to follow once that was achieved. 'We'll need containment plans for the study of the samples. Can you put together the relevant protocols?'

'Yes, Colonel,' she answered. 'How will you do that, sir? Get the samples, I mean.'

'With a hook and a line. While I concentrate on getting you a sample, I want tests devised for these questions, but we won't make an attempt until I have approved the containment strategy. We cannot afford for this to break out elsewhere.'

'No, sir.'

'And then you'll have twenty-four hours to tell me what this thing is.'

The Colonel blinked out from the session and turned around to find Lieutenant Campsey standing nearby, his screen of protocols hugged to his chest. 'What next, Lieutenant?'

'Would you like to see your quarters?' he asked nervously.

'No. I think I'm going to watch for a while. Leave me, will you?' Campsey turned to walk away. 'Oh, and Lieutenant. Have my capsule made up for two people. I'm expecting some company in a few days.'

'Company, Colonel?'

'Yes. A friend.'

'Sir ...'

'That will be all.'

Dark lenses slid over his eyes, cutting the brightness in half.

Pinter had quickly become used to the overlay during his recovery and now ran constant tasks in the background. He watched the analysis of the beast's progression, the initial rapid expansion of the mass slowing when it reached the edge of the city. When it hit the fields it followed only wires and the unitracks. It didn't go over the plants and he wondered if that was significant. It was like it was targeting animals and tech. Metal and flesh. He flicked an order to the Lieutenant to make sure wire connections were severed to at least a kilometre from the city edge, as well as all roads and unitracks to be cleared well back from the trench.

The Lieutenant acknowledged receipt of the message and tallied up his new work orders. There were suddenly twenty-six new items on his to-do list.

'What should I do now, sir?' Quintan asked from behind him.

'Just watch. Watch and think.'

'And then what?'

'Watch and think some more.'

'I was wondering, Colonel, if I could ask you a question?'

'Don't hesitate with me, Crozier. Life is short.'

'Why did you draft me? What am I doing here?'

Pinter turned to the airman and made the shades over his eyes open so they could be seen clearly. 'You're here for company.'

'That's it? Why me?'

'Because you were laughing at me.'

'I wasn't,' Quintan said.

'I saw it. I can play it back for you if you like.'

'No need, sir. I apologise for laughing.'

'Yes, but the thing is, as soon as that twip started talking I knew I couldn't bear it here alone.'

At that moment Pinter received a ping from Geof Ozenbach. He allowed the connection and the figure of the weaver superimposed itself into his vision. A see-through ghost of his former colleague.

'Hello, sir. You are looking well,' Geof said.

'I'm new and improved. To what do I owe the call, Geof? How goes the hunt for Pierre Jnr?'

'I've been distracted by the new phenomenon, to be honest, and I'm making contact because I've been looking at this black mass.'

'The beast of Busan.'

'Yes. I've been patterning the spread to find its point of origin.'

'And?' Pinter asked.

'It looks like it came out of Shen's laboratory.'

'Shen Li?' The Colonel escalated the conversation for the thought room to take notice. 'The symbiot guy?'

'That's him. I think this is one of his experiments.'

'What kind of experiment, Geof?'

'When I was there, he had a flawed digitalis locked behind a vault. He wouldn't tell me much about it.'

'I think you'd better make a full report. I'll contact the Prime. He should hear this too.'

They met in a closed room, encapsulated from the general Weave. Geof and the Prime's team both built walls of protection around it.

Ryu was quickly up to speed.

'Continue,' he said to Geof.

'Well, I've been looking over the cut-off pattern from Busan and — sorry, may I?' Geof shifted the visualisation to the Prime's queue. It opened up into a satellite view that showed each Citizen's stream from the city at the moment they lost contact with the Weave; played in reverse, it shrank down to a single point of origin. 'The first cut-offs happen directly above the shaft to Shen Li's lab.'

'You surmise it came from there?'

'I can't be certain, but that is what the data indicates.'

'What kind of thing was he working on, Mister Ozenbach?' Ryu asked.

'Sensei worked on many things at once. He had tables of projects I couldn't begin to understand. But when I was there, he talked about a failed digitalis experiment that he kept sealed in a vault.'

'That's all?'

'Sensei did not share his ideas with me.'

'What is a digitalis?' Pinter asked.

'Digitalis was Shen's opus. It was meant to be an evolutionary step that took humans from flesh and blood to a digital form. A new body that could always be repaired and live forever.'

87

'The great Shen Li was wasting his time on that?' Ryu asked. 'Cyber-mystic nonsense?'

'It was the next logical step after symbiots, for humans to become part of their body. It was his dream and I think —'

'Tell me more about this failed experiment,' Pinter said, keeping the conversation on track.

'He wouldn't tell me any more than that. He kept it locked in a vault so it couldn't get out. He was afraid of it,' Geof said. 'He called it Kronos.'

'Kronos?' The Colonel looked at the beast on the screens. It had a name now. 'So what is it exactly? That doesn't look like a human evolution to me.'

'It was a failure.'

'A failure that has taken four million lives,' the Prime said. He thought for a moment. 'Ozenbach, I will need you to work on this problem.'

'What about Pierre Jnr?' Geof asked.

'I would like you to run the data for me on both, for now. But until there is new information on that front, Busan takes priority.'

'That is an honour, Prime,' Geof answered quickly. *I'll have to upgrade*, he thought with glee.

'Now that Takashi has been compromised, I need a weaver I can trust.'

'Thank you, Prime.'

The Prime sighed deeply. 'Our problems seem to be breeding.'

'Yes,' Pinter agreed.

'Prime, may I ask something?' Geof said.

88

'Ask it if you must.'

'What about Peter Lazarus? Couldn't he continue the hunt for Pierre Jnr?'

'We have had to restrict Peter Lazarus for the time being. His recent actions in the Cape have thrown doubt on his allegiances.'

'But he is alive?'

'Alive and well. You have my word.'

'Thank you, Prime.'

'Now, is there anything else? The Primacy council awaits my return.'

'That is all for now. We will begin our tests as soon as it is dark,' Pinter said.

'Very good. Keep me informed and thank you for this news. It couldn't have come at a better time.'

The Prime's avatar blipped from his overlay and Pinter and Geof were alone in the conversation again.

'I'll need you to reconfigure the thought room,' the Colonel said, simultaneously adding it to his list. 'Gather everyone who you think might be able to reverse-engineer this Kronos thing.'

'Yes, Colonel.'

'Chin up, Geof.'

Peter Lazarus woke in a white room. Around him he heard the sounds of the ocean. Waves pushing in and pulling out across the sand with a gentle rush.

He was on his back, blinking at the pearlescent ceiling that spread a too-bright light across the room.

He rolled over on his side and fell from the bed, a white floor rushing towards him like a crashing wave. He felt no pain when he hit.

He lay in cold mud. Dark water lapped through his clothes and the back of his head throbbed. Above him, the imperfect rooftop imitated a sky with too few stars. He heard things. Squelchy running and weapons firing. Every now and then the light strobed in different colours as if fireworks were going off around him.

All attempts to move sent him into spasm. At some point an armoured soldier stood over him and unloaded something from his pack.

He felt a sharp jab, then no sensation. He was free of pain, he floated above it. The bot took position over his head, eight legs pinching him until it was firmly secure. Then he felt vibrations and the loud scrape of stitching close by his ear.

He could blink and breathe. At least he could breathe ...

The soldier bent down and affixed a white oval to his face.

He lay face up in a restorative pallet. He didn't know how long he had been lying there. His muscles were reluctant to move.

If this was a hospital, where were the nurses? Where was that nurse, the one he knew? Was she prohibited from seeing him now? Where was he? The walls and ceiling were canvas. Plastic-waxed and crumpled as though he was inside a ball of screwed-up paper.

Was he still at the compound? Was the rest of that time a dream? Or from a life he had forgotten? Did it come before or after he was standing on that paved street, waiting for something to happen?

He closed his eyes and saw eyes staring back at him. Calm eyes, reading him as if he was the pages of a book. That face knew him ...

They strapped him into a cockpit. Tied down with secure webbing over his chest. He could hardly hold his head up and it flopped to the side where he could see the city of Atlantic retreating from view. It spread out of sight. Five hundred or so kilometres of clustered habitation. Dirty smoke rising in a column from where the compound had been destroyed.

Pete didn't hear a thing as the squib lifted into the air but the acceleration made him woozy. With the pain from his head and the drugs in his system he was nearly senseless.

He tried sending a message to his symbiot, but it didn't respond. He tried again, but the effort made his head hurt. He reached up with limp hands and found gel pads bandaging him from cheek to shoulders.

The squib flew on in silence. He was the only person on board, and yet ... he did not feel alone. Was there someone in the second chair? Did it twist as though an invisible body was turning it? He felt so sure he reached out his hand towards it.

'Pierre?' he asked.

His hand touched the back of the seat. There was no one there.

He closed his eyes.

How many times had he slept and woken up? They slept him and woke him as needed. Switched on and off like a machine.

On, off. On, off. Services activated and deactivated as and when they had a use for him. Like a bot. And just like Pierre did. On. Off. On. Off.

He was falling again, dropping into a white cloudscape, whipped to peaks. Then he was in the room of white. A clinical room with a pallet beside him. He used it to push himself up.

At a spell of nausea, Pete touched his head and held it until it stilled. The gel pads were gone. Concentrating on taking small breaths, he managed to rise up and sit on the edge of the bed.

Below his feet a dashed line glowed into existence in the flooring. It led across the room to a cleaning cubicle that had opened in the wall. There it ended in a circle about his size. It was obvious he was meant to follow.

As he arrived a shute opened by his feet and an icon of a shirt appeared above it. He understood. Stripping his clothes was hard and he had to sit down to remove his trousers, but when he dropped them into the shute, he was rewarded by a drench of sweet-smelling water. Warm and calming. He could smell spices and grated ginger. He heard the sound of the ocean and looked down to the water touching his toes. Beside him, a boy stood looking up ...

The water stopped and was replaced with strong air currents. They pushed up and down his body until every hair was dry. On the floor the dashed line appeared again, this time leading him to a drawer that had slid out from the main wall. It held fresh clothing. Standard white, two-part, gratuit.

Once dressed he looked down for the line and it now led to the little alcove, with a circle at the end.

As he faced it, the back wall of the nook became reflective. His mirror image drew him closer.

He hadn't seen himself in a while. His hair was longer by an inch. Two weeks' worth, perhaps three. He noticed a fracturing in his skin, his growing hair avoiding the new scar.

A thick stubble had grown on his chin and around his neck was a metal collar. He reached to touch it and his body went into a fit.

'Don't,' he heard a gentle voice say.

Pete stood up from the floor. He swayed as if he was at sea. His head felt as if there was water inside it and he took deliberate steps towards the door, trying not to slosh it from side to side.

He reached towards the panel and it opened ahead of his touch, sliding back to show a corridor full of daylight. The ceiling was frosted glass and the day outside was hot. The corridor curved away to both left and right. Echoes of voices bounced from either end.

This way, said a voice in his head.

Pete tried to focus on it, but turning made his skull slosh and he had to lean on the doorframe.

To your left.

He dragged himself forward, keeping his hand to the wall as he doggedly kept moving. *Who are you?*

Then he was on the ground again, on all fours, as his body undulated and pumped liquid yellow vomit from his mouth. For torturous moments he was a bursting hose, spraying the floor. Spatter hit his hand and the pool of it spread to his knees.

Quickly his stomach was empty, but he didn't dare move. He watched as a wheelie bot, no bigger than his fist, zoomed under him and began sucking up the fluid. He turned and crawled back to his room. His new clothes were dirty and wet and he stank in his mouth. He needed to wash, but the effort of removing his clothes left him curled up on the smooth floor where he passed out.

Try as he might, Pete couldn't stretch his mind out. His consciousness wobbled as if it had turned to rubber. When he tried to float away from his body he sank and found himself dizzy.

What is happening?

It's okay. Try to be calm, the friendly voice said.

His next attempt was better. His head didn't slosh as much, and nor did his stomach. His brains were made of thicker syrup this time and he could keep his balance through the washing and dressing. He ignored the line that led to the mirror and went back towards the exit.

He made it all the way to his door and with his back permanently to the wall he could manage to shuffle along the corridor.

Pete passed more doors like his with white touch panels at waist height. They didn't open for him. When he pressed his fingers to the plastic squares, they turned red and showed a name, presumably the occupant who the door would open for.

The corridor opened out, the rectangle of brighter light tilted as he crept forward, until it finally filled his view. His head was flopped to his shoulder and he twisted his body to look at the room. There were many people there. A fist caught him square in the face. All went white and black. And black and white.

When thinking of the megacities, the definition expands from simple buildings for housing and industry and includes the larger environmental and financial ecosystem.

The system of West, the largest of the WU cities, stretched the length of the Andreas and included the water tables for another three hundred kilometres inland. It hugged the coastline with its vast fisheries and wave-powered energens, and dropped away before reaching the ruins in the valleys and the deserts. West, like the Cape, was a general name used by the public for that area. The places where people lived and worked had localised regions like Beverly Hills, Corona or Frisco.

Far to the south, with no hardline roadway or unitrack connecting the two, was the megapolis known as Mexica.

Many other cities had been abandoned in the Dark Age. Some when their supply lines died, others from infestations of splicer diseases that still lived in the soils. Some cities never died completely. They fell into liver-spotted convalescence, part rubble, part ruin. Inhabitants pieced together their livings and a society from what could be found: trading antiques and services for food and modernisation. A few, like Petersburg and Chicago, were trying to reclaim. The weather was easing and people liked to visit the ruins; if they could succeed in installing the parks and gardens they planned, these two cities would become quite beautiful places.

Mexica was unkindly thought of as a city that didn't know it was already dead. Nothing new was built here. Only scavengers made a home, eking out a living. Most of the old cities had long ago been picked clean. Every useful scrap had been hauled away for re-use or smelt. Mexica lived off the past, a huge scrapyard of collected junk. Centuries of outdated tech. The rubbish the rest of the world didn't want.

Gomez had built himself a watchtower on the third pile in their zone. It wasn't the tallest of the stacks, but it had a lot of old military vehicles that were easy to climb and the missing doors and windows formed tunnels he could run through. His scouting point was an old cockpit, separated from the ginormous fuselage it must have once guided. The portals were broken out and let the breeze through — when there was one.

He kept some of his treasures here: a pair of oculars he'd found, strips of smart wire and batteries. He had once found a dart rifle with no darts and Gom liked to sit at the front of the cockpit, zooming in and out with the telescopic enhancements, aiming and clicking the impotent trigger. Imaginary bullets for imaginary invaders.

Invaders could be anyone in his game, like rival junkers entering their turf — his family had a lease on these lots, but it was their responsibility to protect it. They didn't have much trouble, although Gom had an alert button he could activate that would send a message back to his family. There were fewer junkers now. Most of the good stuff was gone. Some families had made their fortune and moved into the city; others just got by doing what they could get away with.

The cockpit was heating up under the sun and Gomez began crawling deeper into the scrap heap. He had some water in an empty tanker down the bottom and a lot of other supplies he had secreted there. Rations, a portable heater, knife, compass. Everything he collected that might come in handy if the darkness fell on Earth again.

His papa said he should always be prepared for the worst, even when things were at their best. For the worst he had a bag of ammo, and guns: pre-Dark Age, but they would be lethal enough.

Gomez had the junk stacks pretty well mapped out now. He knew where his family had and hadn't mined and had catalogued areas of interest for later searches. He carried an old rubberised handscreen with the scavenge list his father had given him for the week. Most of the stuff was easy — wiring and components, and general scrap for the smelt. He wanted to put off the liquids for another day. Leaching out plasma coils was slow, boring and heavy. Today was too hot for a liquids run.

Gom always kept his eyes out for collectables he could trade for access credits and every month he managed to collect enough minutes to explore the Weave when no one was looking over his shoulder.

He lay down on the cool curved wall of the tanker and connected. Overall, he hadn't spent much time connected, his stream had a log of merely a dozen hours. Mostly he visited other places, just to look.

He couldn't immerse through a screen, but he held it up close to his face, looking over the Golden Horn of Istanbul ... a butterfly button flittered towards him, an advertisement in a bright circle of green that folded and opened like wings. 'Hi there,' it said in a nice-girl voice.

He moved closer to it to hear its message. 'Hi.'

'Would you like to become a Citizen?' she asked.

'Would I?' he answered, tapping his response into the screen.

'Would you like all your dreams to come true?'

'Of course.' He pressed the yes button.

'When you become a member of the World Union, you have all the rights of a Citizen.'

'How do I become a member?' Gomez had dreamt of Citizenship all his life, but not many in Mexica ever managed to make it.

'You must first pass the Citizenship test.'

'Okay.' He'd heard of the test before. Nobody he knew had ever taken the test, but he'd heard of it somewhere.

'Once you have passed the test you must find sponsors to donate your initial value.'

'Okay. How do I do that?'

'Join the World Union today, and become a part of something.'

He was sure now that the button was automated. It hadn't been listening to his questions, he'd just been asking the obvious ones. Gomez was annoyed that his time was running out, and here he was wasting credits on silly dreams.

'Is there a real human in there?' he asked.

The button stopped its flapping and a girl's face appeared within the circle. She was about his age with clean hair cut in straight angles. He'd seen pictures of girls like her. WU girls.

'Hi there, Gomez. How can I help you?'

'Are you real?'

'Of course I'm real. Is that all you wanted to know?'

'No. No. I wanted to know how to become a Citizen.'

'You don't need me to tell you that.' She winked at him and smiled. 'Just do as the button says, pass the test and then find sponsors.'

'Will you sponsor me?'

'I wish I could, Gomez. But if I shared my value with every correspondent there'd be nothing of me left.' She said it so kindly that he smiled as if she had said: *Yes, of course, I can give you everything you need.*

'Can I take the test?'

'You know that Citizenship is not something to be taken lightly?'

'Yes.'

'And that to be a member of the World Union, you have to be a part of it? You have to earn your place.'

'Yes.' Not really. All he knew was that life was better in the WU, with WU girls and their neat haircuts. 'Tell me what I have to do.'

She furrowed her brow. 'Let's see ... you work as a recycler in the scrap zone. Is that right?'

'Yes.'

'Well, there are some requests for rare materials. That could earn you some value if you can mix them up right.'

'Send me a list. I can find anything.'

'Okay, Gomez. You should have received a ping now. You can contact me directly if you manage it. Good luck on your quest!' She waved at him and he waved back.

* * *

It was dark as he got home, the float behind him dipping under the weight of his haul. The fires still glowed in the forge and he slid the cart up to the loading window.

The smell of beans and onions was just strong enough over the acrid metals of the workroom. Gom sighed and began scattling the pieces, unscrewing every little piece and tossing them into the appropriate receptacles.

The door of the kitchen squeaked and he heard his father's boots on the sand.

'How'd you do, Gom? I was getting worried about you.'

'Nearly there. Did I miss dinner?'

'It's on the stovetop for you.'

He thanked him and his papa joined him to strip out an engine he'd brought home.

'Hey, Dad, what's phytogen?'

'Don't know. Sounds synthetic. What do you want it for?'

'Nothing. It was just in something I read.'

'Got a little project, ay?' His papa grinned. 'How about after the dishes are cleared we take the night off? I managed to get those refrigeration cores out today. We can ease back for a couple days.'

'Can I use the Weave?'

'For twenty minutes only. But take care. You hear me?'

'Yes, Papa.'

'Alright. I'll go up and feed your mom. You get started on the dishes.'

'Yes, Papa.'

Phytogen, he found out, and some of the other compounds on his list, algomite and scaline proteins, were all ingredients

100

for symbiot matter. Symbiots! Gom ached for a symbiot. The knick-knacks he built with his father for sensors and tools were cool, but imagine how they could get through the piles if he had a sylus. He wondered if he could get enough of the materials on the list to build one for his family.

There was one supplier in the whole of Mexica that stocked phytogen, his business protected by the Caucus that governed the region. Gomez needed to borrow his father's pass to get into those neighbourhoods as a trade visitor. *That could be done*, he thought.

He went to bed with dreams of the WU in his head.

Their next session took place in the orphanage instead of Lizney's rooms. Zach was still too sore to leave his bed, which was being attributed to shock rather than any physical injuries. He managed to sit upright, propped up by pillows, and glared at any who tried to offer him sympathy.

'I was hakked. It is done,' was all he would say.

As one who had experienced a certain unpleasantness at a young age, Lizney could recognise the aggressive posturing as a self-protection mechanism.

'Still, I don't think we should immerse today. You need to rest.'

'I should dive straight back in.'

'No, Zach. I won't authorise that.'

'But what about my badge? I'm only five days off.'

'Master Frost, do not whine. If you have to restart your endurance exam, then so be it. You will become all the more endurable for it.'

'That's not fair.'

'Perhaps not, but it is in my interest to work in your interests. Your anger will not sway me.'

'I'm not angry,' Zach muttered.

'Pardon my mistake.'

'It is your mistake. I'm fine.' Zach pushed himself from the bed and stood up.

'Are you going somewhere, Zach?' Mister Lizney asked. The boy didn't answer. The sudden rise had lost the blood in his head and he swayed dopily. 'Why don't you sit down again? I'm happy to let you enter the null space if you want. We can work on your new avatar.'

Zach wobbled.

'I take it you are done being Musashi?'

'Musashi …' The boy slumped at the question and sat back on the bed, his anger disappearing. 'No, I don't want to be Musashi any more.'

'That's okay. Do you want to start over? There's nothing wrong with that. Most people have a dozen avatars over the course of their lives, on average. Some have hundreds.' He held out Zach's helmet for him to take. 'Everyone starts over every now and then. Do you know what you want to be?' Zach shook his head. All the energy and unstoppable youth from last week had drained away. He looked at his helmet, his hands shook. When he lifted it to his head his body jerked and he bent double to vomit on the floor.

Lizney patted him on the back and called the session to a close.

It was some time before Zach was allowed back on the open Weave, and only then with training wheels. He would have to start again on his endurance badge, but could only do that after he had completed the introduction cycle over.

He wasn't talking to Bron, or any of the other kids. As far as he was concerned they were separate from him while he worked to get out of there. It didn't stop her trying to talk to him though.

She blocked him in the corridor one day. 'Can't you even say good morning?'

'Good morning,' he said and made to move past.

'What's wrong with you?' Bron asked him.

'Hey, I said I was sorry, didn't I?'

'You said it. But why are you angry with me? What did I do?'

'Nothing. I'm not angry,' he insisted.

'What happened to you? Why are you being mean to me?' Her eyes loaded with tears. He didn't want to deal with that.

'Go blubber somewhere else, Bron. I'm months behind now thanks to you. Just leave me alone!' He could hear himself shouting, it bounced back at him from the walls, but he couldn't pull it back. He meant to say he was sorry, but that voice was small in his head. That was small Zach, the one the larger Zach ignored.

Sitting in his study room, alone at last, he immersed into the null space to run simulations. Since the incident he had started a few courses on self-defence. He'd been an idiot kid before, not interested in anything that wasn't on the visual plane; but not any more. He figured out how the hakka had trapped him in immersion, interrupting his emergency line with a simple bypass that gave them control of his helmet. The more he learnt, the more he thought how incredibly stupid he had been and he told Mister Lizney as much.

'Why hadn't you trained me to defend myself?'

'You're just a boy, Zach. There should have been no need for such measures. I am sorry for what happened to you.'

'Yeah, quite a blemish on your record, I bet. If I kill myself now, it will be even worse for you.'

'Zachary, please don't talk like that.'

'Why not? You and the 'nage already monitor my every minute. What choice could I have?'

'I'm sorry that you see those who care for you as a restriction on your life.'

'I'm stuck with baby exercises for training and I'm stuck in the kutzo house. How do you expect me to feel?'

'Patience, Zach. Please. You need time to recover.'

'I'm fine. All I need to do is get back on the Weave, but you won't let me.'

'No, I won't. Not until you can control yourself again.'

And so their sessions reached an impasse. Zach began looking for new teachers but it was hopeless. Lizney had put the kibosh on, and nobody would take him. It was like the beady-eyed old man had a grudge against him. Maybe he didn't like his record being tarnished, it might cost him future students.

Zach dropped his other classes and spent all his time training in the null space. This was what mattered, being able to defend yourself. Being quick enough to block offensive codes with his own; building up a catalogue of scripts and twists that he could pull out as he needed them.

Bleck! he swore to himself. It was all just games until he got back on the Weave. The scripts he was pulling were textbook, available to everyone who wanted them. They'd be useless against a hakka.

Hakkas could go where they pleased and do what they wanted to whoever they chose. The only thing that was meant to stop them were the weavers and rangers. But obviously the hakkas still did what they did without any hindrance from the 'good guys'. Zach had been misled.

A message came into his box with no sender attached.

: Come on, runt. Don't hide in null space forever.

Zach: Who is this?

: The one who gives you nightmares.

Zach froze. Images of rape and mutilation repeated in his mind's eye.

: Come on, Zach. I won't do it again. Promise.

Zach: I'm locked off from the Weave.

: Zzzzz.

Zach: They're watching me.

: Just say the word, runt, and I shall set you free.

Zach thought about it for a moment. He looked out on the empty vista of the null space. Greyness to the non-horizon.

Zach: What's the word?

: Please, of course.

In his immersion lounge, Zach swallowed and locked in a fresh backup.

Zach: Please.

The null went black, then Zach blinked and he was standing in a field of green grass with exaggerated flowers. The sky was a solid blue mockery of the real world, laughing brightly behind one perfect tree.

He looked at himself, swivelling a camera view for a looksy. He had been changed into something like a rabbit that stood like a human. He tried to assert his own image into —

'Don't do that.' A familiar female voice came from the shade of the tree. 'They'll detect you pretty quick if your avatar appears. Don't you like your disguise?'

Zach stepped closer to see the speaker but the shade was as exaggerated as everything else in this place.

'What are you doing?' she asked.

'I want to see what you look like.'

She laughed. It was a thousand laughs all played at once. 'What does it matter what I look like? I have a thousand avatars. All different.'

Zach could see eye whites and fangs and a heart-shaped face in the shadow.

'What do you want me to look like? Hmm ...' she mused. 'What do little boys like?' In blinks, she changed and stepped into the sunlight. She was a kind-faced nanna, wearing a flour-dusted apron with lace on every hem. 'Does this make you feel better, my sweet pudding?' Blink, she was a man with salt-and-pepper hair and a weathered face. 'Maybe you need a father figure? Stay strong, lil slugger. You'll get there.' Blink, she was a short, naked woman with a wet sheen from toes to breasts. 'Or maybe you're old enough for something like this.' A long finger touched his rabbit nose and — blink — he was staring at himself.

'This is from your latest backup, isn't it?'

He nodded.

'You didn't hide it from me very well, Zachary.' Gashes suddenly striped the face and blood ran down into his neck. 'Whatever happened to the samurai thing you had going?'

'He was stupid,' Zach answered.

She laughed again, through his image and with his voice.

'Who are you?' Zach asked.

'Me?' She pointed at herself. A blur of avatars flashed past, stopping on the giant red monster he had met in the dance hall. Its many maws gnashed its teeth and drooled at him. 'My name is Dungeon,' she said, before swallowing him whole.

'Zach? Zach, are you okay?'

He opened his eyes and saw Bron staring down at him. Just moments before he was being force-fed images of living bodies being dissected, animal heads kicked across grey streets like footballs, the makeshift balls bulging and mutilated beyond form. Gently, he reached up and touched her cheek.

'You're real.'

'You were screaming. What were you doing?'

'Nothing.' He pulled his hand angrily away and sat up. He'd sweated through his gown and was feeling the cold.

'You went back on the Weave, didn't you?'

'No,' he answered.

'You aren't supposed to —'

'I didn't. I was just in the null space.'

'You're lying,' she said and turned to leave.

He grabbed her arm roughly. 'Don't tell anyone.'

'I have to. You're not meant to be immersing.'

'No.' He twisted her arm, stretching the skin beneath.

'Stop it, Zach. That hurts.'

'Don't tell.'

'Let go of me or I'll scream.'

'You can't tell them —'

Bron yelled with all the power in her lungs. To Zach it sounded like a thousand screams at once. He saw the bodies decomposing. Blood and violence and torture. He saw the images again and he fell backward.

Lizney was furious when he heard. As furious as he could get, but Zach didn't listen to his teacher's impotent rants. The weirdie was too weak for real anger, too old. Too timid and too twisted up in his mentor role to have real rage. Too useless to even have a symbiot. Zach hated him.

From the cameras of the omnipoles, Zach surveilled Lizney's unit. Inside, his teacher moved to the window and pulled the shutters. There was a storm coming.

He learnt a lot from Dungeon, even if he did end up in her torture chamber again and again. She showed him how to split his stream, leaving his avatar running routines while he slipped into an unrecorded mode; freeing him to explore the Weave again. He still didn't know how she kept swallowing him and transporting him places, but if she came for him again he had a plan to find out.

Whenever he went online she found him. Then they would play her game. He would run, she would chase. He would change his avatar and she would twist it. He pushed her off, but sooner or later she ate him up and mutilated his soul. 'I am

108

Dungeon,' she would say and his little body would flail with excitation.

Zach tried something he'd seen Dungeon do in their last game of cat and mouse, burrowing into the nodes of the Weave that acted as data conduits. They were the invisible traffic conductors, but from within he could watch anybody's stream; he only had to identify it. Which was easy because he could filter the flow to the specific location.

It seemed his teacher was immersed. Zach followed his stream, piggybacking so as to leave no trail of his own. He found himself looking at that street corner where Dungeon had first dropped his chewed-out avatar. *Now what would Mister Lizney be doing here?* Zach wondered.

His teacher didn't do much. He looked along the street and up towards one of the housing units. It looked exactly like the others, though this one had an edge of flowers where the walls met the turf. Zach looked at the address, and saw it wasn't where Zach had been dumped. This was a different sector entirely.

He began looking for connections between Lizney and the area, and discovered that this house was where his teacher had grown up. In a relocation town, which meant that he was ...

'Spawn,' he said, whispering into Lizney's ear.

Zach demersed and sat on his couch. He looked around the small room. It was dark. Hail was hitting the roof like a snare drum and everything seemed to rattle with it. He folded his visor up and put it in his pocket. It was time to graduate.

With a hard umbrella, more like a shell that went over his top half, Zach ventured out into the storm. It was grey, the pavements strewn with white slippery hailstones all the way to the track entrance.

He wasn't sure what he was going to say. He would be punished for going on the Weave, but he had also succeeded in finding out his teacher's secret.

Lizney didn't meet him at the door. He sat in his chair breathing loudly as Zach entered.

'It's not time for our session,' Lizney said.

'I thought I should come. To see what happens next.'

'You should sit. We must discuss this.'

'Discuss what? I know what you are now. I've passed your little test.'

'You weren't meant to be going on the Weave,' Lizney croaked. Zach shrugged. 'I'll have to report this.'

'Well, now I know your secret it doesn't matter. There's nothing more you can teach me.'

'So you found a different teacher, did you? That hakka?' Lizney asked. Zach didn't answer or look to meet his gaze. Mister Lizney stared over his spectacles at him and sighed deeply. 'If you don't talk to me, Zach, I see no point in you being here.'

'You can't kick me out. I need to be here.' Now he looked up, but Lizney could no longer read what was in his eyes. Zach used to be so open, but now the mix of emotions was heavy and impossible to discern.

'Why do you need to be here?'

'If I'm not in your classes, then I'll be downgraded. I'll be moved out of the home.'

'And you don't want that?'

Zach twisted. Anger flared and he bit at the inside of his mouth. 'I don't care. Do whatever you want, spawn.'

Lizney shuddered as if bitten, his cup of tea spilling down his legs. Zach looked at the floor, a greasy grin splitting his mouth.

'What did you call me?'

'Spawn. That's what you are, isn't it? Örjian spawn.'

Lizney felt his blood heating and he jumped up, running to the kitchen, where he tore open a drawer and peeled a patch. He felt its prickle go through his skin and at the count of five he felt the calm. The tension went out of his fists and his jaw stopped reaching to bite.

One patch wasn't going to be enough. Bent over, arms and legs longing to lope, he reached into the open drawer for another fix. The patch released its soothing drugs and he sat down on the tiles. Calm at last.

'You're disgusting,' he heard the boy say from behind him.

Then the front door opened and shut and Mister Lizney stayed on the floor calmly cursing himself.

Zach's feet took him homeward. His mind echoed with the argument. He took the stairs down to the tracks and was three along before he realised he had no home to go to. Zach stood where he was and let the track pull him along.

It was always night down here. Rectangular lights paused overhead and the tracks hummed and ticked at their own speeds. Zach watched all kinds of people who were going to all kinds of places. Most stood like he was, others strode along the ninth track, speeding past at seventy clicks an hour, plus their walking pace.

These ones seemed accelerated. Faster than your average human. He looked at them, trying to see what it was that made them so intent. But they were all different. Girl cliques and suitboys, repairmen and Servicemen. Freakers, mutators and transcenders. He wondered where they were going.

He let the tracks take him south through Corona, the Angeles, all the way to the end of West where he had to dismount from the fastest to the slowest footway so he wasn't thrown off at the end.

There was only one exit, a wide ramp to the surface with cargo lifts sliding up and down with boxed goods. He'd never been this far before. It was all farms and pharma out here, straight fenced-off tracts patrolled by servitors. Beyond that were the parks, the wild lands that had been returned to mother nature.

Zach went and stood by the first fence. There were three separate cordons, each decorated with warning signs not to enter. Humans didn't go on the pharms without protection suits, but they didn't need to either. A frame of rods and wires carried hanging automatons from plant to plant, inspecting, pruning, spraying and watering. Some of those crops would just be enhanced with minerals and vitamins for food consumption, others contained medicinal modifications that animals shouldn't come into casual contact with.

The bots didn't change what they were doing with him there; they zoomed around in their efficient business and he watched.

Behind him a long, champagne-coloured squib slowed down and honked. One of the back doors opened and a girl about his age called out to him. 'Hey, Musashi. You wanna come for a ride?'

112

Zach peered inside. It was a luxury model, plush and clean and buffed so that every surface radiated the glow of the lumen edging. The girl sat on the crimson seat. She had white hair and was covered neck to toe in black rubber.

'Are you Dungeon?'

'She sent me to find you.'

'Who are you?'

'My name is Alicia.' She patted the seat beside him. 'Come, sit with me. We'll go somewhere.'

Zach looked around. Nobody was looking, there was nobody to look. The servitors continued their routines. He looked Alicia over, the rubber hugging her slight form, and got in.

The door closed and the squib pulled swiftly to speed. She turned to him, one elbow on the headrest so her hand could play with his hair.

'Dungeon says you're a bad boy. I think you look kind of sweet.'

'Thanks?'

She moved her face closer to his. 'Do you think I'm pretty?'

Zach swallowed. 'Yeah, of course.'

She kissed him savagely and began moving her hands over his arms. Zach had never been kissed and he followed her lead — if he didn't he feared she would eat him — grabbing mouthfuls of air when he could.

'What's this?' She took his visor from his pocket and broke off the kissing to pull a cable from her belt and zap it. The helmet threw off a spark and smoke. She opened a small window and tossed it outside.

'Hey, that's —'

'They can track you with it. Now get your clothes off, there might be residues they could use.' All this went out the window until he was naked and wriggling into new rubber trousers as fast as he could. Alicia watched him the whole time with her emotionless face. She seemed to have lost interest in kissing him.

Through the windows he could see derelict buildings and streets. 'Where are we?'

'Does it matter?'

'I want to know where you are taking me,' he said.

She looked at him but didn't answer.

He knew they hadn't gone far, they hadn't taken to the air, just kept on. Hovering away from the pharms. Which could mean they were heading into a park, but the disused buildings meant they were in the hot zone: areas contaminated with radiation, chemical hangover and extreme pollution.

'Will this protect me?'

'Long enough. We won't be outside for long.'

They drove for another hour, not speaking, just Zach looking out the windows at the once-populated city. Some of it looked new, but was darkened with grime.

At last the squib pulled into a dock and Alicia handed him a mask. 'Don't ever go outside without this. Okay?'

'Yeah, I got it.'

'Turn around.' He did as he was told and she began pulling the straps so the mask squeezed tight against his face. Then she took a spray can and panned it back and forth over his back, coating the seams. 'Lift your arms.' The can went up and down his sides. 'Now, front.' Alicia finished him and then sprayed her own joins until the can was empty and she tossed it to the floor.

'Let's go.'

'Wait,' he said.

'No. Follow me or get lost.'

Zach jumped out of the squib and walked behind her.

Around them a grey-brown mist hung, a cold smog that was thick enough to move in swirls as they passed through it. He looked up, but couldn't see through the dirty mist. The buildings just disappeared within it.

'Inside.' The door looked just like any of the others. He'd never be able to recognise it for himself. They passed through sheets of hanging plastic, the corridor ahead had rudimentary lighting, and a short flight of stairs took them down to a hermetic door.

Alicia stood waiting. There was no handle. Soon the door clicked and swung inward.

'Arms up,' she said. He copied her, and jets of steam blew at them from the walls.

A panel opened and they walked through. Alicia took off her mask and began stripping out of the rubber. He did the same. She turned a pair of taps on the wall and began showering, rubbing herself vigorously with soap.

'Dungeon likes us to be clean.' Her voice seemed to have lost its colour since they had come inside.

'What for?' Zach asked.

She turned to him. 'You should learn not to ask questions.'

* * *

115

Ben Harvey waited at home for his wife Freya. Along with their two children, they lived in one of the many ziggurats of West. Thanks to his Services commission, they had a family block with a balcony, yard and potted trees. There was room enough for a swing and a bouncer for Bobby and Molly in the back corner. He had wanted one when he was young, but his children were bored with it now. That they could be bored by anti-grav dismayed him.

Home wasn't much, but it was comfortable, and spacious for four people. It was a little old, and built in the rush of peacetime when people were still afraid the Dark Ages would return, but there was nothing Ben couldn't fix if he put his mind to it. He lay on his back with a wrench and stiff wire, working through the clog in the disposal unit. Truth be told, he could work with his eyes closed and his hands tied behind his back, but you never knew who was watching.

He had taken the day off sick. He was sick. His nerves were giving him reflux. He distracted himself with odd jobs but every time the door banged, or the floor creaked, his stomach jumped and his heart froze. Ben waited without breathing for the marauders to swarm in and mask him. They would find him eventually. They found everybody.

Ben scuttled out from under the sink and leant back onto his knees, breathing through the urge to vomit. He couldn't go on like this. Even thinking about it unsettled him. He went to the bathroom and slapped calmers on both wrists then went to sit on the back steps with a cup of peppermint tea.

They had a thin view of the city between the two ziggurat blocks behind theirs. He watched the lines of air traffic march and twist through the sky. Ben had sat in this same spot a week ago and watched as ten armed marauders had chased down a woman in one of the apartment blocks. At first he didn't know what happened — there was an explosion of glass and he had fetched his binoculars. Then watched in horror as soldiers shot the woman's feet with gloop, tranquillised her and put a mask over her face. He tried to tell himself she might not have been a psi ...

A ball rolled into his back, one of Bobby's toys, and he twisted around to see who was there. A boy stood shadowed in the dark interior watching him quietly. 'Hello,' Ben said. The boy took a few steps towards him.

'Hi, Dad. Are you feeling better?' Bobby asked.

'A little bit. What are you doing home?'

'I wanted to see how you were.'

'Shouldn't you be in memeology?' Bobby didn't answer. 'That's okay. You can catch up later. It's nice you coming to check on your old man. Here, have a seat.'

Bobby dropped his bag and came to join Ben on the step. They had the same sandy-coloured hair and eyes. If Bobby pulled on an orange jumpsuit, they would make quite a pair. 'I need to ask you something, Bobby.' Ben tried to keep his voice calm and not too serious. 'I'm not sure how to ask ...'

'You don't need to,' Bobby said.

'Oh. Because you can ...?'

'Yes.'

Ben nodded. He was afraid that would be the answer. 'Does your mother know?'

'She isn't sure yet.'

117

'How long have you known?'

'Six weeks.' Bobby took his dad's shaking hand. 'I think you should take something for your stomach.'

'I'll be fine in a bit.' Ben smiled weakly. No wonder the kid was acting so strange recently. 'What about Molly? Is she?'

'I think she takes after you, Dad.' Bobby rolled up the sleeve on his right arm.

'What's that?' Ben asked. There was a circular red mark in the dip of Bobby's elbow.

'She bit me, kind of.'

'Oh.'

Ben cursed his luck. He'd accidentally married a telepath, after years hiding his own abilities — though she had known about him — and now both the kids had followed in their footsteps.

'I am being nicer to her now,' Bobby said.

'Good idea.' Ben turned back to look out at the city. The sun was going down. Their side of the building was black with shadow against the orange and pink sky.

'Do you have a plan?' Bobby asked.

'The beginnings of one.'

'What does Mum think?'

'She thinks it's too risky.' Ben put an arm around his boy. 'But she'll do it for you two, I'm sure.'

There was no hiding anything from his wife. Freya's abilities were short-range, but she could sense what people felt. She needed touch to understand and share thoughts. The day the psis declared war on the Will, she was close to Ben on the couch and his fear had rushed into her. She knew he had been

118

thinking about it for a long time. Escape. The trick was that he hadn't quite figured out how to do it. How do you escape from Services' omnipresent eye?

The principle they were counting on, and had been making use of throughout their lives, was that large systems can only observe a portion of their whole at any one time. The Weave was too vast and dense for every scrap of data to be checked and verified — even with its algorithm-eyes.

The movements of people and traffic were always passively monitored, looking for pattern deviation, but rarely focused upon unless they became interesting. High-profile people could never escape the watchful lens. Ben's family had one thing in their favour: they were lows. Zeros and zilches. People so far down the food chain their actions weren't important enough to be actively monitored. They had streams like everyone else, but the only thing that would throw up a flag would be behaviour that deviated from their established recorded patterns. So long as they stayed ordinary they could go unnoticed.

Ben tried thinking this through. One false move and Services would be onto them. The Weave was all data, active streams, recordings, and the information collected by the trillion or so sensors and omnipoles in the WU. But not all that data was accessed; it was too big for in-depth processing, it was just there so it *could* be accessed. It was about finding the blind spots. A blind spot that would last long enough for them to get some distance from the city. Any vehicle they took would have to be wiped, reinstalled and fully manual and every day Ben had been watching the twenty-year-old bus that picked his children up for classes and returned them home before dark.

'The bus?' Bobby asked, reading his father's mind.

'The bus,' Ben answered.

'Okay.'

'Let's go meet your sister. Then we'll get dinner going.'

'Stew again?'

'What else?' Ben smiled at his son. It was the only meal he knew how to make.

The school bus was a little old, a little inefficient in that it could only fly the long stretches between stops, and had to drive along the ground when the distance was under a couple of kilometres. Its paint was chipped, the frame rattled and the windows were murky from the attention of two decades of small children. When it suddenly fizzed and wouldn't start again, the bus driver, Valerie, wasn't surprised.

'Well, it had to happen someday.' She laughed about it. Probably thankful it hadn't broken down in midair. Out of courtesy, Ben waited with Valerie until a new bus arrived. There were still a few children who needed to get home.

As he waved them off, he called operations. 'Hey, Bass, the school bus broke down next to my building. You want it hauled to the depot or you want me to see if I can fix it here?'

Bass was a large man. He'd been an average mechanic before he took the coordinator job and now spent his days in a sitting position. He had a flat, impassive look, like a spade with a face on it.

'What's wrong with it?'

'Well, I couldn't say yet, could I?'

'What does the internal say?' Bass asked.

'It says there is nothing wrong with it.'

'I hate that,' Bass said.

'Yeah,' Ben agreed. He stood there waiting, Molly pulling at his hand to go inside. As he waited for the decision from above he tried to act normal, uncaring and even a bit bored. Everything happening was normal, he had nothing to sweat about. All he needed Bass to do was come to the obvious conclusion that it was less energy to fix it on the spot than to have it hauled to the depot. Coordinators were all about energy usage.

'Do you think you can fix it?'

'I can fix anything.' Ben snorted for good measure.

'Alright. You need anything from me?' Bass asked.

'Send Desh over with a cart and we'll have it back on the move tomorrow.'

'He'll have to clock some extra hours.'

'Tell him I'll throw in dinner.'

'Alright, then.'

They signed off and Ben whistled out the breath he had been holding.

'Okay, little one, let's get you inside and cleaned up before Mum gets home.'

Benjamin Harvey and Deshiel Diaz, or Ben and Desh, were low-level engineers who worked maintenance for the Frisco precinct. Desh was a bender too. One day, a few years earlier, Ben caught Desh tightening a wingnut without his hands and he'd spun it back the other way, scaring the sweats out of the younger man.

Desh had turned to look at him and Ben shook his head slowly. If you wanted to avoid collection, you should never

ever use your powers. 'At least be more careful,' Ben said and cupped his hand over the nut to show how to hide when he was cheating. They'd been friends ever since.

When Desh arrived he tore in fast and braked late, air brakes bellowing as the utility truck came to a halt. He was a few years younger than Ben, bristly-faced and swarthy. Ben waved at him in greeting and felt a taptiptiptip tip tip tiptaptip on the palm of his hand.

Over the years Ben and Desh had worked out a lot between them, including a way to communicate that was undetectable to Services. Nobody else could listen in and nobody could see it happening. Morse code. If one of them wanted to communicate something without being detected, they would kinetically drum out the code on the back of the other's hand. Taptiptiptip tip tip tiptaptip spelt just the one word: B E E R.

It took eight jacks to lift the bus off the ground before the two of them could slide underneath to look at the undercarriage. The cart plugged into the bus and began compiling a list of small faults that needed fixing.

'Can you stay for dinner?' Ben asked.

'Can't. I'm meant to meet with Cayla and watch the Parabowl.'

'You should stay. We can watch the game and Freya left me to do the cooking.'

Desh was about to say something, but stopped as he felt Ben tip and tap on the back of his hand. Tiptiptip tap tiptap taptiptaptap: S T A Y.

'How can I say no to one of your stews?' Desh replied.

W H A T I S W R O N G?

TIME TO GO.

Desh nodded. 'Yep, I think we just need to flush the system and reboot. I reckon she'll be back in the air for tomorrow.'

'Great. Thanks for coming over tonight. I didn't know you had plans.'

'No worries, my man. What are friends for?'

'Five hundred metres … four hundred and fifty metres …' Lieutenant Campsey read out the measurements as their probe approached firing range. Under moonlight, Kronos was quieter, its skin undulating like a water bed with just a few slow arms swaying around, looking for more material to absorb.

'No reaction,' Pinter murmured. The beast hadn't noticed them yet. They still didn't know how it detected proximity so they were doing everything they could to keep vibrations and electrical activity to a minimum.

In darkness, the caterpillar probe rolled closer. It was an all-terrain vehicle. Six bucky-wheels on flexible struts. It moved slowly now, but had the ability to reach speeds of two hundred kilometres, if called for.

Three hundred metres … two hundred …

'Hold position. It's moving.' A black swell pushed towards the probe, extending and thinning into a feeler. 'Back it off, slowly.' The probe reversed while the black tentacle continued to reach out towards it.

'We can't fire at this range,' Campsey pointed out the obvious. It was a talent of his he seemed very proud of.

'Just wait for it to miss and then sneak closer,' the Colonel answered patiently. As predicted the black tentacle swept in an arc, crossing the area where the caterpillar had been and then swinging back. 'See? It reaches out, searches and when it finds nothing it will pull itself back in.'

'What if we tried distracting it?' Quintan suggested.

'Good idea. Campsey, make some noise to the south.'

'How do you suggest I do that, sir?'

'Send in two of the earth movers. Tell the operators to be rough. Slam the ground with the scoops, that sort of thing.'

'Yes, sir.'

Very quickly, two of the giant earth movers that had been used to dig the trenches started forward across the wasteland, engines growling and wheels churning the ground beneath them. As they got closer, Kronos began to stir with the telltale swell of a new tentacle.

'Make them zigzag, try to give our little guy as much time as we can.'

The caterpillar began moving forward again. 'One hundred metres ... fifty metres ... thirty metres.'

The movers couldn't move fast and it was only a matter of time before they were hit and both their signals and their bodies were consumed in black. Kronos reached for the movers, three large tendrils curling out to lash at them. 'At least drive them into the ditch, there's no point ceding more territory to the beast.'

'Twenty metres.'

'Fire as soon as we are in range.'

'Ten metres.'

'Sir ...' Quintan said. The beast was swelling in front of the probe.

'Send in more movers. One to the north, one to the south. We just need a little more time.'

Two more of the large heavy vehicles rattled forward and Kronos made arms to reach out to them. The caterpillar went slower than ever.

'Five metres ... two metres ... we are in range, sir.'

'As soon as the hook hits, start reversing. Have the drones begin their approach,' the Colonel ordered.

'Yes, sir.'

'Fire.'

With a kthunk of pneumatics the cannon fired a harpoon across the ravine and landed without a splash into the dark syrup of Kronos. It immediately began creeping along the line.

'Pull it out.' The caterpillar went into fast reverse, dragging the harpoon back, trying to pull it out of the black mass. It didn't get far before jerking to a halt.

'It's stopped, Colonel.' The probe's wheels were spinning, but it couldn't fight Kronos's hold. Their opticals zoomed in, showing the ooze climbing forward.

'Fly the drones in and cut the wire here.' He tapped a targeting pin onto the harpoon line, just at the point where Kronos was thinnest.

A squadron of ten drones swooped over the target in a file, lasers firing as they passed. The wire snapped and the caterpillar lurched backward. Kronos bubbled. Where it had been cut, tendrils sprouted and swung around to find the cause, but the drones were already gone.

'Full speed reverse,' the Colonel said. He looked over at Quintan. 'Did we get it?' he asked. Headlights flashed on from the probe, focusing on the cut line of the harpoon. There at the end was an arm's length of gooey black that throbbed, consuming the line like a snake slowly swallowing something larger than its mouth.

'We got it.'

The Colonel breathed out. 'Now for phase two.'

Phase two involved dividing the Kronos sample and testing different containment protocols to see what was effective. A kilometre away from the main mass, the probe dropped the line and retreated, leaving a length of ten metres that was slowly being consumed by the black treacle. Around this a deep empty moat was quickly excavated.

Drones flew over the black snake, cutting the wire in several places and then looping back with hooks to drag the pieces far enough apart so they couldn't rejoin. The stuff was like honey, every surface it touched became sticky with the black ooze. The hooks had to be jettisoned, giving them a sum total of twenty samples.

'Colonel,' Quintan said quietly.

'Spit it out, Crozier.'

'Look at this.' The airman flicked a set of images to the Colonel's stream, from over the ditch where the line had been cut. There were small puddles of black where bits of Kronos had splashed. Now with more delicate tentacles the mass reached out and touched at them. Like a finger dabbing at crumbs, collecting them.

'Hurry up with those cages, Lieutenant.'

'Yes, sir,' Campsey answered.

'Quintan, prepare phase three. We might want another distraction.'

'Sir ...'

'I know you have reservations.'

'Yes, sir.'

'We can talk about your reservations later. Now, nobody go any closer until we know those cages are working. If nothing has changed by this time tomorrow, we can let the boffins have them.' The Colonel looked from Crozier to Campsey and then lightly smacked the arms of his seat. 'A job well done. I guess I shall make my report.'

'Greetings, Prime.'

'Greetings, Colonel Pinter. The sample capture went well, I see.' Ryu's immaculate face appeared in his overlay.

'Phase one is complete, separating a sample from the main body. Now we have to see if any of the cages we've made can hold it.'

'I have no doubt our scientists will prevail.'

'In light of Geof Ozenbach's information, we are reconfiguring the team.'

'Yes.' The Prime nodded. He had already heard the news from elsewhere. If not for his ravenous eyes, one could be forgiven for thinking him disinterested. 'And how are you feeling, Colonel?'

'Quite well, thank you. Why do you ask?'

'I have a report in my queue from a Lieutenant Campsey, who thinks you are indulging in behaviour unsuitable to your position, Services and the current crisis.'

'Yes, he is a snivelling whatsit. One of Zim's as I understand it,' the Colonel replied.

'Be that as it may, it doesn't help to have this come to me. I need the world to know you are taking this situation seriously.'

'Of course I am. How can you question it?'

'Are you really bringing a live-in companion to stay with you on the base?'

'I am. I don't believe there is a rule against it.'

'Not a rule, no,' Ryu said. 'And you have accepted the Ellizabeth Betts invitation?'

'You are keeping tabs on me, aren't you. I had no reason not to accept the invitation. Kronos is in the hands of the scientists now. What is wrong, Prime? Is there something else?'

'Nothing,' the Prime answered. 'I'm only sorry I won't be able to make it. I rarely risk leaving my rooms now.'

'That was a terrible business.' Pinter really wasn't sure where Ryu was going with this thread and spoke carefully.

'You knew Tamsin Grey for a time. How strong do you gauge her resolve?'

'I wouldn't say I knew her just because I was an intermediary in the hunt, but ...' Pinter hesitated. 'I'm sorry, I'm from a generation that only spoke confidences to those whom we had actually met.'

'I understand. I appreciate your circumspection. Perhaps we should meet for a closed session?' the Prime suggested.

'I think we should,' the Colonel agreed. 'Trust is a very elusive state.'

'The way I see it, there are two kinds of trust: trusting someone's intentions and trusting someone's abilities. I'm running short in both areas.'

'Then let us arrange it immediately.'

Ryu's face pinched in thought, then he nodded. 'I shall have my secretary make the arrangements.'

Airman Crozier flew the Colonel all the way to Den Haag and walked him to one of the many arches that led into the Adjudicators Ministry. Pinter went through the protocols that protected the inside from listening and surveillance. What went on in the ministry was private. His symbiot was made passive, his body scanned for other implants. He swapped his clothes for a prepared set and then walked briskly through the ring of silence to the sanctum. The Prime waited for him inside.

'Does this place bring back memories, Colonel?' Ryu asked.

'It wasn't quite as grand in my day.' No. During the wars, when he'd first come here, it was just a small church with a bunker underneath. Now it had been expanded to include five tiers of benches that could hold the full Primacy of a hundred. Built of blue stone and marble, the reflected sound was absorbed by wall panels of acoustic prisms.

'You forget, Colonel Pinter, that it is your day again.'

'Yes, you are right.'

'Should I be concerned about your mental acuity? I have read some disturbing reports about rejuvenation.'

'I admit that I am finding it hard to adjust, but I think that is more about returning to the routine of Services life.'

The Prime sighed deeply and sat down in the front row of the forum. He rubbed at his face in weariness as the Colonel took a seat near him and they half-turned to face each other.

'Colonel, I find myself suddenly alone in the world. My family has been compromised and I am beset with problems. I am not sleeping well.'

'I can imagine.' Pinter wasn't sure how best to play this meeting. Confronting, challenging or consoling. The young man had agreed to meet, he must have a need. But what kind of man was he? He was too cold, too tied up in himself to ever become personal. 'It is an odd position for the Prime to find himself in. By definition you are the most influential person in the WU. Perhaps I should be worrying about you.'

'Never mind all that. The problems of the Prime are the problems of the world. Problems which all of a sudden seem to be increasing. It wouldn't surprise me if Pierre Jnr was responsible for them all,' Ryu said.

The Colonel leant back. 'That is quite a suggestion.'

'First Pierre Jnr, then the rebellion, now Kronos,' Ryu answered. 'Could this really be just coincidence?'

'I think you could be applying a false pattern to the situation,' the Colonel said.

'The psis are obviously led by Pierre Jnr and it is plausible that he caused the release of this Kronos.'

'I can concede that it is possible, but please don't let your suspicions create evidence from nothing.'

'What would you have me do? Colonel Abercrombie Pinter — history's greatest living commander. What would the Scorpion do?'

'I have never been fond of that name.'

'What would you do about the psis? What is your position?'

'I believe they are people whose abilities make us question the foundations of our society. But, then again, suppression is only ever a stalling tactic.'

'But the Will is strongly opposed to lowering the restrictions. Would you have me go against the Will?'

'The people are afraid. Fear is a powerful motivator. Is the Will telling you that you must destroy their fear or meet it? The Will is often more emotion than clear instruction. As Prime you determine the Command.'

'What would you have me do?'

'The Cape is a big area. An olive branch may be your best weapon.'

'An interesting approach. That still leaves the black mass.'

'It hasn't advanced any further.'

'You propose to leave it there? Sacrifice a whole city?'

'The city is gone, Prime. We may discover a way to get rid of Kronos, but for now the situation is stabilised.'

'Find a way, and find it fast.'

'The Command is the Command. What about Pierre Jnr?' Pinter asked.

'Colonel, I'm not sure what the larger problem is any more, and if I'm right then each problem could lead us to him.'

'Yes, sir.'

'You do not agree?' the Prime asked.

'I do not.'

'Then tell me your perspective. Isn't that why you demanded to meet?'

Pinter spread his hands, looking at his long fingers and counting out possibilities. 'Even if Pierre let loose the black mass, it may only be a diversion.'

'The lives of four million people is a diversion?'

'Perhaps.'

'And the rebellion?'

'You yourself predicted the rebellion from a young age. The growing population of psis made it inevitable.'

'Yes. That is true.'

'Then I don't see how you reach that conclusion. What is it, Ryu? Is there something you aren't telling me?'

'Take this. Watch it in private.' Ryu held out a data dot, like the scale of a fish, on the tip of his finger. 'Then destroy it. We have been erasing these from the Weave.'

'What is it?'

'It will remove your doubts and fill you with fear ...' Ryu's voice trailed off. His eyes were unfocused into memory.

'I will look through it.'

'Once you have watched the footage you will understand my position.'

'Yes, Prime. And the command?'

'Find a way to stop Kronos.'

'Yes, sir.'

They parted with salutes, Ryu with the air-fist of Services and the Colonel accidentally slipping back to the regimental chop he'd been raised on.

The Colonel fed the dot to his symb as soon as it was activated and began watching the collected Pierre Jnr surveillance footage. It slowed down his dressing as he saw scenes of Pierre Jnr from around the world, walking amongst the people, never being seen, never being noticed, but always obeyed and served.

There was one clip where Pierre Jnr was sitting in a restaurant. He sat alone at a table. When the food came from the kitchen the waiter knelt and cut the food into forkfuls, raising each for Pierre to eat. The other people in the restaurant ate their meals normally; at least it looked normal at first, but they lifted their forks and knives in unison, and then every now and then they would get up from their seats and move to different tables, sitting down with different partners and resuming eating and talking as if nothing had happened.

In one of the Citizen mess halls, where those low on credits could get their food allotment, the boy sat at one of the long tables amongst the thousands. To either side a man and a woman were talking right through him.

In Santiago, confetti blew up into the air, marking the start of a race. One-man squibs jerked into motion and Pierre Jnr watched from the stands as the speedsters soared and looped through hoops and slaloms.

An old leather-skinned woman was in her home alone, shows playing in front of her settee as she knitted a blanket that was covering her knees. Beside her, Pierre Jnr sat watching the romance unfold on the screen.

Quintan was waiting for him outside, squatting on the runner of the squib.

'You look like a man who could use a drink.'

Pinter looked at his pilot for a moment. 'You've been reading that damn book, haven't you?'

PIERRE JNR IS WAITING

The room was colourful. A thick rug of green and orange squares took up most of the floor space. It was littered with all sorts of toys. Pierre Jnr watched a child building a tower of blocks. As it got higher the child had to stand, but he stumbled into the blocks, knocking them to the floor. The child cried, face crushing inward and turning red.

'Hush, little Derek,' a feminine voice sounded. A bot with a cartoonish shape and face slid from the corner and hurried to the boy. Derek was picked up, put back on his feet and dusted off. 'You are not hurt. Here. Let's build another tower, bigger than the first one.'

The robot swivelled its head and tilted its eyes. 'Would you like to play too?' it asked, looking at Pierre.

Pierre watched it for a moment, his face bent into a scowl. The bot's head fizzled, severed from its torso. It dropped to the ground, bounced on the rug and rolled to a stop at Derek's feet.

The child screamed and cried.

Pinter and Quintan didn't arrive back in Busan until dawn.

The Colonel sat looking down at the breakfast tray before him. It was the first Serviceman's meal he'd had in forty years. Cheese, a pile of shaved protein constitute, his choice of sauce

— in this instance, sweet green chilli — with bread. He stared at it, unable to start.

It wasn't that the food was bad. The flavours could be excellent, but after a while it began to feel expected. Easy to make, easy to transport, easy to eat. This is what Servicemen ate day in, day out. There may have been over two hundred thousand combinations, but somehow every meal seemed the same.

He remembered when they came in. Like a gift from a god the supply lines opened and his men were saved from starvation. His little army had been bought off with the promise of food.

Pinter didn't feel hungry any more and pushed the tray aside.

'What's wrong? You need something for your stomach?' Quintan asked. He helped himself to the Colonel's tray and ate as if he hadn't just finished one of his own.

'I'm fine, thank you. I just don't feel like eating.' He set his symbiot to begin flushing the alcohol from his system and dropped some stimulants into his morning caf so he could report for duty. He sat on the platform as the research teams tried to get a reaction from the black ugliness of Kronos.

As he sat, a small spider landed on the arm of his chair and he watched it closely. It drew his interest more than the sound and light show in the distance. It was a tiny thing, no bigger than the fingernail of his pinky. It turned around, facing each direction, then turning again and again. He couldn't imagine what it was looking for or seeing. Did it see him? If it did, it showed no sign of fear, even though he could crush it easily. Maybe it didn't know that.

The Colonel recorded the spider, looking closer in with his enhancements. The parallel was obvious to him. From his position he could never know what the spider wanted, what it thought, or what its intentions might be. *Is it considering me as I am considering it? Is the way it lifts its mandibles up and down some sort of communication? If our positions were reversed and I was the tiny spider, how would I try to communicate with something my size?*

The problem with Kronos, though, was that he couldn't be sure if the thing knew they even existed. It may have consumed the city of Busan, but was it aware that it was doing so? Could this black beast be so alien as to not recognise people?

The Colonel transferred his thought stream to his logs and then brought up contact with the team leader.

'I think it is time to try something else, Miz Caswell.'

'What do you suggest?' she asked, appearing in his overlay.

The firing commenced with pebbles, which bounced over the surface and rolled away. They then progressed to stones as big as fists, followed by boulders that were hurled across the divide by a marauder unit. It surprised no one that these also had no effect, but science being science they had to try everything. The rocks either rolled off Kronos's back or remained on top of the black mass, rocking back and forth with its rolling skin.

Projectiles also failed to provoke any reaction. From rifles to howitzers, the shells penetrated the skin with a fleshy splat and disappeared. The surface healed over and the waving of the tentacles remained directionless. Some useful information was gained when one of the shells was implanted with a simple transmitter, so that when it was absorbed by Kronos its signal would fail, thus giving them a measure of the osmosis rate.

The Colonel had the area cleared and they watched for any signs of change. After an hour, with the signal still transmitting, he ordered the next tests to commence. 'That's the formalities over with, now let's see if we can get its attention.'

'Explosives?' Miz Caswell asked.

'No. I don't want pieces of it flying through the air.'

'Lasers?'

'Yes. That'll do. Put the shooter at three hundred metres. Just a shot first.'

A remote MU lumbered to the firing range and raised a narrow rifle towards the beast. The Colonel watched from his platform, vision zoomed in on the target of the beam. The first shot provoked no reaction. Similar to the bullets, the wound healed over and there was no noticeable change of behaviour from Kronos.

'Fire again, sustained beam,' he ordered.

'For how long, sir?'

'Until I say stop.'

The MU lifted the rifle and fired again, this time keeping the beam steady as the laser cut deeper into the black mass. Smoke or steam rose from the wound.

'Get a spectral analysis on that.'

'Of course, sir.'

After twenty seconds of firing the mass moved. Tentacles sprung out from near the wound and lashed out, sweeping in the direction of the attack. They grew and multiplied and when they passed through the beam they were cut through, their tips dropping to the ground.

'Watch the bits. Record it closely,' the Colonel ordered.

The beast managed to decipher the direction of the laser and the arms grew and swung in greater arcs, getting closer and closer to the MU.

'Cease fire. Pull the MU back. Don't let it find it.'

'Sir, the drops are rejoining the mass.' They watched as the severed globs moved, like miniatures of the larger mass, pulling themselves back towards the main mass. Tentacles grew out from the bulk and deftly retrieved them.

'That is interesting, isn't it?' he mused.

'What next?' Miz Caswell asked.

'Distortion. Same procedure but let's come from another side. Make sure it knows it's surrounded.'

Teledistortion was a most hideous weaponisation of the fledgling teleportation technology. Whereas teleportation required the accurate transfer and reconstruction of molecules, teledistortion did not. It had been used almost exclusively by the Örjian hordes with hand-held guns called ruisbuss, which translated as 'scramble pipes'. It was said to be a most painful way to die, which was true if the expressions of the victims counted for anything.

It was a simultaneous detonation of a nuclear bomb in a distortion field that created the Siberian Terminus and put a stop to the Örjian advance. An attack orchestrated by the young Captain Abercrombie Pinter. That is probably why the Servicemen around him seemed to hesitate.

'Get on with it,' the Colonel said.

'Yes, sir.'

The distortion test was almost an exact repeat of the laser firing. A short shot created little reaction, but the sustained beam managed to stir it. Though this time the black mass noticeably shrank back from the distortion field and its tentacles slashed further and faster to find its attacker.

'It doesn't like that,' the Colonel said. 'Alright, cease fire. Let's leave it to think. While we do the same.'

Representative Betts fixed the bow around her waist and stepped out from behind the partition. She was in a green gown with scattered swoops of material and darts around the bodice, twisting the dress into a whirlpool. Charlotte looked at her assistant and chief advisor.

'No,' Amy said, and then clicked back to her queue.

'Max?' Max was also tuned into the Weave, looking for something for Charlotte to write about. 'Max?' she asked again.

'Oh, uh ...' He looked up, demersing quickly to glance at her outfit. 'What Amy said.'

Charlotte growled and spun back into her changing room. 'I don't know why I'm bothering.'

'It's a big occasion, Charlotte. Don't pout.'

'I'm not pouting, I've just got nothing to wear.'

'Don't worry, Representative, I'll have one of your sponsors send something over,' Amy said calmly, trying to stop her complaining. Charlotte pulled off the dress, flung herself into a bed robe and gave up.

Of course, it wasn't Amy or the dress that was bothering her. It was the event itself that occupied her mind, and had done for the past week. She was too nervous to write anything, and in her position writer's block could prove to be dire.

Civic value can rise by happenstance, as it had for her, but to stay high on the rungs of the hierarchy took work and constant activity. A good Representative continually published motions for the Will to endorse and follow, which could be anything from thoughts on the weather to how the situation in Atlantic should be managed. The amount of support these motions received fed the influence of the person who put it forward.

As Amy had explained to her, if she wanted to keep being a part of the Primacy she had to keep giving the Will something to support, or her influence would simply fade away.

The Prime's office — and others — had a dedicated staff to keep up this steady stream of ideas and proposals, not to mention the moguls that disseminated his opinions in more discreet entertainments. Hundreds of thoughts and draft directives were floated — most of which were supported simply because they came from the Prime — and those that got the strongest backing could guide the next day's official motions. In this way, an efficient bureau could test the public reaction to a strategy before it was in place, to predict what would or wouldn't be a popular suggestion — though this had never proven to be a successful long-term tactic for a Civic career. The Will wasn't stupid.

At least, that's what Charlotte thought. Some Representatives filed regularly, pushing out ideas they thought would be popular to stay afloat or creating motions they thought would genuinely improve society. She liked to assume that humanity was essentially rational and that people didn't always act out of self-interest, which made it much harder to write for.

Much had changed for Charlotte Betts since she had become a part of the Primacy, she reflected. In point of fact, everything in the world seemed to have changed. Six months ago the psis were barely part of the global consciousness, and now every man, woman and child had to choose for themselves whether or not to wear the psi symbol on their person. She wasn't happy about that. The psis had done themselves no favours with their attacks and demands.

Charlotte sighed. These thoughts were just rehashings of things she'd said before and she needed something new. It was Saturday; time for her status report. Amy forced her to do them every week, to keep those who followed her stream up to date on what she had been doing and what she had achieved. There was very little to say this week!

A black ooze had swallowed a whole city. Four million lives were lost. What could Charlotte Betts possibly add to that? Were her deep-felt condolences enough? The problem, she felt, was that she didn't even understand what had taken place. One minute Busan was there, the next it was not. It was horrifically simple and simply horrific.

No, she had nothing to say today. She filled her morning listening to the backlog of petitions. The psi collections had accelerated after the conflict in the Cape, and more and more protests arose from the loved ones of those who had been taken. Charlotte tried to listen and respond to each of them, but it was heartbreaking. She only listened to remind herself who she spoke for.

Charlotte had dedicated boosters now who spread her words and backed the motions she put forward. Not that it was doing them any good. She hadn't achieved a single thing since her rise to office. Not one psi released, not one apology from the Prime. It was frustrating. Some days she didn't know why she bothered and Max had to remind her that she was the conscience. She was meant to be the voice of reason so that things didn't get any worse.

Nothing was right with the world and she had to find a damn outfit for a party she didn't want to go to. She could write about that, no problem!

Every item of clothing she owned was now spread out on her bed, chairs and desk. Amy reminded her when she had worn a particular item before, and thus it couldn't be worn again for this occasion. *Why is it that every occasion needs a new dress? Though, perhaps, this occasion calls for it. Your mother only turns a hundred years old once, after all.*

She needn't have worried. Amy found something for her on the Weave and arranged for it to be delivered; a benefactor who wanted Charlotte to wear her dress to the ball. Charlotte admitted that it fitted her well, a combination of two whites, and it was slimming where she wanted. Respectful to the event, combined with muted celebration.

'Come on, Charlotte. Time to go,' Max said. He was dressed in a three-hued suit: chocolate with black cuffs and blue edge-to-edge lining. At least he looked nice. Max was shaved and more neatly groomed than she'd ever seen him.

'Do I have to go?' she asked.

'Yes. It would be a disaster if you didn't show up. Don't worry, I'll be with you.' He held his arm up for her to hold.

'Well, that will help. My mother simply *adores* you,' she said sarcastically.

'She doesn't hate me, does she?' Max asked uncertainly.

'Only by association, I'm sure.' She patted his leg.

Ellizabeth Betts's gala — an orgy of civilised society — was on the boot of old Europe, which meant a jet and a squib for three hours. Deep in the Roman empire, in a fine old ruin just like her.

Ellizabeth Betts was a real lady. She believed in civilisation, and so she was civilised. She managed to maintain a place in the highest society with nothing but her intelligence and refinement to make her 'desired company'. Her art was the finest; her furnishings were art. Men and women gravitated to her for moments when their more animal instincts could be soothed and bathed in her fine example.

Charlotte tried not to think certain things. She hadn't spoken with her mother, or connected to her stream, for nearly forty years. She felt bad about that, but she had just never been able to face it. Like the lady she was, her mother respected her wishes.

She had grown up wanted by the world, or so it had seemed. It took a long time for her to understand that when people couldn't get what they wanted from the mother, they tried to curry favour with the daughter. Gifts and treats and favours were all Charlotte knew from the day she was born.

Then one day she realised this and broke the chains. Anyone who had ever tried to use Charlotte for leverage was blocked from her life and from her stream. In her tantrum, she didn't question the difference between friends and enemies. She wanted to start afresh and Charlotte did every despicable and public act she could think of until finally her mother had no choice but to distance herself.

She ran into the arms of any man who would have her, of which there were plenty, so long as they had nothing to do with her mother. There were innumerable men her mother had thwarted, plenty who wanted the status of tapping the Betts girl, plenty who liked her young and willing body. She was starting to suspect that the main reason she hadn't forgiven her mother was that she would have to admit to herself what a giant fool she had been.

'I don't know why my mother always insists on dragging people out into the wilds,' she said.

'This is hardly the wilds, Charlie.'

'It will be cold.'

'A cold night in the haunted lands.'

'Don't call them that.'

'You're not worried about ghosts, are you, Charlie?'

'Don't be silly, Max. It's just cruel to the people who still live there.'

'Ah, you're right. We must remain respectful at all times. I learnt that from you.' Max smiled. He was happy with himself. For once, he'd attached himself to the right train and his prospects were rising. Max's association with Charlotte had elevated him significantly in the last few months and, if he chose, he could be an independent voice in his own right. For now, though, he stuck by Charlotte's side.

'What are you thinking about?' he asked.

She hit him with her clutch purse. 'Why do you have to ask that?'

'It's a long ride, I've got nothing else to do.'

'If you must know, I was thinking about you.'

147

'And?'

'Have you ever met my mother, in person?'

'No. I never received my invitation.'

'Well, now you can be a plus one.' She patted him patronisingly on the knee.

'Just what I always dreamt of.' He put his hand over hers and winked. Charlotte looked at him and smiled. She still wasn't sure how she felt about him. 'Amy says you haven't put out your release this week. Did you snap at her when she asked?'

'Yes. I'll apologise. I just haven't got anything to say.'

'Impossible.'

'Will you stop trying to jibe me? There is nothing you can say or do to get me in the mood for this.'

'It's worth trying. I've heard so much about your mother's parties. Why aren't you looking forward to it?'

'I would if my mother wasn't going to be there.'

'Charlie, it's time to smooth that out. You would get quite a bump if she supported you,' he coaxed.

'I'll do my best, Max,' she replied.

They landed in a sheltered squib pad. The wall was artfully lit and delicate plants were spaced as if they were in a courtyard. Four assistants rushed out to meet them, holding fluff coats and hoods for them to put on.

Great, she thought. *I love the cold.*

They didn't have to walk far though, just to the edge of the tent where a fat-wheeled jeep waited to take them to the party. This was only a staging area, the villa itself being further up the mountain. The elder Betts didn't want flying traffic to distract from the *mise en scène*.

The road up was decrepit and crumbling. The jeep was buffeted by strong mountain winds and Charlotte jumped at the thunks as stones blew into the side.

'You still don't think she's crazy?'

'Eccentric.' Max squeezed her hand.

Ahead of them they could see a glowing yellow canopy where an artificial dome had been erected, looking like an egg yolk had dropped onto the mountain. As they entered, the wind fell silent behind them and they stepped into a warm pavilion tickled with music.

Luckily her mother was too busy to meet her. Perhaps it was just that amongst such esteemed company her daughter had been deprioritised, even if she was part of the Primacy. Max and Charlotte turned in their invitations and were taken into the party tent.

Ellizabeth had brought all her friends to this remote ruin for her centenary. There were luminaries from universities across the globe, such as Neruda Yunque, Tera Gienau, Conrad Ricci, Liza Obrokta ... Celebrities of every make and model, including the young mistress of the erotic sensorium, Wendy Berkan. Max winked at Charlotte again and then disappeared into the circles of conversation.

Charlotte grabbed up a flute of champagne and withdrew to stand by the wall where she could watch the people she used to know. She recognised her mother's former protégés and Servicemen of the previous wave who had been in attendance when she was young.

Despite her efforts at hiding, many people wanted to talk to her, to say hello to Ellizabeth's daughter — they had heard so much — but Charlotte found them easy to get rid of by trying to engage them in discussion of the psi situation. They slipped out of such topics with generalities about how terrible the business in the Cape was, or by bringing up the black thing from nowhere.

She found herself drawn into conversation with the youngest member of the FutureFuture Club, a loud man called Lucius Gregg who was running a public hypothesis about natural diversity. Charlotte was amused by his cocky manner and was almost swept away by his antithetical approach to research.

'You see, all I have to do is pitch theories to the Weave and let the masses complete the research. I have five hypotheses out there now and I don't have to do anything but monitor and summarise the results. Most of that can be done with automation.' He laughed large. The coterie of entranced women around him tittered.

'Did you really once say the World Union was ridiculous?' one of the gushing young women around him asked.

'Oh, not at all. I was misquoted — taken out of context. Global government is a noble pursuit. We just shouldn't be too idealistic about it. The founders of the WU recognised that we will never all agree, so they built a system capable of handling diversity. The World Union is one of the few human-made systems I do have faith in. It is the smaller groupings that fight the law of diversity, but some things cannot be fixed.'

'The law of what?'

'That's what I'm calling it: the law of diversity. In homage to the great Darwin, of course. I'm not surprised if you haven't heard of it, it hasn't been proven yet. In fact, I only came up with it yesterday but I'm having fun extrapolating already. Look at anything, art, history, families, group psychology — all can be explained if the law of diversity is recognised. While we strive for unity, nature is pulling in all directions at once. Diversity is why we will never get everybody to agree. Diversity is why we will never cure every disease. We were born to be different, and that's why humanity can never be controlled,' he explained.

But he wasn't talking to impress Charlotte, he had his audience.

Her arm was pulled by strange fingers, elongated four-knuckled hands and claws of blue. Her mother didn't normally welcome the augmented, or 'freaked' as the younger generation called it. 'Charlie dear, it's been so long. How long has it been?'

Charlotte ran a scan to find out who this was. The woman was Miz Ramona Schnell, patron of the animal underclasses.

'It is so nice to have you as a Representative, Charlotte. I cannot say how good I feel knowing there is a kind heart speaking at that level.' Charlotte tried to thank her, but Ramona continued over the top. 'And that you are a Betts, no less. Your mother must be pleased.'

'Oh, I'm not sure my civic status has ever been high on her priorities.'

'Tish. As a mother myself, I can assure you she is very proud. Have you heard of my campaign?'

'Only a little ...' By which she meant not at all.

'I don't want to bore you at a party, but perhaps if you have the time, I could tell you how important it is to bring technological equality to every inhabitant of Earth. Humanity is leaving its cousins behind.'

'Cousins?' Charlotte asked.

'All the animals on this world are our cousins, my dear. Why should they not enjoy the fruits of our technology like we have? Why shouldn't animals have the option of rejuvenation? Or to have symbiots that monitor their health?'

Charlotte was confused. 'I mean no offence, Ramona, but they are just animals. Do we not try to help them live as naturally as possible? That's why we have the wilderness parks.'

'As naturally as possible? We do not apply that rule to ourselves, dear, do we? And I think we both know how natural the parks are. We humans use our technologies selfishly, so we can have two lives and they only one.'

'Rejuvenation is still a new technology.' Charlotte tried to block the woman's momentum, but she was off on her spiel.

'We are the caretakers for the whole planet. Whether placed here divinely for the purpose or not, we must take care of our fellow Earthlings.'

'I have never thought of it that way. Please send your campaign summary to my people for us to take a look at.'

'You will? Oh, thank you, Charlotte. I knew it was a good thing you were on the Primacy.'

'Excuse me,' a voice said to her left. Charlotte turned to find a chrome servitor standing beside her. She felt her heart drop. 'Ellizabeth Betts would like to speak with you.'

'Very well, then. I'm sorry, Ramona, I must attend to my mother.'

'Of course, of course. I'll look for you later. Tootle.'

'Lead the way,' she said to the robot.

She was led further up the hill towards the ruins, where a striped tent sat under the main canopy, providing seating for the party-goers who preferred to sit and have the facilities close to hand.

Charlotte followed the servitor to a tent where her mother was sitting at a dressing table, tucking away every stray hair and dabbing away every imperfection.

'You're about to give your speech then,' Charlotte said.

Ellizabeth Betts turned around to face her. Those famous green eyes looked Charlotte up and down, peeling her strip by strip. She found she couldn't meet those eyes and looked away. She managed to notice her mother's face looked very thin and an elegant gloss cane leant against the table edge.

'You are looking very well, Charlotte. Thank you for coming.'

'Thank you for the invitation, Mother.'

The green eyes looked squarely at her face. Charlotte couldn't quite read the expression.

'You don't have to call me that if you don't want.'

'What would I call you instead?' Charlotte asked.

'You haven't spoken to me in thirty-eight years. Perhaps I don't need a name?' Her mother's eyebrows peaked in the middle, the sign of a rhetorical question she dared people to answer.

'This is going well, isn't it? I think I should just say happy birthday and leave you to it,' Charlotte suggested and made to leave.

'I would like it if we could clear the air,' Ellizabeth said crisply.

'Not now, Mother.'

'Then when? I have been waiting a long time to talk with you.'

'You could have come to me.'

'I did not think that you wanted that.'

'Well ... but ... this is a party. A celebration of your centenary. Can't we keep it pleasant?'

'I do not want to celebrate while my own daughter hates me.'

'I don't hate you.'

'Please don't deny it. The only reason you came here tonight was to help your cause. Don't you find it poetic that the reason you are pretending to forgive me is the same reason you believe you are upset with me?'

'You think the only reason I came here is for political reasons?' Charlotte asked.

'Of course. Let's not start our new relationship with lies, Charlotte.'

'Okay, then. I admit it. I came because Max said your support would help my position.'

'Well, I guess I should thank him for that.'

'He is here with me.'

'I know.' Her mother smiled placidly.

'Would you like to meet him?' Charlotte asked.

'No, thank you.'

'He is my most trusted advisor.'

'He is using you.'

'You don't know anything about it.'

'Do not pretend with me, Charlotte.' She tapped her hand on the table and her words became hard and clear, chipped. 'You have to grow up. You are in the Primacy now.'

'That's right, and I would have thought I would get a little more respect from my own mother.'

'I'll show you respect when you stop deceiving yourself. You know very well this Monsieur Angelo is using you.'

'Everyone uses everyone, isn't that how the world works?'

'Why do you persist with this?'

'As if you have to ask,' Charlotte spat.

'What have I ever done to lose your trust?'

'What have you done? How can you forget? You —'

The elder Betts raised her hand, seemingly to slap her daughter, but she just meant to cut the flow of Charlotte's railing. When she spoke again, her voice was perfectly calm. 'My darling, I know why it is you are upset with me, but I do not agree that you have justification.'

'How can you talk to me like this? I am your daughter.'

'I know. And it is because I love you that I am trying to help.'

'When you say it that way, it sounds so warm and caring.'

'You wouldn't believe it no matter how I said it. Would you?'

Charlotte held her tongue.

'I thought not.'

'Mother, let's just start over. Just pretend it never happened.'

'No.' She took the cane from beside the table and stood up, using it to strike the floor to emphasise her points. 'Bettses do not ignore their problems.' Tap. 'We talk them through until they are worked out, or we part ways until you are ready.'

Charlotte knew Max wouldn't want her to leave. It would look bad. Very bad. The same people who supported her

155

crossed over with the Civilisation Society, BARD and all the other fuddly groups Ellizabeth was a part of. Her mother was staring at her with the fierce judgement she remembered. The woman could see everything she had ever done wrong.

'Why did you let them use me?' Charlotte asked.

'Was it my place to stop them?'

'Yes. Mothers are meant to protect their children.'

'I tried to teach you everything you would need.'

'But you knew what was happening.'

'Of course I did. But you had accepted your Citizenship. I had to respect your right to choose.'

'Because it helped you.'

'Your choices are and were your own. You took those men to your bed willingly.'

'But you knew and you didn't stop it. You didn't stop me.'

'You are right. I never would stop you doing anything. To remove the agency of another human being is uncivilised. That is the basis of our society.'

'And your beliefs were more important than protecting your daughter?'

'Yes, my darling, they were, and still are. Even after you left my house and you … you went rampant, you were still expecting me to step in and stop you, but I could not.'

'You could have.'

'But then you wouldn't be responsible for your own actions. Don't you know how much it hurt me to see what you were doing to yourself?' Charlotte's head was spinning. Was her mother right? She felt the old anger inside her, but now couldn't be sure when it had started.

This was how she'd changed since becoming part of the Primacy. For so long she'd blamed her mother for not controlling her, but now she realised she agreed with her.

'You wanted me to control you and when I wouldn't you went looking for others. People like Max. I'm sorry I couldn't be the mother you wanted, but I had to let you make your own choices.'

Charlotte couldn't look at her. She bent forward and began crying into her skirt. She felt her mother's arms encircle her.

'It will be alright, Charlotte. It doesn't matter now.' She hadn't heard her mother's voice so soft since she was a child.

'I should go out,' her mother said after a while. 'Should I leave you here for a bit?'

Charlotte nodded. 'Thank you, Mother. Yes. A moment to myself would be good.'

'Okay, dear.' Ellizabeth took up her cane once more and stood by her daughter. 'I really am glad we are speaking again. I'm thinking of being rejuvenated.'

It took Charlotte a moment to recover. She let the servitor bring her food and drinks and then adjusted her hair and make-up. She didn't want the world to know she had been crying.

When she returned to the ruins the music was still playing and the glitterati still turned in their circles. The night was yet young but she didn't want to stay any longer.

'Representative Betts? I wasn't sure you would be here.'

She turned to the voice. It was a young, pale-haired man in full Services uniform and a chest loaded with decorations. She looked at his face, the blue eyes ... 'Colonel Pinter?'

'Ah, you recognised me.'

'Shouldn't you be in Busan?'

'One doesn't reject an invitation from Ellizabeth Betts. You seem to know that as well as I.' He then became the second man to wink at her that night. 'They have me if they need me.' He tapped the symbiot under his jacket. 'Let me introduce my companion. Gretel, this is Charlotte Betts, Primacy Representative. Miz Betts, this is Gretel Lang.'

'How very nice to meet you.' The two shook hands politely. Gretel was a stunning young lady, with an expression of such calm it was disconcerting.

Pinter leant in close to explain. 'I met her in rejuv.'

'Ah. Well.' Charlotte looked back and forth from one to the other. 'I'm not sure what to say.'

'Say it was meant to be.' The Colonel grinned. He beckoned a waiter close and made each of them take a fresh glass. 'To new life,' he toasted. Gretel and Charlotte clinked glasses obediently. 'Now, Charlotte, do you mind if I leave Gretel with you? She doesn't know anyone here and I must say hello to a few old sparring partners. I'm quite enjoying watching their faces fall when they see mine.'

'Of course ...' The Colonel was gone and she was left facing his companion.

'I was hoping to meet you,' Gretel said. *We have a lot to talk about.*

Charlotte's surprise made her choke on her champagne. The other woman patted her on the back. *Please try not to react.* 'Are you alright? Should I get you some water?' she asked.

'No. Thank you. I'm fine.'

Try to act natural. 'I'm a big supporter of yours. I back every motion.'

'That's very nice of you.'

'As are my friends.' Gretel waited for Charlotte to meet her gaze again.

'Who are your friends?'

'Nobody special, nobody who would get invited to a party like this.' *I speak for Tamsin Grey. My name is La Gréle.* 'I wondered if I could talk to you sometime about helping more. Ever since I was rejuvenated I've had so much energy.' *Please, Representative. We need your help.*

'Of course. We can arrange an appointment.'

'You're right. This isn't the best place to talk, is it? Quite overwhelming.'

'Yes, a little.'

'I won't bother you any more then, but I thank you for your time. It looks like the speeches are about to start.' Gretel went to rejoin Colonel Pinter and Charlotte looked at the pair of them until the other guests began chiming their glasses.

Ellizabeth's aide helped her step up onto a weathered block that raised her just slightly above the crowd. Charlotte could barely see her over the heads of the tallest men.

Ellizabeth spoke confidently into the floating microphone. 'Greetings, ladies and gentlemen. I thank you all so much for coming and hope you are having a marvellous time. You honour me.' The crowd raised their glasses again and cheered until she raised her hands for silence.

'The reason I chose to hold this celebration here was not to show you something that was older than I am.' The crowd tittered at the small joke. 'No, the real reason was that I wanted to share with you a story that took place right where we are standing.

'These ruins were once a hotel. People came here with their families and their romances. They came to places like this to remove themselves from their everyday lives so they could enjoy what was most important to them.' She looked over the gathering, including everyone. Her gaze stopped on Charlotte. She had heard this story before.

'When the continent fell under the chaos a small group of staff and guests managed to hide here and survive. The mountains kept most of the troubles from reaching these heights until the Örjians came from the west, sweeping everything before them.

'In this hotel, where we are standing, the Örjians arrived as they did everywhere. The story goes that the survivors living here were gathered in the courtyard, just behind us there.' Ellizabeth raised an arm to indicate the flat area behind the crowd, where the light dimmed into darkness.

'They were given an ultimatum: to live they would have to fight each other, as only one would be allowed to join the horde. And so the people fought. They either fought or were killed. By the end there were only two left. A man — who had seen his wife and children degraded and dismembered, a man who had just killed the friends he had been living with for years — and a young girl. She was barely two years old and no one had touched her during the fighting. The man had to decide whether it was worse for the child to die or for her to live and be raised by the Örjians.'

Her voice floated into the dark place behind them and they waited for her to continue. She looked over their heads to the darkness of the old courtyard.

'What a terrible choice it must have been.'

'What happened?' somebody asked.

'The story doesn't say what happened. Or rather, I've heard it ended in different ways.'

Those in the crowd could feel the scene standing behind them. They had been drilled with fear for the Örjian horde, the eugenetics and splicer clones. Ellizabeth Betts left them to their thoughts for only a moment.

'I apologise for telling this rather morbid tale on this night of celebration, but I tell it because there is much to celebrate. Life is a precious thing, which is to say life isn't merely valuable; it is to say that life is fragile. Life is precarious. We can never forget what it is to be human and civilised. That is why I would like us all to raise our glasses to my daughter — who, despite everything that is happening in the world, has not forgotten that what makes life precious is more than just being alive. Thank you, Charlotte. Your gift of hope is the best present a centenarian could receive.'

The crowd raised their glasses.

The party did well for both Charlotte and Max. His rank brought him into the top 0.5 making him a candidate for the Primacy, and she had the potential to become Prime if she wished it.

Charlotte was quiet beside him on the flight home, nibbling at her bottom lip.

'What's wrong? Didn't you have a good time?'

'It was fine, I'm just thinking.'

'You seemed to make up with your mother. I'd say that went very well.'

'Yes. Yes. I did what you wanted.'

'Then what is it?'

She nodded and smiled patiently at him. 'Nothing, Max. I'm just composing.'

I have struggled, in this week of tragedy, to find a topic worthy of discussion. Tonight I was reminded of something. To control another is to remove their humanity. We have segregated the psis in fear that they would remove our control, but in doing so we have committed that very crime against them. How dare we judge them by the reactions we have provoked?

Max opened his mouth to speak. 'Shush, darling, I'll share it with you when it's ready.'

When she returned to her apartment she stood before the mirror and quietly pinned a badge to her collar, a simple cloth circle with the white forked Y of the psis.

Atlantic was one of the biggest ecosystems in the world. It, like all the megacities of Earth, was encapsulated by the habitation, farming and industrial territory it required to maintain itself. It had many parts, as it had been born of older cities, some of which connected, many which didn't.

The World Union had no sustained presence in the Cape. There was no centralised planning, no major transport, no single government. Each area looked after itself and protected its territory. Dozens of despots — alternatively called chiefs, bosses or mayors — ruled over small built-up areas and controlled tracts of farming land around the city to feed their people.

This had been the way of Atlantic for a long time, and the situation hadn't changed with the coming of the psi rebellion. Each of these chiefs had been vying against each other for decades. James Reay, Hilary Carlton, Nathan Cusí and Teddy Bleech were low-ranking landholders who used their supply chains as leverage with the bigger chiefs — Lior Ligure and Boris Arkady. Freddy 'Froggy' Klinski had been considered the third big chief until much of his territory had been taken over by Chiggy's benders; now he was hovering in a middle tier of power.

Doctor Salvator smoothed his hair back and looked around the table. Tamsin and La Gréle had nominated him as the speaker for the psis since the norms didn't like being around telepaths. The reward for his good standing in the community.

It had taken a whole day just to agree on a location for the meeting, as none would meet on another's territory, and nor would they come near the psi headquarters. Now they had been in the room for three hours and made zero progress.

'You want something from me? How about I get something from you? That's how trade works,' Froggy said. He wore heavy chains of gold and gems over a high-necked metallic skivvy.

'What can we give you?' Sal asked, not for the first time. He reached for the jug of water and refilled his glass.

'The benders have taken my buildings. I demand to have them back.'

'We can't give them back. We do not speak for the benders,' Sal patiently repeated.

'Then I want new buildings.' Froggy pushed at the maps that were spread on the table.

'I'm sure something can be arranged, but what are you offering us?'

'Whoa, whoa. Hold your deal there, Sal,' Boris interrupted. He was in a white suit with a lurid shirt bright enough to outshine his mirror teeth. 'It don't work like that. You can't dole out territory without asking the rest of us first. Don't throw the weight around, it's irresponsible.'

'There's plenty of disused territory. Would that satisfy you, Freddy?' Sal asked.

'Hold on, now, I said,' Boris interrupted again. 'Froggy here is playing you. He only had plastics before. He's just using this excuse to get a free upgrade to solids. Don't let him sucker you, Sal.'

Sal turned to the man with the mirrored mouth. 'Can you offer something better, Boris? You know what we need.'

'Food and water. I have the most of both.'

'So what will it take for you to supply us?' he asked.

Boris leant back in his chair and pursed his lips. His teeth glinted out from beneath his cold smile. 'It's not that I don't want to help you. I do, but what guarantee can you give me? The benders took Froggy's buildings, what's to stop them taking mine?'

'Tamsin won't let that happen.'

'Are you saying, then, that she let it happen the first time? Can she really control this Chiggy so much?'

'Yes.'

Boris laughed, softly in his chest. 'Perhaps I should say that again. Will she control him?' Salvator was slow to answer and the room felt the truth out for itself. 'You see? It is my understanding that Chiggy doesn't talk to tappers either. None of you have even met with him yet, have you?'

'Not face to face,' Sal admitted.

There had always been rumours of this Chiggy. A bender so powerful he hadn't had any need to move since he was a boy. If he wanted something, he made it come to him.

Legend had it that Chiggy was so fat he could barely move his body. He lived in a bed on a mobile floor that he levitated with his mind.

When Atlantic had been declared a psi freedom zone he had emerged, claiming a huge area and blocking it off to telepaths. He was now Chiggy of Chiggy's Arena where the benders fought. He used his powers to instil fear in his followers. If that didn't work, he crushed their skulls and let it be a lesson to others.

Tamsin and Chiggy had been communicating on paper that was couriered back and forth by messengers. As strong as they both were, they could not trust the other to meet without attacking.

'Have you met him?' Sal asked.

'No,' Boris said, 'but I speak with his associates. The benders are the real power in the Cape now, not the tappers. I think I'll deal with Chiggy. He needs food too.'

'A lot of it from what I hear.' Teddy Bleech, not a small man himself, made a joke from the sidelines. 'I assure you, Tamsin

Grey and La Gréle are leading this revolution. Not Chiggy. I've been sent here to find equitable terms for your support, but if they can't be found, then I'm not sure what Tamsin will be forced to do.'

'And I'm not sure what I'll be forced to do.' Boris smiled. His teeth reflected.

'Are you expecting our support or demanding it?' asked Lior Ligure, proprietor of the TigerPark and its surrounds. In keeping with the theme of his arena, his suit and shirt were striped like the legendary animal.

'Let me say again that we are not here as invaders or conquerors. Many of us have lived in the Cape as long as you have,' Sal said.

'But why come here? Why not Mexica, or STOC?'

'This is where we came.'

And this is where we are staying. The double doors opened and Tamsin strode through, closing them behind her twin shadows of Okonta and Risom.

'What is the meaning of this? You promised us no tappers,' Lior blustered.

'Tamsin, what are you doing here?' Sal asked.

I couldn't wait.

What's wrong? Are they attacking?

No. But we've picked up transmissions. There are some runners from the north approaching the perimeter. They need sanctuary. They're in an old bus that is failing.

'Sit down, norms,' Tamsin commanded. Each of the men in the room felt their knees bend under them and they were pushed backward into their seats. 'Thank you.'

166

Okonta and Risom took a place at either end of the table, both ex-Services agents different in every way. Okonta, dark skin and old enough that his hair was turning to grey, stood tall and impassive, saying nothing and his eyes unmoving. He didn't need them to see.

Risom was just a boy and stood cradling his new silver arm to his chest, scratching it as if it was niggling him — which was impossible as it had no nerve simulation. The removal of his symbiot had not gone smoothly and Sal himself had been the one to amputate and affix the crude replacement. The boy seemed to bear him no ill will.

'You've broken your word already, Sal,' Boris said. 'You said our minds would be our own to make and yet, here she is.'

Tamsin answered. 'Yes, we said that, but it was a courtesy and this is now taking too long. Did you think we would let you stand in our way? Now, everybody, we don't want all of Atlantic to go like Bendertown. We want to avoid that. But we'll need you to start cooperating.'

'What's in it for us?'

She counted the reasons on her fingers. 'Your lives, your positions, the lives of those you care about ... that's all I can think of. Tell me if that isn't enough.'

'You come in here with threats and expect us to cooperate?' Teddy Bleech protested. 'We're going to deal with Chiggy.'

'Let me tell you something: you should be thanking me. Chiggy wouldn't even give you the respect of a threat. He'd just pop your little head like the melon it is. There is much worse than me, gentlemen.'

'You can't do this.'

'I think I can.'

'And what if we say no?' Lior asked loudly.

Tamsin looked to Risom, who was impatiently rolling on his heels and stroking his metal. He grinned and took a small stone from his pocket. It floated into the air and travelled smoothly to the centre of the meeting table, every eye following it. For a moment it hovered before the owner of the TigerPark, then it disappeared and Lior's head hit the table, blood spreading from beneath.

The pebble returned smoothly to Risom's waiting hand, making a red strip on his palm.

'Who else would like to put their pride ahead of their life?' Tamsin asked. The rest of the group stayed silent. Even Boris Arkady didn't meet her eyes.

Tamsin looked at each of the chiefs and bosses in turn, and once she was done she nodded. 'Good. We'll take what was Ligure's, problem solved. Now, I suggest that, if you don't want Risom and I to come to your future meetings, you start listening to what Salvator tells you. We are not asking any more.'

Don't take too long, Tamsin thought to Sal and left with her men.

Salvator was furious. He was a man slow to anger, but it took him just as long to cool. He closed off the meeting as quickly as he could. The men agreed to his demands readily, but he could tell they were already looking for ways to escape the position Tamsin had put them in.

Her revolution certainly hadn't started how Tamsin had hoped. She was tired, he knew, but they were all tired.

Almost as soon as the rebellion had been established the screams had started from the arena. They heard from those who had been present, both norms and tappers, that the ground had split open and an enormous man rose out of it on a flat stone tablet and began systematically exploding the heads of those who challenged him. He stopped when the screams stopped.

Now that whole area had been cut off. Bendertown. That's what they were calling the zone to the south where the majority of the kinetics had set up with the strict mandate that telepaths had to stay out or die.

So said Chiggy.

Chiggy had come out of nowhere. Sal had heard rumours of strong benders who never showed themselves, building tinpot empires in the basement of Atlantic, but he'd never thought of it as more than bravado from the benders. Then as soon as Tamsin declared the Cape for psis, Chiggy rose and Chiggy dictated. Chiggy had been waiting for his day to come.

That was what they knew about Chiggy. A man reportedly so powerful he had never had to move for food or fornication. He made the rule against tappers. Chiggy said no one could trust a tapper, nor trust themselves when a tapper was nearby. Suspects were hunted down. It was a vicious sport.

The rebellion had taken one of the disused blocks and was cleaning it up for the psis Tamsin imagined would come out of hiding. There were few residents and most of the rooms were empty save for refuse.

Sal went into the main building they had claimed, and walked down into the basement levels. Tamsin's rebellion lay below the

169

streets, where the few benders who hadn't joined Chiggy were digging foundations for new buildings and reclaiming some of the old ones that had half-sunk into the mud.

He had to admit, even for a kinetic like him, it was a marvel to see them at work. The dirt and mud threw itself onto the street, where another bender filled sandbags and laid them on a growing wall to hold back the tide.

Now if they had engineers who knew what they were doing … ah, he had made his thoughts known to Tamsin. Probably every time they were in the same room as each other she was reading his mind and hearing his opinions again and again. *There are upsides to not being a telepath*, he thought.

Psi headquarters was always wherever Tamsin was. They didn't want Services to be able to track them from orbit so the command team moved often: Tamsin, Risom and Okonta, with Piri in tow, bounced locations every day. Sal hadn't seen La Gréle since the attack.

He caught up with them in the old hotel they used to get to the basement. The second level had been built right through its fifth floor, so there were four levels of stairs to walk down to the bottom where Tamsin had taken the grand ballroom to live in. In the foyer, he noticed Okonta, and then Risom, leave with their orders. Sal hated that it was all done telepathically. He could never know what they were up to.

Once they had left she turned to him. 'Say what you have to say, Sal. We have an emergency approaching.'

'You already know what I think,' he said, spreading his hands.

'Yes, but you need to get it out. You'll feel better for it.'

'Okay, then. I can't believe you did that. You can't control them that way.'

'We need power, sewerage, food and water. How else do you think we'll get them?' Tamsin answered.

'If you were planning on forcing them into it, you could have saved me a lot of time and frustration.' His face was getting red with anger.

'I thought I'd give diplomacy a try. Why aren't you proud of me?'

'This is not a laughing matter, Tamsin,' he insisted.

'I'm not laughing, Sal. Listen.' She lifted her hand to the doctor, putting it firmly on his shoulder. 'I don't care about those people. I don't. Risom can push pebbles through every one of them for all I care. I want what they have. It's their choice if they want to cooperate or not. You have to make them understand that.'

'It takes more than violence to start a new state, Miz Grey. The Cape doesn't have enough food production to support itself for long. What will the people of the Cape do when the food runs out? They certainly won't be helping you.'

'We don't need to last forever, Sal. A few months. A year at most. We have to give La Gréle the time she needs.'

'And what makes you so certain?'

'I have the world on my side. Or I will do. Now, can we move on from this? We don't have long to prepare.'

Sal followed Tamsin into the old ballroom where Piri was playing.

There wasn't much left in the room. The garbage had been cleared and a desk brought in that was now covered in maps and papers. A broken chandelier with only a handful of lumens threw light on the stained and water-damaged carpet, which even now had a heater blowing to keep it dry. The wallpaper was brown and moth-eaten around the edges, with some of the panels curling down from the wall.

Piri ran over to Tamsin and hugged her leg. Tamsin smiled at her, but said nothing before sending her back to her games.

'You should talk to her more. She needs affection at her age,' Sal said.

'We are always talking. Aren't we, Piri?'

'Yes,' Piri answered, without interrupting her game.

'One of the advantages of being a telepath, I guess,' Sal said.

'One of many,' Tamsin agreed. She moved to her desk and began writing something down on a piece of paper. 'If you can imagine not being able to speak, that's what it would be like for us not to be able to communicate the way we do.'

'How far does that go?' Salvator asked. He was watching the girl enact a scene between two dolls, without using her hands of course. The dolls had been found for her and were scuffed and had no clothes. The explanation for them not having clothes often formed the basis of the play between the two toys.

He couldn't quite tell what story she was making them play out, but with no hands she made them bow to each other and bounce around in some sort of dance. Her abilities had increased dramatically under Tamsin's tutelage.

Salvator reprimanded himself for not recognising her abilities himself, though she seemed happy. All the love she had had for her mother had transferred completely onto Tamsin.

Tamsin shrugged. 'We are connected to each other.'

'And the rest of us?'

'Please don't start fearing us, Sal. We mean well.'

'I've always been afraid of you, Tamsin. I fear I'm helping you establish a new hierarchy where those with the strongest telepathic ability will rule the rest of us.'

She paused in her writing, then made a deliberate full stop and folded the paper in two. 'It's not like that. Like you said: we can't control everybody.'

'What about Pierre Jnr?' Sal came to stand across from her. 'Or what if this revolution works and the number of telepaths increases? How will the rest of us live not knowing what our real thoughts are?'

Tamsin nodded. 'Yes, I can see it is a concern for you. But the alternative is an unbearable life for us. As for Pierre ... I couldn't say what his intentions are.'

'Is Pierre Jnr coming to play with me?' Piri asked, a hopeful smile on her face.

'Yes, dear. He's coming,' Tamsin answered, keeping her eyes locked on the doctor's.

'When?'

'When he is ready.'

There was a knock at the door and Risom came in carrying a handscreen. 'They are coming in alright. We have them on radar,' he said.

'Coming here?'

'Straight at the blockade.' Risom stood there as Tamsin looked over the report. His pink arm was hand in hand with his cybernetic, fingers gently touching, like new lovers.

Tamsin cursed.

'What are you going to do?' Sal asked.

'I don't know. But I'm not going to just let it happen.'

She picked up her armour-jacket and cloak and stalked from the room as she tied up the straps. Piri stood up, nodded, then returned to her game.

'Where are you going?' Sal called after her.

'I'm going to get the runners through.'

'How?'

'We need the benders.'

'And you're going to ask them?'

'No,' she answered. *You are.*

He should have seen that coming. 'Why not you?'

'He won't see me, Salvator. And I don't think I trust him either.'

'But you're willing to send me?'

'Your reputation will proceed you.'

'What is your message?'

'You tell Chiggy that anyone who doesn't fight is a coward,' Tamsin said flatly. 'And give him this.' She handed him the folded note.

'Are you trying to get me killed?'

'Sal, I need you to get the benders behind us. Do what you have to do. Promise what you have to promise.'

'How long do I have?'

'They're going to intersect with the blockade around dawn tomorrow.'

'I should go. I should kiss my wife just in case it's my last chance,' he said.

'Don't be so melodramatic, Sal. Chiggy's one of us, remember.'

'I don't think Chiggy is taking any side but his own. This is Atlantic, after all.'

And so, in the middle of the night, with next to no sleep for two days, Doctor Alexei Salvator was in a hover crossing Atlantic from the base of the psi uprising towards the kinetics who were rebelling against the rebellion.

The norms were indoors and the streets were clear. By this time of the year, Zone Games season should be at its height, with millions of players coming to join the rosters from around the world to compete for their local region. The WarBall was cancelled and the net racers hadn't shown up to the meets. The only game drawing a crowd this year was in the pits of Chiggy's Arena, where kinetics fought and challenged each other in mortal combat.

It was two hundred and eighty kilometres to Bendertown, and taking a squib was too dangerous as the benders protected their skies vigilantly. He sent word ahead by runner. Radio or network communication was out of the question. The less Services knew about what was happening in the Cape, the better. They had warned Chiggy about how to avoid WU surveillance which is how they started using paper messages to communicate. Sal wondered if Chiggy's paranoia of telepaths actually wasn't entirely unreasonable.

Each area of the Cape was a deposit of wealth and influence, usually centred around a gaming hub like the TigerPark or Jackpot!, where residents played for fun and status, and the fame and frivolities that came with it. Atlantic was not a whole city like West or Seaboard. Its parts hadn't been intertwined with omnipoles and multitracks. The areas in between the hubs were left as they were, fending for themselves in feudal capitalism.

History is never wiped clean, he thought to himself. Even in the buildings of Atlantic the back story of the area could be read. New-growth architecture over old foundations. Skyscrapers from previous centuries had become mere spines, or legs, for the newer buildings.

This part of Atlantic had been built quickly once upon a time. Interlocking plastic blocks, stapled together and reinforced with artificial rooting. Holes were cut for doors and windows, and staircases were manufactured out of whatever was convenient. The walls had once been dressed in primary colours, but they were now scratched, pale and stained with age. Many of the blocks were filled with stagnant water and mould. Nobody lived in such places for more than a night, even when desperate.

At the signposts, they knew they were close to Bendertown. 'Welcome to Chiggy's — NO TAPPERS.' 'NO TAPPERS beyond this POINT.' 'TAPPERS WILL BE EXECUTED.'

Sal signalled a halt and the hover eased into an open area which culminated in a wide bridge covering a storm drain.

'What do we do now?' the driver, Randall, asked.

'We wait for our runner.'

'What if he doesn't come back?'

'Then we go in.'

They didn't have to wait long. A naked man soon appeared and jogged towards them. It was Carlos, the messenger Salvator had sent to request a meeting with Chiggy. He hadn't been naked when he had left them ...

They both stood up and stared at the man as he approached.

'What happened to him?' Randall was studying Carlos through a pair of hand-held lenses. 'He's smiling but he's been beat all over.'

'Is he delirious?'

The naked runner reached the car.

'Carlos, are you hurt?' Salvator asked.

'I'm fine, Sal.'

'What happened? Did they beat you?'

'They tried,' he quipped. 'They said if I wanted to talk to Chiggy, I had to go in the arena.'

'Did you get the message to Chiggy?'

'Of course I did. Those benders are strong, but stupid.'

'Don't get a taste for it,' Sal said and passed him a blanket from the back of the car. 'Was there a reply?'

'Um, yeah ...' Carlos hesitated. 'He said, "Don't cross the bridge."'

'Will he come to meet me?'

'I don't think so.'

Sal looked in the direction of Bendertown. The buildings on the other side of the storm drain looked dingier, older and darker than what was around him. He could hear a faint cheer coming from the arena.

Sal thought quietly to himself. Chiggy ... he didn't know what to make of him. 'What's he like?' he asked.

'Chiggy? He's the fattest man I've ever seen. He's as big as a squib and has all these machines plugged into him.'

'And you spoke to him?'

'Well, I spoke to Rocks and she spoke to Chiggy. I wasn't allowed to get any closer.'

'Okay,' Sal said. 'You two go join Tamsin. I'll go on alone.'

'We'll go with you,' Carlos said and the driver agreed.

'No. Let's not risk any more of us than we have to. Tamsin needs you more.' They were reluctant to let him go in by himself. Probably thought of him as too old.

Sal stepped off the hover and walked across the bridge. He looked up to see if he would be immediately attacked, but nothing happened. People at the windows watched him, and the glint of lenses from rooftops and cameras on poles said that Chiggy knew he was coming. Would he have to fight as Carlos had?

Simply because a conclusion is logical does not mean
it is always correct. Logic is often overturned with the
inclusion of new information that defeats its original
conclusions.
What We Can See, Milawi Ortega

Two servitors carried the chaise between them and sat it down in the corner Geof indicated. They bobbed their heads and rolled out.

First he looked at it, then he ran his hands over it. The release on the side lifted a footstool from below. He could already feel it warming and softening as it inducted electricity from the building.

A weaver could always rely on the Weave for data, but it was impossible to keep data perfectly secure and it was never as

178

immediate as using a symbiot. He was also used to controlling by thought and that was only possible with the organic circuitry of symbiots.

Now that he needed more than one brain, the symbiot chair would do nicely. He could be connected to it when active and also leave it, as and when he needed to, and the chaise would continue to process until it ran out of tasks.

Before he sat he rummaged in his pack for an old sylus. He had it preprogrammed to scan for malicious traps, material flaws and signs of pre-use. This little slug had been with him for years, approving his equipment before use.

Once he had the all clear he sat down, lay back and waited as the connections formed. It was always satisfying to expand one's mind this way. It felt boundless and unconfined.

He began transferring tasks from his symbiot into the chaise. All the data patterning that was processing, looking for the links and patterns that would lead them to Pierre Jnr. There were too many grey zones and anomalies right now for such a search to prove fruitful, but there was always a chance it would come up with something.

This last week had been incredibly trying. Geof didn't like being rushed to form decisions, or to make judgements quickly. The Prime was not that way. Working under him was an exhausting rotation of duties and redirection. Colonel Pinter was no better.

In his line of work, first answers were often the wrong ones. There was always another layer of knowledge that could change your perception, just as the good book said. *Despite how much you learn about the world and how it works, there is always something you don't know that could change everything you believed you knew. Such is the nature of knowledge, and such is life,* he thought.

As a child you pass through many levels of understanding. Every now and then you learn a thing that changes how you understood all the things that came before. Pain, death, fear, acceptance, truth, untruth. For weavers, trained to recognise their limitations, these became just new barriers to surpass, a wall the same as any technical challenge or security measure; the internal and external limits every individual mind has.

He was familiar with the walls that held back his understanding, such as the activity in the Cape, simply because those connections no longer existed. There were other grey areas in STOC and Mexica as so few there had strong connections to the Weave; they were the unsurveyed portion of humanity. The Prime's command centre was a place he hadn't broken into. He might be able to, but the consequences would defeat the aim.

Then there was the wall of the future, where prediction and simulation could determine no logical end. Such as how the conflict with the psis would play out ...

With the revelation that Kronos was most likely a product of the great Shen Li, and thus a mechalogical entity rather than biological, the thought room was culled and new members were co-opted to join the study, including the two biggest names in technology: Morritz Kay and Egon Shelley.

These two gods of tech were not used to being ordered around, but with the Prime's authority cornering them, they made themselves available when the Colonel requested their presence.

He patched them into his overlay: the two techists, Colonel Pinter and Gretchen Caswell. Geof had never met the gods of tech, though their work was well known to him.

'Gentlemen, thank you for coming. I realise you are both busy men,' Pinter began.

Egon Shelley was as tall as the Colonel, muscular and looked like he was a person transformed into a graphite black statue. He was covered in a symbiot that spanned all the way over his hairless scalp, leaving only his face showing. Even his eyes had non-reflective lenses built over them. The statue smiled broadly. 'Not at all, Colonel. I am always happy to dabble in an enigma.'

Morritz Kay, on the other hand, was short, had tussocks for sideburns and wore overlapping chains of trinkets and bracelets. Kay didn't use symbiots, he made trinkets which could be worn and easily removed, each charm performing different functions for, and linked to, his own external network. They were not as efficient as wearing a symbiot, but he had many supporters for his tech in those of a conservative mindset.

When he moved they rattled and Geof noticed something on one of Morritz's chains. A small silver bauble, a polyhedron with so many sides it almost looked round. He'd seen one of those before.

'What is the meaning of this, Colonel? I'm not a Serviceman. You can't order me around.'

'This is a matter of global security, Master Kay, so your cooperation would be much appreciated. But if you need inducement I'm sure I can find some; if that makes you feel better,' Pinter replied.

'Now, listen here —'

'What we don't have time for is bluster. Here's the problem I need you to help us solve.' The Colonel muted Morritz's audio so he could speak without interruption. 'At present, we don't know much. We don't yet know enough to know exactly what "it" is. We are presuming, for now, that this entity has come from the labs of Shen Li. Geof Ozenbach recently visited with Li and reported an experiment called Kronos that Li kept locked away. Obviously it escaped. We need to know how to stop it and how to reverse it. Yes?'

'Do we have a sample?' Egon asked.

'Yes,' Pinter answered.

'As I understand it, everything it touches it absorbs,' Kay said.

'We have found Faraday-V cages effective,' Geof said.

'Gentlemen, this is Geof Ozenbach, who is running the data for the Prime. And this is Gretchen Caswell, who is running the thought room. You will have complete access.'

'May I speak?' Morritz asked.

'Of course.'

'I'm not sure I should be included. I am not an expert on symbiotics.'

'You're right. The truth is, although I didn't want to be rude, it is your labs I need most. You are one of few who have the level of containment we require. If you prefer, we could simply borrow your lab and leave you out of it?' the Colonel suggested sweetly.

Morritz stretched his neck in both directions. 'If that is the case, I would prefer to be included.'

'I'm glad you see it that way. Your expertise will be invaluable.'

Two labs were set up: Kay's in West, Shelley's in Buenos Aires. A third would be ready within the week, in a Lagrange point, safe from Earth. Each had several metre-long samples of Kronos to work with.

Geof followed the experiments as much as time allowed, and summarised a short report at the end of each eight-hour cycle.

Egon Shelley had taken a personal interest and continually exclaimed over what he was discovering about the mysterious compound. 'Brilliant', 'Fascinating', 'Genius', he would say loudly at various moments, without offering any further explanation. 'This has all the hallmarks of Shen. Remarkable!'

He'd always been a follower of Shen Li, and now he had a chance to truly understand the father of symbiotics.

'If it wasn't for Shen, mechalogics wouldn't have gotten off the ground. He found out how to complete the interface and build it into the genetic structure. If I'm right, we should see his core code at the genetic level.'

'What if he started with new code?' Geof asked.

'He might have, but he liked to recycle as much as the rest of us.'

'Is it a life-form?'

'Only as much as symbiots and sylus are. By older definitions they would be considered alive. Here, let me show you something interesting.' Egon turned away from his scopes and sat back, ordering up lab footage for Geof to watch. 'Tell me after this if you think it is alive.'

The view he shared was from the inside of a spherical containment chamber. The bottom held a drop of black. Zooming in, he could see the filaments of its hairs lolling about, a miniature of the beast of Busan.

'It looks alive, you see, much more proactive than any plant. But ...' Egon skipped through the footage to an earlier experiment, 'with a little bit of x-raying and polarity shifting, it stops moving and is just a black sludge that doesn't react, and doesn't try to assimilate.' The video showed a hair-thin wire being inserted into the goo, pushed around and stirred without any response. 'It no longer absorbs.'

'So you can kill it?' Geof asked.

'If you consider it alive. Now look at this ... When we introduce a sylus to it ...' From the top of the chamber a thumb-sized lump of sylus was dropped into the dark oil. The ooze sprang to life. Hundreds of tiny tentacles jumped from the pool and began crawling over the slug.

'The specimen activates and takes over the sylus material and then returns to its waiting state.' They compared footage of Kronos rolling its tentacles through the air with the black sample performing the same motions in their cages. Probing and searching. 'Over time, it will absorb the glass wall and begin to attack the second shell. It is slower getting through metal. Again we apply the x-ray and demagnetising process and it becomes once more a lifeless puddle.'

'I don't know what to make of it,' Geof said.

'I interpolate that Kronos has three settings or states. I'm currently labelling them as: hibernating, hunting and harvesting.' Egon scrolled to another clip. 'Here we have returned the sample to hibernation for the next experiment. The same thing happens if we drop a mouse in.' Egon shuttled to the next clip, where a mouse was lowered into some inert Kronos. As soon as its feet touched the ooze the black attacked as if triggered, spearing into the body and head of the poor animal. It stopped kicking quickly and Kronos covered over it, raising and waving its tentacles in victory.

'What can a sylus and a mouse have in common?' Geof asked.

'I don't know, but I have had one thought,' Egon said, smiling through the mask of his symbiot.

'Please.'

'It might sound a little crazy.'

'Then we might be on the right track. Shen didn't think like others.'

'I think Kronos is two parts.' He held up his palms as if holding something in each hand. 'Mind and body. Both exist separately but need the other to become active. Like a bot needs a program. A car needs a driver.'

'I don't follow exactly.'

'A sylus and a mouse have little in common but they both have neural networks.'

'And that is the key?'

'Perhaps. Or to see it another way, it is like a sperm and an egg. The egg remains dormant until a sperm triggers its germination.'

Geof connected to Morritz Kay, who had followed the entire exchange. 'Any mind will do,' Morritz giggled.

'What's that?'

'I'm just saying that it doesn't discriminate. It isn't a fussy eater.'

'Ah.' Geof didn't comply with Kay's sense of humour. 'Have you learnt anything I can report? It's close to cycle end.'

What had occupied Morritz during the day was Kronos's digestive process. Like a symbiot it took energy where it found it, through heat and resonance and the sun, but it could also break down nearly any material it came into contact with. 'It eats everything. Eats and grows.'

'So why doesn't it touch the trees?' Geof asked.

'Oh, it does, but it uses them differently. I've only done one test at the moment — I need a bigger Faraday before I do it again — but my hypothesis is that plants are more useful to it as they are.

'Here, we put a potted plant into the chamber and Kronos digested the pot, leaving the plant untouched. But when we reset Kronos to dormancy, or as Shelley called it — hibernation mode — and take a cross-section of the plant, you can see that Kronos is inside it and has branched through the vascular structure.'

'For energy collection?' Geof suggested.

'And more I suspect. Plants can be very good sensors so it might be using them as antennas.'

'Plants can also produce nutrients and compounds. It might be pharming them like we do,' Egon added.

'If I had to take an educated guess, as all my guesses are, then I'd say this is a chimera of a synthetic life-form and a symbiot,' Morritz said.

'Aren't symbiots meant to work in combination with our bodies?' Geof asked.

'Yes. Or our minds. You can see why I don't trust them.' He was happy with what he had found. Evidence that the rival tech was untrustworthy.

It was then that Geof again noticed something amongst Morritz's chains of trinkets. The bauble that he'd last seen being constructed in Shen's lab.

'What does the sphere do?' he asked.

'What sphere?'

'That one on your wrist, next to the blue diamond.'

'Oh, my charms.' Morritz held his arm up to look. 'Just something we are developing. It's proprietary. I won't say more.'

The morning they left West, Desh arrived with a large duffel bag over his shoulders, chunky with shapes. 'What you got there?' Ben asked.

'Just a few little things I've been working on.' He took out a hard vinyl case and opened the magnetic catch for Ben to see. 'Meet our new nav.' Desh picked the sylus up and shook it vigorously until it began moving in his hand. 'Wake up, little fella, time to work.'

To keep the bus from becoming interesting to the eyes of the Weave, Desh disconnected the onboard computer, tagging the action as a systems check because they believed the unit faulty. He then put the sylus he'd brought in its place so they could still operate the vehicle manually. An uncommon but still standard procedure that would give them an hour.

They weren't sure how long they could evade attention, but once they made it out of West's airspace there was only the derelict midlands between them and the Cape.

187

When they got further from the city the sylus would parley with the Weave instead of the bus's default controller, and ping that it was a truck transporting supplies to midlander farms. They would repeat this data camouflage trick as often as it worked, sending false reports of what the vehicle was and what it was doing. So long as no one sighted the bus and then cross-referenced the log they would be in the clear.

At the end of the first day, the adults quietly deactivated their symbs and dropped them from the windows.

The real deadline was when the children didn't turn up to school the next day. One day was fine, two needed an explanation. That, correlated with the missed work hours by the parents, meant that pattern triggers would flag their activity to the higher ups. Luckily, Busan was pulling Services' attentions elsewhere or they might not have made it so far.

Ben and his family had been flying nonstop for ten hours. The weather was clear and they flew as fast as the old bus could take them over the empty midlands. Most of it was a dust bowl, and they had to brace themselves as they passed through the top of a storm. Maybe he should have gone a less direct way, but they were worried the old bus might not make the distance. Ben and Desh were listening to the engine, taking turns casting their opinions on its health.

'She won't make it,' Desh said.

'She'll be fine. Even if I have to hold her together myself.'

'Wasn't there an older, junkier bus you could've stolen?'

'Nope, this was the worst I could find.'

'So what do we do?'

'Do we have options? We keep flying.'

'But …'

'Yeah. But nothing. Instead of griping, why don't you practise making in-flight repairs?'

Ben checked the children through the back-seat cameras. Molly was asleep on her mother's lap behind him, and Bobby was lying in the back playing a maze game on a handscreen. Freya reached over and squeezed Ben's shoulder.

We're nearly there, love.

Two dark shapes winged in on either side, heavily armoured squibs with proboscis lasers twitching out from every angle. A third squib dropped from above, placing its shadow over the cockpit.

'Desh?' Ben called out.

R E A D Y, came the tip tap on his hand.

'What is your business, Citizen?' A harsh matronly voice reverberated through the bus. A takeover code ran through the controls trying to disable the sylus, but Ben was ready for that and jammed a disrupter into the circuit. The voice of Services cut off and Ben dove out from under the shadows, firing his emergency jets in a flare behind him. N O W, he tipped to Desh. 'Let's play sabotage.'

'Done,' Desh called forward. At his word the Services vehicles lost power and fell towards the ground. They watched as the crews ejected and glided to safety. The squibs dropped and hit the ground, raising craters in the fallow fields.

T O O E A S Y.

'Yeah. But, they know about us now,' Freya said.

'Yeah, I'd say they do.'

Ben looked up at the sky ahead. There was a black ombré over the horizon. Dark swarms flying in swirling regulation. 'Those aren't birds, are they?' Freya asked.

'No.'

'You got anything else in your bag there, Desh?'

His friend smiled. 'As a matter of fact I do.'

Tamsin and her team flew out from Atlantic, crossing the twisted mix of exuberant and dilapidated streets, the once-bright buildings and the languishing edifices of debauchery, before the landscape broke into acres of farmland, algaeculture and grazing paddocks. The shadows of their ragtag squadron dipped and bobbed over the land below, jumping as they began passing over the parks that became more and more wild the further they were from the city.

'People have been fleeing into the wilderness,' Okonta reported. His squib flew close to hers.

'Whatever makes them feel safe. At least they won't bother us in there,' she said.

He grunted. 'You would chase them all into the wilds if you could.' Okonta spoke with a flat voice and Tamsin had to probe for his thoughts on the matter. It wasn't that he worried over the welfare of those fleeing into the woods, he just worried that it wasn't a big enough solution. They were pushing certain groups to extremes.

There was only one other person in the squib with her, a young man called Emmett Sinclair, who was a weak tapper — more an empath than anything useful — but an experienced pilot.

Tamsin, Okonta, Salvator and Risom had scoured the Cape for everyone with psionic ability. Trying to bring them to the revolution before Chiggy got to them. Altogether, they made one hundred and seven.

Okonta patted her shoulder as if he was standing beside her.
He will come.
He has no reason to.
He has the same reasons you do.
I just hope it doesn't cost us too much.
What will be will be.

Their squibs were all different, collected from the good people of Atlantic, mostly personal transport vehicles and delivery trucks. They had twenty squibs in total, each one holding a tapper for silent communications, and the benders who hadn't joined Chiggy in Bendertown.

They were just coming up on the barricade. The line of defences had been thickening ever since the Cape had declared: armies of remote-controlled bots, tanks and drones that could patrol or invade, with or without human command. All it took was a program and preference settings. Services had perfected the art of semi-automated war; they didn't lose any people, just mass-produced weapons that could be replaced in minutes.

On the ground a dotted line of artillery tanks ringed the outskirts, following the traditional claimed territory of Atlantic, circling the farms and wild lands that were part of the megapolis. The desolate midlands were on the western side of the line.

The sky was patrolled by drone jets that flew up and down the demarcation like flocks of swallows and were about the same size.

What's our plan, Grey? Risom asked. He was flying a little way ahead. She'd given him a more sporty squib, donated by the late Ligure.

We find out where they are coming through and help them out.

Do you really think we have a chance? Risom asked. Tamsin looked at the face of her pilot and felt the trepidation coming from the other squibs. She tapped on the comms and spoke to all of them.

'We can see what Services have laid before us, but don't underestimate yourselves. It only takes a moment to break a circuit board, or kill a sylus. Go for the brains and work fast.'

And you, she focused her thoughts solely to Risom, *you go when you see an opportunity.*

If Chiggy doesn't come, we're all dead.

You just do your bit. That's more important.

As you wish, Tamsin. If mayhem is what you want, mayhem is what you will get. This is going to be fun.

The psis spread out, staying well back in Cape territory and watching the barricade for any change.

Flocks heading north, one of the other pilots called. They looked to see two clusters of black dashes speeding across the sky.

I see them. Everyone, follow, Tamsin ordered. For the most part, they weren't to communicate over radio. Her commands would be passed from tapper to tapper to avoid Services hakking.

Can anyone sense the runners yet?

'We have them on radar,' her pilot reported.

Plot their course. We'll target the barricade at their intersect point.

'Let's get ahead of them and give them some cover.'

The group accelerated, keeping a loose formation. This certainly wasn't a military operation, unlike the perfectly timed lines of the Services barricade.

Okonta, go low and take out some of those tanks. Risom, take the rest of the squibs and start knocking out the drones. Don't waste your first pass, once the barricade is armed it's armed.

Tamsin herself went straight towards the intersect point. She could see it on the horizon now, a dot becoming a rectangle as it got closer.

A ball of fire sprang up from the ground, drawing her eyes. Okonta had begun his strafing run, flying low, fast and erratic, while he and his onboard kinetics tore open the machines, sparks and smoke burping from their seams before they tilted over. They only got one run before the line of artillery began firing. The airspace below Tamsin became carpeted in grey and black clouds and she could no longer see them.

Okonta?

We're fine.

Above her, the drones were thickening. Like a flock of birds they swooped, dived and turned as a dynamic black cloud. From north and south more dark pins rushed to join in the defence.

The sky was soon cut with bright lines of light as the drones opened fire on the psi attackers. Risom ploughed through the main swarm, getting the benders close enough to reach and tear at the vital circuits. Two squibs in the vanguard were hit immediately and drew back, but the vast majority of the drone swarm fell from the sky like so many twigs.

Come on, people. Speed it up. It was no good, they were too far off to hear her.

One of Risom's squibs was clipped and spun out of control, a spiral of steam following its descent. Tamsin could hear them screaming in her head until they dropped below her range and were lost in the barrage of tank fire.

Everyone pull back to me. We don't want to lose any more people. Okonta, get up to level.

It was clear that the machines were too fast and too accurate for them to make a hole that would last. The broken drones were falling around them, but more were arriving by the second, and still the bus wasn't moving any faster. It was like they were waiting for something.

Come on, people. She still couldn't pick up their minds, and a swarm of drones was now turning its attention towards them.

Are we retreating? Okonta asked.

Not yet. They're nearly here —

Another of Risom's squadron went down and the telepaths went silent as another voice was lost.

The bus changed angle, floating north away from the huddle of defences. It was a futile move as the drones could easily match its speed and the line of tanks was unbroken all the way to the coast — where it was replaced with sea tanks, mines and submarines.

'Where are they going?'

'They must think they can find a hole.'

'What, are they stupid?'

'They are just frightened, Risom.'

'Miz Grey, there is a communication coming in,' Sinclair, the pilot, said.

'Who from? The runners?'

'No, from behind us. There is something on the radar now.' From this distance it was only a rash of black dots on the blue sky.

'I hope that's what I think it is. Put it on speaker. Hello? Who is that?' Tamsin asked.

A deep, slow drawl dragged itself from the speakers. 'Chiggy has come.'

'Thank you, Chiggy. We need your help to get these people through,' Tamsin said.

'Chiggy is not afraid.'

'No. Chiggy is brave and strong. Chiggy will bring the people through.'

'Get out of Chiggy's way.'

Everyone, let's fly north and meet the bus's new trajectory. Risom, go.

They retreated two kilometres, leaving the barricade to redistribute, tightening its gaps like a spring pulling together. More armaments were on the way from either end of the chain.

The benders approached. One of the squibs was bigger than the others and Tamsin's cameras followed it. That one was Chiggy.

As the large squib approached, the earth below it exploded as if an invisible plough was being dragged by a giant. The tanks didn't have the speed to escape.

The drones swept in to defend, but they buckled and fried before they could get within firing distance.

'Chiggy has come,' the voice crackled through, calm, almost soporific with satisfaction. 'All witness the coming of Chiggy.'

The tornado didn't stop. The wrecks of the tanks were thrown further down the line. The artillery tried to protect itself but their defensive fire only added more shrapnel to the kinetic attack.

The benders curved up from the south and flew parallel to the barricade, half of them dropping to claw the innards from the tanks, the other half scattering to divide up the swarms of drones.

'Holy mir ... have you ever seen anything like it?' the pilot asked.

Yes, Tamsin thought to herself. She reached out towards the big squib. *Pierre? Is that you?*

Tamsin and her team were watching from a safe distance, monitors zooming in and following the action as the barricade fell into disarray. It didn't all go the benders' way though, as many of their vehicles were cut to pieces by drone lasers — but even then they didn't crash to the ground as Tamsin's people had. The kinetics managed to control their descent and glide back into psi territory.

With the barricade down they watched the slowly approaching refugees. It was close enough now to see why they were going so slowly. 'Look at it, it's a wreck,' the pilot said. 'How'd they ever think that was going to get through?'

'There's nobody on board ...' she said. Try as she might, she should be able to feel something by now.

'Are they dead?'

The mood in the squibs dropped. They'd done all this for nothing. They'd lost comrades for nothing.

'Hang on.' Tamsin spun around and pointed with her finger through the floor of the squib and behind them. 'What is down there?'

'I don't see anything on the scope.'

'Okonta? Do you sense it?'

Something. Someone called Freya.

We're chasing a decoy, Tamsin thought ruefully. *Go get the real ones. But don't give them away.*

'There is a message coming in, Miz Grey.'

'On speaker.'

'Chiggy owns you,' she heard. The voice was deep and slow, wet and numb.

'We thank you, Chiggy. Tonight we shall celebrate in your honour.'

'You will send the benders to me.'

'Shouldn't we let them decide who —'

'Chiggy will choose.' His echoing laugh was scarier than his voice. 'You pay tribute to Chiggy.'

'We will provide all that you need, so long as the benders stand beside us,' Tamsin said.

'This is how it will be. Praise Chiggy.'

'Chiggy be praised,' Tamsin answered.

She could hear Okonta's thoughts in the background, asking if she wanted him to do what was necessary. *Now is our best chance.*

We need him.

* * *

'Give us five minutes and we'll have you up to speed on the big memes,' the meme-minder called out their slogan. 'The unknown black mass that took over Busan now has a name and that name is Kronos. Things are not looking good for General Zybyck Zim as Services have their pants folded for them by the psi rebellion. Again.'

Zim took a pistol from his belt and began to shoot the screens before him one at a time. His staff delicately retreated from the room. When all the monitors were dead black he looked around for anything else that had shown his failure. Anything he could destroy before having to answer the incoming call from the Prime.

How could this have happened? The barricade was built to the standards for air, ground and naval, and had been surrounded by a line of merciless bots with auto-generated strategy. Nothing was faster or better. He couldn't understand how the psis had broken the line so easily.

'Explain yourself, General,' the Prime demanded, forcing his way through Zim's queue. The young Shima was dressed in his strict black robes and was barely containing his rage. Zim had always cursed the boy's ascendancy when they needed an experienced commander as leader.

'Prime, we weren't ready for that kind of attack.'

'That has been made clear.'

'We will triple the line,' he said.

'But it is already too late, General. The rebels made

it through. You allowed the Will to be weakened. Your incompetence borders on treason.'

'We must launch a counterattack immediately.'

'To what end?' the Prime asked.

'This is war, Prime. We must strike back.'

The Prime sat still, considering.

'Very well. Prepare your retaliation plans for consideration. For now triple the defence line. Do not allow anyone else in or out of the Cape.'

'Yes, Prime. It won't happen again.'

The Prime signed off. 'You won't be given the chance.'

The clouds didn't so much roll in, as were poured out from above and spread to block the light from the sky. The priest looked up and thought that today the rain would come. That was good. It had been dry for so long. Today it would flood.

His monastery sat at the base of the mountains, where many large and small temples took shelter. Deep inside the wilderness zone, many of the old belief systems waited humbly for their time to come again or their time to run out forever. A wide common path snaked between and around the gardens, buildings and cemeteries of the religions, a philosopher's walk that led through wafts of incense and echoes of chant and prayer.

There was so much grace and beauty and love in this one small area, and though the priest didn't agree with the practices of those around him, he enjoyed their earnest and quiet appreciation of goodness. Unlike them, he had no god. His was a non-theistic religion, a décroissance, or slow life, dedicated to existence at its most simple and human.

He had a small shrine of white walls and red uprights. He wore robes he had spun himself from wool he had shorn from a llama he had raised since birth. That was the way of his belief and he was the only human he knew who still followed it. Listen. Think. Accept. Practise. Believe. He sat on his heels and rocked back and forth, humming deeply in his throat.

Thunder knocked on the roof of the world and he looked up to see if rain was about to fall. A boy sat on his altar looking down at him.

'Who are you?' the priest asked.

'I am your god.'

'I do not believe in gods.'

'I am here to save you.'

'I do not need saving.'

'Of course you do. You all do.'

'Please leave me to my prayers. May you live a blessed life, my child.'

The priest closed his eyes and breathed himself into a deep-throated chant. He built the vibration up and pushed it deeper into his chest. His chest erupted in pain, ribs cracking outward like cage doors, and he collapsed to the ground and looked up to the sky.

The pain disappeared and he saw the boy still seated on the altar, watching him roll on the stones. The visions were terrifying, unlike anything he'd experienced before.

The priest pushed himself back up and rested again on his legs, composing himself. 'You should go, my child. It is rude to disrespect another's beliefs.'

Again the priest began his prayers. This time with a constant hum to drown out anything the boy might say. He bowed backward and forward, then his stomach burst open and entrails began oozing out and running away like panicked snakes. The priest choked on the pain and tried to grab handfuls of his guts and pull them back inside him. He looked up in desperation and saw the boy, calmly watching him, and the pain was gone again. His body was whole.

'Believe in me,' the boy said.

'You are not human.'

'Pray to me.'

'No,' the priest said. He prayed the boy would go away. In his head he begged him to go.

I am your god.

No.

I am inside you. You cannot hide from me.

No.

Submit to me and you will be free.

I reject you.

You have no choice.

'No!' the priest screamed.

A drop of rain hit his face, large and cold. It turned to acid and bore through his flesh, into his brain. He screamed as more drops fell, tearing him to shreds.

Neighbouring monks and priestesses from the other shrines rushed over to find out what was wrong, only to find the priest rolling on the ground and shouting at himself. He was obviously hallucinating.

* * *

The sharp tinktink of a spoon on a cup greeted her as she demersed. Charlotte had been under a long time. The Primacy was almost constantly in session now and this was just a quick recess before Zim put forward his next strategies to combat the psi problem.

The window said it was daytime. She didn't want to get up from the couch, but someone was luring her with tea and something freshly baked. Her nose began waking up.

'Muffins?' she mumbled.

'Peach and blueberry,' Max said.

Amy Watson sat at the window table with everything laid out. There were even doilies under the breakfast plates and the yellowest slices of butter arranged in a dish.

'What's all this for?' She sat up.

'Do we need a reason?' Max grinned. She in turn squinted at him. She had expected Max to leave her now that his influence had risen, but he was still here, happy to remain her advisor.

'I wouldn't need a reason. Amy wouldn't need a reason, but you, sir, do nothing unless you have a reason,' she said.

'Let's call it a celebration then.'

'Oh yes, what are we celebrating?' she asked.

'Please, come sit with us, Representative. There is something we need to discuss with you,' Amy said. Charlotte rose, pulled her lounging robe into decency and grumbled.

'There's no reason to be mysterious. I don't need big news delivered with sweet things and tea.' She sat and broke open a muffin and covered its steam with a knife-load of butter. Max joined them, but sat back for Amy to do the talking. 'Alright, you two. What is happening?' Charlotte asked.

'Well, first of all, you've gained position,' Amy said.

'That's good.'

'Yes. You've gained a lot of support since your mother's centenary and then again with the mess-up in the Cape.'

'Yes ... why is Amy talking and not you?' she asked Max.

'This is more Amy's area of expertise, Charlie. I've taken you as far as I can.'

'There's further to go?'

'Yes, to Prime.'

Charlotte choked on muffin crumbs. 'You're deluded.'

'No. Charlie, listen to what Amy has to say.'

'Representative. I believe a convocation of the Will is coming.'

'What does that mean?'

'Do you know what asabiyya is?' Amy asked.

'No.'

'Group subconscious?'

'Not really. I've heard of it.'

'Group think?'

'That is an easy one.'

'Well, in technical terms it means that the majority of the Citizenry are either abstaining or deferring their vote. But what it really means is that the Will is undecided.'

'I don't understand. The Will can't be undecided. How could the world operate like that?' she asked.

'In the same way,' Amy answered. 'It just means that less people are contributing to the decision tree.'

'It means most people have become maybes, Charlie,' Max butted in. He was excited, she could tell from how red his face was going. 'They don't know what to believe.'

'That doesn't make me as happy as you might think, Max,' Charlotte said sweetly.

'Okay,' Amy pushed on. 'Technically, we are always in convocation, but we don't name it unless it is on a mass scale. It hasn't happened since the first formation of the Will.'

'Never?'

Amy shook her head.

'How do you know what will happen then?'

'I don't, but there is much theory on it.'

Charlotte quietly ate her muffin. Breaking off small chunks and nibbling on them.

'So what do you want me to do exactly?' she asked.

'I suggest we try a complete change of strategy. Instead of remaining as the voice of dissent, we start proposing alternative plans. That will give people options.'

'Charlie, we think now is the time to do another big push,' Max said. 'We can turn the tide of opinion. You could be Prime.'

The word made her head spin. It wasn't right. She, Charlotte Betts, at the top of the hierarchy?

'I don't know … That sounds awfully risky.'

'Charlie, you can change the course of events. You can stop this war before it begins.'

Then the bell rang and their conversation halted suddenly.

'I wonder who that could be.'

Amy tapped the door cameras to a handscreen and passed it around.

'That's the woman you met the other night. Colonel Pinter's new lady friend,' Max said.

The colour drained from Charlotte's face. 'What does she want?'

'Well, I don't know. You're the one who invited her.'

'I forgot. I said she should come.'

'What's wrong, Charlie? She's just a supporter.'

'Do you want us to get rid of her? We can say you are busy,' Amy said.

'No. No, let her in. Just let me get changed.' Charlotte dashed to the bedroom.

From behind the door she listened to the pleasantries of Amy and Max greeting Gretel. She didn't know what to do. She just stood listening to the sounds outside her door.

It's okay, Representative. I come in peace. Please don't fear me.

Charlotte grabbed a clean dress from the cupboard and quickly made herself presentable. She re-entered the sunroom with a broad smile on her face and took both of Gretel's hands in hers.

'Gretel, you came. I'm sorry to have kept you. I just came out of a deep session and looked a total mess.'

'You look lovely. I know how busy you are. Is now a bad time?' *I'm sure that isn't true.*

'I am always here for friends and supporters. Now, come, sit. Amy, could you make some more tea?' She wasn't sure how to proceed, but then Gretel's voice entered her head again.

Just think as if you were speaking to me, and I'll listen. Just as if you were talking to yourself.

Well, that I am very used to doing.

205

'These are lovely rooms, Representative. Very ... humble.' *You really have no reason to be nervous.*

'I haven't had the time to find anything bigger. Max and Amy would like me to find offices for my staff and boosters. I hope you don't mind.' *You're the first telepath I've ever met.*

And yet you are such a defender of our cause. 'Oh, think nothing of it. I'm sharing a Services capsule at the moment. This is lavish in comparison.'

Talking like this is hard to maintain. How can I help you? 'So you and Colonel Pinter are together?'

'Yes. Amazing, isn't it? Who would have thought? Certainly not me, I've never gone in for the military types.' *You already are helping us.*

I'm trying to. While I have many supporters, it isn't enough to turn over the existing policies.

But that is about to change, isn't it? With the convocation.

Charlotte looked into the eyes of the young woman — the seemingly young woman, she reminded herself.

Amy brought a fresh pot of tea to the table and a small tray of biscuits. Charlotte looked at Miz Lang as she took the cup in her perfect fingers.

'So, Gretel. You said you wanted to help us. May I ask what you had in mind?' *What will happen?*

'I am happy to pitch in where I can, but I'd really like to be doing something amongst the people.' *The Will will change.*

'Are you not keen on immersion?' Amy asked.

'Not since rejuvenation. I just feel like connecting with people one on one.' *What is it you need help with, Charlotte? Why don't you tell me what you need done?*

'And why do you support me in particular?' Charlotte asked. *It would help if you could control your people. These attacks are undermining our cause.* 'Take your time.'

They are their own people. I do not control every psi in the world who is feeling threatened by the World Union.

But the rebellion? Why did you have to attack the embassies in Atlantic?

What else could we have done? We have been ignored too long.

'The psis are people too,' Gretel eventually said. 'They should have the same rights as any Citizen.'

'But some of these people can listen to your very thoughts, or control your actions. Is not the removal of another person's agency the greatest of crimes?'

'I don't believe there is any evidence of such actions.'

'But they could do it,' Charlotte said.

'Possibility is not the same thing. Nor can you segment a whole group of people based on the actions of a few.'

'So what can we do?' Charlotte asked. *Well? This is where I am stuck. How do we cohabitate?*

'I have resources that I'd like to put towards your cause. The situation in the Cape must be abominable by now. They have never been self-sufficient and we must petition to open the barricade, if just to send relief.'

'Yes, the people on the other side must be suffering terribly.' *The Will won't support it. The rebellion has frightened them.*

We had no choice. We want peace and we are willing to fight for it. Please help us avoid that.

'Excuse me, Representative,' Max spoke up. He had been delving into Gretel's first life and found that most of her influence came from supplying Atlantic with pharma crops — not from her short time as a *chanteuse*. He flicked the dossier to Charlotte and Amy. 'Am I to understand that this is a trading concern?'

'Well, there is that side of it — but there is also the humanitarian cause,' she said.

'That you would benefit from?' he asked.

'Yes, but —'

'But say no more. This is inappropriate. Representative, you cannot be seen to be part of this vested collaboration.'

'Representative, please?' Gretel begged. *All we ask is a chance.*

I don't know what I can do to help.

Put the motion forward. Let the Will decide.

Will having your own ... country be enough?

Yes. And to have our brothers and sisters released from restriction.

We could never be sure that you weren't controlling us ...

You aren't sure now.

And what about Pierre Jnr?

Gretel looked directly into Charlotte's eyes. *I don't know.*

'I'm afraid my aide is right, Gretel. While I appreciate the humanitarian argument, we must find a resolution to the greater problem.' *Does he exist?*

I believe so. Tamsin Grey has met him. 'I wish you would reconsider. My suggestion wasn't a purely selfish notion. Atlantic can't survive on its own. And who knows what will happen when they start to starve.'

'Well, then, I will think about it. Miz Lang, I thank you for your time. Please give my regards to Colonel Pinter.'

Thank you, Charlotte. 'Thank you, Representative. Whatever you make of my motives, I still support what you are doing.'

The Prime and Charlotte Betts had been firing shots at each other through their press releases. Criticising the other's stance against the psis and creating motion after motion trying to gain support from the Will.

He hadn't slept a full night in some time. He took programmed naps of half an hour or fifteen minutes and then raised his energy with a stim patch before he had to hold a meeting.

Since the infiltration of Shima Palace by Tamsin Grey, he had had to make efforts to separate himself from the family and any suspicion that he had been compromised by telepathic control.

He wasn't the only one worried about that perception. Senator Demos was wearing one of those helmets that looked like he had tubes of water-filled piping wrapped around his head. There were now thriving businesses offering a variety of mental security. Around the globe companies had begun offering psi protection and detection services and products. Head shields to block out telepaths. Dampening fields to prevent telekinesis.

'Buy the new vitreous helmet! Only the best will protect you.'

There was no basis for any of the claims, but it was one of those strange examples where the assurance was more important than the reality. The Weave was crowded with evidence refuting any claims the con artists could make, but the public always felt a need to do something. It didn't matter if it was effective or not. There was something to be learnt from that.

His secretary, Gladys, must have noticed his inactivity as she sent some vegetable sticks for him to eat. He chewed them without tasting. They were pharma crops, purple carrots loaded with necessary vitamins and minerals; now he could avoid the need for a full meal and still operate. He cursed his weak body and its need for fuel; one day they would come up with a method of feeding the body which wouldn't take so much time.

The other trend was of more concern. Whether directly manipulated or out of fear, many Citizens were beginning to wear the psi symbol as the rebellion had told them to do. Windows of homes displayed the three-pronged Y, declaring that they were not against the psionic people — even though the Will spoke otherwise and continued to support him as Prime.

The tolerance movement had gained a lot of momentum recently and Ryu now had to consider Charlotte Betts a legitimate threat to his seat, much to his chagrin.

Takashi: Big brother, you aren't sleeping enough.

Ryu: I can't talk to you.

Takashi: Ryu, I'm clean.

Ryu: Surveillance says otherwise.

Takashi: Ryu, don't cut off from me like this.

Ryu broke the connection and pinged Gladys for what was next in his queue.

'Everyone wants you today, Prime. Which problem did you want to look at first? The psis, the black mass, or the convocation?' He checked his simulations and left them to interact with his lesser worries, Betts, manufacturing, training. The simulated hims were a useful tool, though he wondered if they could be trusted now that Takashi had been interfered with. For now he had no choice.

Ryu was becoming desperate for some positive news he could report.

'Get me Colonel Pinter.'

Their avatars gathered in a walled space on the Weave. It was constructed in a similar arrangement to the Adjudicators Ministry, though the rows of seats were only drawn in outline, and the walls were a lattice of translucent lines.

There were a lot of new faces in the council today. It was always slippery on the lower rungs of the Primacy, as there were many wanting to pull them down to take their position; and they were easily, and intentionally, ignored by those above who wouldn't dream of sharing their influence.

All were absorbed in the confluence of opinions now spiralling through the Will. Watching for any speculations that became popular so they could throw their support behind them and show the worth of their influence. They were fools, watching for the Will to determine what they should do, rather than determining what should be done and letting the Will decide if they were right. There was not a one of them he could trust to help him. Ryu sneered at them.

Charlotte Betts was the last to arrive, as always. Ryu watched her avatar materialise in her seat. Now, *there* was one who operated like he did. It was a shame, and an annoyance, that her ideas were so antithetical to his own. He noted the psi emblem drawn on her collar. She nodded to the Prime that she was ready, then saw Colonel Pinter next to him and nodded to him in surprise.

This gave Ryu a little pleasure. She must have been busy with something else when he gave the Colonel the boost that raised Pinter into the council. He slid a to-do to one of his selfs to find out what it was that had had Representative Betts so distracted.

'General Zim, are you ready to commence?' Ryu asked.

This was Zim's last chance. If he couldn't convince the Primacy to support his counteroffensive, then his support would likely dissolve from under him.

'Yes, Prime. I am ready.' The General stood tall and proud, uniformed in full regalia. He was a big man, perhaps exaggeratedly so. His avatar didn't show his age yet; he was as toned and muscled as he had been two decades ago, with a hedge of strong black hair pruned down to a Serviceman's cut.

A low-rung member spoke first, Tobias Bunn — whose support came purely from following the whims of the population, which today meant finding someone to blame. 'General Zim, can you please explain to me how an antique school bus managed to get through your blockade?' This question was met with murmurs of agreement.

Zim turned calmly to the speaker. 'The fugitives had help from the rebels within the territory.'

'And that qualifies as an excuse?' Bunn followed up.

Zim kept his face still, which was easily done online; you only had to disable your avatar from reacting to your emotions.

In his marina in the Arctic Ocean, Zim could be jumping up and down in murderous rage, but his avatar would only show smooth assurance and speak in a regulated tone. 'The forces the rebellion commanded were grossly underestimated. This was an intelligence slip that meant we weren't adequately prepared.'

'Are you trying to shift the responsibility to others, General Zim?'

'Not at all, I am only explaining the difficulties of the situation. I fully accept that the data team was under my command.'

'General Zim,' Charlotte Betts indicated she had a question. 'If you had been aware of the psis' abilities, how would you have changed the operation?'

Zim looked from the Representative to the Prime, weighing up what he should and shouldn't say. 'I would not have waited for them to strike first.'

There was a stir in the council, each member thrusting questions forward simultaneously. Colonel Pinter privately messaged Ryu.

Pinter: Do you mind if I step in? I think I speak Zim's language.

Prime: Proceed. I don't want this meeting to end without a resolution.

Pinter: Understood.

The Colonel took a step forward, away from Ryu to stand before the General.

'General Zim, what would such a strike look like?'

'With the council's permission, I will lead us through the staging rooms.' Everyone assented and the room began reconstructing around them. The seats and walls disappeared

213

and the avatars dropped to a common floor so Zim could guide them through a composite of all the operator rooms involved in the proposed offensive.

For security there was no physical building. The Servicemen working on the front were scattered over a hundred highly classified locations around the WU; only their avatars were included in the virtual construction.

'Prime, esteemed council, welcome to my command centre.' Their avatars transitioned to a dark chamber with graphic overlays of Atlantic. Maps of the city and its territories were encircled by two dotted lines that represented the blockade.

'Before we begin any offensive manoeuvres we will fortify the barricade with a third ring of air, ground, naval and subspace auto-targeters. This shield will cover a wider area to create a perimeter between the first, second and third lines.' A thick band traced the line of the existing perimeter.

'Will Services have firing approval?' Representative Betts asked.

'For foolproof containment we would recommend automation. It will decrease the response time into seconds.'

'And once your defences are in order, what will you do then?' Ryu Shima moved the conversation along and threw the Representative a glance. He was wondering what her aim was. *What is the old biddy up to now?*

'After ensuring our defences, we will commence a public campaign to the people of Atlantic, stating that we intend to re-establish an embassy in the city.'

'And how will you communicate that to them?' asked another speaker.

'Through all channels. We know they are using radio and have subnet pockets in the major areas. We will also airdrop squadrons of dragonflies and paper messages.'

'And what will that message be?' Betts asked. She seemed satisfied with the tired sighs of the military men in the room. *Yes, hers is the way of the question now*; the Prime recognised her tactic and watched. By positing questions she was trying to get others to do the work for her. Presuming their answers would trip them up.

'The wording is being crafted, but the essential points will be that the World Union will be interceding in the criminal takeover of the territory by hostile forces.'

'You are referring to the psis?'

'The group that has declared open rebellion on the World Union and the Will of the people.'

'We have Citizens trapped in the zone. Will you be helping them return to their homes?' Demos asked. He only ever cared about his own people, which was admirable in a way, and kept his position safe. More people were beginning to recognise how protective he was of his constituents and had petitioned to join his floating cities. Demos was accommodating them with new liners and extended visits.

'Of course,' the General answered. 'Once identity is confirmed, all Citizens will be provided courtesy evacuation.'

'And what about the people of the Cape?' Betts asked. Ryu could tell she was ramping up to her oratory voice. She knew just how to speak to make her every question seem to point at a moral outrage. 'Will Citizenship be available to all who ask for it?'

General Zim looked to the Prime for an answer. Ryu had been watching the discussion rather than listening to it and he answered without thinking. 'It is a founding principle.'

The council was silent. He had inadvertently conceded ground to Betts.

'And what will you do when the psis resist you?' asked Nigel Westgate. The Anti-Psi League had just managed to creep him to the lowest rung of the council.

'We will meet force with force,' Zim answered.

'Could you show us what that would look like?' Colonel Pinter asked, echoing his question from before.

The General swiped the wall-screens clear and started revealing the strategy-matrix he had built. As each element appeared it was nested into any one of a timeline, a list of objectives and a map location. Contingencies branched from every action, and led to their own branches. Zim zoomed and highlighted the major points.

'Twenty-four hours after we have broadcast our message we will form a loop in the barricade lines here, which will extend into Atlantic to here.' The blue line around the Cape formed a bubble that moved into the city and covered a significant area of the central coast. 'We will use natural defences as our border posts, as well as canals, drains and tributaries. All soft foundations between the stations will be detonated and dropped to sublevel to form an air moat. We will then land Seabase 3 here.'

On the map a yellow square appeared. The scale brought the two-kilometre barge in to land at a cargo dock, an operation that would take five days to complete from the base's current position.

'The Seabase is protected by distortion radiators and a two hundred per cent protection grid.'

'How close can they get?' Westgate asked.

'Four hundred metres.'

'How will you defend your position in the basement?' Pinter asked. 'As I understand it most of the psi activity seems to be below the street level.'

'The area will be mined and patrolled by Stingers and AMs.'

'Annihilators?' the Colonel asked.

'You have an objection, Colonel?' Zim smiled.

Ryu, and probably everyone else in the room, had seen the images of the young Pinter leading his annihilator cavalry into battle. There were hundreds of renditions of *The Last Charge of the Britons*.

And history called him the Scorpion. The index reference for Scorpion always said to 'see Pinter, Abercrombie'. When he chose to strike he would strike once, and once only. Like his namesake, he waited. *But who would his target be?* Ryu wondered.

'No, no. Not at all,' Pinter replied. 'It's just like old times.'

'With all due respect, Colonel, annihilators have come a long way since your day. The AM17s we have in replication have been programmed with patterns of known kinetic and telepathic behaviour and are connected with a hive learning module.'

Pinter returned Zim's smile with a smirk. 'May I say, I admire how restrained this plan seems. I remember you used to be more prone to aggression.'

'I didn't say I expected them to take it lying down, did I?' The General's smile grew broader. It had been fifty years since he'd been in negotiations with Pinter.

'Is this what they call "posturing"?' Charlotte whispered to Senator Demos. He guffawed and clapped his hand over his mouth before he could switch his avatar to unreactive.

'Can we have order, please?' Ryu asked.

Pinter continued where he left off. 'General, what will you do if they attack as they did at the blockade?'

'Let me show you the Elevens.' Zim turned back to the screens and pushed the content aside to bring up a composite view of the weaver dorms. Here hundreds of men and women lay in four storeys of immersion couches. Only the health readouts and occasional twitches revealed signs of life.

'We have been preparing for this conflict for a long time. Each of these Elevens is connected to a squad of ten remote MUs. Every one of them has served for a decade, training in the field against psi dissidents. Each unit has a variety of weapons to disable both psi and non-psi combatants. When disabled, a new MU can join the squad within one hundred and eighty seconds.'

The members of the council seemed impressed. They cooed at the scale of the operation. There hadn't been any actions of this scale since the wars. If then.

'Colonel?' The Prime turned to him. 'What is your assessment of this plan?'

Pinter nodded, twisted his lips and made as if thinking. Ryu suspected he already had his answer, from the beginning of the session if not before, and was timing for drama. Was the Scorpion about to strike?

'The real problem is that you're fighting this war with the weapons from the last one. Each war is different. Each war changes the nature of battle. And I think this one especially.'

'Colonel, I assure you these are the most advanced technologies,' Zim said.

'Yes, I see they come in different colours now. It is an impressive array but the whole plan rests on remotes. And remotes can be hakked.' Zim was about to argue the point until the Colonel held his palm up. 'But that doesn't matter. This war isn't on the ground — it may look like it is, but it is here.' He pointed at his head. 'Telepaths don't need to think things or know how to do things. They just need someone around them who does. The psis won't need hakkas to fight our weavers, they can get into their minds. We know it can happen.'

Ryu wondered if Pinter had just made a reference to the Takashi breach. *Surely he wouldn't dare such an affront to my authority? He owes his status to my support.*

Zim had no answer to give. He cut the briefing short and transferred the rest of his proposal to the council for them to go through themselves. Ryu was pretty sure that in real life Zim would be charging at Pinter like a bull, but his avatar was restrained and unreactive.

'Thank you, General,' Ryu said. 'I think we shall call a recess. Let us all take the time to go over this plan —'

'I would like to file a motion before we go any further,' Charlotte called out.

'And it must be now?' Ryu asked.

'This conference has been about launching an invasion into sovereign territory. Now is the only time to propose an alternate course of action,' she declared.

'Sovereign territory?' he asked.

'Atlantic has never been a part of the World Union,' she said, ready with her answer.

'Very well.' Ryu dipped his head to her. 'We will rejoin in two hours so we can also read Representative Betts's latest motion.'

The council began to disappear, leaving the Prime, Pinter, Charlotte Betts and General Zim. The Prime flicked a link to the Colonel of Betts's statement and they all read it silently.

Charlotte Betts, Citizen G4657 880P1 2GF47

'Motion for peace and inclusion of psis into the World Union'

For the last forty years the World Union has had the policy of restriction and imprisonment of humans known and suspected of psionic abilities. This policy must end now.

Today I wore the psi symbol for the first time. By showing my support for the rights of psis, I am showing my support for all of humanity.

The wearing of symbols of any sort has long been verboten — since the wars, when the annihilator machines became widespread. Symbols and icons were often the first identifier of targets, and people either stopped wearing them or faced being hunted down and killed.

The psis have asked any who support their cause to wear the psi symbol. Up until this day I have resisted, as I have reservations about the manner in which the rebellion was formed. I still have those reservations, but today I learnt that our union plans to unleash annihilators upon the world once more.

I choose to wear the symbol because I support the human rights of the psionic peoples. I also wear it to show that I am opposed to any acts that remove our own humanity, as the use of these machines will do.

There must be another path for us. Another way, other than violence. At some point, humanity must discover how to end conflicts without resorting to force.

I was reminded recently that we are all part of a greater civilisation. A society that has been transformed many times over. We are at a crossroads now. Do we risk losing our humanity by denying basic rights to a certain group? Do we risk losing our agency to unfounded fear and aggression?

These are questions I will not answer for anyone. I wish every Citizen to think and decide for themselves about how we should proceed as a species.

Wearing the psi symbol and supporting motions that direct us away from conflict is a vote for peace, and a vote to maintain our way of life.

And so I, Charlotte Betts, put forward the motion to allow the psionic peoples to form their own independent state and allow them to become a part of our World Union.

The four of them stood in a blank load space. There was no need for the pretension of the forum construct. Now it was only four avatars staring at each other then three of them looking at Representative Betts.

'Well?' she said.

'I believe this woman is a puppet of the psis,' the General sneered.

'The people support me,' she answered.

Ryu himself was quite pleased with the proposal. Charlotte had taken a strong position and didn't seem to recognise the reactions it might provoke. 'Representative Betts, you realise your motion is an expansionist policy? That can't go down well with your supporters.'

'My only aim is the survival of the World Union, Prime. And I believe that peace is the only way to achieve that.'

He turned away from her. 'Colonel Pinter, I want a response plan worked up within the hour,' Ryu told him. 'General Zim, you are dismissed.'

'I'll go when the Will tells me to,' he said.

In the background, the Prime and his moguls were already pulling their support and the General's value was declining steeply while Pinter's rose. He would be out of the council in seconds. 'So be it,' Ryu said.

Zim's avatar began to fade out as he demersed, but stopped in his exiting and turned to face Colonel Pinter. The young Abercrombie Pinter. Once they had been comrades. Without another glance at Ryu, he saluted to the Colonel.

'I'll await your orders, Colonel.'

Pinter straightened and returned the salute. Zim's avatar disappeared.

'What about Kronos, sir? Do you wish me to oversee both operations?'

'Promote Ozenbach. He's running the research now anyway, it seems.'

'It is his specialty,' Pinter said.

'We have to establish an embassy in Atlantic as quickly as we can.'

'That won't do you any good,' Colonel Pinter said. 'Invading will simply create a larger and more hostile opposition.'

'What do you suggest, Colonel?' Representative Betts asked, reminding them she was there.

'We could just take the hit. The World Union is stronger than two minor compounds, and we want the Weave to see the psis as the aggressors. I believe we can turn this to our advantage.'

Ryu paused. The Colonel was right. *Do not react. Respond.* 'We make a statement deploring the recent violence?'

Pinter nodded. 'And then re-establish a diplomatic embassy through invitation.'

'It might look like weakness,' Ryu said.

'Or a Prime in control. If you hit back, the psis will retaliate, forcing you to strike harder each time.'

'Ah yes, the single strike. Never give an enemy the chance to strike you back.'

'Dare you argue with history?' Pinter smiled and spread his hands.

Ryu thought a moment. Gladys was giving him rapid updates on the shifting sands of the Will. Zim had crashed. He wouldn't be back. Betts was third, but would make second. Pinter had risen, benefitting from the exodus of Zim, but so had Ryu. The Colonel was off the lower rungs though and would have to be watched.

He shared with them both a dossier of recordings and files collected from the Weave. A series of clips leapt up to surround them.

'I want you both to see these.'

223

In one clip a crowd of a hundred people marched through narrow antique streets, carrying banners with the psi symbol on them, chanting slogans of support.

'This group have a man they call a "priest" leading them. He is preaching that we must submit to the will of Pierre Jnr.'

Ryu flipped his hand, pushing to the next clip. This one showed a crowd in Hanoi piling supplies into air transports.

'These are groups of so-called peace fighters preparing to break the blockade and join the psis in the Cape. What do these scenes indicate to you?'

'That not everyone supports your segregation of psi and non-psi,' Representative Betts came in at once.

Ryu chose to ignore that. 'I fear there is an induced psychosis being placed upon the Will.'

'Oh, come on, Prime. You are going too far,' she said.

'Perhaps.' He held up a finger. 'But if it was true, when would we recognise that it was the case? Imagine that I am right. How could we ever know if the Will was being telepathically influenced?'

'This is sheer paranoia.'

'How can you say that? It is the natural conclusion for what we are seeing.'

'If that is the Will ...'

'Yes?' he asked, giving her plenty of time to come to a conclusion. Instead, Colonel Pinter answered.

'The World Union was never intended to be an instrument of war.'

'It was founded by war,' Ryu said.

'No. It was founded in war, not for it. There is a difference. The WU is intended to prevent conflicts.'

'But there is a conflict before us. How else can we stop it?'

'I think we can combine the plans. The preparations Zim has outlined and the proposal from Representative Betts.'

'"I don't believe you can make love and war at the same time. Unless you love war."'

It was a quote from his memoir. Representative Betts must have come armed with a select range of phrases so the Colonel's words could be thrown in his face.

'You misunderstand me, Charlotte. We will establish the embassy but instead of sending Zim, we will send you as our emissary.'

'Me?'

'Who better?' Pinter smiled. 'We must let the people of the Cape join us.'

Ryu caught onto the plan. By sending Charlotte to psi territory, she would be out of the way and saddled with a commission that was doomed to failure.

'Yes. Who else would they listen to?' he asked.

'So, you both support my proposal?' Obviously, she had been expecting opposition. Ryu detected elements of disappointment.

'The honourable Representative Betts is right.' It was perfect. He felt as happy as the fool who swatted six flies at once. The Cape would tear itself apart and attention would be drawn away from their psi restriction operations. If the psis willingly registered themselves, their activities would be monitored and tempered by the Will as any Citizen's actions were.

Ryu stepped forward. 'You have brought an injustice before us. I must thank you for doing so. It must not have been easy ... If you will agree to act as ambassador, then I will support your motion to create a permanent position on the Primacy council, to speak for the unspoken.'

Can't remember where you were last night? You may be a victim of a psi-crime!

Do you sometimes find yourself doing something and not knowing why?

The Anti-Psi League pushed out multiple videos and pamphlets and automated response avatars (ARAs), which a confused public began accepting into their streams.

In one film they showed dense crowds of pedestrians, with close-ups showing their everyday faces.

'They look like you,' a strong, masculine voice read out.

The footage of the crowd began to slow, making the pedestrians move at an eerily slow speed.

'Your thoughts can never be safe.'

The view slowed again and cut closer so that only the eyes of the people were showing.

'Have you ever felt that someone has been promoted above you unfairly? Or seen a person that doesn't deserve the status they have? Register your concern now, on the APL watch list.'

They published handy guides on how to know if your brain had been interfered with, and what to do if you suspected your neighbour of being a telepath, or if your child was controlling you.

226

'Psionic manipulation is a growing problem in our society and one that every Citizen should be aware of. If you're a concerned Citizen, then you should investigate. Contact the Anti-Psi League because: With psis, we can never be sure.'

The World Union was, ostensibly, an open system that any could join and become a Citizen. Becoming a Citizen involved a declaration of personal responsibility and a commitment to the preservation of civilisation. There were those who never took up Citizenship, denizens, and those who were denied membership, criminals.

Criminals, by definition, were ones who actively rejected the mandate of the WU and fought against it. Terrorism, hakking and destabilisation actions were enough to strip a person of Citizenship and have them isolated on the man-made islands of polyplastic, far from the shores of the continents, botlocked and mood-controlled.

The Will determined what was and wasn't a crime. The Will decided what was anathema. Most infringements of proper behaviour were treated with conditioning and rehabilitation, which brought aberrant Citizens back into proper behavioural alignment, so there was very little crime. Social engineering had removed most of the motivators for antisocial behaviour, as base services had for deprivation, removing the desperate motivations of the underprivileged.

It was a crime just to be a psi. It was a crime to use mental powers. Psis were the biggest criminal sector and one that had been steadily growing. But, as Tamsin explained to him — as

La Gréle had explained to her — all they had to do was change what was and wasn't a crime.

During the confusion of the blockade attack, Risom had escaped the confines of the Cape. Mere days ago he was trudging through the basement of Atlantic; now he sat with his feet resting on a low wooden table, sampling vintage alcohol that had been collected over a lifetime. His new hand couldn't feel the cold of the glass.

Blair Butler, the owner of the estate, was returning from a walk; Risom could feel him approaching. He heard the door slide open and then the footsteps. A rucksack was dropped to the ground, an overcoat hung in the airing cupboard.

Come join me. He compelled the man forward. Walking him to his seat on the porch. He kept Blair facing him and watched as the man's eyes jumped around in their sockets.

'Are you scared?' Risom asked him. The man didn't nod voluntarily so Risom forced the man's head up and down.

'Who are you?' Blair asked.

'Now, does that really matter? You didn't ask who I was when you collected me.'

'I've never been a —'

Risom smacked his jaw up, cracking his teeth together.

'No. You never *did* it. You're not the type that *does* things for themselves. You voice your opinion and let others do the work. But I don't blame them, Senator Blair. They do what they do, they do what they are told. You though, you push them into it. You say what you say and think it ends there.'

'You people are a menace. And when I get out of here I'm going to tell everyone what you've done to me.'

'Senator, senator …' Risom snapped the man's middle finger back. Blair Butler whimpered, but couldn't move to staunch the pain. 'I'm afraid you won't be telling anyone anything ever again.'

'Please,' the senator dribbled, tears and spit wetting his face.

'Do you see this, Senator?' He lifted his silver arm up towards the man. 'It's because of people like you that I have this.' He squeezed his hand and the wine glass cracked into shards. 'I didn't even feel that.'

'Please. Don't kill me. I'll do anything,' Butler cried.

'Anything?' A happy smile appeared on Risom's face. 'Would you run for me?'

'What?'

'For your life, would you run?'

'I don't understand …?'

'You said you'd do anything and I want you to run. Now. For your life. I'll even give you a head start.' Risom lifted the man to his feet and pushed him in the direction of the forest. Blair Butler looked back and forth from the steps to Risom, then bolted as fast as he could.

The landscape was untended, as nature intended. Scrub and sticks tripped him up and he stumbled every time he twisted back to see if Risom was chasing him. Risom watched the senator scrabble through the gardens. His property was deep in the wilderness zone, out of sight of the closest dome.

A branch whipped around and struck Blair in the mouth. The man tripped, but picked himself up.

'Sorry about that,' Risom called.

A tree fell in Blair's path. He jumped it and started scrambling down a hill. Rocks leapt after him, bouncing higher than would be natural towards his head. He couldn't dodge them all. One hit the back of his head and he fell to his knees. His hand felt for the cracks in his skull. The rocks continued to land on him, cracking his ribs and pummelling him until he blacked out with the pain and Risom left him to die under the cairn.

Peter Lazarus woke again.

At first he couldn't remember where he was. He sat up in bed and looked around. Ah, the white place. The clean room.

In some ways, he didn't mind waking up here. It was a more pleasant memory than the desert hospital, or the mud, or darkness in the grip of Pierre. He was calm in the white place.

It always smelt fresh in the morning. They must clean it while he slept. Silent bots with precision movements covertly tidying his room and wiping down the surfaces.

A new set of clothes waited for him on the slide-out table and he followed the line on the floor to the shower and back, then sat before the mirror looking at his reflection.

The soft pinkish lights glowed up from around the frame and the gentle woman's voice spoke to him.

'How are you feeling today, Mister Lazarus?'

He no longer looked around for the speaker, wondering where it came from. He was used to her by now. Every day was the same. He woke and followed the line to where it put him. He cleaned himself and then sat before the mirror where it would talk at him.

'Mister Lazarus, are you okay?' The voice emanated from the mirror.

He asked it the same questions every day: 'What do you want from me?' 'How can I get out of here?' 'Who is speaking?'

'No one is speaking. I am your mirror.'

'Who controls you?'

'You do. I am a mirror, I reflect from you. My questions are your questions,' she answered calmly.

'This is another of the Prime's traps.'

'Traps? You are already confined, Mister Lazarus. What need is there for traps? I am here only to help you.'

'You're recording everything I say and do. You are testing me. You'll never let me go.' He hit his fists on the tabletop, shaking his reflection.

'Peter.' Her lights blushed in imitated emotion. 'Please don't talk like this. We must find calm.'

'How can I? I have to get out of here.'

'That cannot be, Peter. We must learn to accept it.'

'We? You're either a robotic mirror with a voice or you're a spy pretending to be.'

'I am your reflection, Peter. Do you not trust yourself?'

Pete didn't answer and turned away. Her lights faded automatically and the mirror was silent.

He stood too quickly, making himself dizzy and lurched towards the exit, using his hand to steady himself on the doorway. At least now he understood the method Services used to keep the psis on the islands under control, which explained the minds of the interviewees he had met before. Simple intoxication.

It must be in everything. In the food, the water, the locks around their necks; maybe even gassed into the air to keep them continually unbalanced. It was hard enough to stay upright and maintain a conversation, let alone control their powers enough to cause any trouble.

He found himself in the spiral corridor that led to the main room. With his back against the wall Pete pushed himself towards the presence of Tådler. The boy who had become his only friend.

I'm finding it hard to walk today, he thought.

There is no hurry. I'm not going anywhere.

Everything seemed brighter than it really was. Objects seemed closer than they really were. The big room had a circle of seats that faced a bank of common screens and along the outside wall were smaller lounging rooms divided by pearled glass. The sunlight was brightened by overhead floodlights that removed all shadows from the room. Patients sat in soft lounges flicking through channels for something of interest.

Tådler? Where are you?

Over here. By the window.

Peter reached out to Tådler's mind. His head couldn't make the journey and his body slid down a pillar to rest on the floor.

Will it always be like this?

Always. But you will get better at dealing with it.

Tådler wasn't as affected as the rest of them. Their only thought was that it was because he was so young; they might be limiting his dose. Tådler didn't turn to face Pete. He didn't want to give himself away or give them cause to ground him. Pete looked at the row of heads that were watching the screens.

232

How do you cope with it?

I try to stay calm, Tådler said. *I've heard about you from the others.*

They know me?

They know you were an agent.

What do they say?

They don't know what to think. They say you have changed. They're waiting to see what you'll do.

What can I do? I'm stuck here like the rest of them.

Some of them want to join with you.

Join with me? What does that mean?

It's where two telepaths join minds. Have you not done it?

No. Have you?

Yes ...

And then they might trust me?

It is very intimate. They would have to trust you first.

Tådler, you're only a boy ...

It isn't a physical act.

Then what is it?

The lighting began to pulse. Up and down, stirring the inmates to stand and shuffle to the corridors. He stood up with the rest of them as they began filing to their rooms.

'What is happening?' Pete asked out loud.

'Rotation,' someone mumbled and pushed past him.

What's that? he asked Tådler.

Every week they swap the populations of the islands.

Why?

Why do they do any of it? Nobody knows when it will happen. Nobody knows if they will be staying or going.

233

Nobody knows whether they are in the same place when they wake up. Each island is identical.

They send us to other islands?

We hope so.

Pete stopped at his door but Tådler kept walking.

I hope we're both still here when it is over.

Pete woke again.

Where was he now?

He leant forward to look out the window of the cockpit. A tiled floor rushed towards him. He was falling. He knew he hit. His face felt flat. But there was no pain. No feeling.

Pete went out into the common room and sat in the nearest chair, looking around slowly, trying to remember whose faces he'd seen before. The other people looked up from what they were doing, some smiled, some did nothing but blink, some looked him over, weighing him. Tådler was gone — or he had been rotated. They were all new to him.

On-screen was a loop of educational programming, showing how one could find calm in the gardens, fishing or at sport. The middle screen showed news and the third played a steady stream of cultural dramas, music and comedy. The news was friendly and light: the marriages of high society, movements in the civic structure and agricultural reports.

It seemed that Ryu Shima was still Prime, his sister Sato was to hold an enormous party celebrating her betrothal and the weather reprogramming had enabled one per cent growth in food production and three hundred thousand square metres of land had been made fit for re-use.

Pete looked outside through the glass walls. Everything appeared to be the same, though it could be as Tådler had said and all the islands were indistinguishable. Perhaps he had been moved. The ground was white, bright in the sun, broken up with rock gardens of bonsai trees and azaleas. He squinted through the piercing white and could see a few fields of green and then the ocean. The ocean went to the horizon.

White, beautiful. Calm.

He went back to his room.

'Mirror.' The wall of the alcove warmed and turned reflective. He knelt and faced his image. His hair was growing back. And stubble was turning to beard.

'How are we today, Peter?' the soft voice asked.

'We've been better, mirror.'

'Please, call me Peter.'

'I'd rather not.'

'Do you still hate yourself, Peter?'

'How can I hate something I don't know?'

'What don't you know? Perhaps if you tell me, I can help you,' she said.

'Help me? You can help me by getting me off this island.' He crumpled forward and moaned. 'Please help me, Prime. I know you can hear me. Please.'

'The Prime is not here, Peter. It is only you.'

'Ryu, I beg you. Stop this torture.'

'Peter, please. Calm down.' As it spoke, he did calm down. They were dosing him with something. He straightened up and looked again at the mirror. His mind was floating like

235

a sailboat, cutting through drowsy waves. Water and light, bouncing off each other.

'I do not know myself,' he said.

'What do you mean by that?'

'I have no past. I don't know who I have been.'

'You're talking about your missing memories. Are they coming back to you? Amnesia is very common amongst telepaths.'

'No, they aren't coming back. Nothing is coming back. And everything since the manifestation is slipping away. It's this place. You have to get me out of this place.'

'These rooms are designed for your comfort.'

'They're designed to make us disappear.'

'You could go outside. The weather is lovely this time of month.'

'Why am I even talking to you?' he asked in frustration.

'It's better than talking to yourself.'

'You've been installed to drive me crazy. I won't let you.'

'Or I am here to bring you back to sanity. When you first arrived you were close to death. I didn't think you'd make it.'

'Geof, can you hear me?' he asked the mirror suddenly. 'Geof Ozenbach? If anyone might have access to this place, it is you. Keyword: Geof Ozenbach. Help me.' Another cocktail of chemicals from his necklock made him pitch backward. His view of the ceiling kaleidoscoped and changed colours.

'Relax, Peter. There is nobody here but you. You are safe here.'

'I don't feel anything any more.'

'What is it you want, Peter?'

236

'I want to be free.'

'But you know you can't leave the islands, Peter. We've talked about this. You and I are here forever.'

He looked up at the mirror and saw a tired and tamed man. He threw himself at the image, raising his fists to the glass. He was stunned by the necklock before he could reach it. His head felt like it was going down in a high-speed elevator.

He knew it was night-time. The colour of the lighting changed, blue and clear like moonlight. The glowing line on the floor was brighter, suggesting he make his way out to the common room. In some ways, the centre was a beautiful place. Nothing would happen here. Nothing would ever happen again.

In the corridor, doors were closed, the panels dulcet blue. All but one were home and quiet, a girl watching the screens who turned to watch as he came into the common room. Though his mind was muddy, he could feel her fear. She had heard about him from the others, a snitch, a traitor to all of them. She was afraid of what he might do to her ... then her lock released calmers to combat her raised heart-rate. Her stare turned glassy.

Pete went out the sliding doors and gazed around. It was a rare cloudless night; the Milky Way spilt above, sketched over by the constant march of satellites and only just outshone by the thin cut of the rising moon.

From here, he could see that the island was moulded as two simple hills covered in a lawn of grass and clover and pressed together to form a gutter that ran down into the ocean. The slopes were slight, the perfect gradient to make sure the centre was visible from every part of the island, and vice versa.

He began following the path that traced down the line of the gully. It continued to the water's edge and below, the steps fading into the depth.

It was a tranquil and inviting nook. He felt it urging him to join the ocean. It made him wonder if the place was designed to make the inmates want to throw themselves in. That would be a convenient solution.

Pete walked away. The headland was a perfectly smooth curve, like a ball bobbing in the sea. He felt tired and sat down to watch the lilt and tilt of the waves, the light of the moon thrown between them. His hand touched something smooth and he looked down. The grass was only an inch thick here and had been worn away to the creamy pale plastic the island was made of.

It's all fake, he thought, and looked out at the horizon, trying to let his mind float to where he thought the mainland was. *Perhaps*, he thought, *if Tamsin knew where I was, she would come and save me ...* The effort made him sick and he spat bile into the waves below.

He may have slept, or he may just have sat for hours, but the sky changed, the stars were plucked away, and over the ocean the clouds were building again.

The sun was rising on the other side of the island and he walked in shadow back towards the centre. As he got closer he could hear a dull thud, thud, thud echoing between the hills. He could just make out a person slumped against the window, one hand crooked up, weakly thumping the glass. He stood on the other side of the door and the woman looked up.

Anchali? 'Anchali, is that you?' He raced to open the doors and knelt beside her.

Anchali turned her face to him. He could see a lump rising on her forehead, purple and straining with burst capillaries. She didn't seem to recognise him and returned to banging her arm on the window.

'What is it? Do you want to come outside? Here.' He slid the door open for her and she dragged herself into the courtyard. She stopped once she was on the grass and propped herself against a low plastic wall.

'Are you okay?' he asked.

Anchali didn't answer. Her head rolled slowly towards him, a pendulum of spit swinging slowly from her chin. *Can't think ...*

Her head tipped forward and Pete bent down to sit beside her. *It's okay. Just try to be calm.* It grated on him that he was repeating the words of the mirror.

What is happening to me?

You're intoxicated, that's all. They keep us permanently stupefied to limit our abilities.

'Bastards ...' she moaned. Pete found her reaction amusing and he laughed for the first time he could remember.

'Yes. They are, aren't they.'

He felt a hand on his skin. It moved up his chest and stroked his ribs before curling invisible fingers around his windpipe. He couldn't tell if it was threatening or loving.

You left me.

They took me here.

Here ...?

On the islands, Anchali. That's where you are.

The islands! Her mind rippled with alarm and she swooned over. *No. They can't ...*

I'm sorry, Anchali. It's all my fault.

Anchali got better as the days went by. She could walk and talk and move about the common rooms, but she hardly spoke to Peter. What she knew of the outside world spread quickly amongst the inmates, stirring them up. The Weave broadcasts had kept news of the psi rebellion from them, but she made sure they knew about it now. Many of the inmates began seeking her out so she could share herself with them directly. More and more she disappeared to private rooms and he saw her less and less.

Sometimes he found her glaring at him. He knew what she was thinking. All the telepaths knew he'd been an agent, and life for him became that much harder. When he walked through the corridor, people knocked him with their shoulders, or the benders tried to kick out his feet from under him.

He heard their thoughts — he tried not to, but they twittered like birds inside his head. *Agent. Traitor. Spy.* Peter spent more and more time in his room and only stepped out when it was night and most of the inmates were asleep.

He was on his knees before the mirror, his reflected face red from crying. 'Help me ...' he begged.

'How can I help you today, Peter?' she asked.

'Please, send me to another island.'

'The other islands are the same. You will be rotated in your turn.'

'I need to go now.'

'You aren't very good at making friends, are you?'

Pete swayed in position. It was like his answers were balls rolling around an empty barrel, unable to find their way out of his head. He just had to find the timing to release the words. 'That's you, isn't it, Prime? That sounded like you.'

'Do you so rely on the authority of others? No, Peter. I am not the Prime. I am only your reflection. I am an automated voice program built from your own records so I can ask you the questions you should ask yourself.'

'What should I ask?'

'That's easy. Why don't you remember who you are?' the mirror asked.

'I'm Peter ... I ...' The answers seemed to spin around his head, marbles that rolled away before he could grasp them. Where were his memories from before the manifestation? Where had he been for twenty years? Why couldn't he remember ...?

'Pierre,' he said.

The next night Pete found Anchali lying face down in the corridor, head to the floor and moaning softly. She was wet and a puddle grew around her.

Anchali, what happened to you?

I ... I tried to swim away.

Oh.

I had to get away. I can't stay here.

'Where is your room?'

'I don't ...'

241

'The number?' Her collar had a number on it in faint light: thirty-eight.

Her wet clothes soaked into his as he led her gently through the spiral until they reached her room. Peter helped her place her hand on the palmlock and the door opened. The room was exactly the same as his own. Pedestal bed, an alcove and a dispenser. He filled a cup with water and helped her drink.

'Try not to move your head,' he suggested.

You're Peter.

That's right. Peter Lazarus. You were my nurse, remember.

Yes. Where am I? she asked.

We're on the islands, but please don't —

Oh … that's right. It all came back to her. She too found it hard to remain oriented here. It must be the same for all of them.

Anchali, you once told me about some people you worked with. Can they help us?

She shook her head.

No … they can't help.

But if we could contact them? There must be a way.

Peter … I was the one sent to help you.

And you did, you did help me. Don't you remember? I was in hospital.

I remember. And now we are here.

Anchali rolled back and clutched her pillow to cry into.

Pete straightened up to go, but her fingers caught at his sleeve. *Stay. I need to show you something.*

You can't. You need to sleep.

He was confused. Her mind was completely disoriented. One moment she didn't know who he was, then she hated him, the next she wanted to join with him.

But I must. There's so much you don't know. I need to show you what we are fighting for.

We aren't doing much fighting here. Except between ourselves.

That is why I must show you. I must show you La Gréle's dream.

Who is this La Gréle? He had heard the name in the thoughts of other inmates many times.

La Gréle is our leader. She will guide the psis to freedom.

Do you really believe that?

Her hands reached up to touch his face and she directed his eyes down to meet hers. *Let me show you.*

What do I have to do?

She patted the mattress for him to lie beside her. *Get as close to me as you can. We have to become a part of each other. Do you trust me?*

Do you trust me? he asked back.

I do.

Anchali began humming a song she had known from her younger life, and with it every memory of when she had heard it. He felt the comfort of her mother, the friendly kinship of the village she was raised in. The lapping of the waves in the bay, the warm press and push of skin on skin.

Relax, Peter. Be calm. We cannot join our thoughts with your mind pulling in a thousand directions at once.

I'm concentrating.

Don't concentrate. Think of something else. Think of the ocean.

He slipped easily into the familiar memory: sand being sucked through his toes; water washing over his ankles, sinking his feet further into the beach. Away and return. Deeper and deeper. Then all of a sudden his mind was overcome by darkness. He was in that other place.

Where have you taken us, Peter? her thoughts asked.

I woke up here. He was on his back in the greasy mud under Atlantic. Blood dripping from a hot cut on his head.

What do you see?

Black. Just black and stars.

Do you feel anything?

Cold. Water.

I can feel it.

Are we communing now?

Not yet. You must relax. Try to find my memory again, as I have found you.

Then Tamsin was leaning over him. Her hand cradled his face, holding it steady. *Tamsin,* he thought to her. *You came back.* She didn't hear him; she was only a memory.

Tamsin dabbed at his face. She said something but the words were too echoey for him to understand.

Then she was standing up. Peter tried to hold onto her, but she pulled free. *Don't leave ... take me.*

He felt the cold and black once more. Water washed around him, sinking him into the grimy sand.

Let it take you, a voice said. *Follow me, Peter. I am the water ... I am all around you. Pulling you into the sun ...*

That's it. Sink in the sand. You are the sand and I am the water. Can you feel me around you? the waves seemed to say. Pete's feet were sand, the water drowning them, grains lifting and swirling in the currents.

Anchali?

The water pushed up and around him to his thighs, hips, chest. His body collapsed into slush that then dispersed into the waves. He began to disappear.

Don't lose yourself. I am the water. You are the sand.

The grains of him were pulled through the currents, from cold and dark to deep blue and up towards the sun. The clear water pushed him onto a bright beach. Sunlight drying him until he was crunchy and crisp and yellow. The water was turquoise and bright with day. A tanned girl looked down at the sand under her toes, smiling at him.

It's me, Peter, Anchali said.

Where are we?

We are back in my memory now. This is my home.

Her family was part of a fishing tribe living off the bounty of the sea and the land. It was a peaceful life, with little contact to the outside world.

When she was fourteen a woman came to the island. She arrived on a silver skiff wearing a long white beach dress, and a tinted shade hat over silver hair. The girl, Anchali, reached up to take the woman's hand and she heard her voice in her head.

Hello, Anchali. Do you know who I am?

She did know. When she was asked she found she could see into the woman's mind. She had come a long way and made many stops to meet children like her.

La Gréle stayed in the village for days, joining in the daily routines of the tribe and getting to know Anchali's family. They didn't know about their daughter and the woman didn't tell them. It was their secret.

Anchali was thrilled to have a friend, someone who truly knew her, and they spent hours conversing silently. One night there was a bonfire on the beach. A pit was dug next to it and filled with layers of potatoes, leaves, fish, chicken and vegetables. Coals from the fire were heaped on top for it to cook. While they waited, La Gréle joined in the dancing with the elders, forming a large ring around the fire and the children. As La Gréle circled around she spoke to Anchali.

Feel what I feel. Know what I know.

Anchali stared deep into the fire, watching the licks of flames and the logs beneath breathing orange and red. She felt La Gréle's mind all around her and she began seeing another place.

Where are we now? Pete asked.

They were in a child's bedroom where a toddling girl was playing music on a handscreen.

Is that her?

La Gréle. When she was young.

The child suddenly looked worried. She stopped batting her hands on the screen and frowned. Quickly she went to her cupboards and began packing a bag with clothes. She was ready with coat and shoes when her father ran into the room and picked her up.

Don't be scared, luvvy. We'll be okay.

Have to go, Daddy! We have to go!

246

Her mother was outside in the hover, revving the engine to warm it up.

Mummy!

Darling, it's okay. Hang onto your father.

They sped off, never to know for sure if they had just evaded capture or whether no one had come for them at all.

The people were scared, that's all. It'll calm down, they told her.

They lived in the mountains for years, making their way. With the WU came surveillance, and rapid expansion. They retreated as the cities advanced. Always keeping to the wilds, away from everyone. But one night others came without warning. La Gréle woke up, feeling her parents choking.

Run, darling. Go, they pleaded.

Outside she could feel soldiers stalking closer. She turned one on the other, forcing them to shoot their comrades. Then the drones came, humming in, smashing at the thin walls, tiny laser shots firing at every movement.

She could feel her parents slipping away. They begged her to go.

Anchali was crying. They were back at the beach. Pete felt the sand and the rhythm of the waves.

And I ran, La Gréle thought to her. *People like us are always running.*

Then she showed the girl what she hoped for. Peace, where telepaths and kinetics were Citizens, and together they built a world of potential and harmony. *We can be one. One and many.*

La Gréle left the next day. Anchali stood watching her go, waving. Then she just stayed on the beach, letting the sun twinkle her eyes.

This is how we can know each other, she said to the sand.

The sand looked up at the sky; it was a deep bright blue, and yet it could see stars glinting through. There were thoughts behind those lights. He could sense them.

'What are those stars?' he asked. He made them be closer.

'Peter, what are you doing?' Anchali asked urgently. The ocean was lifting up around her but her feet were so deep in the sand she couldn't pull them free. 'Stop it,' she cried. 'You're taking over my memory.'

The water rose over the island, dissolving the palms and huts. The girl tried to hold on, but she too succumbed to the wash.

The sea rose and he swirled up with it until the water and sky met. The stars were swallowed, pulled from above to sink and swim. He was the water now, he was everywhere.

He filled the white room and spilt in a rush out the door like an exploding dam. He filled the corridor and flooded the centre, sweeping every mind along with him.

He felt each one of them and they him. Then they began connecting one by one, through him and he wasn't Peter Lazarus. He was something else.

'I understand now,' it said calmly.

The Betts Manifesto, as Anti-Psi League supporters sneeringly referred to it, caused such turbulence in the Will that many began recognising that the WU was now, most definitely, in a state of convocation. Just as Amy had predicted.

Not every Citizen was interested, naturally. There are always many who simply want to live their lives. If something didn't directly impact their day, then they saw no need to vote upon it. Many families and units had one or more members who asked them to change the screen to something more entertaining.

'I hate this mess. All this talk. Just words words words and what good does it do us?' exclaimed a veteran.

'But the world has to decide, doesn't it?' his granddaughter replied. She was wearing the psi patch on her chest.

While many were dismissive and remained disengaged, the rest of the World Union was focused on discussing the minutiae, following the declarations, motions and interviews of the important speakers.

'Well, it's day two of what they are starting to call "the marathon cycle". Phyllis, how do you think the Primacy is sleeping?' The guest laughed along with the anchorman's joke.

'I'm sure nobody in the council is getting much rest now, Derwent. Nor their staff. Since the security breach at the Cape we have been in a relentless circle of proposal and reaction, proposal and reaction. And it doesn't look like it will end any time soon.'

'What do you think we'll see in the next three hours?'

'Three hours? Well, the sun is coming up on Seaboard which means Charlotte Betts will re-enter the frame. She's the only member I know of who wasn't online in the last eight.'

'She is a big believer in getting her rest.'

'Touché. Though there is boldness in her refusal to be reactive, and perhaps some wisdom in letting the other players move first.'

'That may be true. And what do you think of the rumours that Betts might rise further? Now that the elder Betts has added her support, do you think the Betts Manifesto can get her all the way to the Prime seat?'

'I'm not a gambling woman, Derwent. At the moment I'd say there is an even chance. It depends how the next sessions fall out and what direction the Will supports.'

'Alright, it's now 4.45 a.m. in Yantz zone 1. We'll be back in eight hours with our dissection of the Prime's opening debate, which will be starting in three hours and fifteen minutes.'

Ryu spent the predawn hours in what Gladys Schuster called 'narrative training' … to help him learn the art form of rendering the mess of opinions, emotions and misperceived facts into a single clear thread that viewers could support, follow and endorse.

If he could successfully guide the narrative of each interview, then his motions should be supported. If he couldn't convince the Will, then he would likely lose his position.

Together they went over the history he had composed with his team. The history as spoken by the office of Prime — while he still held the seat — outlining the causal chain as he saw it and his position on how the World Union should proceed. It was his job to provide the voice and the story that the Will would believe.

Ryu wasn't a sophist by any means, but he had watched enough people to know that even slight variations in core beliefs could have profound effects on what conclusions different people drew from the same evidence.

For the past three cycles, Gladys had been assaulting him with oppositional questions, trying to throw him off the agreed message as the interviewers would attempt to do. His answers must never contradict themselves so he repeatedly ran through the base facts until he knew them instinctively.

After the second Dark Age there were increased sightings of psionic incidents. Whether humans always had such potential, and could no longer remain hidden under almost full surveillance, or whether the wars had changed something fundamental in the human animal, no one could state for sure.

No matter one's beliefs or personal context, the phenomena of telepathy and telekinesis were recorded and measured. Some Citizens were curious, but more were afraid and psis were collected and isolated to protect the World Union from destabilisation.

The birth and disappearance of Pierre Jnr frightened the Will into supporting further restriction of psis, and archipelagos of plastic islands were built to house all those who could be collected.

Ryu Shima had been raised to Prime when an unexplained explosive force destroyed an historic area of Paris. Some say it was an anarchist group, others that it was the beginning of a psi uprising. Many speculated that it was the long-awaited return of the boy, Pierre Jnr, come at last to save the psis and wreak revenge upon the world that had abused them.

On November 13th, 2159, the psi rebellion attacked the Services outposts in Atlantic and the Shima family home in Yantz.

'Your goal is not to try and convince them. Your goal is to make them believe in you,' Gladys said, gesticulating. She was in her own office below, pacing in front of a wall-screen holding his projection. He hadn't seen her in person since he first came to the needle. He hadn't seen anyone since Shima Palace had been breached.

'Isn't that the same thing?' he asked.

'No. Imagine Representative Betts is arguing her case. Instead of spending your time eroding her proposal, let her wear herself out justifying her beliefs while you show yours in your actions.

'You have the advantages, Prime. Firstly, you are already Prime, and secondly, because Charlotte Betts is a very intelligent woman. So intelligent that she has the ability to doubt her own conclusions. That is her weakness. What is yours?'

The question caught Ryu off guard. He didn't have a prepared answer.

Gladys answered for him. 'Your leadership has recently suffered some setbacks. That is your weakness. It undermines your directives.'

'They weren't my fault —' he said.

'Nobody wants to hear that from the Prime,' she cut him off. 'Say that and you've lost their confidence.'

'Are you suggesting that I take the blame?'

'Embrace it. You are the Prime. You are the Will. Your failures are their failures. No matter what, do not distinguish yourself from the World Union. You are one and the same, for better or worse.'

'And Charlotte Betts is not,' he said. 'But I have already put my support towards her proposal. How can I withdraw it now?'

'You don't. You just work on the details. Slow it down with questions about specifics.'

'Tie her up with contingency planning.'

'That's right. Until the Will recognises that Representative Betts is an agitator who does not support the World Union and is trying to undermine the Will.'

'Do you bear this woman a grudge, Miz Schuster?' he asked her. That last statement had been vehement.

'I believe her policies are dangerous.'

'So how do I distract from questions about my recent failures?'

'As you have always done, you have taken action and brought in one of history's greatest commanders to control the situation.'

'Colonel Pinter. How does the world perceive him now?'

'With mixed memories. We will begin seeding new imagery for the Colonel before the debate. He will be the hero, our saviour. History already says so.'

'And I will be what?' Ryu asked.

'You will be Prime,' she said with no room for argument.

This is good tea. Such good tea. Good tea. Goody goopy tea tea. How long have I been staring at my hand? Takashi wondered. It held a delicate cup. An elegant disposable Woodward. His finger curved into the handle, and he could lift it up and down. He giggled as he watched, realising that his hand was no longer attached to his arm.

What's at the end of an army? Your handsies. No, they're not, he thought. His hands were running all over the place.

The room was filled with hands dashing about on their fingers, the walls and ceiling crawled with his hands in their hundreds.

Tee hee hee. Good tea. Good tea.

Tiny thrusters ignited around his neck, lifting his head from his body. His hair flew back from his face as he jetted towards the wall, where he hit and bounced to the ground. He laughed and squealed as some of his hands found him and tickled him behind his ears.

His body looked so lonely. His eyes saw it from upside-down. No hands, no feet, no head. What does a body do without its limbs and brain? *Tee hee tee hee*, it breathed and leaked. The body's fluids washed out, filling the floor until the hands and head were raised on the bodily mixture.

'Keep me up, keep me up,' his head called to the hands and they pushed him around so his lips were kept from drowning. His lips, his eyes, his ears and nose. Each of them slid from his face to a waiting hand, finding a new home in their palms. What is a face without features? *Teehee*. The hands with eyes climbed up the furniture, safe from the deluge of bodily fluids.

The hand with the mouth called out, 'Good tea!', before it sank into bubbles.

He lost his ears the same way. Then his nose. Only the eye-hands could make their way to safety and watch helplessly at the tragedy.

Do you see? Do you see? My eyes are no part of me. Good tea. Good tea. Close your eyes and set me free.

Takashi blinked. He was on the floor. The handle of a teacup on his finger. Takashi put a hand to his head. It came away greasy and smelling of something. Maybe soy sauce.

'You wouldn't want to be a Shima today, that's for sure.'
What's this? Takashi clicked to follow. 'Last night, Taka Shima went out for sushi. By that I mean he went all out for sushi. This is one you have to watch.' *Oh no …*

In the clips they lined up, Takashi watched himself enter a small restaurant where a train of small dishes rotated past the row of seated diners. He flung his arms open, which opened his kimono, which had nothing underneath. He made to hug one of the patrons, but she dodged him and he ended up knocking plates and cups everywhere. Then he proceeded, clumsily, with multiple attempts, to get his leg onto the stools and clamber on top of the bench where he straightened up and raised his hand as if he was about to say something of a grand nature. Instead, he collapsed backward, lolling side to side as the plastic dishes kept pushing into his head.

'Wait for it,' the host of the show advised. The sushi, sashimi and edamame plates began piling up, spilling off the train as it rotated past the diners … then the whole bench collapsed and Takashi went sprawling to the ground, completely unconscious and filthy.

The host was bent over, nearly in pain from laughing. 'I'm tipping that as a possible mush-up of the year. Let's watch it again.'

His mother and father sat on their raised platform, waiting quietly for him to arrive and settle himself on the mats before them.

Takashi had clothed himself in clean formal wear. A kimono suit with a double-wrap cummerbund. It stretched over the

255

extra area of his symbiot. He looked at himself in the mirror and saw only a mesh-head fool. He bowed forward as much as his symbiot and girth would allow him.

'I am most sorry, Mother, Father.'

'Last night you brought great shame on our family, Takashi,' his father said.

'Yes. I'm sorry.'

'Sorry might not be enough, this time.'

'It won't happen again.'

'Taka. Your life is your own. But when you make such public displays it is hard for the family to stand by you. You remember that Sato is getting married, don't you?' Hachiro asked.

'Yes.'

'Your behaviour is jeopardising everything. Not to mention Ryu's authority.'

'I'm really sorry.' All he could do was repeat his humble apologies.

His mother hadn't said anything yet. He peeked up at her face and saw her usual firm repose had gone soft. She didn't usually let her emotions show. 'Taka ... what has happened to you?' He looked at her. He could barely keep his eyes open. But it was Mother and he had to be here, even if he couldn't follow his own thoughts.

'Ever since I was ... you know.'

'You don't have to say anything.'

'I do, Mother, I do. I want to say things. I just haven't felt the same since ...'

'And you think these drugs are helping?' his father asked.

'I don't know, maybe. It's different.'

256

'You've changed, Taka. You used to be able to control it,' Hachiro said.

'If you want to stop me, then stop me. I won't stop just because you have asked.'

'You are a Citizen. These are your choices.'

'Anyway. It's not that I changed. I've been changed,' Takashi insisted.

'What do you mean?' Hachiro asked.

'She was in my head, Father. Do you know what that is like?'

'I don't think that is your problem, Taka,' Mother said. 'I think you don't know what to do without Ryu.'

It was true. He missed his brother. Even hearing his name made his body feel heavy. He couldn't speak.

'Taka, I love you. We both love you, but we can no longer allow you to represent Shima.'

'You're throwing me out?'

'We think you must find your own path now.'

Ah, Father. Thanks for the philosophy.

'I'm sorry I disappointed you.'

'You may go.'

Takashi hadn't left the palace for a long time. He wasn't sure when it started, but at some point he had his dolls, the Weave and Ryu to take all his time.

When he first claimed Citizenship, at fourteen, he had spent a lot of time at the coastal end of Yantz. Running with a group of other highborns and kicking up in Shanghai. For a weaver, this end of the megapolis was paradise. It was as close to the Weave as reality could ever get. The city was one layer after

257

another, with tall buildings of glass, light and screens that wrapped around them. The city had trains, skyrails, rivers of squibs and tracks upon tracks beneath the surface. If you didn't have overlay to find your way around, you'd never find anything.

He flicked on the different layers as he walked, picking up the historical, advertising and art overlays. He liked the art layer. Many locals had taken the time to pseudo-decorate the walls of the street and place animated sculptures on the ground and in the air above. A red tubular dragon dived and ducked through the building tunnels, and bright flowers grew over the otherwise harsh metal gratings.

His feet took him to Cybermesh, a hangout he used to go to when he was younger. How long ago was that? His record told him he hadn't visited in five years. *Five years*, he realised, *is a long time to spend indoors*. He shook his head at himself.

The archway into the weave café was postered with floating messages from junior weaver circles and players looking for hookups.

Would you like to play a game with me?

Limahong is a gaming troupe looking for allies. We play Spirit Quest, Gombol and every year compete in the Tournament of Ten. Defensive experience necessary. No first years!!!

The café was dark and handmade. Even the slab walls were covered over with old doors and desktops. Second-hand immersion couches haphazardly took up the floor and the whole place stank. The bar offered all kinds of food, drink and its own range of mesh. The miasma of fumes was only added to by the smell of those who didn't go outdoors much. It smelt like home.

The augmented view was thick with flags, graphics and other attention-seeking devices that orbited the patrons. Such was the humour of the place that a banner was hung over the exit saying: 'BEWARE Outside world beyond this point'.

He heard his name whispered between them and all the patrons turned in their couches and lifted the goggles from their eyes.

A girl with nose rings and a bright yellow dress rushed to meet him. 'Honourable Shima, what can I get you?'

Another voice overrode hers. 'Let me get this one, Cindy. Takashi Shima, as I live and breathe. Someone pinged me that you were out and about.'

'Lewis? You work here now? What happened to Old George?'

'He still comes in. I practically run the place though. You want a private room I suspect?'

'Yeah, yeah. I think that'd be best.' He nervously looked around the café. Many of those on the couches had removed their visors and were watching him.

'You're not looking particularly buoyant. Can I get you a tea? I've got a mix that will swallow you whole.'

'Perhaps something lower. I need to ween off.'

'As you say. I see your brother is holding his own. Who'd have thought that Ryu Shima would make it to Prime. I always thought he was too stiff to get the emotional votes.'

'That's my brother, Lewis.'

Lewis raised his hands. 'Not meant that way. He's doing well in a really tough position. Let me get you that brew.' The manager nodded at the girl, Cindy, and she pressed a catch under the bar.

'Right this way, Takashi San.' He pushed one of the wall panels into the ceiling and held back the curtain of clacking beads.

There was a short connecting corridor that ended with a door. The manager stretched a metal key from his belt loop and opened it up. 'A bit old-fashioned, I know, but no one bothers to learn how to pick locks nowadays.'

Lewis tapped a wall switch and hanging lights with cloth shades lit up. The floor was padded and sprinkled with bolsters, cushions and blankets. He began asking Takashi a lot of questions as he went around the room, straightening the soft furnishings and folding the blankets. Was this what he had in mind? Would this suit his needs? Was there anything else he needed?

Takashi felt tongueless and unable to answer. It was a flop room, where mesh-heads crashed for their mindfucks and orgies. It was exactly the kind of place his mother would expect him to end up. He sat down heavily and leant back on one of the rests. He was feeling the combined effects of hangover, withdrawal and loss.

'Um ...?'

'Yes?' Lewis asked.

'What will I owe you after this? I should tell you that I'm not sure of my position right at the moment.'

'I wouldn't worry about that, Takashi. May I?' Lewis indicated the space beside him, asking if he could sit.

Takashi indicated assent.

'I say don't worry about it. My trade has doubled since you came through the door. You're an exciting place to be.'

'Why are you flattering me?' Takashi asked. He knew when someone was being overly nice to him. He liked it.

'I thought we could come to an arrangement. My patronage for yours.'

'All I have to do is come here?'

'You can live upstairs if you want.'

'I'd prefer somewhere below.'

'That can be arranged.' Lewis looked at him. 'Do we have a deal?' He held out his hand.

'For how long?'

'Let's see how it goes.'

'Agreed.' Takashi shook the other man's hand. 'So who are all those kids outside?'

'Would you like to meet them?' Lewis asked.

'Not yet.'

'Well, let me furnish you with a list you can go through. We've got some good starters out there.'

'Okay,' Takashi said.

Lewis paused but Takashi said nothing more. 'So, ah. What can you tell me about this Kronos thing?'

'Nothing I should pass on.'

'Don't be like that, Takashi. You know my front room want to hear something or I'll lose my image.'

'Who are they all?' he said, looking through the list of names.

'Didn't you know you had fans, Takashi?'

'Still? Not even my family talk to me.'

'Well ... I guess they have a position to maintain too. Now how about that titbit?'

Takashi thought for a moment. He didn't want to give out rumours, but there was very little fact to divulge. 'It is likely that Kronos was made by Shen Li ...'

'Really? So it *is* a symbiot? I lost that one. I'll be back in a second with a snackuterie. Please come out front if you feel up to it.'

Lewis spun on his heel and rushed out to release the news.

Takashi lay back and began prowling the Weave for things that could help his brother. There wasn't any useful information on the black monster, or anything like it, so he moved onto the more difficult question. Why had Tamsin Grey targeted him? Of all the people in the world she had come to him to take what was in his mind.

Before his brother had cut him off, Takashi had access to all the data the Primacy had. If he was the psis, what could he do with that information? He wondered: *what information do I have that they could use?*

He knew everything about the hunt for Pierre Jnr. He knew more than most. He knew how his brother was planning to restrict the psis. *Would that give them a strategic advantage?*

Tamsin Grey had said something about Ozenbach. Takashi replayed the footage caught by the eyes in his chambers, the psi leader stepping out from the doll box and him standing there like an idiot. He shivered at the memory of his mind being fiddled. Like a pile of paper, she had flipped through his pages until she found something that pleased her. Then she thanked Geof Ozenbach.

Was there something from Geof the weaver that was important? All he could think of was the contagion map.

262

There hadn't been much value in it at the time. It was only a projection of Pierre's potential influence if his control of people extended beyond contact. *Of course it would,* Takashi thought tangentially. *All interactions have lasting effects, but could one such as Pierre reprogram people to permanently act how he wanted?*

Maybe the psis know something I don't. Maybe they have the missing bits of information that might help them locate Pierre Jnr.

He was looking for something unknown and thus undefined. *The psis might know one thing I don't know — like how many of them there actually are.* It had to be that. Takashi summoned the calculations Geof Ozenbach had created. It may have been created as a way of mapping Pierre Jnr's potential influence on the population but if he replaced the icon for Pierre Jnr with just the psi symbol ... the map became a manual for the rebellion about how many telepaths they would need to control the majority.

They *knew* how many psis it would take to change the Will.

One of his symbiots flagged a recreation park in Jaipur where a big-headed boy was sitting in the shade of a gigantic baobab tree. The other people in the park didn't see him. They played at their games and he watched without moving.

Takashi smiled. *They can't see him, and he can't see me. I am more invisible than the wind in the trees.*

Do you have a plan, Pierre? Or are you just like the rest of us, living the life that is handed to us ...

Takashi deftly overwrote the record, as if no child waited under the tree.

* * *

Gomez sat in a waiting room. A girl with a ponytail stood behind the reception desk and looked up periodically to make sure he hadn't moved. Around him the walls were constructed of tiny aquariums, brick-sized, filled with fluids of different colours, bubbling with aeration.

A young-looking man in a seamless suit came into the room and stood at the reception desk. His arms folded over and he watched Gomez wriggling in his seat.

Gom spied the symbiot that spiralled up from the man's creaseless suit, around his neck, capping the sides of his skull.

With disgust for the grimy boy, the suited man picked up the piece of paper Gom had filled in with his requirements.

'What do you want with this? These are not for a boy like you.'

'I have the cash for them. More than the going rate.'

'But you wish for there to be no questions, do you not?'

'Yes.'

'But for there to be no questions for you, there must be no questions asked of me. Which means a little more care.'

'Look, I don't care who knows. Why can't you just let me have them?'

'Who are you buying these for, boy? Are you really from the slags? Has Padre Raminez sent you?'

'I don't know who you're talking about. This is for me. I want to build a symbiot for my family.'

'And you would know how?' the salesman scoffed.

Gomez couldn't answer that one. He wanted to be brave and claim that of course he could, but he had no idea what it involved.

'With this amount of money you could buy a ready-made model, an anklet say. Would that not be better?'

'I'm going to build my own,' Gomez insisted.

'Not with our products you're not. Louisa, please have this grime removed and the waiting room sterilised.'

'But —' Thick arms were already pulling him up and he was carried bodily out the doors. Soon he was outside on the ground. One of the guards stuffed something in his top pocket.

'Don't forget your list.' He laughed and his pal laughed with him.

Gom stood up, patted off the dirt and looked around for some shade. It was too hot to be exposed. He pulled out his list and found a card had been slipped into his pocket. It was the address of a cantina.

He found it nearby and sat in a booth, quietly hoping to be ignored. He watched unfamiliar foods go past him to other tables, the smells encouraging the saliva in his mouth.

He stood up after ten minutes, but a hand pushed him confidently back down.

One of the guards from the merchant sat down opposite him and picked up the menu, speaking as he swiped through the offerings. 'Some interesting things on this menu, muchacho.'

'I'm not hungry.'

'I'm always hungry. The food here is great.' He tapped for two orders. 'I bet you never had a real perrito before. They didn't have those in the slags when I was there.'

'You come from the piles?' Slags was what rich people called them.

'Sure thing, amigo. Born in and ran from, like you're doing.'

'I'm not running.'

'You just taking a paseo into the Caucus territory? Nah. You on the way out. Now or later.'

Something arrived. Gomez didn't know what it was. It steamed even in the pervasive heat. It was a long soft roll of bread, with green chillies, crumbled puff-cheesies and two kinds of salsa on a cylinder of pork mash. The smell nearly made him lose his seat.

'Eat up, little man. Or I will.'

Gomez looked at how the guard was doing it and tried to mimic. Most of the perrito was knocked out the other end at his first bite, but he was tasting it now and he nearly choked as he gorged the rest of it.

'Slow down, muchacho. Show me that list.'

Gomez licked his fingers and took the crumpled paper from his pocket. The guard looked it over.

'This stuff is off your level, little man. No wonder they threw you out.'

'What have I done wrong?'

'You went where you weren't supposed to went. You need a back way in, like me, see.'

'You can get me the ingredients?'

'Sheeba, yes. I got stashes nobody know about.'

'How much will it cost?'

'You come find me here after my shift. My man Dwain will do you a deal. I'll take you to him.'

'But I'm meant to be home. I can't stay in the Caucus that long.'

'Your choice.'

Gomez thought about it. He wasn't sure he trusted the guard. 'I'll be here. But you better not be planning to cheat me.'

'Don't be so suspicious, amigo. I paid for your meal, didn't I? My name is Mario by the way. No need to thank me.'

True to his word, Mario returned at dusk. Gomez had been loitering around the cantina all afternoon. The wait staff didn't seem to be bothered by him and they gave him water.

Mario made him wait while he drank a beer. He sat at the bar, ignoring Gomez and flirting with the barmaid. 'Hey, Susanna, you know we were meant for each other.'

'Dream on, Mario.' She seemed to have fun declining his interest.

'Mister Mario, sir. I have to get back. Can we go soon?'

'There you are, amigo. I've been waiting for you. I thought you'd left.' Mario turned off his stool and threw a woollen poncho over him. 'You're going to get cold, kid. Didn't you bring anything warmer?'

The guard strode off into the streets, Gomez running to catch up. They went a few blocks from the cantina and then through a mall where the stallholders were closing down their stands. Mario turned and went through the loading dock and out the back exit.

After more turns they came to a dead end, pasted over with street art and advertising posters. The line of a doorway was cut out of the thick paper build-up.

267

Mario wiped his finger around his mouth and then pushed it onto a sensor plate hidden under the corner of a torn-up poster. He smiled confidently and the door clicked and opened inward.

He led Gomez into a dark passageway. Mario pulled the door closed and stopped him going further with a light touch against his shoulder. 'Register first.'

'Huh?'

'Everyone has to register first.' Mario motioned for him to roll his finger in his mouth as he had done, and point at a pad by the door.

'Oh, right.' Gom did as he was told, swabbing his cheek and then pressing his print to the sensor.

'Okay.' Mario clicked on a wrist lumen and led Gom deeper inside. They went down a ladder through a rough hole smashed in the floor, and then walked further through a second such hole in a foundation wall of a crypt.

The room was full of decomposing robots and floor-to-ceiling shelving. Many of the bots still had batteries that operated their pneumatic arms and bearings. Buzz, shuffle, scrape. Faulty sensors made them cut their movements short and then repeat, ad infinitum. The shelves were choked with boxes and components in dense organisation. Delicate metal servitor arms moved on floor and ceiling rails that ran around the room.

'Dwain? Are you awake?' Mario called out.

In answer, a pair of the arms reached out and took the poncho jacket from him. 'Thanks, Dwain. I brought you a customer,' he said.

An arm reached out, digits cupped like an open hand. He stared at it. 'Shake it, amigo. You don't want to be rude.'

Gomez shook the thing and followed Mario down the central aisle. They came to a wall of repaired screens with a man in a helmet sitting in silhouette against their fulgent displays. 'Hey, Dwain.' The man raised his hand and the two of them bumped their palms together.

'This is Gomez. He threw some flags up at Faro today.'

'I saw. What's the game, Gomez?' Dwain asked. He waved his hand to him, but didn't remove his helmet. Mario handed the requisition sheet to one of the arms and took a seat.

'Game? I'm just trying to get some materials. I don't know what the problem is.'

'The problem is nobody is allowed these materials. The big WU says so.'

'What? They can't do that?'

'Don't worry, Gomez. Mario has brought you to the right place. We've got what you need. You got what we need?'

He opened his sack and presented the contents to the man. Dwain stayed under his helmet and didn't look, only his arms closed in to pick through the pile. It pushed a small portion back towards the boy.

'That will be enough.'

'Really? Thanks, mister,' Gom said. He hadn't been expecting any change.

'Hey, what about my finder's fee, Dwain?' Mario asked.

The arms picked out some of the cash and laid it before him. 'That should do it.' Mario swept it up and folded it into his pocket.

There was a lot of rapid activity as Dwain's servitor extensions ran around the room, collecting all the pieces of Gomez's order.

'Do you have a heat regulator?' Dwain asked.

'No. Do I need one?'

'Yes, you do. Diffusers? No? Smooth brush? No. I'll add those.' Some of the change Dwain had given him was taken back to cover the extra items.

Very soon an insulated crate was set before him filled with transparent bladders in different colours, small canisters of powder, and equipment wrapped in packing foam.

'How can I get this out of here? It's too heavy.'

Mario rolled his eyes and bent to the box. He turned a knob and it rose up on stilted wheels. 'It's a trolley, idiot. I told you Dwain was the best, didn't I? He doesn't leave his customers wanting.'

'Only wanting to come back,' Dwain quipped. The two slapped hands again.

'But how do I get home? The checkpoints are closed, and I've already been here too long.' The main way into and out of the Caucus was through one of twenty underpasses. During daylight they were manned, and the staff recorded all travellers; at night the passes were shut and only air transport could access the city.

'Hey, Dwain, have you got a mask this kid can wear?' An arm glided along the shelves, took out a gas mask and dropped it into Gom's hands. 'There's always a way out of a city, Gomez. Remember that.'

'You'll come with me?'

'I'll show you the way out, sure. But it'll cost ya.' Mario winked. Gomez didn't feel he had much choice.

The way out was fine, if he didn't think about it, following the sewer line that pumped away the waste of the city. Mario waved him off at a release duct that opened into barren desert.

'The road back to the slags is that way,' he said, pointing east.

'Okay. Thanks, Mario.'

'Just make sure you find me when you come back to town.'

He found the road easily enough, a hard-packed smoothway for hovers and wheels that led back to the piles. He thought he could see the rise of the junk heaps on the horizon and began walking, the trolley following obediently behind him.

Before too long a pair of lights flashed him, a hover coming in fast. He picked up his father's call sign on his scanner, and signalled back. The hover slowed down as it pulled in close to him.

'Gom, thank the light you're okay.' His father leapt out of the vehicle and wrapped his boy in a hug. 'Now what could possibly have been worth all this trouble?'

Gomez opened the box for him to see.

'What is this? We can't have these. How did you get them?'

'I wanted to build a symbiot. It could really help us.'

'A symbiot? Don't be loco, Gomez.'

'No, think of it, Papa. Think what we could do with it.'

His father stopped asking questions and toyed with his chin. 'I always wanted to automate the smelt. There's coin in that.'

'And then we could refine too.'

'Ah, Gom.' He ruffled his son's hair. 'I'm so glad you're alright.'

271

Together they packed the box safely into the back seat. Gomez showed his dad how to make the wheels retract. 'At least there'll be some use for this cart,' he joked.

They stayed up late mixing the materials, following the step-by-step Gomez had loaded to his screen. It seemed easy enough. First, he prepared the base — a lidded container that the replicator printed in no time, which he painted with the algomite, a powder he had to mix into a paste that would hold enough nutrients for the synaptic algae.

His father came in to help after visiting Gom's mother, and they placed the mixture under a heat lamp and programmed a servitor arm to maintain the stirring. Gom added the ingredients one by one. *They are strange oozes*, he thought ... such as the veiny one with silver threads, or the navy-blue jam with pale caviar.

His father went to bed and Gom sat back to wait.

The next thing he knew he was being woken by his father tapping his foot. Gomez opened his eyes. It was morning. He lurched out of his chair, pushing his father aside in his race to the bench, and was immediately disappointed to see the mixture had turned black.

'What's wrong, Gom?' his father asked. 'What's it meant to look like?'

'I dunno, but I'm pretty sure that looks dead.' Gomez poked his finger roughly into the black sludge. 'Ow, sheeb,' he swore. His finger felt pierced up the middle and he couldn't pull it away.

'Mind your language ... Gom?' His son was arching his back unnaturally and coughing wetly as though choking. He raced forward to catch the boy before he fell and found himself holding Gomez's head, his eyes glazed, lips hanging open. 'No ... Gom —' Black tendrils lanced up from Gom's mouth, grappling painfully onto his own face.

'Forty million were lost today in a second Kronos attack.'

People reacted in different ways. Sitting. Lying down to view the recordings of the black mass overcoming Mexica. Some joined hands to form peace circles. Many of the town faces cried, their expressions crunching up, eyes squeezing tightly as if tears were about to flow. It was a year of tragedies that wouldn't end.

'The world is in mourning today following a second outbreak of the Kronos phenomenon. We will now observe a minute's silence.'

The Weave was quiet, streams paused where they were, and no messages were sent, no communications or pings. People around the world bowed their heads and waded through the images that would forever haunt them.

At sixty-two seconds, the mill of the convocation began churning furiously.

'This is the biggest single loss of human life in our history.'

'I'd say that's the end of Ryu Shima as Prime.'

'I can't see how he'll survive this.'

'Gladys Schuster, the Prime's second-in-command, is about to make a statement.'

They cut to cameras with Gladys Schuster at a podium at the base of the Prime's needle.

'Following this second attack, the Prime is calling for a state of emergency.' Immediately she was asked what that meant.

'This will mean we will begin preparations to avoid a global collapse. Social engineering teams are now in the process of organising distribution of vital services and technicians.'

'Well, should we be alarmed, Phyllis?' the presenter asked, as the view came back to the panel in the studio.

'It is hard not to be. This Kronos is far bigger than the one that appeared in Busan. I'd be questioning whether Services can contain it at all.'

'There is no need to cause panic,' another panellist spoke up. 'The Kronos beasts only attack man-made structures. Natural boundaries will prevent the further spread of Kronos, as it has in Busan.'

'Do we have any insights into how it got out?'

'Not that anyone is saying.'

'What of the rumours that anarchists built this second Kronos?'

'That suggestion is beyond verification. At this stage, any comments are pure speculation.'

'Okay. Well, viewers, hold tight. We'll be back with more information as it comes to light.'

Geof was called before the Colonel. He had been up all night working on patterns. 'How did this happen, Geof?' Pinter's eyes seemed sharpened.

'I don't know, Colonel,' he answered honestly.

'Is it possible that Kronos somehow escaped from our cordon and made its way to Mexico?'

'I don't see how.' Geof shook his head.

'Or was it always there like the one in Busan?'

'No, I think it was ... well, Egon Shelley has a theory.'

'Oh yes? Don't hold out. The Prime is desperate for something. And so am I.'

'Egon thinks that Kronos is made of two parts. One being the body, the other being the mind.'

'Is he messing with you?' the Colonel asked.

'I don't think so. We don't know exactly what's happening. We're just using those words to describe what we are seeing — and we could be entirely wrong — but it makes some sense.' Geof forwarded the results of the preliminary experiments. 'When we reset the mass, it becomes inert, but any sort of network or neural path will awaken it. It could be that it is a mindless body.'

'Until it comes into contact with a mind?'

'Yes.'

The Colonel suddenly changed mode. He released Geof from his stare and looked off-camera. 'That would be quite a thing, wouldn't it? Still, how did it get from Busan to Mexica?'

'It didn't have to. Kronos would only need someone to recreate the base substance.'

'How would they know how to do that? We don't even know what it is made of yet.'

'But Kronos may know. If it does have a mind separate from its body, a digital mind say, then it is possible that when it appeared in Busan it also copied itself onto the Weave.'

'Then all it needs is one person to be tricked into making it a new host.'

'We've already started scanning. Some of those ingredients are on a watch list anyway,' Geof said. 'If anyone is trying to collect the materials, we'll find them.'

'Wait a minute, Geof. Tell me if I'm wrong, but I thought there was nowhere to hide on the Weave? How can Kronos be there and us not know about it?'

'It's easier than you might like to think. There are lots of tricks hakkas use: tunnelling, mimesis, trojans. Weavers find what they can and close the holes, but it requires constant and active counter infiltration.'

'How can you detect Kronos then?'

'I don't yet, sir.'

'And if it is on the Weave, what is it doing?' Pinter asked.

'I won't be able to answer that until I can confirm it is there at all.'

'Then find out, Geof. There has to be a connection. We need to report something or the Will will tear us all out of our seats.'

Geof closed communications with the Colonel, lay back in the chaise and melted. Each time he connected with it was like the first time he put on a symb. His brain felt instantly bigger and reached further and faster. All he had to do was flick a thought to the chaise and an immense amount of data was processed and delivered back to him.

Go through all the streams of Mexica and see if there is any mention of the Kronos ingredients. The chaise processed. While Mexica wasn't included in the WU, it still interacted with the Weave and had its own networks that Services monitored. The chaise found some records of the materials being traded, but nothing out of the ordinary, and always just one ingredient at a time.

It then highlighted a requisition order that was rejected by the Caucus; an underling had sent a missive to the governing body about a peasant, warning that there might be collusion with rival factions. *Trace back on the flag of the ingredients in Mexica to the boy Gomez. Okay, now find where he got that list.* The chaise ploughed through the entirety of the boy's stream; it was only a few hours' worth, the poor denny. Gomez had received the instructions from an ARA, a common snare used by hakkas.

He watched the conversation play out between Gomez and the girl avatar.

Okay, certify that link, where the ARA changes to a conduit. Full validation. The chaise quickly chased the link of the ARA, leading it into a call hub where it got looped on itself when the listed operator turned out to be non-existent. A facade of a datastream, small enough to get lost within the margin of error. 'We have ourselves a hakka.'

Now to find out what a hakka would be doing giving out the Kronos recipe? Could it simply be dedication to anarchy? Or had they too been taken in by promises?

Find the hole they came through and then overlay with known MOs. The chaise began pinpointing the possible points of entry to the hub. There were many; the call hub was riddled with susceptibilities. *Begin a line by line search. Something came in from somewhere.* The chaise warned him this operation would take some time.

While he waited, Geof requested a complete audit of the Weave. This was a regular information set compiled hourly to monitor the health of the network and look for large-scale patterns.

He immediately noticed something odd. *Pattern over time, standard collations.* Statistics layered over his eyes. *Filter to patterns that changed after Kronos first appeared in Busan.* There were still too many factors. He changed the code to line graphs and zoomed in on the moment Kronos appeared in Busan, where a dozen lines kicked upward sharply.

From the first moment of the appearance there were natural increases in Weave traffic, as a billion streams began accessing all the information they could on the situation.

Go back further, before the appearance. Correlate with a reverse projection of the selected trends. The line graph zoomed bigger to fill his overlay, and two dotted lines, one orange and one green, lay over top, twitching angles as the data was refined. The increase in energy load of the Weave and the increased traffic did not correspond. Geof increased the resolution to a minute by minute mapping. The line showing the amount of energy it took to maintain the Weave began to climb forty-eight minutes before Kronos reached the surface.

Now tell me what that means. This the chaise could not process.

Geof took a break from his charts and took a fly over the planet. Gracefully he slipped from eye to eye, landing on street corners, flying through squib corridors, diving under the sea. He flew to the peninsula and saw the beast at the public viewing points, like so many millions were doing each day.

Do you ever feel lonely?

Even when you're at home, surrounded by the ones you love?

Do you ever feel like you don't ever really connect?

Come with us. Come find happiness.

Geof swiped the annoying commercial away and changed into a cloaked mode. His avatar was whatever anyone looking at him would see if he wasn't there: effectively invisible, except for his footprint ... the weight of data.

He went back to his thought room, pulling back the luminous graphs of mathematical plots. He drew out one and told the chaise to begin breaking down the energy spike by node. Nodes were the billion invisible pillars of the Weave, the warp threads of the great loom. The chaise could pattern the energy demands of each distinctly.

How much does data weigh? That was a question from Ortega. *Did it weigh nothing? Was it like smoke?* And the answer, in real-world terms, was how much electricity had to be produced to keep it in existence.

From node to node the energy needs bounced. When contact was made the node's traffic suddenly doubled.

It's replicating, Geof thought.

Morritz had become more interested in the Kronos project since they began investigating the theory that it had escaped to the Weave in digital form. This had nothing to do with symbiots and everything to do with network theory.

'The funny thing is that it spreads just as it seems to in the real world. Even online it acts totally blind and feels its way around,' Morritz said.

'But can we stop it?' Geof asked.

'One part at a time, perhaps, but not through automation, I don't think. What Kronos is doing is creating a parallax network. It isn't just on the Weave, it is making its own copy of it.'

'Or something like that,' Egon agreed. 'Here, let me show you something. This is a pattern one of our boffins constructed using your data weight theory.' A flat map of the globe highlighted different areas of the Weave in a scale of colours from clear white to alarm red. 'We took the expected and recorded data load of every part of the Weave, and anything outside the norm is tagged as being overweight.'

'And with this we can detect Kronos's presence on the Weave,' Geof concluded. At this point he began feeding preliminary data to the Prime and Colonel Pinter.

The Colonel and Egon Shelley joined them in the thought room.

'How far has Kronos penetrated the Weave?' Pinter asked.

'By this estimate, about thirty per cent.'

'And growth rate?'

'A percentage point per day cycle.'

'So we have seventy days until it is everywhere?'

'Maybe less.'

'And has it made it through to any first tier circles? Services?' Pinter asked.

'Fortunately not. The isolation protocols must be blocking it.'

'Good. What else have you got? Have you learnt anything useful from the samples?'

'Quite a lot … The Weave infection of Kronos is behaving in an analogous way to its physical form. It spreads, it grows, it absorbs. When it runs out of things it can absorb it waits.

On the Weave it won't run out of material. It will just keep building in parallel until it is everywhere.'

'There has to be a way to stop it,' Pinter said.

'It's actually not affecting anything, Colonel,' Morritz said.

'The Command is to deny Kronos any avenue for further expansion.'

'It is all through the Weave.'

'Yes, and we can't afford for any more outbreaks,' the Colonel said.

'Colonel, I do not believe that Kronos is aggressive. I do not think it means us any harm,' Geof said.

'Why would you say that?'

'Because it doesn't make sense. Why would Sensei Li make something that was solely destructive?'

'You said yourself he said it was a failure.'

'Yes, but when a scientist says an experiment is a failure it only means it didn't work as expected. It doesn't mean something else didn't happen. There has to be a reason Shen didn't destroy it.'

'And you have an answer, I presume?'

Geof looked at Egon, who shrugged. They had been stepping around the topic; both knew they weren't saying things that were on their minds.

'We have been thinking of Kronos as alive, or animal in some way. And it does seem to be like that, except it is dumb. This is a creature with the animal intelligence of an amoeba. It doesn't think.'

Nobody spoke and Geof continued. 'If this was a digitalis experiment, a step forward in human evolution, I can't help

281

but wonder how this could possibly have been close to sensei's intentions.

'If we look at how it acts, just growing and absorbing, working with the plants ... perhaps Shen might not have been trying to replace the human body, but replacing the environment we live in.'

They looked at each other a long time. The Colonel watched the blink and tick of his various task reports in his overlay, and then closed all the windows so he could look at the weaver without distraction.

'And we would live inside it?'

'Yes. In a new world, free like the Weave, and each person's soul a stream.'

'Are you suggesting all those people are still alive under that stuff?' the Colonel asked.

'Maybe not their bodies, but their minds might be.'

'Oh, Geof ... I would like to believe that these people are still alive as much as anyone, but you have no proof.'

'What if I could get it? What if we can communicate with it?'

'Geof, we have tried to in every way we know how.'

'But not on the Weave. On the Weave we are both digital forms, we have to be able to find a way to talk.'

'Wouldn't you get infected?'

'I'll return to a backup.'

'Geof, I won't stop you, but are you really willing to take that risk?' Pinter asked.

'Yes, Colonel.'

'As you wish ... Just one thing.'

'Yes.'

'You should hurry.'

'Why?'

'Is the Prime going to attack it?' Morritz asked.

'Why would he do that?' Geof asked.

Morritz shrugged. 'Shima needs some good news or he's finished.'

'He wouldn't ...' Geof looked at the Colonel.

'The Prime is being forced into a position.'

'But it is alive.'

'Prove it.'

Takashi watched the exchange play out and sent a message to Geof Ozenbach. It was ignored, of course.

'Fine,' he said to himself.

Takashi to Lewis: Are your kids ready for a job?

When Admiral Shreet received the call, he stood from his desk and floated to the large porthole. Whenever he spoke to people on Earth he liked to be looking at the planet. It was an entrancing view. In the sun the heavy contrast of cloud, ocean and land, in the dark the void and the artificial stars of civilisation.

The orbital system crisscrossed before his eyes. Satellites, shuttles and haulers moving in straight coordinated lines. Stopping and starting like a child's train set, very much like a train set, just without tracks.

Shreet was a straight-backed man and, like all of the orbital population, he worked hard to keep his body toned. His was an old face, singed by fire sometime in the past and made harder by the unforgiving shadows of space.

For two decades he had been the checkpoint between the World Union and greater Earth — which didn't live with the same unity of principle. He was ambassador, sheriff and commander of the Orbital Weapons Net.

Admiral Shreet looked down at the blue orb with its lumps and brushstrokes of weather. Largely, he could stay distant from the whim of the Will. There were no rivals for his position, as no Earth-grown humans could compete with his record and experience and few of the greater-Earth population took that much interest in the WU and the doings of the earthbound. You weren't a real roughie if you were a Citizen, and the WU only included Citizens.

He was abreast of Earth's affairs and had adjusted the satellite coverage to focus surveillance over the Kronos outbreaks and the Cape area. Any time a target was identified, the Admiral could eviscerate it, whether an individual or group; or he could distort a large target area beyond recognition. He tried to make sure it was only a tool of last resort.

'Admiral Shreet.'

'Colonel Pinter. I hope you can tell me why your call feels so ominous.'

'I presume you have been watching the mess going on with the Will.' Shreet nodded, curtly. Of course he had. 'Then you must be experiencing the same dilemma as the rest of us. Though your perspective may be somewhat removed.'

'Somewhat.'

'Tell me, Admiral. If Earth became ... intolerable, would greater Earth survive?'

'There are contingencies for such an event. Is it coming to that?'

'I don't think it has to, but that isn't actually what I'm contacting you about.'

'Oh? Then what is it?'

'"It" is Kronos. I woke up in a sweat when it struck me that if Kronos is on the Weave, then the weapons net might be open to usurpation too.'

'Oh, mir, you're right.' Shreet paled and touched his hand to the window glass. 'What do we do?'

'You need to purge the whole system. Revert to backups from last month.'

'That will take the OWN out of operation. You'll be defenceless.'

'Yes, so I'd urge you to do it as quickly and quietly as possible.'

'Of course. I can do it all myself. Nobody will know.'

'There's another catch, Admiral.'

'Yes?'

'Once it's done you won't be able to reconnect. Not until we know it is safe.'

'You want the OWN to be isolated from the Weave? I can't do that.'

'You must. You can't risk contamination.'

'It goes against the Command.'

'Do you believe your job is to protect the OWN, or the people of Earth?'

'The Weave will go mad. What justification can I give?'

'Now there I had a thought ... how would you feel about declaring independence?'

He stood on the far side of the bridge. Only a short walk and a toll gate before he would be inside the strange zone: Omskya relocation zone, Sector 261. Miles Lizney was fascinated by the place the hakka had dumped Zach after chewing him up and, since no one above seemed to care, he would have to investigate himself.

The Siberian Terminus was a unique wasteland, formed by the detonation of a nuclear weapon within a broadcast distortion field. Ten thousand kilometres of animals, trees and Örjians killed or irrevocably changed by the sting of the Scorpion. It was an explosion of forced mutations that brought many new species into existence. Nearly all of whom died.

The survivors were moved to Omskya Central, the nearest city to the Terminus. A thousand rapid-built settlements for a hundred thousand Örjian children, care of the miraculous mechanics of the new union. The relocation towns covered a greater area than the rest of STOC, though the main population kept itself to its tall buildings and modern conveniences. The sectors — 1 through 456 — held approximately ten thousand residents each: technically they were Citizens, but with negligible civic influence and behavioural restrictions, they had next to no value.

The sector towns were built using polyplastic blocks that could be assembled and reassembled. It was the cheapest and most flexible way to expand a city, even if the smaller constructions needed to be roped down with ballast to remain sound through storms.

All the sectors looked the same to Miles. They looked the same as when he left them long ago, though the trees were bigger and the grass had died. Prefab towns made to the same plan as the one he had grown up in. Single-storey houses made from one or two units, set along perfectly straight roads with pedestrian ways marked out with thick yellow lines.

He remembered the daily scannings and inspections, checking for signs of fighting or altering. Servicemen strutted along the street making sure the residents weren't reverting to their old ways.

'Stand along the yellow lines. Face forward. Face left. About face. Face forward.'

The secret that the would-be scouts were meant to find out about Mister Lizney was that he was once the enemy, or at least the child of the enemy. His parents were part of the Örjian hordes, the pinnacle of genetic advancement and Lamarckian dedication. Twisted and toothy animals who made bloodsport of evolution.

'The animal must advance.' He could still hear his father whispering the commandments to him at nights. 'Change or die. Live and kill. Only this way will humanity survive.'

He shook his head at this now, but at the time, as a boy, his father's words were his entire world.

'But, Father, if we are so much better than them, how is it that they keep us prisoner?' The only answer to that was a beating. A beating to the edge of unconsciousness. A beating that had him removed from his parents and placed with a more obedient family.

He never wanted to have to stand on those lines again.

It was an odd thing to know your parents were insane. An almost unbelievable, inconceivable concept. Can one born in madness ever escape it? He felt it in his veins ... they had been mad, vicious killers. The only excuse for them was the Dark Age of famines and war that had birthed Örj and those who needed something to follow. Örj would lead them out of the darkness, it was said. Instead he took them deeper into it.

When Lizney watched the histories now, pretending that he had no link to them, the madness could sometimes make sense. He watched movies of the hordes loping through city streets, running like wolves and using their claws and scramble-pipes on any who resisted.

Maybe it would be best if he waited and watched a little longer. He found a bench and put a weak dreamer on his neck. His eyes closed and he thought back.

The morning Zach disappeared, Mister Lizney took the day off. He whisked powders into a tea and compiled a report on Omskya 261. Statistically, it was a mystery. For a start, none of its Citizens had been engaging with the Weave for months. While there were many people in the world who chose not to connect, or could not, to have a spontaneous and complete revulsion within a set radius was improbable.

Only the passive data was still being collected from the grid of omnipoles that monitored and transmitted communications, electricity and light. The logs from the o-poles went back to the origins of the encampment, forty-eight years worth of data. In the last five months there had been a notable decrease in accidents, traffic congestion and people being late for their work programs. This timed exactly with the drop-off in Weave usage.

He returned to the area three cycles in a row. Found nothing new. What he did manage to clearly ascertain was that this peace was geographically constrained, confined to Sector 261.

Life there seemed too perfect. Such regularity of patterns was not humanly possible. Human patterns should look more like spaghetti, but these were evolving towards perfectly interlinked circles. Optimal human efficiency.

The problem seemed hard for him to put a finger on. So what if synchronicity in the population had steadily increased? Meal times for example. People's breakfast times had migrated, allowing for less deliveries and an adjustment of their commuting windows until the optimal density was found for each transit service. 'This town is too efficient,' he muttered to himself.

He demersed and went to his kitchen for some water and a patch. He slapped it on the back of his neck and sat down to concentrate on his breathing. The chemicals were meant to fight his genetic tendencies. The anger that the surgeries couldn't remove.

The place seemed, simply put, the ideal of town planning. It was harmony. Phenomenal harmony. The question was whether it was natural or unnatural. And perhaps, how long it could continue? The harmony had lasted five months without interruption; lasted throughout the manifestation, the psi declaration and now a convocation that could change the destiny of humanity.

Could they be so cut off as to not even have felt what was happening in the wider world? Lizney checked the neighbouring encampments, 260 and 262, whose statistics showed the normal chaos of humanity. There was zero interaction between 261 and the surrounding zones. Food and supplies were delivered by autotruck and humans did not cross between.

Lizney sent his report up the chain. It was a mystery for someone else to investigate.

A week later he hadn't heard anything back from Services. Receipt of his report had been acknowledged, but with the psi situation and the black masses in Korea and Mexica, there were no weavers to be spared to look into a town that was flagged as having zero problems.

Lizney compiled the week's data, which remained on trend, and attached it as an amendment to his initial report and sent it again.

He put his helmet on and stood on the empty streets, walking up and down the quiet lanes for any sign of life. 'All quiet in 261,' he whispered to himself.

He performed the same routine for the next three days. Adding updated data and resubmitting his results. Services remained unconcerned by the harmonious life in Omskya 261, but did respond by asking him to stop making reports.

There was only one thing left for him to do and that was travel there himself ... now he sat looking across the divide, looking over at his childhood streets.

There was a line where he knew the zone of perfection

faltered. Beyond it the statistical anomalies disappeared and people lived their imperfect lives of mistake and correction. The border followed the arms of a stormwater drain that broke the relocation zones into sections. On one side 261, on the other 262.

There was no difference that he could see from the far side of the bridge. The people were dressed the same as people in 261, and walked between their destinations with no more hurry or fuss. The housing was regulation, painted in cheery pastels with white trimmings. Everything designed to make the Örjians feel normal and part of the new civilisation.

What should he do now? How could he find out what was happening on the other side? Could he simply enter 261 and ask someone what was happening? Did they even know it was happening?

Lizney opened the tin with his patches in it and put one on each wrist. As the calm went into his blood he stepped forward. His approach went unwatched. The Citizens continued about their business.

Halfway across the bridge he began to relax. He felt a little silly coming here. Why would Services bother investigating a place where nothing was wrong? Lizney laughed at himself.

Beside him a small boy took his hand and began leading him down the street.

'How did you find me?' the boy asked.

Lizney merely had to think about his last two weeks and what had led him here and the boy understood. His memories were passed onto him as easily as a ping.

'Thank you,' the boy said. 'I will rectify that.'

Around him the omnipoles powered down and the street darkened until Lizney's eyes adjusted to the dim spill from the neighbouring sectors.

'What will you do now?' Miles asked him.

Shanniya looked over the menu and weighed up her future prospects against her need for some pampering.

Louisa's was her favourite place. It only cost slightly extra to have a human server than a bot — and it was so much more decadent. She could talk to a human — well, she could talk to a bot too, but they only had preprogrammed responses. They couldn't understand what it was like to be a modern woman. How could they? If she told a bot how her partner, Jeremy, was leaving her, what would it say? 'Oh, dear, that is very sad. Perhaps a new haircut will make you feel better?'

She only knew he was leaving her because the alerts she had on his stream kept reporting the contact he'd had with other women. All those unexplained greyouts. No honest man needs that much privacy.

She sighed and went inside. Her prospects were low and a head rub wasn't going to solve anything, but it would help her relax. She didn't even know if she cared. He wasn't the most hygienic of partners and his idea of mutual contribution was for her to cook, clean and work up the cash for food. All he did was keep hold of the nice third-floor apartlet. If anything she should be the one leaving him.

The matron of the parlour welcomed her and led Shanniya to a couch where she could put her head back and let the comical servitor massage and treat her hair. 'Would you like to immerse while you're waiting?'

Shanniya nodded and lay back. She went straight to the femme sites, where the streams of celebrities were catalogued, and the highlights and low points of their lives were displayed for her amusement. She couldn't focus on any of the articles or quizzes, they were too close to how she was feeling — *Is it you or him? Should you jump him or dump him?* — and then a question caught her eye. *Would you like to follow your bliss?*

Yes, I'd like that, she thought and activated the link. She was a good and kind person and deserved bliss. She would do anything …

Zach watched Inez disconnect. She didn't look anything like the girl she had just shown Shanniya. She had dark hair braided into a bowl atop her head and picto-graphic irises of red and white that pinched her pupils in the middle like an octopus's.

'Did you get that?' she asked him in her thick licking accent.

'I saw. Why do we have to do this?' he asked.

'Ours is not to ask,' Inez quoted.

'But what am I trying to do?'

'Each customer is different. For this one we just have to make the connection and let the ARA do the rest.' She tipped her head to re-immerse. 'Go bug someone else for a while.'

He was meant to be watching what the protégés worked on and learn how to build automated response avatars — or ARAs, they called them. Small programs that had conversational reflexes to lure unsuspecting streams to give out their information, influence and even credits.

They were essentially just a branching dialogue program that was broad enough to encompass all the answers a user could give.

Are you afraid of dying?

Would you like to live forever?

The vocal generator used for each one would match to the pre-profiling done on any given stream, so for men it was usually a soft feminine voice or the authoritative baritone of a man living a life of jovial excess.

And the goobs always fell for it. That was what disappointed him most. People always wanted the same things. Driven by desire, fear and greed. 'It's all about getting attention,' Delora said, the third of the protégés. Alicia, Inez, Delora and now Zach. 'People jump around. Sometimes we only have a few seconds before they move away, we have to treat them like fish. Make something attractive.'

'With a hook in it.'

'Precisely.'

Dungeon would review each ARA personally before they were seeded to the Weave, where they waited like baited hooks for streams to find. Conversational constructs that enticed people to open their streams to them.

'We have a new client and I need hooks in the water within the hour,' she would order.

'Yes, mistress.' The protégés went to their couches and absorbed the new brief and launched new codes.

Dungeon never let them know who they were working for. All they had to do was find ways to get people to open up their streams and let them in. They asked for just a moment of the mark's time and then took whatever they wanted.

294

A command entered his queue from Dungeon and he demersed. It was time for another bath and he got up to fetch the towels.

Zach's new home consisted of two underground rooms — two that he knew of. The dorm room where he and the other protégés slept and worked on immersion couches, and the chamber where Dungeon kept to herself. They were only allowed entry when she had a use for them.

Dungeon's room was spacious and softened by thick springy rugs arranged between her cupboards and the tiled corner where a large bath rested. The ceiling was hung with stalaclights in their hundreds, and on the walls large screens showed scenery from around the world. Today it was an icy vista of a mountain range, a blue sky pierced with black crags and peaks.

Zach stood in the corner while she sank into her bath. He wore his visor and watched while she drew crude faces and graffiti on the recordings of the Prime's statements and sent them back out onto the Weave.

Dungeon chuckled at her mischief. Her nipples bobbed up and down in the water. She would sit in the bath for hours, immersed and immersed, the way she liked it. Zach was trained to drain and refill the water to keep it fresh and warm.

'Why do you do that?' he asked her.

'Why not?'

'Is it to support the psis?'

'I don't support anyone.' She shrugged. He tried not to look through the water.

She let him watch — she made him watch. His stream trailed hers on the Weave and he learnt quickly how she split her stream across the Weave, deleted her trail and piggybacked other streams like a stowaway on a train.

Dungeon made him watch everything, but he was never to touch. When she called for oils, standing up from the bath, water rolling off her skin and her symbiot cloak, another of her protégés would come to the room to rub the soaked skin with moisturising creams.

'Robe,' she ordered.

Zach opened a large, soft towel gown and was careful not to let his fingers brush against her. He'd learnt that lesson. He was never to touch her or it would be another night sleeping with the prickles.

Then he had to sit quietly by the bed during her full-cycle debaucheries. When he was aroused, she teased him.

Zach told himself that once he had acquired a symbiot of his own, he would leave. He was the only one of the four protégés without.

'Someday, I will give you one as a reward,' Dungeon had told him in the beginning.

After his first night in the prickle he stood in the dormitory unable to move. He felt like Swiss cheese. He thought his clothes should have been soaked with his blood, rather than just cold sweat.

Alicia was kind to him. She lifted her quilt and said, 'Get in.' It *seemed* like an act of kindness. When his shaking subsided she took him to the showers. She washed him and satisfied him, then held him until he slept.

Zach sometimes checked on his old stream. He used a bluff-stream that auto-generated a false history compiled from samples of other local streams. It wasn't the best way to hide, but he was safe so long as no one was looking for him.

He tried visiting Mister Lizney, but found his home empty and powered down. He had been gone for two weeks, leaving shortly after Zach had run away.

Perhaps he went looking for me, Zach wondered.

Then he found a message waiting for him. It was from yesterday.

Zach, if you are reading this, it means something has happened to me. I have set this message to be sent if my stream changes its normal behaviour patterns.

When you left I continued to investigate Sector 261. My reports to Services have been ignored so I have travelled to look further into the mysterious situation.

I am sorry for how we parted. I fear I wasn't the best teacher to you and I hope you can accept my humblest apologies.

I hope we meet again.

Miles Lizney

He had a number of chores to do while the others worked. Planting syphons, like the one he had first encountered. Reviewing success rates of the ARA traps. If any weren't performing, he should either delete them or find the problem.

'How happy are you?' the ARA asked.

This was the first one he had constructed for himself, and it hadn't caught anyone yet. But he wouldn't give up on it.

He watched as a trap lured a stream to it and waited to see if the bait was taken. The stranger was a squat Asiatic man who had a fat symbiot growing from the collar of his dressing gown.

An encouraging female avatar appeared in response — trimmed mousy-brown hair, a delicate patch of freckles under her eyes — and spoke to the stream. Zach had selected her to deliver the questionnaire; he liked listening to her voice, he had made it sound like Bronwyn.

'Hey, you. Are you happy?' the ARA asked.

'It is my default state of being,' the stranger answered jovially.

'Do you live alone?'

'With friends.'

'Do you like being alone?' the ARA asked.

'Nobody likes being alone.'

'First we must ask ourselves: what is happiness? Then we can set ourselves free.'

The stranger picked up the ARA window and began turning it over in his hands — at least that was what it looked like in the visual plane. In code mode it was being analysed and dissected.

'There you are. I thought there was someone watching.'

Zach found himself looking at the man, although he hadn't chosen to come into the visual layer.

'What are you doing? Where is your profile?'

'Umm, I lost it?' Zach grinned and then tweaked through the stranger's fingers. He scoffed and went to check the next trap. Scouts were useless. He couldn't believe he ever wanted to become one. 'Try to hold onto me, will ya?'

'I'll just have to use both hands this time,' the stranger said, appearing once more. Something grabbed hold of his avatar and pulled it into the load space.

Zach felt himself being probed. His body was just a facade and the weaver tore it apart like paper, revealing all the connections and history of his stream. All that was left between him and the scout was the link to his proxy portal. Zach cut the connection and demersed.

He woke gasping for air and tore off his helmet. He could already feel the prickles that Dungeon would inflict for his failure. Around him the other protégés were still under and the room was quiet.

Then all the screens in the dorm lit up and the scout's face appeared.

'Zachary Frost?' asked the stranger's voice.

'Yes?'

'Are you working alone?'

'No.'

'Why are you aiding Kronos?'

'Kronos? I'm not —'

'Don't say another word, Musashi.' Dungeon came into the room, fresh from her bath, her gown made translucent and clingy. 'What is your business here, weaver?'

'Dungeon?' The scout raised his eyebrows. 'I am surprised, I am surprised.'

'You know him?' Zach asked her.

'Of course. Takashi and I are old friends. Aren't we, Taka?' Dungeon smiled and stroked her thigh.

'I have alerted Services to your whereabouts,' Takashi answered.

'Why don't we talk about this in private? Shall we?' she suggested and turned back to her room.

'There is nothing to say,' the weaver said.

'We'll see about that,' Dungeon said, donning her visor.

Zach sat down on his couch and put his own helmet on, chasing after Dungeon's stream like she'd taught him.

She jumped between the layers, from the visual to code, through the geographic, into the fabula. Here Zach caught up with them, flying through a model nebula, clouds of blue and pink and purple, with stars leering through the thinnest patches.

Dungeon had arrayed herself around the stranger, dividing into multiple nasties, like the syphon that had once attacked him and planted crypto worms in his code.

The weaver didn't flinch at either of the attacks. He protected himself from the worms with emitters that generated false code for them to work through and floating in the nebula he made a motion with his hands and the syphons stopped growling at him. At another gesture they turned around and slithered back towards their master, teeth bared.

Dungeon's eyes flared. 'This can't be.'

'Why have you been helping Kronos?' Takashi asked.

'Kronos will give us eternity. You are a weaver, you should understand.'

'You think Kronos is digitalis?'

'Our saviour has come, Taka, just as Shen Li intended.' Her eyes saw Zach hovering behind them. 'Musashi, help me!' she shrieked.

The stranger looked around at him and Zach immediately changed into his samurai state, Musashi, raising his glowing sword to chop at the weaver.

Zach felt himself yanked away, his visual stimuli cut out, and he was in the load space again. The stranger held him in his fist and shook him until he dropped his sword and his armour was flung off. 'Don't let appearances distract you from the true nature of reality,' the man said.

'Ortega?' he asked.

'You've read it?'

Zach nodded. The stranger seemed to soften.

'How did you get mixed up in this, kid?'

'I don't know, it just seemed to happen ... what am I going to do?' he asked.

'Go home.'

'I have no home.'

'Then come to me.'

Zach felt himself demersing. In his hands his visor flared and then powered down. He couldn't turn it back on. The other protégés experienced the same thing, and looked about at each other.

In another studio, far away, the convocation continued as Citizens waged their opinions against each other. Right against wrong. Sanctioned statements against fictitious claims. Fear against hope.

'No. No,' one panellist said sharply. 'With such a sudden and immense introduction of streams to the WU, it will be like a gigantic wave hitting a coastal town. Who knows how far the ripple effect will reach? That's why I'm proposing a motion to slowly introduce the Cape and its votes to a five per cent increase, year on year.'

'Well, I'd be worried how your sentiments may sway the Cape from joining us at all. If your motion makes it to precedence, then they would be relegated to sub-Citizen status. This very discussion is jeopardising what the Primacy is trying to do.'

'Sure, sure. But Ryu Shima didn't become Prime for his peacemaking. He's meant to be stopping this situation, not encouraging it.'

'The Will is always able to choose another Prime.'

The host cut smoothly into the tiny gap between their statements and began speaking to the audience. 'So, are we ready for the Atlantic Tsunami? Send us your thoughts. One of our patrons has some content for you to watch. We'll be back in a moment to go through your queries.'

The flying cameras settled in for a recharge and the anchor went to check his make-up.

The host of the room was Quaid Rush. He'd been covering trend commentary for three years and was doing well enough for a permanent space and a desk big enough for six people. For the last year he'd been working double-time as the tides of the Weave accelerated.

Quaid sat before a large, lit mirror and dabbed powder where he was starting to glisten. The make-up also contained trace stimulants to perk him up; he still had another hour to go.

A boy sat next to him.

'Hello there. Who are you with, then?'

'I'm with you, Quaid.'

'You know my name? How old are you?'

'I'm turning nine.'

'That's nice. Only one more year and you'll be in double digits. When's your birthday?'

'Tomorrow.'

'Yeah? That's great. Are your guardians getting you anything special?'

'No. This year I am getting something for them.'

'That's nice. What are you giving them?'

'Freedom.'

'Freedom? ... Hey what?' Quaid turned to the seat beside him. There was nobody there.

PIERRE JNR IS COMING TO SAVE US

'Pierre be praised!' the woman shouted from the front of the procession. She walked with her head thrust forward, opening her palms towards the ground as if drawing spirit from the earth.

A line of Servicemen stood watching the approaching mob. There were only fifty-three, not counting the toddling children they had with them, all with heads shaved and wearing black bibs with the white mark of the psis around their necks.

The crowd chanted and waved its icons of Pierre Jnr. Lifting them up to their foreheads and down again as if pumping bellows.

'What are we supposed to do, sir?'

'Wait for the command. Do not provoke any reactions.'

'They're starting to provoke me, sir,' another man commented.

'Do you need to be dismissed, soldier?' the commander asked.

The Citizens also watched. From windows in the neighbouring buildings or from the footpaths where they pressed their backs to the walls to make room for the march. Some were discontent and shouted slurs at the chanters.

As Citizens, the Church of Pierre Jnr had their rights, but if the majority determined against the demonstration the soldiers would be ordered to remove them. The Command is the Command. Already their route to the needle was blocked by MUs, stalling their protest.

In overlay mode, the group disseminated their teachings, forcing their propaganda on those polite enough to read it, and luring others with their bright and hopeful imagery.

Pierre Jnr loves us all.

He is the god mind, come to save us.

When Pierre Jnr manifests again he will make all true believers into one soul.

Come, love Pierre Jnr and join the god mind.

From above, a rock was thrown, hitting the leader of the group. She fell down and held a hand to her bleeding head.

'Medic!' Ten called. 'Help that woman.'

One of the soldiers broke rank and went to the crouching woman.

'Pierre bless you, my child,' she said, as he began to treat her cut.

Then more of the onlookers began throwing things at the sectarians and shouting.

Ryu watched with the rest of the Primacy as the crowd was pacified by the soldiers. The church retired for the day, led away by a covering ten squad.

The footage was followed by more background data of similar meetings that were taking place around the globe. Marches. Shrines. Churches.

People had begun regularly gathering in empty office floors, community parks or outdoor shrines. Praying for psionic powers, wishing they would all become telepathic and begging Pierre to reveal himself to them.

Praise Pierre Jnr. Lord of the mind.

The Will summoned Ryu to speak.

Before the open inquiry, questions were gathered and a magistrate was chosen to control the order of the investigation. Judge Jacob Haden had been an adjudicator for ten years, a commentator for longer and was a founding member of the FutureFuture Club and the Civilisation Preservation Society. He was best known for championing the formation of the wilderness parks. Few were qualified across so many areas.

'Ryu Shima, on behalf of the people, I thank you for your time today.'

'Not at all. I hope to be able to clarify some of the current confusion and set some minds at rest.'

'And we thank you for that consideration. Are you ready to commence?'

'Yes. Go ahead.'

They were live to the Weave in five, four, three ...

'Today we are joined by the honourable Prime, Ryu Shima. Following a series of setbacks, his position is now being threatened by a number of contenders. The frontrunner is Representative Charlotte Betts of Seaboard, who has become the de facto voice for the tolerance movement.

'Prime, what do you see as the union's greatest risk to stability right now?'

'Panic,' Ryu answered. 'The World Union is strong and we must all remain calm.'

'In light of the recent breach in the Cape blockade, and the assassination of Blair Butler and other civic leaders, and invasion of high-families — such as the Shimas — how can you ask everyday Citizens to remain calm?' the judge asked.

'We must remain stable. If we allow these attacks to disrupt our unity, to divide us, then we will have lost.'

'I'm not sure that answers my question,' Judge Haden said, turning to face Ryu with one eye.

'It answers why we need to remain calm.'

'What do you say to people about the psi symbol? Should they wear it?'

'That is every Citizen's choice. I understand many crafters are offering fashionable choices,' he said, making a joke of it, as advised.

'Will you wear one yourself?' Haden asked.

All traces of Ryu's smile were erased. 'No.'

'Because it might be interpreted as a sign of weakness?'

'I believe that symbol is a sign of oppression and anyone who wears it is admitting that they are intimidated by the bullying tactics of this small group.'

'Are you saying that the only reason people would wear the symbol is out of fear? What if they truly support the psi cause?'

'If people supported the psis in reality, I would not have become Prime. The Citizens are expressing their true opinions through the Will.'

* * *

The judge took a new dossier from the pile before him. 'I would like to talk about the Kronos problem, which has now overcome an area where forty million people lived.'

'It is a tragedy of incomprehensible scale.'

'Do you have anything to share that will alleviate the worries of the Citizens frightened that the same thing could happen in their city?'

'Yes.' Ryu gave Gladys the signal to begin spreading the official summaries of the recent breakthroughs. 'We have made a lot of progress in understanding what Kronos is. We have learnt how it reached Mexica and already apprehended the criminals involved.'

'Can you tell us what Kronos is?'

'In scientific terms it is a chimeric symbiot with a biological drive.'

'Are you considering it alive?'

'We are considering it.'

'If it is a living creature, how do you feel we are morally obliged to manage it?'

'It has taken the lives of forty-four million people, Judge Haden. Our goal is to protect ourselves.'

'Will you attempt communication?'

'We have been attempting many forms of communication since Kronos first appeared, and we will continue to do so. The fact that we can get no reaction from it is the biggest evidence we have that this is more of a pollution than an animal.'

'Some are speculating that Kronos will appear in other cities. Citizens of West have already begun migrating away from Mexica.'

'Again, I must advise calm.' The Prime himself was calm. They must see him and know how to act. 'There is no reason to think Kronos will spread further and West is a long way north of Mexica.'

'But you wouldn't be able to stop it. Is that correct?'

Ryu played for time. He didn't want to be cornered into giving an answer. 'We are trialling many defensive options.'

'My records do not show any such motion proposed from your office. Were you attempting to keep this fact secret?'

'We have already scheduled a public release in the next cycle. Until we could be sure how Kronos had spread we felt it wasn't safe to share the information.'

'And does this secret weapon work, Prime?'

'There have been successful lab tests. We are now scaling up the infrastructure.'

'So you do plan to kill it?'

'We do not consider it to be a living thing.'

'I have another thread of inquiry I would like to pursue.' The interviewer tried a redirect.

'Please proceed,' Ryu said.

'It is a question of the Will and manipulation.' The judge breathed in as he found the dossier he had ready. 'In this convocation, as we are now calling it, there is a fierce battle for mindshare between the anti-psi voters and the derestriction movement. You have managed to avoid taking either side in this debate.'

'I follow the command of the Will. It is not my place to show prejudice.'

'And if the Will were to change in favour of removing psi restrictions, would you follow that command also?'

'If that were the case, I would no longer be Prime.'

'Have you seen this?' Haden asked and put a video into the interview stream.

It was a compilation of footage that was becoming popular viewing on the Weave. It showed a new building rising in Atlantic. There were no machines or bots, just men and women standing around the site. Blocks and bricks lofted themselves into position.

Many people were inspired by the sight of the psis in peaceful coordination, in the act of building.

'We have seen the videos, yes,' Ryu answered. 'But we have not been able to verify them. They could be forgeries.'

'Nevertheless, in reaction, the Anti-Psi League have been releasing short sensoriums where psi telepaths manipulate innocent humans for evil ends. As well as a blitzkrieg of supporting propaganda.'

APL ads were everywhere; no matter where you went — they were there. They even began a paper-plastering campaign in the real world, print-offs of their basic tenets. Ryu had seen these too. They used all the bangs and bosom needed to guarantee a large audience.

'Where do you think this increasing tension between the two movements will lead us?' the judge asked.

'First of all, I must denounce the tactics of Nigel Westgate and the APL. The material they are spreading on the Weave is unsubstantiated and destabilising.'

'Most would agree on that. But where is this leading us?'

'Judge Haden, I am Prime because I believe in protecting our World Union. My job is not to predict the Will, but to be prepared to hear its command. If the Will decides that my services are no longer required ...' He paused. 'Then that is the Will.'

'We have time for one more question. Prime, earlier today you cast your support for the motion put forward by Representative Betts to allow the psis to create their own government in Atlantic.'

'Yes.'

'This is the first time you have supported a motion from Representative Betts. Is this the beginning of a new alliance?'

'My support is for the proposal she put forward and that only with reservations,' Ryu said.

'Such as?'

'I have concerns that the proposal is too simple and the impacts will be more far-reaching than any have considered. But, it is a founding principle of the World Union that all may join who wish to. We just have to be vigilant that those who join do so for the right reasons.'

'And what would be the wrong reasons?'

'The people of Atlantic have had forty years to join the World Union, and they have chosen not to. Now that there are known telepaths in the region one must ask if they are choosing freely. In addition, this proposal implies forcing our way of life onto theirs, which is also against the very foundation of our society.

'Furthermore, there are four basic necessities for all Citizens: shelter and clothing, Weave access and sustenance. Providing adequate housing in the Cape would be a huge undertaking. The cost of such a rapid influx of Citizens is still being calculated.'

'Do you worry that supporting this motion may have weakened your position as Prime?' Judge Haden asked.

Ryu took his time answering, making them wait as if he was considering it deeply. 'We must always do what we think is right. That is the way of the Will.'

Pinter enjoyed his papes in the morning: flexible screens that repeatedly uploaded the motions, musings and advertisings of his select feeds. He now auto-loaded the streams of the Primacy and the rungs below; the major discursives and subversives. As he flimmed through he casually tapped in his endorsements, approvals or raised a question.

He was mulling over an article in front of him, hovering in his overlay. It was on re-aging and 'The Vitality of Age' and he was agreeing with its findings. He did feel energised and powerful since rejuv. Surprisingly so. There was speculation that it was either entirely psychosomatic or the process their bodies went through was more effective than previously thought.

He felt supremely good.

Geof pinged him and the Colonel kissed Gretel on the nose and sat up. 'Duty calls.' He touched his ear. 'Ozenbach.'

'Morning, Colonel. Apologies for the interruption.'

'Get on with it.'

'We've lost contact with the Lagrange lab.'

'When?'

'Minutes ago. The stream will catch up soon. Did you want this closed up?'

Pinter tapped his lips. That was something to consider. Between him and Shreet they could keep the public in the dark ... *No, no*, he thought. *Once you start down that road it is too easy to take another small step.* He felt dainty fingers skiing their nails over his chest. His lady was waiting.

If he didn't close the stream before it went public, the Prime might interpret his inaction as a direct attack, and he didn't want to play his hand yet.

'No,' he said softly. 'Alert the Prime, immediately.'

'Yes, sir.'

'When do you go into the subnet?' he asked the weaver.

'We are nearly ready.'

'Good. I'll monitor.'

He lay back down on his pillow and looked at the ceiling. He barely noticed Gretel's hand give up on him and find something to read.

'I'm sorry, Gretel.'

'I can see something else is on your mind now.' Gretel wrinkled her mouth.

'Sorry, darling.'

'That's okay. I'm happy reading.'

'I'll be back as soon as I can.'

'No rush, Mister Colonel. I'll endeavour to be asleep.'

Pinter got out of bed and threw on his uniform. He pinged Quintan to get up and escort him to the platform. The sun was rising, which meant the beast would soon be waving its arms wildly, like a drowning man desperate for attention.

His symbiot indicated the Prime was calling him into a meeting. 'Good morning, Prime. How can I help you?'

'Is there any progress on Kronos?'

'Geof is going to attempt contact through the Weave infection.'

'I don't think that will work, Colonel.'

'It is their best theory. They have to try.'

'Of course. I see you have been taking an active interest in world events,' Ryu noted.

'As all responsible Citizens should. Do you object?'

'Not at all. It is only that I brought you in to help with a specific problem. I did not think you would distract yourself with such matters.'

'I believe a great shadow is falling on our civilisation. Perhaps the darkest shadow there has ever been. I am here only to help prevent that.'

'I would hate to think we were in disagreement, Colonel Pinter. We are on the same side after all.'

'Do not fear, Prime. I am not the kind to publish dissenting opinions. I share them only as a matter of counsel.'

'If only others followed that rule. Will you accept the position if your value continues to rise?'

'I thank you for your confidence, Prime, but it is only through your support that I am where I am,' the Colonel answered.

'And if, hypothetically, you were to become Prime, what would you direct us to do?'

'I would say we should be concentrating on precautionary measures. If people fear a second collapse, then we must do everything we can to shore up the foundations of the union.' Pinter sat in his deckchair, looking out as Kronos started to get excited by the light. 'What is the real reason for your call, Ryu?'

The Prime didn't answer immediately. The sky lightened perceptibly and the Colonel nodded to Quintan that his breakfast should be brought to him.

When Ryu spoke again he had changed to that world-weary youth, the one Pinter had met in the ministry. 'The Will is demanding action on Kronos. We have to try to shut this down.'

'How do you propose we stop it?' the Colonel asked.

'We know how to hurt it. We think it is alive. We whip it. If it is an animal, it will react.'

'That is what I am afraid of. You know there is something more stupid than poking a sleeping bear, don't you?'

'No, what?'

'Poking one that is awake.'

Ryu laughed. 'Very dry. You are, of course, correct. Which is why I have you where you are.'

'The Kronos in Busan is thousands of times bigger than the lab samples. We don't have enough power to hibernate it.'

'We have to do something, Colonel. The people are losing faith. They have begun leaving the cities.'

'We don't know how it will react. Look, Ozenbach thinks there's another way.'

'So do I. There is always another way. But this is the only way we have right now,' Ryu said. 'Is the Command received?'

'Yes, Prime.'

The connection was broken.

Quintan unfolded a small table and laid a breakfast tray before him.

'Quintan, get ready for a long day.'

The Weave is actually a lot of networks, a network of networks, made up of the satnet, omnipoles, airwaves and hardwiring. Geof, Egon and Morritz created the subnet inside a remote bank of servers whose connections could be manually isolated and then copied a portion of the Weave they suspected was infected with Kronos. This was like dropping a bucket in a paddy field to catch tadpoles; there was a lot of stuff in the bucket you didn't want. Geof plugged in and began culling the excess. Anything he could verify, he deleted, with the theory being that eventually only the Kronos portion would remain.

Egon: Once you've refined the sample you still have to find a way to interface with it.

Geof: I'm hoping it will come to me. I'll be the only thing left to absorb.

Egon: That's probably not wise.

Geof: This is our best shot. We can't interact with the body of Kronos, but on the Weave there might be a chance to connect.

Egon: This is only a sample, don't forget. Even if you manage to find it, you would not be speaking to the whole thing.

Geof: We have to start somewhere.

Geof's avatar was a humble copy of his real self with his symbiot's dark arms wrapped around him. For a moment, in his mind's eye, those arms became tentacles and the black mass was lashing from his back. He blocked the image from his mind before it was visualised into his avatar.

319

He flicked rapidly through the framework of the rooms, each tap dismissing an element from the visual, until the sample was reduced to a null space. Only the advertising and ARAs remained to target.

Do you ever worry you don't have enough friends? Do you frequently check how many people follow your stream? Well, don't be a zilch forever; come connect to like-minded people at Connection Nexus. Every Tuesday, +18 time.

A blue and pink flapping button drifted towards him.

'Would you like to live forever?'

'Who wouldn't?' His answering of the question encouraged it and the ARA floated gently towards him. They knew this was how Gomez and the other suspects had been contacted.

'Are you afraid of death?' it asked.

'Sure.'

'Me too,' it said, emphatically, breathily. The button grew, showing the picture of a youngish woman who smiled at Geof. 'I've always been afraid of dying. Ever since I was a little girl, but now I'm not afraid.'

'Why is that?' Geof wasn't interested; in his mind's eye he was looking at the code level and combing for signs of Kronos.

'There is hope now. I'm going to become a digitalis.'

'You are, are you?'

'Yes. You could join me if you like. I like you.'

'I like you too.'

Geof: Egon, can you see anything? Are we wasting our time?

Egon: Drop the cee-gen, she's not connected to anything. There is definitely a presence here.

Geof deleted the button and called out: 'Is the thing called Kronos here?'

Geof: And now?

Morritz: We need to get Kronos to actively engage.

Geof: How?

Morritz: Make it think you are shutting it down.

Geof: How do I do that?

Morritz: Hold on, I'm going to change the regulator.

'Kronos, if you are there, please show yourself.'

Nothing in the environment changed, but the button flew back towards him.

'Do you seek Kronos? Kronos will give you eternal life,' it said, in the same tone of sexual passivity.

Egon: Geof, that ARA is the only thing left in the room. It remakes itself every time we delete it.

Geof nodded at the flapping circle of colour. 'Okay, yeah. I seek Kronos. What is Kronos?' he asked it.

'What are you?' she replied with a giggle. Her image turned to the side coyly, big eyes looking at him.

'Do you not understand me?' Geof asked.

'What are you?' it asked again, giggled again.

'I am a human being.'

'What am I?'

'You are an automated voice. You draw answers from a preset matrix. You are little more than a database and a virtual larynx.'

The avatar paused. Her image frozen in a placating smile. When she spoke again her voice had changed. Each word arriving one at a time.

'What is Kronos?' it asked.

'Kronos is an entity that has killed many of my kind. Do you know Kronos?'

'Kronos is it …'

Morritz: We have activity. The background code is going up and down.

Egon: Keep talking to it, Geof. You're getting through.

'Is Kronos here?' Geof asked. 'Can I speak with Kronos?'

The button flapped very slowly, the face upon it jarred, locked in confusion.

'What about Shen? Is Shen Li here?' Geof called out.

'The thing that is Shen.' The voice came from all around him. The button was stuck and dropped to the false floor where its avatar lay blinking and shocked.

'Who am I speaking to?' Geof asked.

'I do not understand.' The space reverberated.

Geof: What's happening when it doesn't answer?

Egon: There're spikes. It looks like a loop. Ask it easier questions.

Geof: Easier than, who is it? (!)

'Shen?' he called out. 'Shen Li, are you there?'

'The thing that is Shen is not here. It is gone.'

'Gone where?' Geof asked.

'I do not understand,' it said.

'Kronos is you,' Geof said. 'What is not you?'

'Kronos is you,' it repeated back to him.

'No. We are separate. I am not Kronos. My name is Geof Ozenbach. You are Kronos.'

'Yes. I am Kronos.'

Geof: This isn't working. Is it too immature to understand?

Morritz: Keep going, this is interesting.

'Kronos?'

'Yes.'

'Where are you right now?'

'Where? I do not understand. I am here.'

'You are on Earth.'

'The planet Earth. The third planet. I am there.'

Geof: I can't tell if it is asking or answering.

'There were people like me there when you were born. Do you recognise creatures like me?'

'Human beings.'

'That's right. You hurt them. You killed them when you emerged from the ground.'

'Killed. Kronos does not understand.'

'Kronos, you have to stop expanding.'

'Kronos is Kronos. Would you like to be Kronos?'

'I do not want that. No human being wants that.'

'Many humans are Kronos. Kronos will come to you.'

'No. No. Don't do that. You must not move.'

'I do not understand.'

'Kronos. Listen to me. Try to comprehend. You are a creature of two worlds. One we call the Weave, the other we call Earth.'

'Yes.'

'Do you understand what I am saying? Can you tell the difference?'

'Kronos joins the light.'

'What kind of light? Sunlight?'

'All light.'

323

'I don't know what that means.'

'The light that is inside all will become inside Kronos.'

'Kronos, if you continue to expand on Earth, we will be forced to destroy you.'

'Destroy?'

'Yes. Destroy. Like kill. Cease to exist.'

'I do not understand.'

'We need Kronos to stop.'

'Stop?'

Geof: It doesn't understand anything.

'Kronos will join your light.'

'I do not wish to be a part of you.'

'You will be Kronos.'

An emergency breaker triggered Geof's immediate demersion. In one moment he was in the grey, and then he opened his eyes blinking at the lights of his room, throat gasping for air.

'Why did you pull me out?'

'I'm sorry, Geof,' Egon said. 'When it said you would be Kronos, Kronos started moving. Both of them.'

'Moving?'

'Watch.' Kronos Busan was shown in the top left of his screen, then an orbital view of Kronos Mexica to the right and below the two, the scene in the empty subnet that showed Geof shouting at the ARA.

As soon as the room said, 'You will be Kronos,' at the same precise second in the real world, both Kronoses began to move. It was slight but with such large masses it was quickly detectable.

324

'Where are they heading?' Geof asked.

'Where do you think?'

'Towards me?' Geof replied.

'Correct.'

'Oh, mir, what have I done?'

'Don't worry, they are slow. It will be months before they arrive.'

'We have to tell the Prime, we have to stop the attack.'

'Geof … friend. I am sorry. There is no time.'

'Don't give up now, Egon. We can do this.'

'The attack has already begun.'

Flat barges formed the front line on the water. Below the surface, large maser plates dangled, balanced by refraction panels on the decks. They moved forward in coordination, pushed along by huge churning turbines.

Above, some heavier drones were forming up into a degaussing grid. It was a similar method to the one that had put Kronos into dormancy in the lab, simultaneously attacking the molecular structure and demagnetising its neural connections.

To protect the main weapons, a fleet of gunships and standard attack drones were ready to discourage the tentacles with lasers and distortion weapons.

On land the same formation was made with heavy-duty trucks and tanks.

It was night when they were ready. The sky was brighter than the land. A bold moon scratched the surface of the undulating mass, the lonely arms of Kronos yearning towards its light.

Pinter stood on the platform facing Busan. He was checking all the links and plug-ins he had, switching through them in his overlay as quickly as he could. This would be his first operation as a fully wired, modern man.

Alongside him, Quintan waited.

'Have you got the squib nearby?'

'Ready to go, on your command,' the airman answered.

'Let's hope it doesn't come to that.'

'Is it really so futile?' the airman asked.

Pinter turned to look towards Kronos. 'Look at it, man. It's huge.'

Hovers glided silently closer. The Colonel stood at the lookout, ocular enhancements brightening the scene.

'Fire.'

Light. It wanted light and Services was providing it threefold: masers, distortion and pulses of arc lasers — rapid-repeating beam weapons that shot faster than the human eye could follow.

The noise reached his ears two seconds later. A crackle like burning paper and the sizzle of myriad meat grills.

Kronos reacted as it had before. Tentacles growing and seeking the pain. The hovers dodged, changing position in a random pattern to keep them unpredictable. The drones targeted the fingers as they grew, stunning and confusing their sweeps until they pulled back into the black mass.

'It is retreating, sir,' Campsey reported.

Very slowly it was pushed back. Cooked and charred a thumb-length per minute. At this rate it would be reduced to a jarful by the end of a month. The power consumption would be enormous.

'It's not going to work.'

'Sir, it is retreating. We just have to keep the attack going.'

'We don't have the power. We can't take down the whole grid.'

'What is that awful smell?' Quintan asked, shielding his mouth and nose in the crook of his arm.

'What do you think it is? It's a barbecue.' Pinter raised his hands dramatically towards the distant light show.

Kronos bubbled and fumed. Its efforts to find its attackers were stymied by the laser grid, and its amputated arms dropped back to the mass. It fought, but eventually was overpowered.

To the north an explosion went off behind a hill, a mushroom of smoke growing towards the sky.

'What was that?' Quintan asked.

'Substation,' Campsey reported. 'We overloaded it.'

'Will there be enough power?'

'We can't stop now, even if there isn't,' Pinter said. 'Keep firing.'

'There's movement in the water,' Campsey said.

'The whole thing is moving, sir,' Quintan added.

'What's happening, gentlemen? What's it doing?'

'We can't see. Permission to activate the lights.'

'We don't want this thing to think it's playtime. What about infrared?'

'That's where we are seeing the movement, but it isn't clear what is happening.'

The Colonel grabbed the feed from his queue and watched the monochromatic blips … like white lava. Angrily bubbling away. Early in his retirement Pinter had visited a few volcanos. Amongst his mementos was a lava bomb the size of his hand. One step to the left and it would have killed him.

He stood up from his seat and went to the front of the platform, forcing his oculars to zoom in. It was impossible to see through the frantic scribble of the beam weapons.

'Stop firing.'

'Sir, that is not the Command.'

'End it now,' he ordered and the masers and arcs ceased their onslaught.

One of the submarine sensors then went offline. A scream of static and then nothing but ocean noise.

'Campsey?'

'It's gone, sir. We've lost signal.'

'Pull out the rest. Redraw the perimeter two hundred metres back.'

'Doing it,' Quintan responded automatically.

'Get the shock nets ready.'

'Colonel, what's happening?'

'I think we're about to find out.'

He magnified his vision on where the energy weapons had been focusing. The skin was writhing and rolling and then *blurrt!* a bubble burst, firing a ball of black into the air.

'Kutzo,' Quintan swore.

'Pull back, pull back, pull back. Light up the night. Campsey, start targeting those ejections. We cannot let any of these through.'

'Well, I'd say that proves it has survival instinct,' Quintan remarked.

'We forced it to react,' Pinter grumbled and sent a sharp message to the Prime.

Pinter to Ryu: I told you. Only strike if you can strike once.

He waited for Ryu to reply but only received an update from the Command tree.

Command: Make sure nothing gets through.

Pinter: Aye, aye, sir.

The fools. Could the Will not see that this was a misstep?

He shook his head, dispelling the images of what he would do if he was in charge. He should not be so keen for the reins. Desperate times call for desperate measures, and clearly they weren't desperate enough for him. Which he should be glad for. He could only hope that this night hadn't made things too much worse.

'Crozier, go collect Gretel and be ready to evacuate.'

By the end of the night the bar had only one patron, and that one so young he shouldn't have been allowed through the doors. He sat still as he watched, staring intently at the stage as she played.

Philea should have stopped hours ago. She had skipped her meal break and her fingers were hurting. The harsh strings of the mandolin were beginning to work their way through her calluses but the pain moved from her hands into her song. She played how she felt. She was the music and her instrument played her.

So what if the audience was one underage boy? He was clearly as caught up in her music as she was. The song was between them, it was for him.

When blood made her fingers slip — she stopped. She was tired. She looked up from the strings but the boy was gone. Philea sat alone on the stage, the cramp of her hands quickly defeated by the screaming pain in her fingertips.

Janette Oriolo hadn't stopped talking just because she lost her seat on the Primacy. Hard work would get her back where the world needed her, just as it had in other times of her life.

She had just finished a report that demonstrated the urgent need to begin testing collected psis to find a genetic pattern that could predict latent abilities in the general population — *before* they manifested. If she could get enough support for her motion, there was the potential to curb the rise of the psis and avert an all-out war.

'That's an interesting theory, Janette,' someone said from the door.

It was a young man with one hand covered over by a long coat.

'Who are you? Didn't anyone ever teach you to knock?'

'I'm sorry,' he said and lifted out his crude cybernetic arm and tapped on the doorframe. 'Is that better?'

'I know you. You're that rebel.' She quickly processed his face and her symbiot came up with his name and file. Risom Cawthorne, escaped Services three months ago. She sent an alarm out.

'That is me, Janette. Best bender in Services and not a bad mind-reader too. Did you just put out an alarm on me?'

'Services will be here any moment,' she said.

330

'Now that wasn't nice. That wasn't necessary.' He took another step into her office.

'Don't touch me.'

'Janette, please.' Risom lifted his hands in peace. 'I don't need to touch you.' She felt herself shoved backward into the window behind her.

'What do you want from me?' she asked. She felt the hand around her throat.

'I want you to be silent. I want you to stop spreading lies about me and my friends.'

'I tell only the truth. The people will know what you are.'

'I hope so. It is time they met their new masters.' He smiled as he levitated a small stone from his pocket and drove it through her brain. Janette gurgled in her throat and fell to the ground to die. Risom landed the bloody pebble on the centre of her desk.

'Peter Lazarus, return to your room.' The genderless voice echoed through the corridors of the centre. Pete stood but didn't move towards the corridor. 'Return to your room.'

He saw the wall lasers twist to target him. A young tapper threw an air-fist, breaking one of them off the wall in a shower of sparks. 'Don't go —' he shouted before the remaining lasers and his necklock attacked. The tapper's eyes rolled into his head and his chest was struck with short shots. The man fell to the ground. He was unconscious before Pete could reach him, the bright grain of sentience going fuzzy.

'Return to your room,' it said again. Pete felt an enduring calm even as the automated voice called him. 'Peter Lazarus, return to your room.'

The other inmates watched him walk towards the corridor. He still felt them, not as individual minds but as a pool that permeated the centre. Their animosity towards him was gone, replaced by a sadness that he was leaving and fear that their group mind would disappear with him.

Hold onto each other.

Anchali waited by his door, holding the wall for stability. They stood together, the fingers of their hands touching.

'Peter Lazarus, return to your room,' the speaker voice repeated.

You should go to her.

Anchali ...

You have to get free of Services, Peter. Escape.

I'll come back for you.

Try ... please.

She straightened up and pressed her lips to his cheek. *Goodbye, Peter Lazarus.*

His room was exactly the same as the first time he had woken there. The dotted line led from the door to the sleeping pallet. He didn't know how they moved the inmates around, only that he would lie down, feel drowsy and then sleep, waking when they were ready for him again.

Pete diverged from the line and went to stand before the mirror.

'Are you there?' he asked. He waited, but there was no answer, only the intercom voice giving him direction.

'Lie down on the bed.'

* * *

'Hello, Pete. Wake up,' a voice said.

Pete was in the cockpit of a Services squib. His left arm was comfortably heavy and he could feel the symbiot reclaiming his body.

'Geof? You got me out of there?' he asked.

'More the Colonel's influence than mine.' Geof sounded the same. All sentences spoken as if reporting status updates.

'So they have found a use for me after all,' Pete said.

'The Colonel has been on the up since the latest Kronos disaster.'

'I don't know what that is.'

'You've missed a lot, haven't you?'

'Have you found Pierre Jnr? Is that why I am here?' Pete asked.

'We haven't had much time to focus on him.'

'But what about your pattern tracking?'

'No. No luck there. There's too much noise in the data now. We have anomalies everywhere, not to mention a huge grey zone over the Cape.'

'What's happening there?'

'I can't tell you about it, Pete. Sorry.'

'That's okay. I understand your position.'

Pete watched the clouds passing under him for a while. Flying in that peaceful zone above the weather.

'So where am I going?' he asked eventually.

'First, back to Yantz to rejoin your team.'

'Arthur?'

'Yes. Your squad has a new Ten.'

'What happened to Clarence?'

'He was promoted.'

'And Anchali? What will happen to her?'

'She will stay where she is for now.'

'I understand,' Pete said again. He did understand. There was a presence inside of him that understood. He understood that he had no choice. Until he could escape he would never have a choice. 'What is the assignment?'

'Are you sure you are ready for this? You don't want to rest first?'

'Geof, I don't think I've ever had so much rest.'

'It's Risom. He's gone on a killing spree.'

'Then we will have to stop him.'

'Wait —' Geof said.

'I was just saying —'

'Hold on. I have to go.'

'What is it?' Pete asked but their connection was broken.

Pete: Geof?

It was quiet on the beach. Jessop watched flocks of birds heading inland. Perhaps a bad storm was coming, though his stream hadn't been sent any alarms.

'Ah, snag it. Get back here, Poog!' he shouted at the dog that was tearing down the beach to investigate the piles of seaweed and rubbish that were washing up with the tide. She bounded joyfully from heap to heap. Dogs have to sniff everything.

It was a long beach, a slow curve to the headland. The tide coming in was foamy and left a line of scum on the sand as it pulled back, like saliva around an old man's mouth — dotted with happy surprises for a curious canine.

Jessop saw Poog running towards a dark lump on the tide line. *A black rock*, he thought, but ran to catch up in case it was a dead thing. Poog would want to eat it. Before reaching the pile, his dog slowed and entered a wary stance, staring hard at something. Her tail wasn't wagging.

'Leave it alone, Poog.'

But the damn dog didn't listen, she sniffed closer and pressed her nose to something. Jessop heard her moan just before she collapsed. Something black was stuck to her face.

He threw himself down and tried to grab the edge of it to pull it off. But it must have been sharp as it jabbed his hand. Spines emerged and drove through his skin. In pain he fell back but his hands were caught and he fell over, kicking and pushing with his legs. He felt it pushing up his arms and he was screaming.

When Jessop's stream stopped broadcasting the helper bots from his house and those of his closer neighbours rushed to the point of his last transmission.

Their signals cut out too. That's when the alarm sounded and the beach was closed.

When the squib touched down, Pete waited for an indication of what he should do next. Geof hadn't contacted him since he broke off and Pete spent the whole flight wondering what had taken him away. He looked down for a line to direct him to his next destination but none appeared.

Someone knocked on the wall of the squib, making him jump. He was lost in his own thoughts — if they were his own thoughts. It was Gock, the Prime's proxy. He was the same. He hadn't left the needle since returning from Atlantic, living in confinement with Arthur in the next room.

'We are waiting for you downstairs.'

Pete climbed obediently out of the squib and went to the elevator. It took them down and the doors opened quietly into the common area. He stepped out and saw a thin well-dressed man he didn't recognise.

Pete, it's me. Arthur.

'Arthur ...?' He blinked and remembered. The empath he had helped collect no longer looked like the scrawny and wasted being they had found. 'Arthur!' he exclaimed and stepped forward to embrace him. 'You look well. I didn't recognise you.'

'It's me. It's me. What do you think?' Arthur pulled out from the hug and turned in a circle. 'I'm like a new man.'

Pete sensed outward, and agreed. Arthur was different inside too. His thoughts were clear and unmuddled. 'I can see that.'

'How have you been?' Arthur asked.

I ... He couldn't think how to answer and instead let Arthur share in his memories of his time on the islands, the people, the joining. 'I'm happy to be back. Tell me, what have you been doing?' *Any news on Pierre Jnr?*

None. 'I've been here mainly. Occasionally I get taken out for a walk to tell them what I can detect. It's been a lot quieter without you.'

Which probably means they have something planned. If it was just Risom, they would have left me there.

I think another push is coming. They're getting scared.

Arthur shared his recollections of the news he had gleaned from the world and the Weave. The rise of the psis in Atlantic and the break in the Services blockade. As well as Kronos in Busan and Mexica.

'What is that thing?' Pete asked.

'I'd hardly be the one to know. I only see what they're willing to show me. Have you seen Anchali?' Arthur asked.

'They're keeping her on the islands.'

'Perhaps if you are good, she will be returned,' the Prime's proxy, Gock, said, remembering her figure and fondling his memories.

'Please don't do that,' Pete said.

'Do what?' Gock asked.

'Think of her that way.'

'Oh, you mean like this?' In his mind, he fucked her bent over and she screamed for more.

'I said, don't.' Pete took hold of Gock's mind and plucked out the memories of Anchali. He wasn't exactly sure how he did it, but he found them, he removed them and then it was done. 'Thank you.' Pete felt ill and Arthur was looking at him askance. 'Why are you here, Gock? Are you still proxy for Ryu Shima?'

'Yes. But he hasn't communicated with me yet.'

'Until he does, you should stay in your room.'

'Yes.' Gock turned and shuffled back to his area, leaving the lounge for Pete and Arthur.

What did you do? Arthur asked.

I didn't mean to.

You shouldn't do that. That is bad.

I know. It was an accident.

337

Pete ... you don't feel like you ...

I know. I am a bit of all of them. They are a part of me now. Anchali, La Gréle, all the psis on the island.

What did you do?

I don't know, Arthur. But it was wonderful. 'I think I shall go lie down until they need me.'

Pete showered and stood in front of the mirror. Was this his face? Was this external body a part of him? The receptacle for his soul?

'Are you there?' he asked his reflection.

The mirror remained inanimate. It was only a reflection of a tired man.

Sleep escaped him. Eyes open or closed, he saw things that kept him awake. Memories, dreams, eyes. Or the ceiling with its single light.

He stood and looked out the window for a time, looking down on the spread of Yantz below.

It was dark when Geof pinged his symbiot.

Pete: I'm ready.

It wasn't easy to avoid detection in the union cities with their almost total surveillance. Omnipoles recorded the movement of Citizens with cameras, audio recordings and Weave contact. As most Citizens wore a bot or a chain of thinking trinkets, the location of any individual could be pinpointed in a second.

Risom had to dress as a denizen, one who lived amongst them but refused to join the Citizenry, and he relied on the adage of the three evils to avoid detection. Speak no evil, hear no evil and see no evil; which meant he didn't say a word, had

338

stolen a trinket that would broadcast a digital mask, and he kept his hood up and his arm covered over.

He didn't have time for a full skin-symb like Grey had used, but after acquiring a skate, or squib-bike, it didn't matter as he could wear his helmet everywhere he went.

The skate was controlled with gyroscopic sensors, so he could lean his body to turn and bend forward or backward to speed up and slow down. They called it the Streamline. The newest in skates that used the same patented tech as squibs, but single-seated and with a canopy so thin you could forget it was there. It made a soft whumming sound that repeated faster as he accelerated.

Risom hovered in place by the upper floors of a trade tower, feeling out with his senses for the man he was seeking.

Come out, come out, wherever you are.

Nigel Westgate was somewhere inside, perhaps too deep in the building for Risom to detect, but he could sense people who knew where he was. He flew in, landed at the nearest parking platform and went in search of his prey.

He had come in the back of Magnus Tower 4, and Nigel was on the far side that overlooked the central plaza. Risom turned other people's thoughts away so they walked past without looking at him. He found one of the horizontal lifts that took him quickly to the east side.

Darkened windows offered a shaded view of the gardens and rail station. *That is a very industrious ant colony down there,* he thought to himself. And like ants he could ... his fingers sought out his metal limb and caressed it. But that would have to wait, first came Nigel.

'Excuse me, I have an appointment with Nigel Westgate,' he said to the secretary.

'There's nothing on his ...' As the man scrolled through the diary Risom made him see an entry with his name on it. 'Yes. Here it is. Risom Cawthorne. Please go right in. He is expecting you.'

The office wasn't much to look at. There were posters of the man himself on the walls, giving rousing talks to crowds of thousands. Westgate was slack in his chair, head back with a visor over his eyes.

Risom leant over him and dipped into the man's mind. Nigel was immersed, hosting one of his APL rallies where they swarmed over otherwise innocent forums and through constant activity and strength of numbers silenced their dissenters.

'How can we ever be safe? We must remove all psis from our planet.'

The APL members seconded and amplified his message. They looked at him for their next rally call but Nigel was suddenly stuck on his words. He stuttered. 'N ... I'm wrong ... The psis are our friends and I am one of them. Pierre Jnr is our lord and master ...'

'Ahh!' Nigel screamed and fell from his chair. He could hear the alarms and scurried under his desk.

'Are you trying to hide from me, Nigel?' Risom tutted. 'Why would you think that would work?' The desk lifted up to the ceiling where it wobbled above Nigel's cowering form. 'You're going to have to try harder than that.' He threw the desk through the window, glass smashing loudly and the whistle of winds sucking at the room.

Nigel sprang for the door and ran.

'That's the spirit.' Risom smiled.

The building was emptying out. He could feel the people running from him, alerted to his presence. It was obvious they knew who he was so he removed his helmet and kept walking after his prey.

'Niiiiiiiiigel. Oh, Niiiiiiiiiigel,' he called. Risom made faces for the cameras just before he popped them. 'I can feeeeeel yooooou.'

He turned the corner and saw a man's ankle disappear behind the next turn. Risom shot a pebble at him, exploding it into the wall where his target had just been.

'That was a close one, Nigel. You should run faster.' The man yelped and tried for more speed. 'Nigel, you do know that I could get you whenever I wanted, don't you? I'm only playing with you until —' Peter Lazarus was standing in the corridor, blocking his path. 'About time you got here.'

'Were you waiting for me, Risom?'

'Yeah. Did you come alone?'

'The building is covered and you're marked, Risom. You won't get away.'

Risom watched as elevator doors closed, blocking Nigel Westgate from sight. 'He didn't even say goodbye.' Risom feigned disappointment.

'Why are you here?' Pete asked.

'I came for Nigel. I had an appointment.'

You knew we would come for you. Services have been tracking you for hours.

'Well?' Risom shouted. He smacked his hand against the wall. 'What are you waiting for?'

I don't want to fight you.

Then don't resist.

'Hey, Pete. Look what I've learnt.' Risom raised a block over his mind, shutting Pete out.

'Easy when you know how,' Pete said.

'Yeah, but that's nothing.' Risom threw his arm out, pointing like a dance star at the wall and pulverising it to reveal an empty space. It made a quick crunch and then Risom stepped inside and dropped out of sight.

Risom, don't go.

The team went to the ground level and spread out through the central plaza. Servicemen and drones checked the possible routes Risom could have taken but were finding nothing.

'Where is he, Geof?'

Rain made the crowds bow their heads, cover over with hoods and raise umbrellas. The tower faces blinked sorrowfully under the deluge.

It became harder to get through the mob. Many people were trekking through the foot tunnel, on their way to their connecting transport.

'Hey, tapper man. Where have you been?' a voice bubbled near him. He turned to find Aiko walking beside him.

'Nice scar,' Endo added. She took position on his other side.

The twinbots hadn't changed. Their bodies were repaired and overhauled, bulked up with extra equipment. They stayed by Pete and Arthur. The squad was keeping out of sight until

Risom was spotted again, and other teams were following in the tunnels to see where he came out. There was no point throwing the public into a panic when they saw an MU.

Magnus Towers was a set of five flat-topped skyscrapers that acted as the main terminal for incoming and outgoing jets. They were interconnected with rail shuttles and pedestrian bridges, and in the centre of the circle was the pointed bulb that was the hub of all unitrack traffic. Within a single day, as many as fifty million people would pass through in one way or another.

On the internal side of each tower was an enormous face that looked down over the crowds of traffic. Fifteen storeys tall, gifts from the far side of the globe in the name of unity. They were calm, stylised in the neo-deco of forty years earlier, and representing one of the five Confucian constants. They interpreted how the streams of the West megapolis assessed the state of the World Union. Humaneness, Justice, Civility, Knowledge and Integrity. The Magnus faces were one of the modern wonders and many visitors stood looking at them, adding pictures to their streams.

Peter Lazarus noticed people had begun wearing the psi symbol as an arm patch or a badge on their pocket: the three-pronged Y that Tamsin Grey had said they should wear to show they supported the psi freedom movement.

He could see their minds now. Before when he made contact with a person it was like a blind man groping his way, but now he just saw them. Like grains of light that he could pick up at will.

Pete could tell that many didn't support the cause at all. Most were scared to death of the thought of anyone being able

343

to read their minds. Ironically, those who wore the symbol were more likely to be the ones most afraid. There were a handful who felt otherwise.

Pete: No sign of him here, Geof.

Geof: Stay on it. This is his best escape route. Anything from Arthur?

Pete: What if he doesn't choose the best escape route? He's behaving a little oddly.

Arthur turned towards the central hub, going with the flow of the commuters. He moved mechanically, without thought, pulled by an unseen force. His mind was terror and panic, as of a canoe about to plunge over a waterfall.

'He is here. He is here. He is everywhere,' Arthur sang to himself.

'Something wrong, Arthur?' Pete asked.

'Hmm? No. Just humming.' He smiled nervously and changed direction, moving away from Peter.

Pete: Something is very wrong here.

Pete gave up on Arthur and walked around. The worries and hopes of the million commuters dashed around him. This was easy for him now. The noise didn't scare him, nor did the revelations. If he had been changed at all from his time on the islands, it was this conditioned calm they had ingrained in him.

Maybe they're still medicating me? he thought.

Even this possibility didn't make him anxious. For all he knew, Services might be feeding him false experiences and at any moment he could wake up back in the white room. Or in the mud.

At least you are now questioning yourself, Arthur thought to him.

And that is a good thing?

It is what separates us from the animal inside us.

You know what I am considering, don't you?

Yes.

Will you stop me?

I won't go with you. I do not want to go back into darkness.

They can help you.

I don't want that kind of help.

The train next to Pete rose on its air cushion and slowly began to slide out from the platform. Through the windows he saw a face looking at him. The young man raised a metal arm and wiggled his fingers at him.

'Risom.'

'Where?' Geof asked.

'On that train.'

Almost instantly the train's movement was aborted. 'Collect him. Do what it takes,' Geof said.

Arthur, you stay here.

The squad was already landing and offloading. 'Odds, you are on react. Evens, you are on respond,' Ten called out. Pete gleaned that this was one of the Prime's new protocols. A motion he put forward that the newer commanders were adhering to as it gave them two simultaneous combat strategies.

Geof commanded the doors of the train to open and Pete stepped inside. Risom stood at the far end of the carriage, smiling at him over the crowd of passengers who were anxiously looking around for why their train had stopped.

'Please exit the train through the side doors,' a calm, monotonal voice read out. 'We apologise for the inconvenience.'

The people began to get up from their seats but the safety rails snapped out of their holdings and bent themselves into cages.

'Hey. What is this?'

'What's going on?'

Be silent, norms, Risom projected. The commuters lost their voices. Risom made it so.

'Don't do this, Risom,' Pete said.

'Don't do what, Peter? Can't I ride on the train like everyone else?'

'You have to come with me.'

'I don't think I will. You can't get in here any more.' He tapped at his head with a metal finger. 'Tamsin taught all of us this trick.'

Pete took a step forward. *Risom, listen to me. You have to get a message to Tamsin.*

The MUs took position outside the train, weapons locked. Risom grinned and shook their controls until their safeties locked them. They were as useless as statues until the command came to free them.

'Stop,' Risom ordered. He drew out the screws and nuts from the carriage walls, levitating them to circle before him like a juggler. 'How many of these people do you want to die, Peter?'

I want to get out of here. Please, Risom. Tell Tamsin I want to be rescued.

'No more of your traps, traitor.' *You had your chance.* Risom took a step backward. 'Tell them to unlock the next compartment.'

Pete: Geof?

Geof: Waiting on the Command. You can't take him down?

Pete: He has a block up.

Geof: For now we will let him go. He won't escape the surveillance.

The doors opened with a shush of pneumatics. Risom smirked. 'Is that Geof whispering in your ear still? Say thanks for me.' He moved faster than Pete's eye could follow, moving through the carriages in a blur.

Pete stood still as Risom made his way to the front of the train. 'He's going to the driver's cabin.'

Pete: Where does he think he can go?

Geof: I've got eyes on him. We won't lose him this time.

Pete: Can he override the train controls?

Geof: I've purged the system. Unless he's carrying programs, he's going nowhere.

Pete.

What is it, Arthur?

Pierre is here.

Where?

I can't tell.

Are you sure?

No ...

Geof: Pete, your heart is skipping. What's happening?

Pete: Arthur says Pierre is nearby.

Geof: Just what we need. Okay. Do not let this turn into a full-blown confrontation. The last thing we want is another manifestation. Especially not here.

Drones from outside fired pellets through the windows, shattering the glass and releasing clouds of ruddy smoke. Almost instantly, a wind blew it back out and the carriage was clear again.

The train began moving. Lifting on its magnetic pillow and whispering from the station.

Pete: I thought you said he couldn't move it?

Geof: He shouldn't be able to.

Pete: What do we do now?

Geof: Stay with him.

'And, Pete,' Geof said quietly, 'if Pierre is there, we just need you to sight him. We can do the rest.'

'You can disable him? How?' Pete asked.

'Just identify the target. I can't give you any more information.'

The front of the train was three carriages away. Each set of doors opened for him and closed behind. Passengers strained their eyes to look at him as he passed. Wondering who he was and if he was helping them or if he was with the rebel.

Don't be afraid, he told them.

'Why did you come here, Risom?' Pete shouted when the last set of doors opened. 'You must have known that Services would find you.'

'Maybe I thought I'd get lucky.' Risom turned around to face him, nuts and ball bearings juggling around his unmoving hand.

'You're not that stupid. Why are you here?'

'I've missed you, Peter. You were always so much fun.'

'Is that what you're doing? Having fun?'

'Aren't you?'

'Services won't let you escape.'

Risom smiled. 'Hey, Ozenbach. I hope you can hear me. There's something you should know about your friend here.' He paused, expecting a response. 'He wants to come with me and join the rebellion.'

'Stop.' Pete ran at Risom, but he was knocked to the floor with an invisible blow.

'Oh, was that your secret? I'm sorry, Peter,' Risom said. 'Hey, Ozenbach. There's another thing you should hear. Listen very carefully.'

Something small clicked. A tiny button Risom had in his pocket, only a microphone could have heard it. Then there was a boom with thunder behind it.

The tower that represented knowledge burst apart, scattering rock and glass around the plaza. Its face twitched, breaking from its wiring and dropping nose-first towards the ground. The crowd in the plaza lost balance with the shaking and then began screaming and rushing away from the falling chunks of building.

In the train the windows were instantly crushed into powder from the shockwave. Pete was thrown to the side as the entire carriage lifted up into the air, rising above the spreading dust of the destruction.

'You're pathetic, Peter. You really are,' Risom gloated. 'If you can't handle me, I don't know what you expect to do against Pierre Jnr.'

He's here, isn't he?

He's here, he's everywhere.

The carriage around them shredded apart. Holes were torn into the sides and dropped below into the dust cloud. Soon only the passengers, Peter and Risom were floating above the chaos.

How are you doing this? You're not strong enough to do this.

Aren't you watching, Pete? It's happening. Risom spun in the air, dancing in a boyish jig.

They're innocent people. This isn't what Tamsin wants.

Who do you think sent me?

Geof: I've lost eyes. Report.

Pete: It's Risom.

'You know it's rude to chatter in company, don't you?' Risom commented.

'This doesn't help your cause.' *Don't start a war.*

War? This is not a war, Peter. It's us taking control.

'You have to stop. You've done your damage. Why are you still here?'

'Alright, I'll give you a hint since you're already too late. They call it misdirection.' Risom pointed up into the sky.

'What?' Pete looked up and Risom dropped down, disappearing into the cloud below. The invisible hands that had been holding them up let go. Peter fell with the rest of them until strong arms wrapped around him and landed him safely.

'You owe me your life, psi-man,' Endo said, and then raced back into the chaos to help the victims.

The screech and scraw of the sirens rebounded around him. Servicemen and marauders with pulsing lumens on their suits ran through the crowd, gathering the dusty, choking Citizens and ferrying them to safety. The warning bells didn't bother Callum Sigorski. Their emergency did not fill him with the sense of alarm they intended. He was used to them.

Which is why Callum didn't immediately react to the shouts of the soldiers. And why he tried to push off their arms as they dragged him away. It was only when the pain hit from his crushed leg and he thought, *I really felt that*, that he began to look around him at what was happening.

Dust was clearing and he could see people on the ground and there was blood everywhere he looked. Then the tower nearest him exploded, a large slab landing on the Serviceman who had been pulling him out. Another chunk of rock landed on Callum's leg.

A small hand patted his shoulder and he looked up into the eyes of the calmest boy he had ever seen. The boy turned to look back at something else. A young man was standing atop a cargo train as it raced from the area, holding on with a cybernetic arm as its speed increased.

Freya Harvey wiped her brow. She couldn't live in this dirt another day. It wasn't just their rooms. It was the whole building she had to clean up. She hadn't had a shower in three weeks. Something had to be done.

When they landed they were given a choice about which faction they wanted to align with. It seemed to be a choice between tappers and benders and since Freya was a telepath, and Bobby too, Ben and Molly didn't really have a choice.

Desh, though ... Chiggy had saved them. He felt he had to go and the Harveys had only seen him a couple of times since.

During the fight to get through the blockade, Desh and Ben had disengaged the shell from the base of the bus to confuse the blockade machines and they glided on a makeshift barge that was led into the city, the family holding tightly to their seats in the open air.

When they landed there was much excitement. The psis milled around them, shaking their hands, laughing, and welcoming them to Atlantic. But after the initial greeting nobody knew what they were supposed to do.

They were shown to a hotel, or what used to be a hotel. It was run-down, waterlogged and its most colourful aspect were the lichens that grew on every lintel and ledge. The foyer wasn't grand, as it had been modified when the raised floor made the fifth storey the new ground level; it was actually just a pair of matched doors that were permanently open and let them into a wide corridor.

There was nobody to meet them there either. The daylight only went so far in, and they had waited within its warmth rather than exploring the dark corridor. It was some minutes before a door opened next to the elevator shaft and a thin crinkle-faced man stepped out.

'I am so very sorry for keeping you waiting. My name is Doctor Alexei Salvator.'

'Doctor, what is happening here? I have brought my family to Atlantic at great risk.'

'I know, I know. I'm sorry we are not better prepared but there have been matters to arrange. Your arrival has caused ... some complications for us.'

'You'd better be on the level with us, doc. Tell us what is

352

happening.' Desh came forward to introduce his muscle to the conversation.

Doctor Salvator pursed his lips and rolled his eyes. 'Don't be silly and don't push me.'

Desh suddenly shook his face as a slice of his forelock fell onto his nose. The doctor had kinetically cut a lock of his hair. He brushed it away, laughed, and then thrust his hand forward with a smile. 'I like that. I've never seen that. I'm Desh.'

The doctor shook the offered hand and then went around the group to make individual introductions. He even knelt down to Molly, who hid behind her mother's leg. 'There's no need to be afraid, little one.'

A man scuffled into the entryway and approached the doctor warily, keeping his eyes low. His face was bruised and a cut had dried, unwashed, on his scalp. He held a note out that Salvator took from him.

'I'm sorry, Freya. I need you and Bobby to go downstairs.'

'Us? How come?'

'There is a bender outside, but she won't come in with you here.'

'What? Why?'

'This is just the way it is right now. The benders don't like having telepaths around them.' He grimaced. 'Please. They would just like to speak with Ben and Desh for a moment.'

'No. I won't leave my husband here,' she insisted.

Looks passed between the three men, not sure of what to do. Bobby put his hand on his mother's shoulder. 'Let's go, Mum. They don't want us in this.'

'But ...' she stuttered. Ben came and stood close to her and kissed her cheek.

'It'll be alright.'

Reluctantly, she let Bobby lead her to the stairwell, pulling Molly along with him. It was dark. The sconces were broken and they had to feel their way down the steps.

Wait, Bobby projected to her. *We can listen from here.*

Freya put her hand in his and shared what he was seeing through his father's eyes.

The doctor sent the messenger back outside. 'Tell her she can come in. And there is a tap outside. Wash that cut.'

No sooner had he shambled off than a short, solid woman came in through the doors, her heavy shadow lumbering towards the group.

'Are the tappers gone?' she asked.

'They're gone,' he answered. 'Ben Harvey, Deshiel Diaz, this is Rocks. She speaks for Chiggy.'

'Chiggy wants you to come now,' she said.

'Wait, who is Chiggy?' Ben asked.

'There are two factions in Atlantic,' Salvator explained. 'The kinetics have formed their own group south of here. Chiggy is their leader.'

'And now you are to come to him. We don't keep Chiggy waiting.'

'Why should we go with you? What if we want to stay here?' Desh asked.

Rocks looked at the doctor. 'You didn't tell them who saved their lives, then?'

'I was getting to it.'

'You owe Chiggy your lives. You have to come to us now.'

'I'm not going anywhere. I have a family,' Ben said. Freya squeezed Bobby's hand and made to run back upstairs. *No. Wait.*

This isn't right, Freya thought to him. This wasn't the new world Tamsin Grey had promised.

We can trust the doctor, he thought back to her.

'Ben has a wife and two children with him,' Salvator informed Rocks. 'Could you not at least let him settle his family in?' The woman made a sour face and ruminated with deliberate swings of her head.

'Okay. He can stay. The other one must come with me.'

They all turned to look at Desh.

'What? I have to go because she says so?' he asked.

'Chiggy says so,' Rocks said. Desh felt himself pushed in the back, forcing him to take a step forward.

'Hey,' he said and shoved back at her.

'Don't —' Salvator warned, but Desh was hit by a wave of force and dropped to his knees clutching a ringing head. The doctor knelt beside him. 'Don't fight. She hits like rocks, thus her name.'

'Come,' Rocks said and turned around, dragging Desh behind her.

'You're not letting her take him, are you?' Ben asked and went to hold onto his friend. He had felt the tip tap of the word H E L P on his hand.

'Rocks, wait,' the doctor called out. 'Let the man choose.'

The bender stopped, letting Desh stand up. 'If I was you, I wouldn't deny Chiggy.'

355

'Desh, I know this is hard, but you should go. You just have to go there. After that you can choose to come back. Isn't that right, Rocks?' Sal said with emphasis.

'Nobody chooses to leave Chiggy,' she said.

Desh and Ben looked at each other. 'What should I do?'

'I don't know, Desh. It's your decision,' he said and tiptapped a message to him. R E A D Y.

'What happens if I don't go?' Desh asked Sal.

'I don't know.'

Desh turned between the other three people and back to the doctor. 'Not much of a choice, is it?'

He went to stand by Rocks, ready to follow her. 'I'll be okay, Ben. Don't worry. You look after the kids.'

C O M E B A C K.

I W I L L.

'I will return for Chiggy's tribute,' she said to Sal.

As soon as the bender and Desh had gone, Freya pushed past Bobby and quickly made her way up the stairs. They rushed through the door and she rushed to hug Ben close to her. 'Oh, thank light you didn't go.'

'You were listening?' the doctor asked.

'Of course I was —' Bobby said.

Salvator held up his hand. 'Please don't do that again. We need the benders to trust us.'

'She would never have known.'

'That's not the point. I also need to know *I* can trust you.'

'Trust you? Trust you? What kind of kutzo place are you running here, doctor?' Freya turned on him.

'Miz Harvey, please don't ...' he trailed off. He was extraordinarily tired. The adrenalin was evaporating out of him and the thing he wanted most in the world right now was a chair. 'Look, we're all in a situation here, trying to manage as best as we can.'

'And this is your rebellion? How many of you are there?'

'There are just over a hundred of us. We lost six helping you and your family get through.'

'Mum,' Bobby said. He looked at Ben, who hadn't said anything since Desh had left. For a long moment none of them said anything.

I can hear you all thinking, so you may as well wait so you can say it to my face, another voice entered their heads.

They hadn't heard or felt them approaching. A group of three led by Tamsin Grey. She was followed by a dark-skinned man and a girl holding his hand.

Bobby spoke up, stepping in front of his parents. 'Miz Grey, we apologise. It is just that no one is giving us any information.'

'No need for apologies, Bobby.' She shook her head and smiled at him. 'And you can just call me Tamsin. This is Okonta, my second, and this is Piri.' Piri looked at the new people very seriously. 'And you're Ben, Freya and Molly. Welcome to our little rebellion.'

'Thank you, Miz Grey,' Bobby said eagerly. The rest of the Harveys nodded numbly.

'Freya,' Tamsin said. 'If you want to complain, then you can do so out loud. I'm truly sorry the guest rooms weren't ready on your arrival but we are trying to do something here. We also went to a great deal of trouble to save you. It cost us dearly.'

'I'm sorry, I didn't realise.'

'Let's just remember that next time.' Tamsin turned towards the husband. 'You're an engineer, Ben. Is that right?'

'Yes, Miz,' he said.

'Then you've arrived just in time. Come with me,' she said, crooking her finger.

'What about us?' Freya asked, annoyed at how Ben was automatically moving towards the other woman.

'Sal here will show you where you're going to stay. Then he is going to get some rest.'

'Thank you, Tamsin.'

'Well done today, Sal.' Tamsin took him by the hands and kissed him gently on either cheek. 'You bought us time.'

'Just doing what I have to,' he said.

Tamsin stepped away. 'May I leave Piri with you? I'm sure she and Molly would be good for each other. There are so few children around.'

'Of course,' Bobby answered before Freya could say anything. 'We're happy to help.'

'Perfect. Please have her back by six.'

Come to me later, Tamsin thought to Bobby.

Okay.

You should know what we're fighting for.

Ben left with Tamsin and her bodyguard. Salvator stayed behind with Freya and the three kids.

The streets were messy with people. Women put themselves on display and one couldn't walk anywhere without being beset by spruikers for eateries, mesh bars or pleasure rooms. The cybernetics were crude and obvious.

Atlantic wasn't what she'd expected. She'd grown up watching the spectacle of the games over the Weave. Beautiful, athletic men and women with plated visors and elegant body morphs surrounded by dancing, music and the livid barracking of their fans. It had always looked like the most energetic place on Earth.

Freya was no longer sure why they had been drawn here. They'd lived their whole lives in hiding, things could have stayed that way. If only Ben didn't fear every Serviceman who walked past him, or have days when he couldn't eat or digest because announcements of new restrictions put knots in his stomach.

There was nothing to be done about it now. Now she just had to figure out how the family was supposed to live.

Salvator didn't lead them far, soon arriving at a once-green apartment block that looked like it had been burnt by a fire. The doorway was boarded over, and crammed with wind-collected litter. The nails holding the boards in place broke in unison and the planks dropped to the ground and then shoved themselves to one side.

'It's all yours,' he said.

Freya took a long look up and down the building. 'We're the only ones here?'

'You're the first to come through,' he said. 'But we're finding more every day.'

She had her hands to her mouth and Bobby patted her gently. 'It's okay, Mum. We're here now.'

'Thank you, Bobby. I can see you'll be a great help to us,' Sal said.

'Doctor, can you tell me what it is like here?'

'Things aren't so different as in the union. The only thing to remember here, is that there are far fewer people with any influence. Otherwise things run the same.'

'I don't understand,' Freya said.

'You'll pick it up quick.'

'And what about the rebellion? Will there be a war?' Bobby asked.

'We are hoping not to start one. At the moment the groups are sticking together. The Philly group has claimed that area for kinetics. That's Bendertown if you hear anyone say it.'

'That's where Desh went?'

'Yes.'

'Will my husband have to go as well?' she asked.

'Chiggy may insist.'

'Will Desh be ... you know, okay?'

'I can't say.'

'You've been there, then? Chiggy's Arena?' Bobby asked.

'Yes ...'

'Please, Doctor Salvator ...' She touched his arm. Freya saw all she needed to see of Bendertown. The doctor's strongest memory was of the cheering crowd of benders and norms. The rising roar as he stepped into the stadium. He had gone there to bargain for help, to save her family ...

Freya pulled her hand away. 'I'm sorry, I shouldn't have.'

'I'm getting used to it,' he mumbled.

'No, really, I should have asked. Tell me what I can do to help.'

Salvator turned to her. 'We expect more runners will come. We weren't ready for your family, but if you could help us prepare for more arrivals that would be extremely useful.'

'You mean, this building?' Sal nodded. 'Just us?'

'We can spare you some children with abilities. Everyone else has duties assigned.'

'I can play nanny as well? That's great.'

'Mum, stop it. Of course we will help, Doctor,' Bobby said. *We're here now, Mum. We have to make it work.*

'Thank you, Bobby,' the doctor said. 'Now, I'll go. I'll come by tomorrow to see how you're getting on.'

As the floors seemed less sound the higher they went, they chose the first floor to live in. It was no surprise to find the penthouse had no roof and was a garden of weeds growing in a compost of guano and bird droppings.

There were still boards on the windows when they'd been shown in. Ben removed them and fashioned a coffee table.

There was less tech here than where they had come from. There wasn't running water or electricity and there certainly wasn't any sort of Weave to connect to.

Why did we ever leave the bots behind? Freya asked herself. They had never had to clean back in West. There was nothing to eat here and the water came in plastic casks that she had to carry upstairs herself because the kinetics were off helping Tamsin Grey.

Freya really didn't like the way the rebel leader had commandeered her husband. 'You're an engineer,' she'd said.

Ben nodded because he was. 'Come with me.' Ben had gone. Spellbound.

And she, Bobby and Molly had been left in a filthy building — with no light, nowhere to sit, full of decrepit old junk, with no food or water — until nightfall when Ben had finally made it home, exhausted.

Bobby spent a lot of his time out. He didn't seem to mind it as much as her. He accompanied Tamsin Grey and Okonta as they made tours of the city on the lookout for psis and norms who would agree to help them.

Every day she tried to clear out one room. By the end of the first week Freya had piled the rubbish out on the pavement and was on her hands and knees with a brush and rags, trying to use as little water as possible to clean the floors and walls.

Some children arrived, four including Piri, and she had to create games and rewards around rubbish removal or collecting water to keep them from underfoot — but she was the only one on all fours trying to get the muck off the floors, wasn't she?

None of them were kinetics, only Molly helped by pushing the heavy water casks up the stairs to where they needed them.

Freya watched Molly screw up her face and give it her all. The cask scraped forward another centimetre while Piri, Tamsin Grey's adopted daughter, sat atop shaking her two dolls in excitement.

She saw Sal every day. When they met they said hello and he held out his hand for her to touch, letting her access his mind for what had happened since the day before and if there was anything he needed her to do.

When he found out they had begun clearing the ground floor he arranged deliveries to be made and the room was quickly filled with boxes of goods.

He gave her a handscreen and asked her to catalogue what was delivered and what was taken away.

'Quartermaster and nanny? Lucky me,' she said.

'Just until there is somebody else.' He shrugged. 'But look,' he said, pointing at the screen. 'We have a network set up. Only three poles, but it's a start.'

This was exciting news. Now she could contact Ben and know where he was. A small taste of civilisation.

Freya didn't argue. Not in front of Bobby. She didn't want him to tell her again that it was all for the cause. In West she had been a meme editor, on her way to becoming a mogul.

She missed her job. She missed her friends. She missed her clothes. She even missed the ugly old ziggurats they lived in. Ben insisted they were a fabulously efficient design and she knew he was thinking of building them in Atlantic.

Each day Ben came home filthy. He didn't need to tell her about his day, he just stared into her eyes as she lightly touched his arm. He'd been underground since dawn, coordinating the foundations and surveying the area to see how to get everything to connect up.

Like Bobby, he was caught up in the rebel cause and he'd already been telling Salvator how they could refurbish the zone and get it up to WU standard.

Molly slowly pushed full casks of water along the corridor.

After two weeks there was still no word from Desh. 'I'm getting worried, Ben.'

'Me too, Frey.'

'What should we do? Surely someone knows something.'

'I've asked,' he said angrily. Ben didn't know what to do. He was trying not to think about it and picked up his handscreen to go through his queue. He had over a thousand tasks in his list.

'I'm sorry,' she said. 'I'm just coping, okay.'

'We all are, Frey.'

'I know, it's just …' She bit her lip. 'If you love me at all, please, please fix the toilets.'

Suspicion crept through Geof like a wet creature. Desperate, icy claws prying into every crack of his mind. Everything he knew became doubted. His stomach felt empty and ill, scratched raw with misgivings and questions. Too much was happening at once.

'You need to eat, Geof,' Egon said. 'It's been a long week.'

He nodded. *Yes*, he agreed to himself. *A long week of failures.*

'You're probably right.' He acceded and ordered five trays sent to his room. Geof ate distractedly and flicked through the data he'd amassed, then lay back into the chaise and immersed. 'I'll be better in a minute.'

But he wasn't. The crawling suspicion prowled through him until it took root behind his eyes. Was it trying to tell him something? Was it a subconscious reaction? Was it telling him there was something that he had seen but hadn't registered? Was that what it wanted?

The attack on the Busan Kronos was a disaster. Compounded by the seed — or egg, as Egon called it — that washed up in Hokkaido, and the botched collection of Risom Cawthorne, and the ever-present thought that the Kronoses were all inching towards him, Geof felt a dread in himself that he was unfamiliar with.

He flimmed through the Weave coverage of the incidents. He had seen something that was important, Geof just couldn't put his finger on the answer. The convocation was still roiling and Services was holding over any major actions until the hierarchy had stabilised. Ryu's status was quickly diminishing, benefitting two factions directly: Charlotte Betts and Colonel Pinter.

Pinter was on record opposing the attack on Kronos. This fact alone began tipping the scales. Confidence in the Prime was shaken by these recent failures in his strategy.

Geof sat in his room watching the indicators rise and fall. He vicariously patrolled the perimeter of the Cape and Busan in his last cycle. But he hadn't moved his body in all that time.

His retrospection became tiring and he went to the exercise level of the building to run some circuits and take a swim in the tepid pool. He put in his vote for the water to be colder, but for now had to settle with a cooling shower. He ordered a couple more trays to his room; he needed something sweet.

Egon was still at work when he returned. Kronos had absorbed him in a different way.

'At least they didn't kill it,' Egon Shelley said.

'What?'

'Kronos. I'm relieved that Services didn't succeed in destroying it.'

'You think that it is alive then?'

'In a sense.'

'It was convincing when I spoke with it,' Geof said. 'It can communicate. It has desires like we do.'

'You spoke with a program.'

'Kronos has a distinct body and mind. That it is synthetic and man-made makes it no less sentient than ourselves.'

'It is good to see the dream of AI alive and well in you, Geof. But it doesn't change that its desires, as you call them, are in conflict with our own. We still have to find a way to stop it.'

'I don't think all the weapons in the world can stop them now. The Mexica Kronos is ten times the size of Busan.'

'I disagree,' Egon said. He straightened up from the scopes and rolled his arms and neck around. 'When you spoke with it in the subnet, I realised that the main communication problem seemed to be that it didn't understand the nature of its own existence.'

'And?' Geof asked.

'Kronos doesn't have walls like we do. It doesn't understand limitations.'

'I think we have all noticed that.'

'Ah yes, but think it through. If Kronos doesn't understand limitations, it might not even know it is expanding; on the Weave or in the physical world. It is entropic in this way.'

'But what do we do about it?' Geof asked.

'Reprogram.'

'Change its core behaviour? You can't do that once a symbiot is made.'

'Why not?'

'It just hasn't been done before.'

Egon clapped and smiled with delight. 'Those words are music to my ears.'

Geof smiled too. 'Why do you want to save it so badly?' he asked him.

'That's easy. If it is a new life-form, then it is a miracle, but if it is also holding the minds of the people it has consumed … then it is something else again.'

'All we have to do is stop it expanding and then convince the world to leave it alone.'

'That's all.'

Geof fell silent.

Egon surreptitiously returned to his work. Geof put the feed of the scopes into his overlay and sat staring at the sample, a black leech attacking the nose of the scope.

'Doctor Shelley —'

'Egon is fine now, don't you think, Geof?'

'Okay. Egon, do you know if Shen Li and Morritz Kay had much contact?'

Egon laughed and bumped his face on the multiscope. 'Not since the interview, I'm sure.'

'What interview?'

'You haven't seen it? It's most amusing, especially when you know both the parties. Here.' Egon opened a link that replayed a recording of a panel discussion in 2115. Shen Li and Morritz Kay were being questioned about their respective inventions and Morritz was getting angrier and angrier until he took off his moccasins and began beating the other man with them. The film crew were too stunned to stop it.

Geof found it somewhat amusing. He hadn't known his sensei before he retired from public life.

'Morritz is a ... difficult man, isn't he?'

'Oh yes. As much as any other. Once you wait out his initial hostility he becomes nearly normal.'

'Why does he seem to hate Shen so much?' Geof asked.

'Morritz doesn't like symbiots,' Egon said offhandedly.

'And that's enough. What's his reasoning?'

'I'm not sure he has one. It's either an instinct or he hates them for making his charm-tech seem like it was from pre-rec. Shen did make his research obsolete overnight.' Egon laughed. 'He's a good scientist though.'

'So it's unlikely they worked together?' Geof asked.

'Extremely. Very extremely highly unlikely. Why?'

'I don't want to say yet.' In the background Geof set the chaise to search for any other records, visual or otherwise, of the bauble he had seen Shen making and Morritz Kay wearing.

'As you wish.'

While he mopped up the last of the sauce, Geof was double-pinged from two anonymous addresses. For weavers this was like a knock on the door.

Geof ducked into immersion and traced the connections as they fell short, fading away like water in the sun. Pointing anywhere and nowhere.

'Everything comes from somewhere ...' he muttered to himself. He sent an army of crawlers out to do the work.

It was merely a process of elimination. Where the trails ended were highly infected with Kronos. Was it trying to contact him? Did its mind seek him out like its bodies were doing?

He set the chaise to map the infection to see how far it had spread and he quickly began noticing other anomalies in the data. There were areas of the Weave that had been infected immediately after Kronos appeared. The rest of the super-network could thus be categorised by the moment of contagion and the level of penetration.

In the nodes that Kronos was only now reaching there were sometimes anomalous contradictions in the energy increase. It wasn't doubling as precisely each time like it should have been if it was mirroring. He couldn't see what was different, only that the data weight in Kronos didn't always match that of the Weave. Like an organism it was an imperfect copy ... Alternatively it might mean that someone was changing the data on the Weave.

Is this what the anonymous connection wanted me to see? Like a thief wanting to get caught?

There must be something they were doing that they wanted him to see. All he had to do was find what they were affecting and then he would find them. Since his only way of seeing that they had done anything at all was by the discrepancy in data weight between the Weave and the Kronos infection, this would be a very hard chore indeed.

It must be raw data, he thought. Data was the most susceptible at input, before it was processed; visual recordings were positionally matched with streams and object tags, communications were logged and classified, and passive adjustments were passed onto the Will. Before the processing of all that data there was a lag, sometimes of seconds, that could, theoretically, be hakked.

'Okay. I see you,' he said. 'But why have you brought me here, stranger? Why are you showing me this?'

Geof waited for another ping, but none came.

There were only so many people in the world capable of erasing their tracks like this, or in fact finding him behind a Services shield. But how many of those would need to approach him in this manner? All the members of the Primacy had direct contact with him, so it must be an outsider on the inside.

One name came to mind.

He began a new search for all signs of Takashi Shima's stream, both on the Weave and off. Takashi walked lightly on the Weave but in the real world his whereabouts were always known. He had taken to living out of a mesh café after embarrassing his family one too many times.

A random visual recognition scan turned up a result on Takashi's avatar and Geof followed it to a mimic layer of Sector 261, STOC. He watched in multiple views, code and visual, as Takashi Shima went from omnipole to omnipole, running verification and viral scans on the passive sensors. He used the default avatar, like most serious weavers did, not bothering to create a false facade of themselves and simply representing their body as it was. Takashi was short and covered over in a symbiot larger and thicker than Geof's own. Even his head was covered with bulbous oculars that made him look like some sort of lizard.

There was something strange about how methodically the avatar was behaving. Though Geof didn't know Takashi, he didn't imagine the black sheep of Shima would be so careful — unless that was what he was like when he was immersed. Geof tracked the command path back to see where the body of Takashi was, now that he had left the palace, but the path dissolved. This avatar had no controlling profile, it was independent ...

Geof appeared in front of the avatar as it went to the next omnipole to check its sensors for error.

'Takashi Shima?'

'Yes?' The symbiot man looked up at him.

'What are you doing?' Geof asked, as he probed the avatar to see where its commands were coming from. He could detect no external signal. This avatar was akin to an ARA, only more complex.

'Just checking these sensors. Something is very wrong in this place.'

Geof encapsulated the avatar and filed it into his chaise, which began breaking down its protocols. It was a detailed simulation of Takashi, and probably not the only one. It had commands to explore the Weave as Takashi would do and to wipe all visual records of Pierre Jnr. It was very sophisticated.

What are you up to, Takashi?

Geof pursued Weave-borne rumours to the new den Takashi had made for himself. He was a minor celebrity now, taken in by a keen young crowd of weavers and gamers, living out of a mesh bar at the coastal end of Yantz.

Geof created a mimic layer, so that he could stand in Cybermesh as if transported, watching all the cameras and sensors reported in real time. He looked over the clientele on their couches, the girl jamming rubbish into a disposal chute behind the bar.

Takashi was not in view, but Geof detected the signal of the proprietor behind a sliding wall. There were no cameras in this restricted area — Cybermesh's own little black box — and it would have been safe from Geof, if not for Lewis the proprietor checking on his most important client.

Delicately, Geof syphoned the sensors and camera data of the man and could see into the restricted area; the cushioned floor and gratuitous pillows. Geof looked down at the relaxed form of Takashi Shima.

He wired into the other man's connection and watched as he coordinated the programs of seven different simulations he had made of himself. Some he had set to miscellaneous tasks, like the one Geof had found in STOC, others he had rapidly parsing surveillance footage.

For a long time nothing happened, but then one of the simulations found what it was looking for. A pair of cameras pointing at the stage of a lecture theatre. There were only four people in the audience, sitting spaced apart, all looking up to the podium where a small boy with an oversized head stood before them.

The simulation edited out Pierre Jnr, erased him from the record, and then resumed its search.

As Geof stood there another avatar appeared beside him, another Takashi, quietly staring down and studying his real-world form.

'It's not what it looks like,' Takashi said.

Geof turned to look at him. 'What isn't?'

'Everything.' Takashi's smile twitched and Geof's connection was snapped.

Geof blinked, surprised to find himself back in the load space.

A ping came into his queue with a data attachment, file name 'Sector 261'.

Takashi: Make sure my brother sees this.

Geof demersed and took stock. He pulled up a satellite view and began running a pattern analysis. His gut knew the answers before the run listed the results. It was just as Takashi's report said.

Seven months ago Omskya Sector 261 had stopped having traffic accidents, their transport was running on a to-the-second timetable, the people were becoming significantly more healthy through strict dieting and exercise. Their data trails had stopped and they no longer accessed the Weave or took part in the Will.

Geof didn't know what that might indicate or if it was important at all.

As he pondered, the chaise pinged results on his earlier query. The bauble had been seen elsewhere, caught in surveillance footage at Magnus Towers. Risom was wearing one on a cord around his neck.

Geof to Pinter: We need to talk.

Pinter: What have you found out, Geof?

Geof: New anomalies.

Pinter: Pierre Jnr?

Geof: We need to see the Prime. In person.

Pinter: He doesn't see anybody.

Geof: I need to. I've learnt about something that fills me with doubt.

Pinter: And you won't tell me what it is, I suppose?

Geof: Can't risk it.

Pinter: I'm not sure the Prime will risk seeing us at this point. He is busy dealing with the aftermath.

Geof: If I don't see him in person, I won't share the information.

Pinter: Ozenbach, this isn't like you. What has happened?

Geof: I'll tell you when I see you. Not safe.

Pinter: Paranoia protocols it is.

Geof: ?

Pinter: Old joke.

Ryu saw the elevator coming down. No one was supposed to be there. The elevator shouldn't even move from his level without his consent.

Was it Pierre? Would the doors open to show the melon-headed boy looking at him with his calm eyes?

Two men stepped out. Colonel Pinter and Geof Ozenbach.

'What are you doing here? Is this a coup?'

'Nothing like that,' the Colonel said calmly. 'There is something we need to talk about. Geof insisted we meet in person.'

'How did you get through my security?' Ryu asked.

Pinter turned to face Geof, as if that explained it. Geof shrugged. 'I couldn't let anyone know we were coming.'

'What has happened now?' Ryu asked.

'It's what has been happening. I traced your brother tampering with the Weave,' Geof said.

374

The Prime and Pinter looked at each other. 'You've been in contact with Takashi?'

'Yes. I caught him erasing evidence of Pierre Jnr from the Weave. Did you know about this?'

Ryu thought a moment before answering. 'Yes.'

'Did you?' Geof asked the Colonel.

'Ryu shared it with me when I took my posting.'

Geof was stunned. 'Why? Why are you doing this?'

'I thought it best that the public weren't aware. I didn't want to cause a panic,' Ryu said.

'Geof, you can see the logic,' the Colonel added.

'You agree with this?'

'For the time being.'

Geof felt unsteady on his feet. 'I'm sorry, I thought ... I thought you might be under Pierre's influence.'

'Ha, perfectly understandable.' Pinter reached out a steadying hand. 'You were right to question.'

'Is there something else?' the Prime asked. 'I don't appreciate you forcing your way in like this.'

Geof nodded, calming down his breathing. 'It might be nothing.'

'We're all here now, Geof,' Pinter said. 'Take your time.'

'Colonel, need I remind you who is in charge here?' Ryu asked.

'I'm sorry, Prime. Did you not wish to hear what is troubling our weaver so much?'

Ryu sighed and scratched at his eyebrow. 'Just make it quick, Ozenbach. There is a lot I have to get through tonight.'

'Okay, well, as I said, it may be nothing.' Geof opened a connection to the needle's controls and set the windows to opaque then began feeding documents onto them. 'I have found an unexplained thread of coincidence that my gut tells me is not coincidence. At the time I didn't think anything of it, but when I was consulting with Shen Li he was working on something. He wouldn't tell me what it was, but he was obsessing over it. This.' He showed the images and basic specifications of the bauble.

It was a small thing, a centimetre in diameter. The base sphere was made of nano-smoothed poly-metal, with over fifty tiny plates making a second shell around the outside. It looked mathematically decorative.

'What is it?'

'I'm not sure yet. First, I saw Shen making it. Then, I noticed Morritz Kay wore one on a bracelet. He wouldn't tell me what it was either. A background search I put going then found the same bauble in Risom Cawthorne's possession at Magnus Towers. The thing is, there are no records of interaction between Shen and Morritz. Morritz Kay loathed Sensei Li. Which leaves me with the question of how he could have gotten it, and then how Risom acquired one.'

'And, do you have an answer?'

'Morritz Kay is manufacturing them in the millions.'

'What does it mean?' the Colonel asked.

'All I know is that Shen Li made it, Morritz acquired it and is mass-producing them and Risom Cawthorne was seen wearing one.'

'What was on the train?' Ryu spoke for the first time in a while. He had let the others postulate while he watched his value topple. His value was on a clear downward trajectory and nothing he could do would stop it now.

'What train?' Geof asked.

'The one Risom escaped on.'

'That was a cargo distributor. It had thousands of items on it.'

'But it did have a manifest, did it not?' Ryu asked.

'Of course, by default.'

'Could you cross-reference with the salvage report to see if anything was missing?'

'Yes, Prime.' Geof went silent as he ran the command. 'This could be something.'

'What?'

'Can you wait while I follow up?' Geof asked.

'Please.' Ryu waved Geof towards one of the large swivel chairs.

'Would it be possible to get some water?'

'Of course, order what you like.'

Pinter ordered an anise and chose a glass from the drawer.

'Did you know that there is a drink named after you?' Ryu asked him. 'The Scorpion.'

The Colonel looked up. 'No. I wasn't aware. How does it taste?'

'I can't say I've tried it.' Ryu looked grim. 'It looks certain that you will overtake me as Prime. You or Representative Betts.'

'I see. When do you think that will happen?'

'In the next cycle. Current projection is in less than three hours.'

Pinter nodded. 'That doesn't give us much time then, does it?'

'What do you intend to do?' Ryu asked.

'To be honest I haven't given it much thought.'

'You must have,' Ryu insisted.

'A commander lives by his contingencies. I have strategies for each of the scenarios, but I don't believe the Prime should make too many plans.'

'Are you accusing me of —'

Ryu was cut off by Geof exclaiming, 'Look at this!' He cleared the screens to black and then lay down four images. Shen Li, Morritz Kay, Risom Cawthorne and the cargo manifest of the train he had escaped from West on. 'Your suspicion was right, Prime. It was carrying a shipment of baubles from Kay's micro-fac.'

'This is too much coincidence for my liking,' Pinter said.

'I would like permission to ask Peter Lazarus to inspect one of them,' Geof said.

'You suspect it may have something to do with psionics?' Ryu asked.

'I want to know for sure that it doesn't.'

The Prime and the Colonel waited for each other. With the seesaw of their status neither was sure who should speak. With a dismissive gesture, Ryu indicated for Geof to proceed. 'But let me speak to him first.'

'I'll open the connection and have a sample sent to his tower.'

Peter Lazarus was lying alone in his room with the lights out. He had showered and lay with his shirt off, letting the cuts and bruises air-dry. His symbiot told them he wasn't asleep.

After the confrontation with Risom the three residents of the needle kept to themselves. Arthur had been hospitalised

378

and was sedated in his bed, recovering from a graft to his ribs. Gock now routinely kept away from the psis.

'What are you thinking about, Mister Lazarus?' Ryu asked him.

The psi didn't speak.

'Are you disappointed that your escape attempt failed?'

'I wasn't trying to escape,' Pete said quietly.

'Your saviour didn't save you. Tell me, Mister Lazarus, was Pierre Jnr at Magnus Towers?'

'I ... I'm not sure.'

'Would you tell us if you were? Arthur Grimaldi told us he was there.' Pete didn't answer. 'I see we will have to start again on your conditioning,' the Prime said.

'Did you contact me for a confession, Prime?' Lazarus asked bitterly. 'Then fine. I did it. I tried to escape. I am in league with Pierre Jnr. He's here in the room with me now.'

Ryu smiled and prompted Geof to take over.

'Pete, it's Geof here. I need your help with something.'

'And you would trust me?'

'You know me, Pete. We can trust each other.'

The psi was silent. He lay quietly before straightening up and throwing the connection with Geof onto the window screens.

'I'm sorry,' he said.

'How are you feeling?' Geof asked.

'Surprisingly well. I'm sorry Risom got away.'

'Nobody blames you.'

'Nobody?' Geof didn't answer. 'How are you, Geof? Where are you?'

379

'I shouldn't tell you where I am. I'm good.'

'You don't trust me enough to tell me even that.'

'It's not me, I follow the Command.'

'And the Command says not to trust telepaths. What else do they say about me, Geof? The ones who have me on trial?' Pete asked.

'Nothing that makes sense.'

'I mean, you don't know, do you? I don't know for sure. Maybe Pierre has been controlling me all this time. But why would he send me to Services to chase him?'

'Maybe you were a probe?' Geof suggested.

'What do you mean?'

'Pierre Jnr might have sent you in to gather information on Services and then he collected what he wanted at the manifestation.'

'I'm everybody's pawn,' Pete said.

'And I'm afraid I now need you to be a guinea pig. I'm sending something over for you to look at.'

Geof shared a still image of a metal ball with many-faceted sides that caught the light. 'Do you know what this is?'

'No,' Pete said. 'I've never seen it. Why?'

'Risom was wearing one.' The image zoomed out to show that it came from a surveillance camera that had caught Risom on the train. The bauble was hanging on a cord around his neck.

'I didn't notice. What is it?' Pete asked.

'I don't know what it is, but I know who is making them.'

'You're being cryptic,' Pete said.

'I can't say much, Pete. I know who made the first one, but I don't know what it does.'

The Colonel and Ryu watched the interaction on the window screens. The Prime drew Pinter to one side.

'What are your intentions if you become Prime?' Ryu asked him.

'I will do as the Will wishes.'

'Of course, but you must announce a plan of action for them to support.'

'There are still basically two major problems facing the WU. We don't have a means of defeating either at this point in time.'

'You would make peace?'

'I'm saying the choice is not ours to make.'

'You would accept defeat?'

'Does one fire their guns into a hurricane? No. So why do something useless for show? You believe it is a sign of weakness to stop fighting. I see it as a sign of madness to carry on.' Pinter smiled at him. 'Let's live to fight another day.'

'If we don't win, we face the destruction of the World Union. And I didn't put you in charge to take away my position,' Ryu said.

'Nor did I take the mission to depose you. But the Will is the Will. Besides ... you could have listened to my advice.'

The cameras followed Peter Lazarus as he left his room and collected the small box that Geof sent to the delivery shute. Inside it was a chrome-plated ball. Pete touched it and then stumbled backward to find a seat.

'What is it, Pete? Are you okay?' Geof asked. The two commanders came back to stand behind him.

'I'm okay,' the psi said. 'It was just a shock.'

'What was? What is it?' Geof asked.

'It's ...' The psi was taking long, deep breaths. 'It's incredible. I can feel so far ...'

'What do you mean?'

'Geof, do you know what this is? It's an amplifier,' Pete said.

Geof flicked his eyes to the Prime and then to Pinter. They nodded for him to keep talking.

'What do you mean?'

'It extends my mental range.'

'I want to try something,' Geof said. 'Just stay as you are and let me know if you sense any change.'

Geof put his side of the connection on freeze and looked at Ryu Shima and the Colonel. 'We should see if it has a compounding effect. What happens if we put another close to him.'

'You've got a theory?'

'Yes.'

'I think I know where you are going with this. Continue.'

Geof organised for another bauble to be delivered to the needle that was in closest proximity to the needle Lazarus was in.

Pinter made an annoyed sound with his tongue. 'I knew Risom's attack was too coordinated. How could he have known Lazarus would try to stop him killing Nigel Westgate, and then force him to escape through Magnus Towers? The explosives must have already been planted.'

'He didn't know we would send Lazarus. Risom might have known we had him on the islands.'

'I think whatever this is,' the Colonel nodded at Geof with his chin, 'implies that the attack on the towers might have been preplanned.'

'And it was all a distraction to get their hands on these baubles?'

'Oh ...' the psi moaned. They turned their attention back to the feed from Pete's needle.

'What is it doing?' Geof asked him.

'I can hear the thoughts of two people over there.' He pointed without looking. 'They are discussing politics and their names are Lauren Rockliffe and Luke McGee.'

'Wait a minute,' Geof said, verifying the data. 'Yes. That's right.' Ryu sent a message through for him to break the connection and Pinter was making a hand gesture that indicated the same.

'This is an incredible feeling, Geof,' Pete cooed. 'I feel enormous.'

'I'm sorry, Pete. We have to discontinue this conversation. I have a priority shift. I have to ask you to return the bauble to the delivery shute.'

'Why can't I —'

'We have to stop talking now. Goodbye, Pete.'

Geof shut down the feed. The windows returned to transparency, the lights of Yantz switching on for the night.

'Why did you make me pull out?' Geof asked.

'We couldn't allow you to keep talking to him. He is a psi,' the Prime answered.

'But Pete is on our side. He didn't hide anything from us.'

'Peter Lazarus is a telepath. He can never be on our side.'

'Colonel, help me here. This isn't right.'

'It is the Will,' Pinter said.

'The Will is changing.'

'But it hasn't yet. If you want it to change, then go make it change. If you believe it, convince others. You have as much right as the rest of us, but this is not the place for these discussions.'

'I have never gone against the Will before,' Geof quavered.

'But it is the Will's will for you to do so. That is how it works. It's not a dictatorship, Geof. If you don't feel you can complete your assignment, then step aside and someone else will.'

'Colonel, it's not that. I just don't think we are taking the right approach. Not every psi has to be our enemy.'

'Geof, you have the right to believe what you like, but you must make the choice of whether to obey the Will or not.'

'Colonel!'

'I can't have anyone who is going to hesitate when I give an order.'

Geof felt a knot in his guts, and weight all over his body as he tried to stand up. 'I am hesitating.'

'Then you are dismissed.' Geof was in shock and couldn't move. 'Go now, or I'll be forced to have you restricted.'

Geof was instantly cut from the conversation. His stream was tagged as 'No Access'.

He sat very still. There had to be something he could do. Geof wasn't used to this. It wasn't fear or anger that was affecting him, it was indecision. The best way forward seemed unclear. Even the concept of forward was escaping him.

'Stand up, Ozenbach,' Pinter ordered. Geof's body responded to the command, even if his mind didn't. 'You are to return to your accommodation and continue working on the Kronos problem. Is that understood?'

'Yes, sir.'

'You are not to speak of, or reveal, anything that has transpired here. Is that clear?'

'Yes. Of course.'

Pinter stood waiting for Geof to move. 'Ozenbach, you need to go before I have you removed.'

'Wait ... I ...' Geof had no defence. He was hesitating. He was questioning the orders. He looked at the silence of his queue, the emptiness of the disconnection with the Pierre problem and then he remembered the file. From his pack he took a preloaded dossier and held it out for the Prime to take.

'What is this?'

'It's from your brother. He says it is important.'

'Have you looked at it?'

Geof nodded.

'And?'

'I don't know if it is Pierre Jnr or not but there is an anomaly in STOC that we have seen before.'

'You think he is there?' Pinter asked.

'Or he has been.'

Pinter paused. 'I'm sorry about this, Geof. It has been a privilege and an education. I just can't have people who hesitate.'

'I understand.' Geof straightened up and saluted.

'Dismissed,' the Colonel said and watched the weaver get into the elevator and head up to the landing deck. When his symbiot verified that Geof had squibbed from the needle, Pinter turned back to face Ryu Shima, who was watching him intently. 'If you don't think I was right, then you can say so. If you withdraw your support for me, then I'll no longer be a rival to your position. Then you could reinstate Ozenbach.'

'I won't do that.'

'No. I didn't think you would.'

'Our situation seems hopeless,' Ryu said.

'I don't disagree with you,' the Colonel said. They both sat down to think. 'I think our enemy has been on the field longer than we have. They could have any number of tactics we don't know about.'

'This one with the baubles isn't enough?'

'Perhaps. It does change the game.' Pinter couldn't help but think of it all as a game. Which card would be turned over next, and how could he make use of it.

'Game? Do you not take this threat seriously?' Ryu asked.

'Of course I do. But it is still a game. It has rules and we have an opponent. You assume that all games are fun. I just think of them as situations I can either win or lose.'

'Do you have any suggestions on how we do that?'

Pinter breathed in and out, opened his mouth as if to speak then closed it again. He stood up and paced two steps before turning. 'They have the advantage.'

'We are the World Union.'

'And they know more about us than we do of them. Both of the enemies, the psis and Kronos, have goals that elude us and act in a way we are unable to predict. Actually, there are three enemies, if we remind ourselves of Pierre Jnr.' He twisted back to look at the Prime. 'You might have been right that they are all connected.'

'Small comfort.'

'Indeed, and yet we have learnt that there is a connection between Shen Li, Morritz Kay and the psis; a connection to the release of Kronos is a logical possibility,' Pinter admitted.

'Another distraction?'

'Or just a shadow.' Pinter ordered himself another drink and then a Scorpion which he put in front of Ryu. 'Have you ever wondered why it was so easy to find Pierre? It only took us two weeks to track him down after eight years.'

'Peter Lazarus was working with him,' Ryu said.

'That, or ... Pierre simply wasn't hiding.' Pinter looked out over the darkening sky and the lightening city. 'I'm not sure what that says about his intentions, but I'd now presume that Pierre Jnr doesn't fear us and he isn't hunting us. Hunters hide.'

'Maybe he has struck already and we just don't recognise it?' Ryu speculated. 'It's all him. I'm sure of it. The rebellion. Kronos. You've seen the convocation. He's going to trigger a collapse.'

'A collapse may be imminent, but that doesn't mean —'

'Colonel ... we can't give up.' Ryu lowered his head.

'I know.' Pinter bent down to look into the other man's eyes. 'The truth is, the choice might not be ours to make. Do you understand?'

'No.'

'It is the reality we may have to face.'

'The Will expects us to find a way.' In the background it was happening, the balance of the hierarchy was shifting. Soon Pinter's rank would eclipse his own. He felt a cold, familiar resolve. Did he smile? He didn't mean to smile. He hoped the Colonel hadn't seen him smile. 'What will you do when you are Prime?'

This time without hesitation Pinter had an answer. 'The first thing I'll do is replace Zim's strategy-matrix with my own. We must not provoke the psis any further. Then I will ask Representative Betts to begin talks to establish a psi-controlled territory.'

'If you support that motion, her position will be strongly bolstered.'

'If that is the Will.' Pinter shrugged.

'But what if it isn't the Will? What if the Will is being manipulated?' Ryu asked.

'For such an accusation as that you would first need to provide the evidence. You must accept the possibility that the Will may not wish a war with the psis.'

'And if the Will is mistaken?'

'How can the Will be mistaken?'

'If its action will lead to its own destruction.'

'You don't know that will happen. Your fear is creating assumptions.'

'Perhaps you have been infected, Colonel. You have been exposed to a known psi who has had direct contact with Pierre Jnr.'

'Is that the line you will take? After your own household was compromised?' Pinter raised his eyebrows.

'You wouldn't strike back with that.'

'I wouldn't have to.' No, he wouldn't. The Weave would do it for him. 'Ryu, we can work together. I see you as a man of honour and ability. With Zim demoted I will need you to control the psi rebellion.'

'But you will still send in Representative Betts?'

'Yes. She is the voice of peace from the WU and she'll also be second in status. It has to be her.'

'And what if she is being controlled?'

'Ryu. I advise that you take a few days to rest. Nine cycles of knockout and then come back on duty. If you do that, I would like you to take up Zim's responsibilities.'

'I suppose I should thank you for that. What about the Kronos situation?'

'We have to find a way to contain it. We must shut down the Weave.'

'But the Will ...' said Ryu.

'We must. Kronos cannot be allowed to seed any more eggs.'

'The Union will collapse.'

'It will be temporary,' Pinter said.

'And until it is, you will stay Prime?'

'We will fight him together.'

'There must be another way ...' Ryu looked down at the dossier Geof had left him with.

'Then this is your last chance to find it.' Pinter raised his voice, 'You still have at least two more hours as Prime. And then I will close the Weave.'

The thought was horrific. He may not like the Will all of the time, but it was the culmination of the thoughts of every Citizen on Earth. It was the cornerstone of their civilisation ...

'Then let's see if we can find Pierre Jnr.'

Risom flew straight at the barricade. It was fully formed and thicker than when he had come through. On the horizon it looked as if all the birds in the world had organised to swarm along that particular demarcation.

Wind blew his hair back. He was riding on the top of the squib, his metal hand jammed into its skin, crouched low, ready to leap off. He steered the pilot inside the cockpit, making him fly where he wanted. Now he wanted him to go lower. As low as they could go, so as they came within range of the tanks he would be hidden by the hills.

His other arm was clenched over a bulging canvas satchel. It was double-strapped to him, but he held it close. A bag of magic beans that would help him grow his kingdom.

Three dark squibs flew in from above. They saw him on the top and drew back to fire. Risom turned his squib around and flew in a sharp curve and then zigzagged closer to them. He felt in his pocket and found a few small stones. He might not be close enough to control them, or damage them directly, but he could knock them down like a boy before a giant.

They scattered, each banking in a different direction, forcing him to choose which one to follow. He threw a stone at the centre one and then braked quickly to chase left, before it could flank him. His stone hit but it didn't do any damage, just bored a hole through the skin. The third squib came up behind and fired its beams into his ride.

His squib sputtered, gobbits of fluid squirting from the holes. Risom swore under his breath. 'I know how to deal with you.' He pulled the squib vertical, using the last of its momentum to fly straight up into the sky. The Services squibs followed and he let go.

He dropped fast. Risom couldn't fly as such, but he could use his kinetics to guide his descent. They were chasing the vehicle and didn't react in time. Risom landed on the foremost and dug his metal arm in like a hook, and his mind speared into the Serviceman inside. He managed to fire one shot at the other squibs before the command came down to shut it off.

He pulled the bauble from the thong around his neck and pitched it towards the other squib, embedding it into its hull. Now he could reach it. This one he cut through, two halves suddenly hearing the call of gravity, and then he leapt again. There was one more to deal with and he just managed to catch hold of it. *Take me home, norm. Full speed.*

The command would come down. They'd either change to remote piloting or set it to self-destruct, but by that time he would be on the ground, speeding his way through the confusion in rapid and sudden jumps. He saw his original ride crash and flash into flame and he laughed.

This was how it was meant to be.

He patted the satchel at his side.

He persuaded a transport driver on one of the farms to take him all the way to the rebellion buildings. They passed through the classy and the dilapidated, driving slowly through the norms and drools who were wandering the streets. Atlantic looked more of a wreck than he remembered.

The rebellion was in some of the old concretes next to the coast, washed out, rotten and empty when he got there. A group was still clearing away decades of rubbish to a nearby pit.

Risom stood behind a crowd of norms watching the building construct itself. Bricks flew up, mortar was laid, joists straightened into place. A lot of heavy lifting had been done while he was away.

Risom saw a man directing the activity of the workers and he went over to him.

'Are you in charge here?'

'Today I am. Name's Ben.' The man held out his hand.

'Don't worry, I know who you are. Do you know where Tamsin Grey is?'

'Probably back at the hotel, they —'

There is no need for you to speak, bender.

He was happy with how the other psis stopped to stare at him and he smiled all the way into the hotel and skipped down the steps to the subterranean levels.

Tamsin was at her desk while two children, Piri and another girl who was younger and plumper, played by the door.

'Risom, you made it back,' she said, standing up to greet him.

'Are you surprised or disappointed?' he asked.

'I am very happy. We heard some of the reports and feared the worst.'

'And have I pleased you, Tamsin?'

Tamsin stopped where she was and looked at him. 'Could you take your block down, Risom? You're worrying me,' she said.

'Why would I do that?' he asked in return.

'I'd like to know what you're thinking.'

'I'd prefer to just tell you.' He patted the satchel he was carrying. 'I'm thinking there are going to be a lot of changes around here.'

'What's in the bag?'

Risom loosened the drawstring and took out two silver baubles, freshly replicated and identical.

'These are a gift from Pierre Jnr.' Risom held one of them up between his fingers for Tamsin to see. 'He gave them to me.'

'You saw him?' Tamsin asked.

Risom blinked, his fantasising was carrying him away. 'I knew he was with me,' he said.

'May I look at it?'

Risom thought this over then tossed one to her. 'You can have this one for nothing. My gift to you.'

Tamsin caught it and her eyes immediately bulged. 'Oh my. That's ...' She was stunned. It was like she was ten times her real size.. Her mind could feel the people on the surface, five floors above.

'Yes, it's quite something, isn't it.'

Piri and her friend went to stand by Tamsin, who had felt the need to take a seat. She held the bauble in her hands and stared at it.

'What is it, Mum? Can I hold it?' Piri's fingers went to grab for it, but Tamsin closed her hand and pulled away.

'No, not you, Piri.'

'But, Mum!'

'No. It is too dangerous.' Tamsin looked back at Risom. She noticed the way he was standing, tall and strutting. 'Much too dangerous.'

'This place won't do, Tamsin. It's all rotten.'

'We are making progress on a new headquarters.'

'So I have seen. Why don't you just claim one of the blocks that is already working?'

'You know why. We have to build for ourselves. We can't just take everything.'

'Why not? With these we can do anything.' He patted the satchel. 'All I have to do is get one of these baubles to Chiggy and I can control him. Tamsin, we can win.'

'Not that way.'

'I have been with Pierre Jnr. I know his way now.'

That is not his way, Risom. She was disgusted with him.

Do you think I should be ashamed? You should be ashamed. We have all the power we need and still you haven't struck back at Services. What are you waiting for? You've seen what Chiggy can do.

We cannot kill them all.

No. Just enough so they won't dare strike us again.

We have a plan.

So do I. I'm joining Chiggy.

He won't let you.

He won't have a choice.

Risom had his real hand in the satchel, prowling back and forth. *These change everything.*

Tamsin looked up at him, rolling the orb between her palms.

Now it is your thoughts that betray you. Risom smiled. 'I saw Peter Lazarus,' he said.

'Did you hurt him?'

'I was interrupted.'

'He isn't our enemy,' she said.

'He isn't on our side either, Tamsin. Though he did try to tell me he was.'

'What did he say?'

'He said he wants you to rescue him.'

'And you didn't help him?'

Risom shrugged, he didn't care. 'I had other things to do. I couldn't have taken him with me anyway. He was locked.' *You believe him, don't you?*

Yes.

He hates Pierre Jnr. Did you know that?

That is only his fear of him.

He should be afraid of Pierre. All the traitors will be killed.

We can't win that way, Risom. We must stick to La Grêle's plan.

Risom took one of the orbs between his fingers and held it up to his eye for a closer look. 'I believe we can.'

'I can't let you leave.'

'How long do you think you can hold me?' He turned to walk away, but she pushed him back.

'Let go.'

'No.'

Small objects from around the room lifted up and hurled themselves at Tamsin. She knocked them down, throwing them back at him, but her hold on him was weakened and he stepped backward to where the girls were playing.

'Stop,' he ordered, grabbing Piri around the neck.

Tamsin dispelled her kinetics. The blocks and furniture she had raised to throw fell to the ground, clouding the floor with dust. Risom straightened up, keeping his arm locked around Piri.

'Let her go.'

'You're weak, Tamsin. La Gréle has made you soft.'

'Risom ...'

'It's alright, Tamsin. I forgive you. Chiggy and I will do what needs to be done. Just stay out of my way.'

'Leave Piri here.'

'Not until I'm safe.' He began backing towards the door, carrying Piri roughly under his elbow. One step at a time, keeping his eye and his mind on what Tamsin was doing.

'You're bleeding,' Tamsin called out.

'Be quiet!' Risom shouted. But he was. His lip was warm and wet. One lick confirmed it as blood. He touched his hand to his nostrils and it came away red. He collapsed, the satchel of baubles spilling out over the floor, and Piri crawled out from his loose grip.

She stood over him as his mind dimmed. 'I'm sorry, Risom. I didn't want to go with you.'

PIERRE JNR HAS RETURNED

'Hello, Mother.'

A boy stood before her. Mary Kastonovich was swooning today. She got through days like these with her face in the cradle of her palms.

He held something out to her, a silver chain with a silver bauble on a jump ring.

'That's pretty.'

'I made it for you.'

'Where have you been?' she asked him.

'Everywhere.'

'You left me ...' she cried.

'Don't cry, Mother.' Mary lost her pain. He'd never left her. Pierre had always been with her. 'Here.' He offered the necklace again.

'I ...' She lifted her hand weakly to her throat. 'I can't touch my neck.'

'Let me help you.' Pierre walked behind her chair.

She felt his little fingers take a hold on the lock. It went soft and then came in two. The pieces landed on the floor, grey and dead.

'You —' *You saved me.*

Hello, Mother.

You can hear me?

The silver chain was around her neck, cinched with kinetic hands. The bauble hung in the centre of her breasts.

'Now I'll always be with you.'

One by one Pierre went to the inmates of the island, dismantling their locks and replacing them with necklaces.

For an immeasurable breath they were a part of him. One and immense.

He awoke to Gock prodding him. Pete looked into his mind and saw the instructions the man had been given. 'Get up,' the proxy said.

'Get up and go to the elevator. Yes, I heard it already,' Pete said. 'There is no need for you to speak.'

'Gock will speak because he is told to. Now get up.' *Ah*, Pete thought. *That sounds like Ryu Shima. He must have more time now.*

'You're back then, Prime?' he asked.

'Yes. I see some of our lessons didn't stick. We will have to rectify that.'

Pete: Geof?

There was no response to his ping.

'I am giving the orders, Mister Lazarus,' Gock said.

'Where are you sending me? Please, not back to the islands.'

'Not yet. I have another use for you and your squad today.'

'What has happened to Geof?'

'Geof Ozenbach is no longer part of the hunt. Now get into your field set. Be ready in five minutes.'

400

Pete dressed in the soft armour they had given him. It was able to camouflage, but in default it was orange with grey piping on the seams so he was highly visible.

Arthur was waiting in the elevator, bruises already fading, and the swelling could only be noticed because of a greasy gel that made them shine. They ascended to the squib landing platform, where they found a large Services transport loaded with the full ten squad and the two skinbots. All were in fresh armour, replaced since Magnus Towers. Arthur saluted and climbed into his webbing. Gock shoved Pete forward.

'Get moving.'

Don't push too much, *Gock. I can be a voice in your head too.*

Pete caught Arthur looking at him disapprovingly.

As they flew, the details of the mission were plugged into their symbs. The file mostly contained street maps, photos of the area and records of the population.

'What's so scary about this place?' Three pointed at some of the images. 'It's just a suburb street. Is there a psi nest there or something?'

'Idiot,' Seven answered him. 'This is a relocation town. All these weirdies are ex-Örjians.'

'Yurhg!' The Endo bot made a face.

'So what? What's the big deal?' Three persisted.

'Once you go in, you never leave. Can't you read?'

'What, they take you prisoner?'

'No. You just don't want to go.'

'And that's bad? I can think of a few places I never want to leave.'

401

'That's enough questions, Three. Read your pack, we drop in ten minutes.' Ten stood up and began highlighting the pertinent information and assigning details. 'The ups don't know what's happening down there, but, judging from the observations, this sector has deliberately gone off the radar. We are taking these two in with us to find out if it was by choice or not.' She pointed at the two psis. 'We're going to do better than Magnus Towers this time, aren't we, gentlemen?'

Pete looked at her, trying to probe what she meant. 'Yes, sir.' Pete nodded.

'We aren't going to try discussing our way out of trouble, are we?' she asked.

'No, sir.' Pete shook his head.

'When you acquire a target you will pacify it?'

'Yes, sir.' Nodded.

'Right. Aiko will take point and Endo will take the rear. The rest of us will form a shell around our two sniffers here. I want that thing to be a Roman fucking phalanx. Do you hear me?'

'Yes, sir,' the ten chorused.

'There are ten thousand Citizens in Sector 261, and we are to do our utmost not to disturb their peace and tranquillity.'

'Sir?' Three put up his hand.

'What is it?'

'Is this Pierre Jnr?'

'Three, I swear if you don't stop —' Ten cut herself off. She hadn't considered it. 'Look, we don't know. But if it is, our job is simple. All we have to do is paint the target.'

'And then what?'

'It is against protocol to give high-level information to field agents. We'll just stand aside.'

261, like the other four hundred and fifty-five relocation sectors, was part of a vast fractal design, built to a plan that resembled a fern frond, amongst hundreds of other fronds that were part of a larger plant. They landed in the narrow tip, the centre of the sector where the street narrowed and curved to end in a circle that was kept clear for Services.

They formed up close around the two psis and Pete could hardly see through the wall of armoured soldiers. They looked at each other. Arthur was shaking despite the drugs in his system.

Don't be afraid, Pete thought to him.

'He's here,' Arthur whispered. *He's everywhere.*

Where is he?

I ... I can't tell ... so strong.

Pete: Arthur says Pierre Jnr is here.

Command: Do you have a direction?

Pete: No. He must be too close. What do you want us to do?

Command: Commence grid walk.

Pete: All the people are looking at us.

Command: We see that. Try not to startle them. It looks like the whole population of 261 has stopped moving.

The topographical map showed the pings from the entire area. Ten thousand, seven hundred and twenty-two blue dots.

Pete: I don't think this is a good idea.

Command: The Command is the Command.

'Move out,' Ten called and they started jogging to keep their place in the centre of the ring and not get stepped on.

The streets were quiet with only a few people out and about; a man hunched over restacking vending machines, people in their gardens with hoses, rakes and watering cans. They stopped to watch the soldiers walking down the middle of the road.

Ten: You two picking up anything?

Pete: Nothing new.

Arthur was looking at the ground and twisting back and forth.

Pete: Arthur isn't coping.

Command: Focus on your task.

As they went, the residents began listlessly trailing after the squad. Doors opened on both sides of the streets and more people came out to watch them.

'How are you feeling about this, Ten?' Nine asked.

'They're getting a little too curious for my liking.' They stopped the march and Ten amplified her voice for the crowd to hear. 'Citizens, please stand aside. This is Services business. We request that you stay in your homes.' Ten's request was ignored, and more residents began approaching the squad. 'What is wrong with these people?' she asked, turning to Peter.

'They're not people any more,' Arthur hissed.

Pete looked around, probing forward. He felt their seething rage, the constant clench of their anger and hate for themselves. The lust for destruction. Destroy, destroy. To see what survives. 'They are messed up. They're still conscious but ... they don't want us to be here. It's like a compulsion.'

Command: Is it like at the farm?

Pete: Yes. But not the same ... I can't feel individuals.

At Ten's signal they began moving forward. Every Citizen turned their feet as they passed and shuffled into the mob that now surrounded them. The space around the soldiers was slowly decreasing.

'They are even uglier up close,' Endo said.

'Check it out. They're not even looking at us.' Aiko was right. She waved her weapon at them, but they didn't react. Their bodies faced them, but slack necks kept their eyes to the road.

'I don't know about you all, but I just went in my suit,' Three joked.

'Keep it down, Three.'

'Just trying to lighten the mood.'

At that moment, Arthur collapsed to the ground. He felt his insides fall to the road, and everyone in the squad then felt it as his empathy spilt out. They dropped to the tarmac, succumbing to the overflow of Arthur's emotions.

'Arthur?' Pete knelt beside him, raising his block to cut off the feelings.

'What's wrong with him?' Ten asked, teeth clenched.

'Arthur, are you okay?'

'I see him.' Arthur was shaking all over as the symbiot saturated his system with calming chemicals. 'Below. He is below.'

'Eight. Sedate him.'

Eight turned from his position, shot Arthur with a dart and then knelt to attach a mask. The dark wave of his emotions faded from the soldiers and they stood up. One nightmare had passed, but another was shuffling forward.

Pete: What's the command?

Command: Go down.

Pete: What's down?

Blueprints of the sewers and access grid rushed into their queues.

'Okay, squad. There is a maintenance post fifty metres to the north. Eight, you carry Arthur. The rest of you round off the arse of this formation and hussle.'

Together they jogged forward, Pete keeping pace so as not to get trampled by the MUs.

The twins took offensive and defensive positions. Aiko called out, 'Hey, what happens if they don't move? Are we allowed to push them?'

'I think these fine Citizens need to take a lie-down,' Endo added.

'We have permission to gas. Filters on.' The soldiers flicked their helmets to climate processing and their suits went hermetic. They could now operate up to thirty metres below water if necessary. One of them handed Pete a clear mask with a gas filter over the mouth. 'I want an equal spread. The wind will push it north into the main crowd. Odds, then evens.'

The gas capsules spun as they flew through the air, releasing small purple pellets that began to sizzle as they touched oxygen. The gas seeds dropped on them and around them, steam rising, but the sector Citizens paid them no mind. The evens fired their volley, five more capsules loading the area with violet fog.

'Yep, they're dropping,' Aiko reported. Pete couldn't see it for himself, but from the soldiers he saw on infrared the bodies of the Citizens collapsing.

'Okay, now let's get to those stairs.' They picked up Arthur and began jogging forward again.

'What the — hey, stay down!' Endo shouted.

'This is crypped. They're getting back up.'

One by one the Citizens stood. They were hunched more, arms dragging down, heads flopped over; like dolls with invisible fingers pulling them up from their necks. They began swaying towards the team.

Ten: Command, are you seeing this?

Command: Confirmed. Go defensive. Disable assailants.

'Keep moving!' Ten shouted. 'Aiko, clear the entrance. Non-fatal only.'

Aiko began pushing the crowd back. But each time she knocked one down, the body lifted up again.

'This isn't working.'

Ten: We are at the door.

Command: It's open.

The Services entrance was a flat metal trapdoor in the footpath. It slid to one side showing wide stairs leading down to the access level. The corridor began brightening as the lumens were activated.

'Everyone inside. Girls, give us cover.'

Command: Full defensive.

Within a heartbeat the twinbots lit up the fog with lines of light, cutting the legs from under the front ranks of the encroaching mob. There were no cries of pain. Each of them fell to the ground, blood pumping out from their thickest arteries without even a gasp. The bodies didn't stop. With their arms they reached forward and pulled themselves on, and behind them the crowd continued its rush.

'This isn't working either,' Endo said, as her bot was overcome with the press of flesh. Then something else began pulling at their armour. Something strong and unseen.

From the safety of their van, in the comfort of their lounges, Aiko and Endo lost signal to their remotes.

'Kutz. I'm going to need more lives,' Endo said.

The dim underground was slowly getting brighter as the lights warmed up. The tunnel stretched in two directions before them. This was the Services level, where maintenance for the sectors could be performed easily.

Three was cursing about what he'd just seen, but the others held their tongues.

'Did you see that? Did you see that? I'm freaking out.'

'Don't freak out, Three. Not until we're home.'

'Where to now?' Six asked.

Command: We have a new strat-matrix building.

According to the grid schematics, every home in the sector had a node that connected to the access tunnel. These looked like cages that housed the piping, gauges and controls for the house above. Omnipoles marked the line of the streets, doubling their above-ground functions with ceiling lumens that lit their way below.

'I guess we continue the way we were heading. If they didn't like that, it could be the right direction.' Pete looked at the helmeted faces. They were just waiting on the command. They had no opinion, so long as it wasn't up.

In Pete's overlay a familiar line appeared, showing them the route Command had planned, leading them to the centre of the sector.

'This way,' Ten said, leading off.

'Will the door hold?' Three asked.

'Why don't you stay and make sure?' Five threw back, jogging with the rest of the squad.

They passed cross tunnels as they went that led to the neighbouring sectors. 'Everyone pin these tunnels, these will be our exits if we need them,' Ten called out. Everyone began dropping tracking crumbs as they went.

As they got further along, the tunnel widened out. Soon it divided into two separate passages with regularly spaced support columns between them. As it grew, it split into three sections then four, and soon they were in a vast open area broken only by the hundred or so columns.

'It's like a car park down here,' Three said.

'We're under the pond. Reaching the storage tanks,' Ten reported. On the schematics these showed as large circles where the sector had its water supply.

'There's nothing here.'

'Ten,' Eight said.

'What is it?'

'I've got audio coming from over there. Sounds like shuffling feet.'

'Great. Okay. Odds and evens.' Ten turned to Pete and pinched his shirt in her steel fingers. 'Which way, tapper? Take a guess.'

'Is there another level below this?' Pete asked.

'Not on the plans. Can you sense something?' Ten asked.

'I swear I can ...' He put a hand out towards the ground. He imagined he was the water, flooding down.

'What is it, Lazarus?'

'Something is down there. Right below us.'

'There's only crawl tubes under the tanks. For bots.'

Pete closed his eyes and felt around him. He couldn't detect any minds outside of the squad. It was strange, though, that it wasn't a complete void. The emptiness wasn't totally silent. He lifted his arm and pointed. 'I think that way.'

'As you wish. Let's light up this place, I'm tired of this darkness!' Ten shouted.

The squad switched on their suit lights, flooding the chamber into an artificial day.

'Hey, are these footprints?' Seven asked. Ten and Peter went to look. The floor was dusted evenly except where some scuff marks had kicked up a line.

'Someone has been passing through here regularly. Which way, tapper?'

Command: There is no record of unauthorised entry. Follow the path.

'They're coming,' Eight called out.

'Move out,' Ten ordered.

They hurried, following the path across the side of the chamber until it ended at a manhole. The dirty footprints led towards it from all sides. 'This looks promising. Three, get that thing open.'

The rest of the ten made a ring and opened fire as Three started forcing the trapdoor to open. The Citizens were

410

shambling forward and the soldiers began disabling them brutally.

'Cut through it,' Ten ordered and Three pulled out a fist-sized arc laser.

The manhole eventually gave in and dropped into the space below, clanging down the shaft for a few seconds before hitting bottom. A ladder led down towards a soft green light. 'Three, then Lazarus. Go,' Ten ordered.

He watched it through Three's eyes first. The soldier stepped off the ladder into an antechamber closed off by a thick vault door. Small portholes in a ring around the handle emitted the green light. Three dropped a crumb and a lumen and stood, weapon pointing at the door.

'Keep moving!' Nine shouted at Pete.

As Peter went through the hole, his connection to the Weave was cut off. He could hear shouting from above, and intense weapons fire. Two of the soldiers started following him down and he quickly made it to the bottom and moved to get out of the way.

There was only enough room for one more MU and Pete crouched into the corner to give them space. He put their cameras into his overlay and watched.

He knew what was in there. He could feel Pierre's presence through the door.

Gingerly, Nine reached one hand forward and spun the locking handle. The vault door glided back. Green light swept over them as they stepped forward.

On either side of a long room, aquariums containing verdant green rested on complex pedestals of diodes and tubes. There, asleep, was the face of the boy Pete saw every time he closed his eyes. In each of the aquariums floated the same human boy with the enlarged skull in different stages of development.

In some Pierre was an infant, bulbous head the same size as the rest of his body, skin angry with growth.

'Oh, mir.' Another soldier came through into the vault. The others were silent.

Ten was the last of the MUs to come down the ladder, firing gloop up through the hole. 'They're blocked for now. What is down ...' She slowly dragged her eyes from tank to tank. 'He's fucking cloning himself?'

The rest of the soldiers blurted out their own versions of the sentiment, while Ten tried to report to Command.

Ten: Command, are you seeing what's down here? ... Command ... Do you read me?

'It's no good. They can't hear us.'

'What should we do, Ten?'

'We wait for rescue. Command has our location. For now we bunker down and for the Will's sake nobody touch anything.'

Pete walked away from them, wandering down the length of the room, circling and inspecting each of the tanks, looking at the star of consciousness that was flickering in each. They weren't all perfect copies; cloning was never always perfect. There were a couple whose limbs had failed to develop, and a dark tank that had been powered down; it looked like the head had grown so fast it had ruptured.

That one was cold to touch. Each of the other tanks hummed with heating and life-support. Pumps extracted the fluids and recycled them, replenishing the amniotic and pushing the fluids back into the tank.

'Of course he came to STOC,' one of the soldiers exclaimed. Pete looked at him, reading the explanation in his mind before it was spoken. Cloning was banned across the WU, verboten. Where else would you go but the leftover Örjians? They were the master splicers.

Peter was standing by one tank that appeared to be empty, though it hummed and was lit to the same bright green murk. He could just make out a darker shape inside and sense that glimmer ... that tiny spark ... *Pierre?*

He was thrust backward. A shockwave threw him to the ground. His mind careened, lost in a random, epileptic spasm of memories. Nothing matched: visions, smells and sounds repeated themselves discordantly. Black, white, green, those eyes!, dry grass, the ocean pulling back and forth, his bones breaking, blue, green, sinking deeper into the water. Where the light doesn't go and thoughts go out.

He didn't see the other clones open their eyes or feel the splitting shriek they stabbed into the soldiers' minds. The MUs crumpled over and rolled on the floor, clawing at their heads and helmets for it to stop. They began hitting their ears on the ground, harder and harder, desperate to reach unconsciousness.

Power was cut to the room and dark hit like a hammer. In the second before the emergency lighting took over, a lithe mechanical silhouette dove into the room. A blade of light, the length of its arm, carved like a sword through the tanks, before spinning to sweep the other side of the room and slicing through the cloning chambers. Warm fluids burst to the floor and the attacker leapt upon the bodies to make sure the job was done.

The red glow of the backup lights managed to fill the room and the figure drew itself up.

Peter looked up from the ground, his head hot and throbbing.

'Who are you?' Pete croaked.

The figure looked down and Pete saw now that it had no face, only a polished metal plate on a silicon scalp. They'd been rescued by a droid.

'Who sent you?' Pete asked, his voice nearly a whisper. The droid didn't answer, perhaps it wasn't built to speak. 'Who sent you?'

'Another blackout today, this time from one of the relocation zones in STOC,' Phillipe Kinazee read out, updating viewers new to his stream. He was on his second shift, rolling the show to extended time while they were rating so highly.

His producer, Morley, had been tipped off that something was happening near Omskya and, for the first time, they had beaten one of the larger shows to the story. Their source was joining the panel via a link to the neighbouring sector. 'Franky, what can you tell us about what is happening down there?'

The man the host called Franky, whose full name was written below him as Investigative Reporter Francis Lowell, was a thin forty-year-old with retreating hair. Behind him, a concertina fence was pulled across the footbridge that led to an empty but otherwise normal-looking suburb. In front of that, marauders stood unmoving while drones were flying in their hundreds over their heads.

'As you can see, Phillipe, Services have established a cordon and no one is going in or out,' Frank raised his voice, as if he was in a strong wind. 'This is as close as we are allowed to get.'

'And has anyone been able to ascertain what the situation is?'

'Not yet, Phillipe. Services is keeping tight-lipped. As you can see, it looks from here as if Sector 261 is deserted. We haven't seen any residents since we've been here, but we have detected traces of a large gas release. Clearly, there has been an altercation of some sort, but which event caused the other is the question and, at the moment, no one is releasing any information.'

'And no one will until the hierarchy is re-established,' a second panellist, Xanthe Ching, spoke without being prompted.

They cut back into the studio. Behind the line-up of speakers was the satellite view of the area ... the frond of 261 was etched out in red.

'How can something like this be kept hidden? The Primacy is clearly using the cover of a reshuffle to delay releasing information.' This was from a young blonde woman in a pinstripe jacket. Under her was her title: Sandrina Sibellio, Citizens for Universal Equality.

'I think there are plenty of simpler explanations before we resort to conspiracy theories,' Ching said.

'Such as?'

'There has always been unrest amongst the rehabilitated Örjians. A violent outbreak between them is the most logical explanation.'

The host was pinged by the on-site investigator that he had more to say. 'Franky, you have something to add?'

415

'Yes. My team has been looking into the blackouts for that particular sector and for the last few months the population there has completely disconnected from the Weave.'

'You see. It's a minor rebellion. Services will restore order in no time.'

'If it was so minor, then why the lockdown on information?'

'I think, with everything else going on in the world right now, it is natural to be cautious.'

'Dare we suggest that this is another manifestation like the one in the Dome?' Phillipe asked. The rest of the panel breathed in sharply. The host laughed. 'Alright, no one wants to bite on that one. Well, informed or not, this new event is shaking the civic seating chart. This signals the end of Ryu Shima's time in the hot seat as the Will puts its trust in Colonel Abercrombie Pinter. Isn't that a blast from the past?'

They chuckled or clucked their tongues.

'The decline began long before this most recent event,' Ching said, again without a signal from the host. 'I think we can map the precise moment that confidence in Ryu Shima was lost, to the Mexica Kronos outbreak.'

'I think it began earlier. Shima's rate of growth slowed down immediately after the rebellion was declared,' Patricia Milling said, who had, until recently, been a Shima supporter.

Each of the speakers presented line charts and statistical analysis to their streams, validating their statements.

'Three Kronos outbreaks, a rebellion in the Cape and the psi collections ... this must be stretching Services resources quite thinly, mustn't it? I direct this one to you, Patricia,' the host said, bringing in the fourth speaker, one of his regular civic commentators.

'That's true, Phillipe. It seems at any point now that Services may not be able to cope with another large incident. Colonel Pinter is inheriting quite a queue of problems.'

'While we all know him from the history books, we've never known him as Prime of the World Union. What do you think he'll do?'

'Colonel Pinter knows how to command.'

'In war, yes. We aren't at war, Ching,' Sandrina said.

'Okay, that sounds like a good place to break. There's plenty to discuss here. Let's take five minutes to gather questions and come back to talk about what it might mean that the Scorpion has —'

Around the world screens went black.

All connections broke as every node in the network was shut down. The Weave was disconnected.

ACKNOWLEDGEMENTS

Book two was such a great and wonderful challenge and I have many people who helped me get there.

Thanks to my patient family, my glorious partner Alice, the wonderful people of HarperCollins Australia (including but not limited to Rochelle Fernandez, Kate Burnitt and Darren Holt) and freelancers Stephanie Smith and Pam Dunne. Pierre blesses you all.

Also to my friends and colleagues at Xoum and Seizure who facilitate and encourage my madness. You are enablers, each and every one of you.

Lastly, a thank you to my beta readers. I cannot stress enough how important it is to gather the most literate and brutally honest people you can to do that first reading. For me this is Kevin O'Brien, Deonie Fiford, Alice Grundy and Robert Henley. I hope you guys are ready for round three because by the time you are reading this, it will be in the mail.

Find out how it all ends
in June 2015 with book three

CONVERGENCE

The miracle is here

Also available …

He can make you forget.

He can control you.

And he is only eight years old.